"Looking for something else is a hell of a lot better than sitting in the shit. Isn't that the mainline, searching for something else?" He grinned. "You two, example. Neither of you is in this just for the money, that's obvious. So you're both looking for something out here. Don't know what it is, and don't care. Hope you find it. But I'm going to be doing my looking in some other solar system. I just have to worry about getting back alive so I can collect and ship out. Probably have to stay off the river coming back, go the whole thing on foot through the jungle. Take me two or three months. Safer for you, too, that way. Maybe when we're finished we can all go back together."

"Ryker, too?" Benedict asked.

"Only in a casket." Gerad gound out his cigarette, lit another.

RICHARD PAUL RUSSO

Benedict is a
First Order Empath—
but his talent
could desert
him at any moment!

INNER ECLIPSE

A TOM DOHERTY ASSOCIATES BOOK

INNER ECLIPSE

Copyright © 1988 by Richard Paul Russo

First printing: February 1988

A TOR Book

Published by Tom Doherty Associates, Inc.
49 West 24th Street
New York, NY 10010

Cover art by David Mattingly

ISBN: 0-812-55256-3
Can. No.: 0-812-55257-1

Printed in the United States of America

0 9 8 7 6 5 4 3 2 1

For Sally, of course

PART ONE
Triumvirate

1

THE TIME HE FIRST SAW RYKER, IT WAS RAINING.

The night air was typical Winterside, warm despite the rain. Benedict Saltow sat at one of the Blue Danuub's outdoor tables, the rain a steady clatter on the clear roof above him. The rain and the clouds high overhead hid Triumvirate's curve and ceiling, helped maintain the illusion he was on solid ground somewhere under an open sky. He sipped at hot Tuskan coffee and watched the people emerging from or entering the spoke terminus less than fifty meters away—passengers recently arrived on Triumvirate or those about to depart.

Benedict looked up and watched the progressions of emerald lights along the spoke shaft that traced the passage of transport pods ascending to, or descending from, the hub. He followed the glittering trail of one until it rose into the rainclouds and disappeared.

He was waiting for something to happen.

He did not know what he was waiting for, nor when it would occur. Today? Tomorrow? A week, a month, or a year from now? Ever? And if never . . . then what? Benedict tapped at the rim of the coffee mug and watched the people at the foot of the spoke.

A grouped tandem of luxliners had apparently docked in the last hour because most of the people emerging from the terminus lobby looked to be wealthy vacationers—"touros" loaded with far too much luggage who stood out of the rain and paid overworked portiers to summon magne-cabs to take them to their hotels or chalets. A long line of cabs waited; the public omnis and hotel shuttles remained empty. Benedict felt slightly ill and drank more of the Tuskan coffee, knowing it would not help.

Most of the tables around him were unoccupied, though the interior sections of the cafe were crowded. Through the rain and the increasing babble from the touros, Benedict caught the sound of approaching footsteps, shuffling and familiar. He turned to see Hadling slip through the walkway gate, a hand raised. Hadling, as usual, wore a dark slick-coat, one or two sizes too large, that matched his wet, unruly hair.

Benedict had been on Triumvirate for just over a year, but Gird Hadling had lived here for more than ten. Hadling had picked up the clipped "native" dialect, and said he would probably stay on Triumvirate until he died. *And why not*? he had asked Benedict once. *Triumvirate a small world, or a large city, what difference it hangs in the vacuum of space, self-contained and self-containing? It is home.*

Hadling nodded and dropped into the seat across from Benedict. He pressed the order stud, and when the click sounded leaned forward and said, "Koaler, over and under," into the table-ear. He released the

4

stud, leaned back. "Hello, Stennet," he said, and smiled.

"Hello, Gird."

They sat in silence, listening to the rain, the quiet voices of the people inside the cafe contrasting with the harsh yammer of the touros and the sounds of traffic. This was what Benedict liked most about Hadling—they could sit for hours without speaking, and the silence would not be awkward.

A waiter brought Hadling's drink, topped off Benedict's coffee so fresh steam rose from the stone mug. For a moment it reminded him of the steam that vented from the slopes of Mount Rakamon on Dante's Eye; then it called up images of smoke from burning houses and governmental buildings on Mesa. His depression increased. Benedict could almost feel his inner paralysis deepen, and he closed his eyes to push away the memories. The images shimmered, threatened to remain, but gradually faded and left him feeling hollow.

"Just a few," Hadling said, "we'll see angry touros there. Happens, luxliners dock, touros can all afford cabs, all *insist* on cabs, before long aren't enough. 'Specially in rain. And dark."

Benedict opened his eyes and turned to look. Hadling was right. The long line of cabs was gone and there was still a crowd waiting. One of the hotel shuttles, from the Triumvirate Marriott, was half full, but the others, along with all three omnis, were still empty, and the remaining touros were not interested in them. A disorganized semblance of a line formed as they waited for more cabs to arrive. The Marriott shuttle sent a twisting ring through the air, the hotel logo on its doors flashed twice in bright crimson, then the shuttle pulled away.

Benedict and Hadling were close enough to hear the touros complain to each other about the poor service, the lack of proper transportation and facilities. The same complaints they always made, Benedict thought, wherever they went. He sensed the background murmur of their anger and frustration, and flipped up his inner screens, blocking out all traces of feeling from the touros.

"Benedict," Hadling said.

Benedict turned, wary and alert. He was not on Triumvirate in his own name. All his identification bore the name Stennet Reese, and that was how Hadling knew him. Benedict rarely used his own name anymore; he did not want to be known as who, and what, he'd been born.

"Benedict Saltow," Hadling said.

So, Benedict thought, Hadling knows. He nodded.

"Since met you, touch of familiar. Couldn't lock it. Did some pic-sorting the Info-Sys outlet. Tried Video Celebs first. Then Musics. Then hunched into Catalog of Empaths. There you were. First Order. Not many around."

"No." Most of the time now Benedict wished there was one less, but there was nothing he could do about that. Suicide was not an option for him.

"Haven't told anyone. Won't. Everyone's right to privacy, by me."

"I appreciate that, Gird. Let's just pass on it, then. And call me Stennet."

Hadling smiled, gave him a quick nod.

Benedict reached for his coffee. Hot pain stopped his motion, a sliver of fear that sliced through his primary filters, it was so intense. Benedict turned in its direction, the fear already becoming his own, though still under control.

The touros had gone silent, and were backing away from the curb, giving room to two men who stood an arm's length apart next to a waiting cab, its rotors humming quietly. A woman had one leg in the cab, but had stopped and looked back at the two men.

The shorter of the two men was about to put a final piece of luggage into the magne-cab's trunk, but had paused, valise still in hand; he now bit the corner of his lip, one hand worrying the shimmering material of his violet jumpsuit. The fear radiated in waves from him, seeped into Benedict, and grew in intensity.

The other man was huge, a full head taller than anyone else around him, and dressed for mountains or desert in high-ankled boots and loose-fitting pants and shirt of a light tan color. The loose clothing did not hide the tensed muscles of his arms and shoulders. His black beard and hair were thick, the hair long and the beard trimmed short. A large field pack rested on the ground at his side. From him, Benedict received a flushed, growing exhilaration cut through with a strange, dark tension.

"I'll repeat. I want this cab," the larger man said. "And I mean *this* cab, at *this* moment."

The shorter man shook his head. "You just came down, you haven't waited like the rest of us. You can't just take this cab, you have to wait, it's our cab." He turned to put the valise into the open trunk.

The other man reached out, grabbed the smaller man's wrist, and twisted until the valise dropped to the wet ground beside them. Benedict suppressed the emotions coming in, but did not cut them off completely. Even stepped down, though, emotion from the two men shuddered through him with a dull ache, and he kept up the screens blocking out everyone else.

"All right, all right!" The smaller man's voice was a

Richard Paul Russo

high, nasal whine. "We can share the cab. It'll be cramped, though."

The big man shook his head. "I want the cab to myself," he said.

The shorter man looked around as if expecting support from the other touros, but they were all trying to blind-eye the situation, and ignored his silent entreaties. Two Fleet Officers in the group looked on, but they, too, ignored the conflict. As usual, Benedict thought. And, as usual, there was no Triumvirate Security around. He waited, wondering if he should step in.

"No," the smaller man finally said. Benedict felt the fear trip up as the man bent over to retrieve the valise. The larger man clasped his hand over the back of the other man's neck and forced him to his knees. The fear from the man doubled, trebled, and Benedict bent over with pain as the fear coursed through his spine and out along his limbs. He'd had enough, too much, and it was time to cut it all off. Benedict tried to throw his primary screens up, but nothing happened. He tried again, desperate now as the fear lashed through him (some of his own?), but another seizure had taken hold of him, just as one had three weeks before, and time and again before that. Screens, filters, and shields collapsed as his ability to block out emotion deserted him once again.

The small man's terror became his own, ripped through him naked and unmasked. The emotions of other people around him began leaking through, mixing with the man's fear, and suddenly Benedict's breath was coming in short, coarse gasps and he broke out into a heavy, dripping sweat.

He felt a hand on his arm, heard a voice calling. "Stennet? Stennet, are you all right?" But he could not respond. And yet, even doubled over with the pain, he did not take his eyes from the scene before him.

The larger man dropped to one knee and forced the smaller man's face down into a pool of water that had formed with the rain. The muscles in his hand and forearm tightened as he gripped harder. The small man reached out with both hands, and fingers clawed at the ground, at the larger man's boots. No one made a move to stop it, and the two Fleet Officers began walking deliberately away.

Hadling stood up from the chair, took a few steps toward the terminus, then turned back to look at Benedict. His face was tight, his brows furrowed. Go, Benedict wanted to tell him; but he could say nothing. Hadling turned once more to the struggling men across the way, then returned to Benedict's side and reached out to hold Benedict by the shoulder.

Panic from the small man cut again and again into Benedict, tearing through his gut, and then a rush of elation and distorted tension from the other man swelled and flooded along with the fear. Without warning, all the few remaining screens and barriers broke down and Benedict was buried under waves of emotion from every person within several hundred meters, buried and drowned by the tumult, nearly blinded as he collapsed from the chair. He would have hit the ground, but Hadling held on to him, pulled him up and supported him against the back of the chair. Benedict saw Hadling's mouth move, but heard no words; then even that was gone as silver and crimson light flashed across his eyes. He thought he was going to cry out, tried to, but in the continuing silence a hot darkness began to flow over him.

Connections clicked inside his head. All feelings

shut off instantly. A cold cloud of relief swept through him as the screens, filters, and shields slid quickly into place, now strong and unbreakable. Hearing and vision slowly returned; somehow, desperate to know, he pushed Hadling aside to see what was happening.

The larger man had raised the other's face from the water, now slapped it twice with his free hand, then shoved it back down into the pool. Still no one around them moved or said a word. The woman, apparently the smaller man's companion, stood frozen against the door of the cab.

Benedict's breath came more easily now, long and deep. The shaking had nearly ceased, so he tried to stand, intending, perhaps, to stop what was happening. Hadling eased him gently back into the chair, shaking his head.

"Let me," Hadling said.

But before Hadling had a chance to move from the table, the larger man released the other's neck, stood, and stepped back a few paces. The other man remained on his knees, coughing and choking for breath, his fingers digging into unyielding pavement. When the coughing eased, the larger man spoke to him in a soft, firm tone.

"I want the cab."

The smaller man nodded, then rose to his feet, his gaze to the ground. He stumbled to the cab and began removing luggage from the trunk. The woman closed her eyes briefly, then reached into the cab and took out a shoulder bag and brought it to where her companion was stacking the rest of their baggage. When the cab was empty, the larger man pointed back toward the terminus lobby. "Take all that inside," he said. "When I'm gone, you can come back out."

The man and woman said nothing. They struggled with the luggage, making two trips to the lobby. After the second, they stayed inside. The large bearded man picked up his field pack, tossed it into the back seat of the cab, then squeezed in through the small door. He closed it, and the cab pulled quietly away and into the night.

Hadling sat, looked at Benedict. "You all right?"

Benedict breathed deeply, then nodded.

"What just happened to you, that have to do with being an empath? A First?"

Benedict nodded again. His mouth and throat were dry; sweat still ran down his face.

"About a drink?" Hadling said. "Like you could use one."

"No, I'm all right. I . . ." He drank some of the coffee, which was cold. He pushed the mug away. "Coffee, though."

Hadling pressed the stud, ordered coffee and a second drink for himself.

"So that's what it's like, being an empath."

"Not really," Benedict said. "It's . . . it's not like that all the time." His own words dug at him, and he wondered if it was possible. Only three weeks had passed since the last seizure. The seizures were coming closer together, and he could not help thinking that it would continue, that eventually he might lose all control. Worse than being skipped into a Tri-Meth. The sweat continued to trickle from his temples.

Drinks arrived. Benedict sipped at the hot coffee as he looked back at the terminus lobby. The touros had settled and calmed, and had re-formed the line waiting for cabs. The two Fleet Officers had reappeared and were talking with a group of touros that had just emerged from the lobby. The man in the violet jumpsuit and his female companion had joined the line, this time at the end. Benedict watched, feeling ill again, and listened to the rain falling from the glittering night above.

2

HIS PARALYSIS DEEPENED.

Two days had passed since the seizure, and Benedict had not left his hotel room once in that time. Someday, he thought, he would stop moving altogether. He would be seated in a cafe somewhere, his fingers locked on the handle of a stone mug filled with Tuskan or Linsok coffee, his gaze fixed on the rising steam. People would speak to him, he would not reply; they would poke at his arms, jab his ribs, and still he would not respond. Finally they would pry his fingers loose, cart him off, then skip him into the nearest Tri-Meth Institute to be observed and prodded and experimented on until he gratefully died.

He was staying at the Slider Hotel on the slope of eastern RimsEdge. The hotel was moderately priced, which meant he had a small but clean room with a single bed, a sitting chair, a desk and chair set in front of the wall terminal, and a narrow balcony just wide enough to stand on.

Late afternoon, Benedict stood on the balcony, fourteen floors up. The Winterside sky was unusually clear and he could see, between the taller hotels and office buildings, parts of the Central Freeway, the multilevel thoroughfare that circumnavigated Triumvirate without a break—an infinite road that passed through Winterside, through the first short transition zone, then along under the bright sun of Summerside, through the second t-zone, and into Winterside again. Benedict considered hiring one of the high-speed private limos, driving onto the Central Freeway, and programming the limo to never exit. He could endlessly circle the interior of the world, hidden behind tinted glass, forever passing from one season to another and back, simultaneously in constant motion and in constant stasis.

The door to his room opened, then immediately clicked shut. Benedict turned quickly, saw no one. Someone making a mistake? He waited, watching the door, listening.

Nothing. Not a sound. Then a faint, familiar odor reached him. His pulse quickened, his breath stopped for a moment. Out on the balcony, he was in trouble. When the expected *chikking* sounded, he moved.

Benedict dove into the room and to his left, covered the back of his neck with both hands. A blur of dark motion shot past just above him, and as he hit the floor he felt the sting as the quirta's tail slashed across his hands.

Christ, he thought. Inside a closed room. Not much better than the balcony.

He came to his feet, saw the quirta swerve and bounce off the balcony rail and floor and back into the room. He dove again, protecting his neck. The slash of the quirta's tail went deeper this time, along the length of his arm.

Benedict rolled against the wall cube, popped it open, and pulled out his cutter. He could just barely follow the flight of the quirta bouncing off two walls, the floor, then toward him. Christ. There was no way to track and shoot the damned thing. It moved too quickly.

Benedict lunged directly at the quirta, felt the rush of wind just past his head as the quirta popped up and over him to avoid a collision; Benedict scrambled for the door.

He pushed it open, swung into the corridor, and slammed the door shut. In the same motion he dropped to his knees and turned, his cutter aimed at the figure a few meters down the hall.

It was the big man he had seen at the spoke terminus two days before, the black hair and beard a mane around his head. The man smiled and held both hands out from his body.

"I have no weapons," he said.

Benedict remained motionless, breathing heavily. He studied the man's clothing, searching for unusual bulges, but could not tell whether or not the man was armed.

"And the quirta?" he asked. "Slaved?"

The big man nodded once. "I can neutralize it. The slaver's in my shirt pocket."

Benedict stood, but kept the cutter aimed at the man. "All right."

The man slowly reached into his shirt pocket, withdrew a slim metal case covered with colored studs. He pressed one, then another. "That's it."

Benedict backed away and the other man, without prompting, approached the door and opened it wide. He stepped into the room and Benedict could see past him to the quirta on the floor, its body quivering. Little more than dark wings, sharp tail, and the stubby legs it used to punch away from solid surfaces, the quirta was not much larger than Benedict's hand. It had no eyes, no ears, and used a sophisticated form of echolocation—the *chikking* sound. The quirta was native to DreamVeil, and exporting the creatures was strictly forbidden. He'd had a few encounters with them several years before on DreamVeil, the only reason he had survived this one.

He aimed the cutter and fired. The beam arced, burned a hole through the quirta, and the creature ceased moving. Benedict walked in and picked up the dead quirta by the tip of its left wing. Still keeping his distance from the other man, he went to the disposal and dropped the limp creature into the chute. A quiet thrump sounded, and the quirta was gone.

Benedict looked down at his arm. Blood dripped heavily from it. He glanced up at the big man, lowered several screens, and quickly made a judgment. This man was not interested in killing him; at least not yet. Then why the quirta? Benedict pocketed the cutter. He went to the bathroom and popped out the medikit; he left a trail of blood across the floor.

"My name is Ryker," the big man said. "Let me help you with that."

Benedict shook his head and set to work on the arm. The cut was clean and straight, as if made with a scalpel or laser. No major arteries or veins were open.

Ryker grabbed the two white towels and started wiping up the blood on the floor. "The quirta was a test, Saltow."

So this man Ryker also knew who he was. Benedict washed the blood from his arm, sprayed disinfectant and local coag into the wound, then pulled the cut together with a string of wing clips. Later he'd go to a clinic, finish it right.

"A test for what?" he finally asked.

Ryker cleaned up the last of the blood out in the corridor, then threw the towels into the disposal chute. He turned to face Benedict.

"To see if you clicked with your reputation. I have a proposal for you, a project I'm putting together. I needed to know if you were as good as they say you are."

"You should have saved yourself the effort. I'm not interested in your proposal, whatever it is."

Ryker took a step forward. "You might not think so, Saltow, but I wouldn't be here if I wasn't damn sure you *would* be. I know a lot about you. What you want, maybe what you need."

"I don't think so."

"I'm not leaving Triumvirate until I've laid out the project for you."

Ryker was a man accustomed to intimidating people with his size, Benedict could see that. He'd seen an obvious example at the terminus, and now Ryker was trying it with him, though much more subtly—the step forward, breathing in to expand his chest slightly, setting back his shoulders, shifting his feet. Benedict was not intimidated, but he realized that Ryker would *not* let him be until he had made his presentation. Fine, then, he would listen to Ryker, reject the proposal, and that would end it.

"All right," he said. "Talk. Sit down, if you'll be more comfortable."

"Not here. We need privacy."

Benedict sighed deeply, but nodded. He was tired of secrecy games. "Let's go." He put on a long-sleeved shirt to cover the wound, picked up his raincoat, and they left the room.

3

THE HOTEL LOBBY WAS CROWDED, AND SEVERAL LONG LINES of dark-skinned men and women waited in front of the main desk, their luggage as worn as their clothing. Two loud arguments were under way at the desk, and most of the people in line were talking among themselves. As he and Ryker worked their way through, Benedict heard bits of Portuguese and Lingala, but most of it was too dialected for him to understand.

Outside, the clouds were beginning to return, and the air felt heavy, smelled of rain. They walked along a busy road lined with restaurants, arcades, and several other small hotels, the walkways nearly as crowded as the hotel lobby. Traffic was heavy, dominated by public omnis and transporters, with a fair number of cabs, and an occasional personal slipster or limo gliding over the road with darkened windows.

Among the crowds, Benedict kept up all the screens and filters, not allowing even the normal background murmur of emotion to enter. After the seizure, he was cautious, though he knew it was irrational. The seizures were coming closer together, but if the pattern held, it would be at least another two weeks, maybe three, before the next one struck. Still, he could not quell the fear completely, and his screens remained solid and intact, an impenetrable wall.

Ryker led the way to an oval bar that jutted out into a park from one of the many cafes along the roadway. A light drizzle began as they stepped under the multicolored awning and ordered drinks to go. Benedict ordered scotch and Ryker asked for a double Ribbon, an exotic drink with high alcohol content.

Ryker lit a cigarette with a blackstone lighter, then pointed to an isolated table by a fountain, the table covered by a slanted tarp. Drinks arrived in disposable containers, Benedict put on his coat, and they went out into the rain, headed toward the fountain.

"I am putting together an expedition," Ryker began. "I need someone like you for this project. I need a First Order empath." He put up his hand as if warding off an expected protest. "I know, you're one of the few Firsts who don't hire out."

"Then you know this is pointless."

"No." They reached the table, water now dripping from Ryker's hair and beard, and sat across from each other on the artiwood seats. "I have something other than credit or cash to offer." He sipped at his drink, then relit his cigarette. He pointed the cigarette at Benedict. "You, Saltow, have become very interested, in the last few years, in the possible existence of alien intelligence. Of an intelligent, nonhuman race of beings. More than interested. You're obsessed. That's why you went to Dante's Eye, hoping those creatures living at the edges of the lava flows might actually be intelligent. You were involved in the attempts at communication, weren't you?"

"Do I need to answer?"

Ryker smiled and drank deeply. "Yes, you were involved. You took a lot of risks. Almost died twice. Then, through a freakish accident, the entire population of those creatures was destroyed. So no communication, no answer."

Benedict turned away, his gaze unfocused. For a moment he saw flame and exploding rock, felt the burning heat and the shaking earth, watched vast gouts of erupting steam, heard the cries of those people who did die. "No accident," he said.

"Probably not. But that's irrelevant, and the question of their intelligence has become moot. The human race is back where it started. Alone."

Benedict looked at Ryker, but said nothing. Alone, yes, and in very poor company, he thought.

"Saltow, why is it so important to find another race of intelligent creatures? To you, I mean?" When Benedict did not answer, Ryker went on. "Well, it *is* important to you, we know that. And important to a lot of other people, myself included. And the people I am associated with."

Benedict sipped at his drink, watched Ryker drop his cigarette to the ground and light another.

"That's what I'm offering you," Ryker said. "Contact with an intelligent, alien race."

More games? "A discovery like that," Benedict said, "and I haven't heard of it? That would have tripped all over the galaxy in gigantic cluster blips. Within days everyone on Triumvirate would have known."

"It hasn't come close to being confirmed, and it's been kept quiet. It's been suspected for three or four years, actually. And word *will* get out soon, a few months from now, a year or two at most. Rumors are increasing, getting more difficult to cap. More people involved all the time, and too much at stake." He paused, as if waiting for a response.

"I'm still waiting to be convinced," Benedict said.

Ryker nodded. "My employers are convinced enough to finance an expedition to locate them." He finished his drink, draining it, then crushed the cup and dropped it to the ground. "There have been isolated contacts, between twenty and thirty over the last few years. There's been no communication, but there have been indications of intelligence, of self-awareness. The creatures have always disappeared, immediately. One was trapped, captured, but died. Probably suicide, which would be another strong sign."

"Possibly intelligent, and someone traps them like animals?"

"Perhaps that's all they are. We don't know. They disappear, leave no traces, no trails. Searches have been made, but there have been no signs of villages, anything like that."

"But indications of intelligence, you said."

"Yes."

"What?"

Ryker shook his head. "You become a part of this expedition, you'll learn more. But for now you get nothing." He crushed out his cigarette, reached for another, then apparently changed his mind. He tapped his thumb against the tabletop. "I'm sure you appreciate the financial potential for those who find these creatures first, and can establish their intelligence. And there are, of course, other types of rewards, though admittedly the people I am associated with are primarily interested in the financial gains.

"We need your help, Saltow. If they are hiding, which seems probable, we may not be able to make visual contact, or even find traces. You, however, might be able to sense them, detect their presence. We have to try everything."

The drizzle had become a heavy rain, and the air cooled slightly. Benedict drank from his scotch, hoping it would warm him. "Why don't you just hire another First?" he asked. "One who *wants* to hire out?"

Ryker shook his head. "You know what most Firsts are like? Shit. Most of them never have to really work their entire lives. They get located at an early age, receive free training and evaluation for years, and when they're certified as Firsts, they pick and choose. They work for governments, corporations, combines. A few become psychiatrists. They are all set for life, instantly wealthy, live in nice safe towns and cities, in beautiful, large houses, surrounded by luxury if they wish, and never worried about making a living from day to day." He turned his head and spat violently.

"No," Benedict said. "I've known some of them. They don't live such carefree lives. They may be wealthy, but being a First . . . There is a price, and they all pay it in some way. You underestimate them."

"They have never had to learn to survive," Ryker replied. "I have, Benedict Saltow, and you have too. We know about you. How you lost your parents, how you grew up in Triskele, what you had to do to survive. We know you're an adept at free-hand fighting, and with short-range weapons. You've been in and out of minor wars and rebellions, one major revolution. You're forty-seven, but physically you're not much older than thirty, in peak condition. Or you were. That's why the test with the quirta, to see if you'd lost too much sitting around here on Triumvirate."

"And did I pass your damn test?"

"We wouldn't be talking if you hadn't."

"A sure truth. I'd be dead."

"Yes. You're resourceful, and I need that. We know what you've done on DreamVeil. On Carthage. On Mesa. And everywhere else. You know how to survive."

Benedict leaned forward. "That's enough." For some reason, he was beginning to get angry.

Ryker went on as if Benedict had not spoken. "Above all is dependability. Another First, even if we could hire one, would not be reliable. This expedition will become difficult, probably dangerous, and it would be too easy for a First to walk out. Too many easier ways to make money. If you come, it'll be because you want to. And you'll stay with it."

A slight breeze kicked in, sprayed them lightly with rain for a few moments, then died. Neither spoke. All Benedict could think of was that he did not want to make a decision like this, not now. Maybe not ever again.

Ryker took out a cigarette, tapped it on the table a few times before lighting it and inhaling. "That's the proposal," he finally said. "You join this expedition, and help find these . . . creatures. We don't *know* they're intelligent, but do you want to chance it? If they are, and you aren't in on it now, it would take years to get anywhere near them. If ever."

True enough, thought Benedict. He studied Ryker, saw a man struggling to maintain control over some inner pressure straining for release. He could sense a dark, edgy tension in the man, and Benedict remembered the same warped, dark tension that had undercut Ryker's exhilaration at the spoke terminus two days before. He was a dangerous man to be involved with.

23

But Ryker was right, Benedict could not risk missing out. More than that, though, Benedict felt the need to act, to move and pull himself out of the growing paralysis that threatened to immobilize him completely. He needed to get off Triumvirate. Reasons, and more reasons. And yet, what he really wanted to do was return to his hotel room and sleep, forget all this.

"How many others involved?" he asked.

"Two others. We leave in eleven days for their home world."

"Assuming I join your expedition."

"I think you already have."

"I have a lot of questions that need to be answered before I can make that decision," Benedict said.

"Don't count on it. I tell you what you need to know, and I decide when. Right now you've heard everything you need."

"I don't like working blind."

"You won't be. Besides, you'll have to adjust. I make all plans, arrangements, provide equipment, supplies, finances, identification. I will allow input, certainly. And discussion. Your knowledge and experience are valuable. But I make all the decisions. I will have final say on everything, and you will do what I tell you." He paused, leaned forward. "We've noted your independent nature. You act on your own, ignore or override the decisions and orders of others."

"I work best that way."

"Not this time. Totally unacceptable. Understood?"

Benedict nodded slowly. "Understood." But not accepted, he thought. Never.

"Then you will join us?"

Benedict still did not want to make the decision,

though he knew that on some level he already had. He did not see that he had much choice—the alternative seemed to be wasting away on Triumvirate, the seizures becoming more frequent, his energy and motivation dwindling until nothing remained. He needed to do *something*. And . . . there was the possibility of contacting alien, intelligent life. That was still, more than ever perhaps, important to him.

"Yes," he said.

Ryker breathed slowly and deeply, apparently relieved. Had he doubted more than he'd let on? "Fine," Ryker said. "As I expected. In a few days I'll have all your identification materials, give you the finalized departure date and flight information. Until then you're free to do as you wish."

"That's very generous of you."

Ryker frowned, the thick brows twisting downward. "It will be much easier if we get along."

"We're too different, Ryker. You won't change, and I certainly won't. I don't like you, and I won't pretend. We'll have to live with that."

The big man hesitated for a few moments, then slowly nodded. "Okay. No illusions."

That's right, Benedict thought, no illusions. All his own had been destroyed, and he no longer had the strength to create new ones. He was stuck with reality.

Ryker put out his cigarette, tossed it with the others on the ground near the crushed cup, and stood.

"I'll contact you when everything's ready."

"Where can I reach you?"

"Nowhere." He turned and strode off into the rain.

Benedict watched him walk through the park and onto a crowded walkway, the mane of dark hair visible until he turned a corner and was gone from sight.

He got up from the table, picked up the cigarette ends and the crushed cup, dropped it all into a nearby recycler. The rain was even heavier now, and colder. Benedict pulled his coat tight around him, buttoned the collar, and headed back toward his hotel.

4

AFTER AN EARLY MORNING SESSION AT A CLINIC, WITH HIS arm in a healing unit, Benedict spent most of the following day trying to make connections with people he knew only indirectly—people he had heard of second- or third-hand over the years, mentioned in passing on some other world. Half the names he could recall did not exist in any of Triumvirate's directories. The others, when he could get through to them, refused contact, even when he detailed the lines of reference. With each attempt, he had to give his true name, which meant that what he had managed to keep secret for over a year was rapidly becoming common knowledge.

Finally, toward evening, he spoke with a woman who agreed to meet him. Her name was Tereze Abouti, and she had been highly praised by Karl Ruhman years before. Benedict had worked with Karl for two years on Mesa, supporting a revolution Benedict did not think about anymore if he could help it; which was why he tried her nearly last. Her name reminded him of Karl, and thinking of Karl threatened to bring back the memories of Mesa. He had to work to keep them suppressed.

Close to midnight, he waited in front of the deserted plaza of the Weber-Solinex building, the office high-rise lit from within, security personnel visible through the tall, wide glass doors of the reception area. The plaza itself was illuminated in dim orange, most of the lights ground-level spots smoking upward through the night mist. Benedict stood in the cover of a large abstract sculpture made of stone, wood, and coal rods. The sculpture looked to him like a diseased mushroom with three stalks and covered with bulging tumors.

An old, slightly rusted slipster glided into the plaza, slowed as it neared him. A window slid down, and a face appeared. It was a man with pale skin and light hair and dark, tired eyes. Benedict left the cover of the deformed mushroom and stepped up to the car.

"I'm Saltow," he said.

The man in the car nodded, withdrew. The window slid up, the rear door clicked and opened. Benedict climbed into the narrow back seat, his head brushing against the ceiling, and closed the door. The slipster pulled away from the plaza.

Two men sat in the front seat—the one he had first seen, and a driver. The first man swung a large rectangular object over the seat, and Benedict took it from him. It was a full-hand crypter; a line of amber dots flashed at him in the darkness of the car. Benedict slid aside cover plates and placed both hands into the deep slots. He pressed down, a pair of green lights blinked, and a high chirp sounded. The man in front studied the dashboard readout for a moment.

"All right," he said. He took the crypter back from Benedict and placed it on the floor.

They were traveling into the heart of Winterside. A half hour later they reached the equator and passed beneath the Central Freeway; the lights of the traffic produced a glowing band extending both north and south. The slipster shunted onto a wide, programmable roadway headed directly west. The driver keyed in a seven-digit code, then lay back against the seat and closed his eyes.

Fifteen or twenty minutes later, the slipster turned onto a narrow street between two tall buildings, and as they left the main road and dropped off the grid, the driver flipped back to manual and took the wheel in both hands.

Speed greatly reduced, they moved along between high walls, tall, dark buildings on both sides. They crossed two more narrow streets, then turned left at a third. The vehicle glided slowly under cones of dim gray light, the mist glistening in and out of the shadows. The walkways were nearly deserted. In the middle of the second block, the driver pulled the wheel and brought the slipster to a stop in an alcove carved out of a dark building.

The driver remained in the idling slipster. The other man got out and motioned for Benedict to follow. When Benedict stepped out, the driver immediately pulled away, turned a full 180 degrees, and moved off down the street.

Benedict's guide stood at a doorway barely distinct from the rest of the dark metal wall. He pushed a card into the door slot, keyed a sequence into the panel, then the card popped back out and the door slid open. Benedict followed him inside.

The near silence of the street was broken as they walked along a dark corridor lit from above by deep ruby light. Through the walls on his left, Benedict thought he recognized the muted thumping sounds of a stunner arcade, and on the right the unintelligible dialogue of a cinedome soundtrack.

They climbed a stairway at the end of the corridor, doubled back along a narrow ledge, then went through a door and into a small room dimly lit by a pair of ceiling globes.

A woman sat at the single wooden table, across from an empty chair. She looked up, and Benedict's guide said a few words in French, confirming Benedict's identity. The woman nodded, and the man withdrew.

She was tall and dark, with long black hair pulled behind her and reaching her waist. She was dressed in brown pants and a dark green pullover. The long, prominent nose and the black eyes looked familiar. Benedict approached the table, and the sense of familiarity increased.

She stared at him a moment, then softly smiled.

"It's you," she said. She shook her head, still smiling. "Hard to believe, all these years, but you. Name was different, so was mine."

Benedict looked at her, and then he, too, smiled.

"Likra," he said.

"No. Tereze. But was Likra. And you were Stennet."

Benedict nodded. Seeing her again brought back feelings of pleasure, but mostly of sadness and guilt, and the bitter disappointments of Mesa.

"Odd," he said. "Karl talked so much about Tereze Abouti, but never told me you and she were the same person."

"And never told me you were Benedict Saltow. Let our covers hold. Watched us, amused, I think."

"I imagine so. He probably enjoyed it." Benedict wondered if Karl ever enjoyed anything again.

They remained silent a long time, watching each other. They had almost become lovers on Mesa seven years ago. But that was the past, and there was no going back. Benedict did not *want* to go back, not to the memories of that world.

Tereze broke the silence. "Why me? What services, and when?"

Benedict looked to the open door. "Is this room polished?"

"As much as possible. We can talk freely."

"Part of what I have to say goes no further than you."

"Of course."

Benedict sat, placed his arms on the table. He was glad she was not a stranger; it would be easier. "I've been approached by someone I know nothing about. His name is Ryker. First or last, I don't know. He's backed by a group of people, perhaps a combine, but again I don't know who they are, where they're based, anything. It's very much a blind project, but . . . I've decided to join it anyway." He paused, feeling for some reason a need to justify himself, but he went on. "The actual team will be four people: Ryker, myself, and two others I don't know and haven't met. It's a . . . search expedition." He breathed in deeply. "Ryker claims that somewhere, again he hasn't told me, there have been contacts with aliens who may be intelligent."

Tereze nodded. "Yes, Nightshade is where they are."

"You know about this?"

"Not Ryker. Name's unfamiliar. But Nightshade, yes. All kept under, word out to few people, most reliable. So far. Several combines, other concerns, have search teams. Most are small." She smiled. "Four people, five. Some a little bigger. Too big, then secrecy problems. If these creatures are intelligent, much power, much wealth to be gained. But only for those in first, only those with control. Interworld laws and treaties? Forget. Fleet's useless, can't enforce damn thing. Nightshade laws? No, Nightshade means Flex, that means too much power and wealth. And an Old Earth expression—possession is ninety percent of law. First one in will possess these creatures, do what they want. Whoever finds them will exploit them. Some worse, but they're all bad." She leaned back. "Maybe an exception, somewhere. And you a part?"

"I want to be there if it's true."

Tereze nodded. "Maybe you can do something, to help these creatures."

"I'm not going along to help."

"Why *are* you going?"

"I've got personal reasons."

"Don't you think, if they're intelligent, they're worth helping?"

"I don't care anymore."

She smiled again. "That's not true." Benedict said nothing. "Tell you, I'm glad you're going. Maybe you'll find a way."

Benedict was not sure *he* was glad. "How could they be on Nightshade?" he asked. "And they haven't been found before? We've been there eighty, ninety years or something?"

"One hundred and twenty-seven years," Tereze said. "Yes, a long time, but. Only three large cities, a dozen much smaller. Most of the planet still unexplored. Contacts have been high in the mountains, deep in the jungle. Far from the cities. The Flex free-lancers have made the contacts. There's been a growing demand for Flex, always is, so the free-lancers have been going further."

It was plausible, he thought. From what he understood, the Flex combines had all the power on Nightshade, kept a tight rein on things. There would be no systematic exploration because the combines weren't interested in anything but Flex.

Flex. It was not surprising the combines had all that power, given the nature of the drug. It was, perhaps, the most intense euphoric anyone had discovered, with a big stimulant kick, and extremely addictive. Unlike other drugs, though, such as the opiates, Flex could lead to a point—the "crux"—beyond which withdrawal was impossible. With someone past the crux, withdrawal, no matter how sloped, meant death; past the crux, the drug itself led eventually to death. And so, as far as Benedict was concerned, Flex meant just that—death.

"Again," Tereze said, "what do you need from me?"

"I need to know more about this man Ryker, and the people behind him. In a few days we're going to meet again, make final arrangements. I want you to follow him, see where he's staying, who he meets. See if you can learn exactly who he is, do some info-searches for background. I'll let you know where I'll be meeting him, and when."

"Done. Like to say it won't cost, but never stir friendship with business." She smiled. "Slash rate, though. And only a small advance. Three thousand. Acceptable?"

Benedict nodded. "I'll be following him myself after we meet, so let your people know. I'll probably lose him, but I want to see what I can get firsthand."

"Fine." She took a slip of papris from a pocket and

pushed it across the table. "Transfer to this account. Leave day and time at the second number."

Benedict picked up the papris, folded it, and put it in his coat pocket. He stood.

"That's all," he said. He wanted to ask her about Karl, but couldn't do it.

Tereze stood as well. "Back the same way," she said. "Direk's waiting outside, and the slipster." She stepped forward and embraced him. "Good to see you again . . . Benedict."

Benedict returned the embrace; her smell brought back the memories once again, fleeting images, shimmers of emotion.

"Maybe when this is over," Tereze said, "you'll come back, no business, we can have a drink, a meal. Talk again."

"Yes, maybe."

She nodded, returned to her chair, and sat. "Go, Benedict. It's late."

Benedict walked to the door, looked back. Tereze was watching him, the smile gone, her face almost entirely void of expression.

"Go," she said again, her voice soft.

He turned away and walked out of the room.

BENEDICT WAITED ALONE IN A SMALL HIRED SLIPSTER, THE
windshield reflecting, in shifting patterns, the lights of
the Sheraton and the enormous fountain in front of
the hotel. The fountain was a triad of aquatic animals
carved from stone, with glowing streams of water
spraying out from eyes and gills in a shower of
color—deep greens and shifting hues of blue. The
closed mouths of the stone animals, combined with
the open, geyserlike eyes, reminded him of the tiny
sand creatures on Mesa that lived by the canals and
river, and spouted streams of sand into the flowing
water as they burrowed along the banks.

He had met Ryker in the Champagne Room of the
hotel more than an hour earlier, thirty-seven floors
above. Ryker, already half drunk and about to start
on a huge, steaming meal, had wanted Benedict to
join him for dinner. Benedict had refused, unwilling
to spend that kind of time with Ryker. An argument
had erupted, with Ryker trying to assert his authority,

and Benedict asserting his independence. It was a useless confrontation, Benedict realized, gaining nothing for either of them. Eventually, though, Ryker had given him all the idents and schedules, and Benedict had walked out, leaving Ryker to his enormous meal, his cigarettes, and his heavy drinking.

Ryker finally appeared, emerging from the central lobby entrance, a cigarette in his mouth, his head slightly tilted to one side, eyes half closed. He stumbled once near the fountain, then walked along to the transport curve, his gait unsteady. He stepped off the walkway as a cab pulled in, and flagged it. Ryker lurched in through the rear door, and after a few moments the cab pulled away. Benedict watched it maneuver through shuttles and omnis in front of the hotel, then started forward and followed the cab onto the main road, forty or fifty meters back.

Traffic was light, but there was enough so Benedict could follow unobserved. The cab turned eastward just short of the t-zone, then began a jagged path, moving north, then east, then north and east again. Benedict had to concentrate to keep track of the cab, and they were already deep inside the t-zone before he realized they had entered the Lido.

Benedict had been in the Lido district only once before. Although Triumvirate law technically applied within the Lido, in reality the Triumvirate Security forces kept only a nominal eye on the district, prepared to intervene only if major excesses occurred. Benedict had stayed away from the district, because he had no desires for anything the Lido could provide, and because it reminded him too much of Triskele, where he had grown up learning that the supreme law was simply to survive.

Traffic became heavier, and Benedict moved in closer. Without warning, the cab pulled to the side in front of a games parlor, and Ryker disembarked. He began walking along the street, steadier now, his carriage erect and firm. Benedict lanced forward, wove through several slipsters and omnis, then twisted into a public autopark, where he handed the slipster's scrambler to the valet, pocketed the voucher, and was quickly back out onto the street.

It took him a moment to spot Ryker, now on the opposite side of the street and moving away. Benedict remained across from Ryker, and kept pace a few steps back. The walkways were crowded, and Benedict easily kept hidden among the people moving in both directions.

The Lido was alive with light and sound, a throb of voices and odors and the jump and flash of color. Building faces were awash with neon and phosphor, deep reds that blended with violet, and harsh orange clashing with the pulse of blue and green. Within five minutes Benedict passed nightclubs, game parlors, bars and stunner arcades, walkside delis and cafes, cinedomes and pain houses, and two of the transient hotels that were hire-by-the-hour, two-day maximum. There were no permanent residents in the Lido, only those who lived on the fringes and shuttled in every day to run their businesses, partake of the services, or simply glide through the hours.

Ryker stopped in front of the Sensei Emerald, looked at the glittering window displays. Benedict had heard of the Sensei Emerald, and understood it to be a dance club that catered primarily to wealthy gay men, both young and old. He was surprised when, after some hesitation, Ryker went inside. Ryker struck him as, if anything, a phobe. Apparently Benedict had misjudged him.

Nearby was an open-air chika stand with several tables. Benedict ordered a half dozen Hi-Lan egg rolls and a pot of tea. He sat at a table back from the street, where he had a view of the Sensei Emerald, and yet was well out of sight.

Benedict ate the egg rolls slowly, methodically, and hardly noticed the flavor. He thought of how long it had been since he had cooked a meal for himself, how long it had been since he had lived in a place with a stove or oven. Almost seven years, since he'd left Mesa. He'd been living in hotels for all those years, moving constantly, never staying at one for more than two or three months. He wondered if he would ever consider anyplace home again.

The food was gone, and his tea was cold when Ryker emerged from the Sensei Emerald. At his side was a young Asian man, not much older than twenty, dressed in black and silver. His hair was straight and dark, cut extremely short on the left side, and long on the right. The hair on the right was braided into two tails. He was tall and muscular, and moved with a liquid grace.

Though the two men did not touch, it was clear as they walked down the street that they were together. Benedict left a cad-note on the table and strolled along behind them.

Ryker and his companion moved into an area closed off to vehicle traffic, and the crowd thinned as it spread into the road. At each intersection the flow of people became a confused web, and once, when Ryker and his companion turned off onto another street, Benedict nearly lost them.

Benedict stayed close as they moved along a street lined with stunner arcades. The street curved slightly, then opened into a large, oval plaza that was accessed by five other streets.

Ryker and the younger man crossed the plaza, headed toward a hotel at the triangular junction of two streets. Benedict watched them enter the lobby, then looked for a place to wait. Although the plaza was lined with outdoor cafes and restaurants, the tables were full at most of them, and some did not have a view of the hotel. Benedict skirted the edge of the plaza, keeping an eye on the hotel lobby. He considered returning to his own hotel, leaving the rest of the night for Tereze's people, but he found an empty table in front of a dark pub, against the outside wall. An artificial candle glowed in the middle of the table, and Benedict switched it off as he sat. With his back to the wall, he could just keep the lobby entrance in full view. He ordered straight coffee, a Niiri muffin to chew on, and sat back to wait.

A news hawker appeared a few meters away pulling a handcart into an open area. People began to gather around her as she set up the portable newsboard, and small groups formed in front of each of the board's four panels. The hawker then walked among the groups with her fee box, and when she collected enough cash, returned to the board, flipped on the power, and the panels came to life.

Words flowed across the panels, a series of headlines followed by general story outlines and major details. Each board covered a different subject area; the one facing Benedict carried news from the worlds of Gemini and Apollo. One of the others, he was certain, carried Triumvirate news, a third probably carried more general interworld news, and the fourth panel would cover something like art and entertainment blurbs. As the newslines flowed, the hawker sat by her cart, selling hard-copy full-text newspads for each of the panels.

Twenty minutes later a wind kicked up, twisted through the plaza in gusts with a biting chill. Awnings glided out over tables, and the benches out in the open gradually emptied. Hats and umbrellas appeared, and within a few minutes the rain began to fall.

The news hawker sold a few more newspads to the dwindling audience, then cut power and broke down the board. She packed it in her cart, covered it with a tarp. Benedict called to her, and when she came over handed her several coins. The woman nodded her thanks, gripped the handle of her cart, and pushed off into the rain.

Although the tables around him were packed with people trying to stay dry, he now had a clearer view across the open plaza to the hotel lobby. Still, Benedict realized he should leave. Ryker could be in the hotel all night, and Benedict could not keep watch indefinitely; that was Tereze's job.

A movement of dark hair on the street to the left of the hotel caught his eye. Benedict stood, twisted to look down the street, and saw a dark head just above the hats and umbrellas of other pedestrians. It disappeared around the curve in the street.

It had looked like Ryker, but Benedict was certain he had not come out through the hotel lobby. A side entrance? And so soon? Benedict decided to chance it, and he pushed away from the table and hurried across the plaza. The rain drenched his hair and face, and he pulled his coat more tightly around him to keep dry. The cold breezes added bite to the rain.

Two blocks from the plaza he caught sight of the dark, wet hair, but could see little else. He kept up a fast pace, and gained ground. Within a few minutes he was close enough to see more of the head and the upper half of the body.

It *was* Ryker, and he was alone, marching boldly along the street. Benedict slowed, matched the big man's pace.

The streets were changing. A few blocks from the plaza the roads were again open to vehicles. The cacophony of noise had dimmed, and the flash of colors dulled from block to block; businesses were less conspicuous, many of them closed. Everything about the streets became darker as they moved out of the Lido. Residential units—apartments, dormers, communals—appeared, then became dominant.

There were so few people on the walks now that Benedict had to stay further back. He kept close to the buildings and in the shadows of alcoves, doorways, unlit awnings.

Ryker slowed his pace to a leisurely stroll, and did not seem to have a specific destination in mind. He would stop at an intersection, look up and down the streets, then continue, sometimes headed west, sometimes north, sometimes backtracking to the south, but his overall course was away from the Lido. An occasional cab passed, some free to hire, but Ryker apparently wanted to stay on foot.

He turned down a narrow street. When Benedict reached the corner and looked around the building, he saw Ryker in front of a bar, beside two very drunk men. The men were laughing, leaning against the building for support, pointing occasionally at Ryker, but Ryker ignored them. He stared in through the window. Above his head a sign flashed "Lucky Red's" in flickering blue light. Ryker pushed the two men aside and walked into the bar.

Benedict crossed to the opposite side and walked slowly along the street. The two drunk men called out twice to him, then became quiet and shuffled down the street through the rain, sharing a single umbrella. At the first intersection they turned the corner and were gone from sight.

Benedict continued walking, very slowly, watching

the bar. A couple went in, and he wondered if they were Tereze's people. Or were they out on the street somewhere, hidden, waiting for Ryker to emerge? At the end of the block, he crossed the street, and stopped at the first doorway. It was recessed enough to provide minimal shelter from the rain, and he pressed himself into it. He could see Lucky Red's, and he settled his weight evenly on both legs, arms folded tightly against his chest.

Over the next fifteen minutes a few people entered or emerged from the bar, but Ryker stayed inside. Benedict decided he would wait a half hour more, but no longer. He was cold and wet and tired, and did not care much anymore what Ryker would do for the rest of the night.

The door he leaned against opened, and a woman appeared in the light from the inner hall. She was in her thirties, he guessed, blond, wearing a purple kimono, and barefoot.

"Need warmth, trickster?" she asked, smiling, her eyes only half open. The pupils were dilated, and he could see she had trouble focusing.

"Just waiting," he replied.

"Waiting for me?"

Benedict shook his head. "Someone else."

She reached out, weakly grabbed his wrist. Her hand was colder than the rain. "Come, find you some Flex."

So that's what it was, he thought. He gently removed her hand from his wrist, shook his head again. She leaned against the door frame, and looked up at him, her skin blotched and pasty. Still smiling, she slid to the floor, one leg inside, the other out on the walk. Rain spattered on the pale, shaved skin.

A cab turned onto the street, and Benedict watched it stop in front of Lucky Red's. Ryker emerged from the bar, arm in arm with a redheaded woman wrapped inside an acrylic shimmer-coat. They got into the cab, and the cab moved down the street, passing by Benedict and the woman at his feet. He did not move. There was no way to follow. Perhaps it was just as well. His head ached, and his stomach felt queasy.

He turned back to the woman. She had reached out and grabbed his ankle, now tugged at it. After a minute she gave up and looked at him.

"No?"

Benedict shook his head. Time to go, he thought. He was tired.

The sound of a door opening came from inside the building and up a flight or two of stairs. Somewhere out of sight, a woman screamed down from above.

"Bitch, back here now! Flex me, bitch, Flex me!"

The woman on the floor rolled her head from side to side and closed her eyes with a moan. She did not get up, and the door above slammed shut. Silence returned. The woman held out her hand, palm up, and let rain fall into it. She brought her hand to her mouth and licked the droplets, then let the hand fall back at her side.

Benedict stepped out of the doorway and walked down the street, watching for a cab to take him back to the autopark, and not caring if one came by.

6

"NICE FRIEND YOU HAVE IN RYKER," TEREZE SAID. "Suggest you pull out, find some other way to Nightshade, or forget it completely."

"I can't."

She nodded. "I know."

They had met again in the same small room, but she had taken Benedict through a series of halls and doorways and out onto the street. Now they walked along a narrow roadway in silence. They crossed an open, flat lot, then went into a stadium where a lacrosse match was in progress. The stadium was less than a quarter full, perhaps ten thousand people at most; he and Tereze had no trouble finding isolated seats in the upper deck. Tereze drank warm ale from a flask, and Benedict declined her offer to share it. Something was bothering Tereze; he could sense a trace of uneasiness in her. He raised a screen to block it off, and turned to watch the lacrosse match below, one team in blue, the other in black.

"How soon are you leaving?" Tereze asked.

"Two days."

"Good. Much longer, the Lido soldiers would probably find him. End of your expedition."

"Why? What happened?" One of the players in blue tripped an opponent from behind with his crosse, and the man in black sprawled onto the grass, then came up swinging his crosse like a club. The man in blue parried the blow with his own crosse. By then, other players arrived and pulled the two men from each other. Benedict noticed that the referees had stayed away from the fight, and now waited for the players to settle to. After a few minutes, the match resumed.

"The Sensei Emerald and its patrons are sacrosanct in the Lido," Tereze began. "No injury, no harm to any of the patrons except by mutual consent. Ryker violated that code. You were there. You saw the young man Ryker left with? Ryker nearly killed him. Brought him to the hotel room, stripped and gagged him, then beat him with his fists, boots, a chair. He did it because Nishikida is gay. Ryker's a phobe, and pathological."

So, Benedict thought, his initial judgment had been accurate. It did not make him feel better.

"How is he?" he asked. "Nishikida."

"He'll live. Probably no permanent physical damage. But he'll be in clinic for at least three weeks."

Christ. Benedict closed his eyes for a moment. It must have been bad.

"But only the beginning," Tereze continued. "Later, he went to a bar outside the Lido, slicked up a woman there."

"I know."

"Cut her up badly while he was . . . what? Enthralled in passion? The woman seemed to think he was more interested in the blood than her body. She didn't care. Flex addict. She even gave him the knife to use on her. Gave her enough cash to keep her in Flex for two months. She's past the crux, she'd die without it. No complaints, won't press any charges, says it was worth it. A sick man, your friend."

Benedict wanted to tell her Ryker wasn't his friend, but he knew Tereze understood that. "Anything since that night?"

Tereze shook her head, drained the flask. "No. He's keeping in, low visibility. He probably knows the Lido soldiers are searching for him."

Benedict leaned back in his seat, no longer interested in the lacrosse match. There was hardly a cloud in the sky, and the few high above them were light and fluffy and drifted slowly past. There was to be no rain for a day and a half.

"Have you been able to learn anything about him?"

"Some names," Tereze said. "Hannes Ryker. Damon Ryker. Relker Hanne. Probably born Hannes Ryker, on Earth. An Earth native who left. They're getting rarer each decade. Very light, what we could find on him. Worked a solo scouter for Amalg Colonies. Didn't find a single optimum, not even a fringe or possible. Found nothing but balls of ice or fire or solid rock, apparently. He resigned after six years, citing his failures. As if every world he scouted had turned bad because he discovered it. Strange way of thinking, your friend." She shrugged. "After that, nothing. Don't know who he worked for later, who he works for now. Has nearly unlimited credit at his disposal, though. Not his, but his to use."

"That's it?"

"Told you, very light. Give me three months, I could do better. For a few days, you have plenty."

"Still watching him?"

"Yes. Just before you leave, call, I'll flip you anything new. You want to know where he's staying?"

Benedict leaned forward and shook his head. He tried to concentrate on the lacrosse match. "Not really."

"Transfer another two thousand five into the account I gave you," Tereze said. "That'll cover until you leave."

"All right." The players seemed to be running chaotically about the field, with random movements, and he could not follow the action. "I should be leaving," he said.

"Wait." Tereze stood, searching the stands. She waved twice, then sat again, turned to Benedict. "Time to meet an old acquaintance first." Her uneasiness (or was it guilt?) had increased, was again coming in through his filters.

"Who?"

She didn't answer. She looked down along one of the aisles. Benedict followed her gaze, saw a man climbing the steps toward them. He wore dark, reflecting sunglasses, and the diffuse, artificial sunlight glanced dully from them. When the man was still ten or twelve rows away, Benedict recognized him. It was Jean-Philippe Blanchot.

Benedict had known him on Dante's Eye four years before. Jean-Philippe had been in charge. He had overseen all the various projects, experiments, and operations on Dante's Eye connected to the creatures by the lava flows. He'd organized and coordinated the physicists, biologists, sociologists, chemists, all the scientists and researchers with their observation teams, and he had run the actual attempts at communication. He and Benedict had not always gotten along; Benedict was too independent, too unwilling to

47

subsume his own ideas and plans. But they had always respected each other.

Jean-Philippe approached, walking along the row of seats in front of them. He seemed thinner now to Benedict, and his hair was almost completely gray.

"Hello, Benedict."

"Jean-Philippe."

They shook hands, and Jean-Philippe sat on the back of a seat, facing them.

"Tereze tells me you're going to Nightshade. With an expedition searching for intelligent alien beings."

Benedict looked at Tereze, but she would not meet his gaze. "Yes," he said. He strengthened his screens, blocking out her discomfort.

Jean-Philippe nodded. "We'd like you to help us, Benedict."

"And who is 'us'?"

"An organization similar to the one we had on Dante's Eye. Much larger now. More equipment and money and expertise at our disposal. We've been rebuilding steadily."

"And waiting for your chance."

"Yes."

"And this is it. On Nightshade."

"Yes again."

"What the hell do you need me for?"

Jean-Philippe adjusted his sunglasses, then scratched at the side of his nose. "We can't go into Nightshade the way we did on Dante's Eye. Everything is different. Before we make any moves, we have to know for certain that these beings *are* intelligent."

A halfhearted cheer rose from the spectators, and Benedict looked past Jean-Philippe to see that the team in black had scored. "So tell me," he said. "Why do you have to know first?"

Jean-Philippe hesitated, then went on. "Nightshade

is Flex. The Flex industry, as you'll see when you arrive, controls everything on that world. Air traffic is limited to three air corridors, all rigidly monitored, deviations discouraged by destruction. The satellite surveillance and security networks are overwhelming. Air approaches to the jungles, either from space or from within the cities, are suicide. The other major access to the jungles, where it appears most likely they'll be found, is by river, and the waterways are just as rigidly monitored and controlled as the airways are. Affiliation with one of the Flex combines is a must. Which leaves exploration by foot, and even that is dangerous. It's also practically without hope, though we are following that line for lack of other options."

"I understand all that. But what do you want from me?"

"You go on this expedition with this man. If you make contact with these beings, and you can determine whether or not they are intelligent, you let us know. Either have a transceiver graft done before you leave, and signal us when you know, or go without it and return to the nearest city and contact us from there when you know something. I'll give you frequencies, times, call codes, links."

"And then what happens?"

"If they're not intelligent, nothing. We pull back, and leave Nightshade. Wait for the next chance, the next world."

"And if they are intelligent?"

"We're prepared to go in with force, which is the only way. We're ready to neutralize the satellite networks, then come in from space, armed to establish and protect ourselves until we can negotiate agreements with the Flex combines."

"A lot of people would die," Benedict said.

Richard Paul Russo

"Which is why we have to know." Jean-Philippe sighed heavily. "How could we justify those measures if it was discovered these beings were not intelligent? That people had died for nothing? But if they are intelligent, we need to protect them, prevent them from being exploited. That's why we need you."

"Why not send your own people in?"

"We've tried. But you can't do much unless you're directly affiliated with one of the combines. We haven't managed that yet. Probably won't. You, though, are being invited in. This man Ryker must be backed by a combine, or by someone with close connections."

"Might not be. Might be a renegade mission, like that."

"Yes, but we've judged that unlikely." Jean-Philippe paused, then removed his sunglasses and looked directly at Benedict. "We won't get another chance like this. You'll be the best shot we have."

Benedict stood, paced back and forth in front of the seats. Christ, another decision he did not want to make. "You realize," he said, "that if I get a transceiver graft, and Ryker discovers it, I'm dead."

"Yes, we know. And if you don't get one, trying to leave the expedition and get back to the city to contact us will be almost as dangerous. We realize we're asking you to take risks. You've taken them in the past."

"I'm tired of taking risks."

"Just going to Nightshade on this expedition, with this man Ryker, is a risk."

"It's for myself. Working for you means taking risks for someone else."

"Will you do it, Benedict?"

Benedict looked back onto the field. The team in

50

black scored again, and another fight broke out. Once again the referees walked away, ignoring it. This time the fight sucked in all the players, and Benedict watched as they beat at each other with fists and sticks, kicked with their cleated shoes. The three referees stood together across the field, smoking.

"I don't know," he finally said.

Jean-Philippe held out a folded sheet of papris. "It's all on here, call codes, people who can help, all of that. When you decide, let Tereze know. She'll contact me."

Benedict took the papris. Jean-Philippe put his dark glasses back on, and once more Benedict could not see any sign of the man's eyes. But Benedict could sense his doubts.

"Good-bye, Tereze. Good-bye, Benedict."

"Good-bye, Jean-Philippe," Tereze said.

He nodded once, then started down the aisle. He turned into a stadium tunnel and was gone.

"I could use more ale," Tereze said. She tapped at the empty flask. "Have a drink somewhere with me?"

"No, I don't think so." The fight on the field had finally broken and the referees wandered toward midfield to continue the match.

"I had to tell him, Benedict," Tereze said. "Maybe I should have mentioned him to you, something. Asked, anyway. But . . . was important, I thought."

Benedict shook his head. "It doesn't matter."

"Benedict, what's happened to you? Was it Mesa?"

He turned to face her, then sat down. "Mostly, I suppose. Mesa, and DreamVeil. New Carthage. Dante's Eye and Triskele and the Lido three nights ago and the lacrosse match right now on the field." He turned and gazed down at the field. All that registered in his vision were tiny dark blurs of motion.

"Why *are* you going to Nightshade, Benedict?"

"Would you believe me if I said I didn't really understand all the reasons myself?"

"I suppose. You must have some ideas."

"Yes." He did not go on. How could he explain?

"Jean-Philippe says you have some fixation, on finding intelligent alien life. Says *that's* why you're going."

"That's a part of it, certainly. A large part."

"But why?"

Benedict breathed deeply, shook his head. "I want escape." He turned and faced her. "After what happened on Mesa . . . I've given up on people. On humanity. Being a First Order empath, which I cannot change, makes it unbearable for me to be alone, to isolate myself. But I can longer bear to be an empath among human beings. So, maybe I can be an empath among some strange, alien creatures instead, on some world away from people. Maybe that would be more bearable. I want escape from humanity."

"Do you really?"

"Yes."

"I'm not sure that really makes sense."

"Difficult to explain. I know what I feel, but putting it into words . . ." He shrugged.

"I don't think you really want escape. I don't think you're really that pessimistic about people. You haven't given up on all humanity."

"Oh, but I have. I don't believe in anyone anymore. Not Jean-Philippe, not you, not even myself."

Tereze shook her head again, smiling this time. "You may not realize it, Benedict, but that's just not true. It's crap, is what it is. You're using it as an excuse to let yourself go to hell."

"I don't need amateur analysis." He turned away from her, tried once more to concentrate on the lacrosse match, but couldn't. "Karl," he said after a long time. "Do you know anything?"

"He's still alive, you call it that. I get blips on him. He's little more than hatred and bitterness and guilt. Physicians think he's kept himself an invalid, that he should heal, but he doesn't." She paused. "Nothing you or I can do for him."

Benedict remained silent. He wanted to leave with Tereze now, go somewhere and have a drink or two, then find a room in a hotel or chalet and spend the rest of the day and night in bed with her. But he was afraid. Afraid he would lose control of the filters and screens, afraid of what he would find deep inside her. It would be easier if Tereze was a stranger, then it wouldn't matter what she felt, it wouldn't matter what happened. But she was not a stranger, and despite everything, it still *did* matter. He stood, looked down at her.

"I need to go."

"You need something, Benedict."

No argument, he thought. "I'll talk to you in a couple of days."

"Are you going to do it?" she asked. "For Jean-Philippe?"

"I still don't know."

She nodded. "Benedict, do what you can on Nightshade. And what you can't, you can't. And come back, see me."

"All right." He turned and walked away, left her sitting alone in the stadium under a dry, gray sky.

7

HE WANTED TO SEE HADLING ONE LAST TIME BEFORE HE LEFT.
But Hadling had always initiated their meetings,
sought him out, and Benedict had always been content with that. He did not know where Hadling lived.

Benedict checked with the residential directory,
and was surprised at Hadling's location, an apartment
number in Trilling Heights. Trilling Heights was two
hours away by transporter, inside the t-zone, an
enclave of refugees from abandoned worlds. Benedict
had been through districts like Trilling Heights before, in both t-zones, had been inside some of the
residences, and knew what to expect. The buildings
were cheap metal prefabs, structurally sound enough,
but more appropriate for laboratory animals. There
was no space between buildings, no privacy between
apartments with the thin walls, and rooms were small,
usually only two meters square in the bedrooms, and
not much larger in living areas. Consequently the
residents spent as little time as possible inside, and

the streets, most closed off to vehicle traffic, were nearly always crowded and noisy.

Dressed in worn, faded clothing, Benedict rode a public transporter through the late morning overcast, the clouds still holding back the rain. He made one transfer at the border of the t-zone, and as the second transporter entered the t-zone, the rain began. It quickly built into a gusting storm, then just as quickly dropped off until the rain stopped completely, clouds twisting overhead and splitting apart to occasionally let in light from above. Weather in the t-zones was more violent, and essentially unpredictable, the price paid for the nearly complete control in Winterside and Summerside. The transporter let him off at the edge of Trilling Heights where vehicle barriers marked the entrance.

The air was warm, humid. Benedict strengthened his filters and screens as he walked through the crowds toward Hadling's building, allowing in a minimal background. People filled the walks and streets, children and adults, many of them milling without any apparent destination. He even saw a number of loose pets—silters, dogs, frizas, and cats—on the streets, playing. The noise level was high, men and women talking to each other, children running and squealing, people yelling to or from windows above the street. Most of what he heard was Portuguese, which meant this was probably a group of refugees from Ibarra —refugees who had been "generously" lifted off when the planet's just tolerable weather went wild, threatening to kill everyone on the small, barren world. A colonization combine, the original settler corp that had brought the Portuguese colonists to Ibarra four years before, ran the rescue, then shipped them to the nearest terminal, Triumvirate, and left them there after Gemini and Apollo had refused immigration.

Most of the refugees had nothing, no way to ship off Triumvirate to another world, no way to earn the fare. They had been on Triumvirate nearly two years, if Benedict remembered rightly. They had no more hope now than they did two years ago.

As he walked, Benedict felt the background tension common to almost all the refugees, the frustration and anger that had been locked inside them for so long. It was a solid undercurrent, hidden beneath the casual conversations, the occasional jokes and smiles. It even ran through the children as they played, though more subdued and vague, unfocused. Benedict was surprised at the intensity of the tension, at how close the anger was to the surface. These people were ready to explode.

Their only real hope now was that some barely habitable world would be discovered, and one of the colonization combines would come in and offer volunteers free passage from Triumvirate to the new world. There they would break their backs trying to produce food from unforgiving soil, work themselves to exhaustion and early deaths forging the way for later colonists, making the mistakes and learning the fatal lessons that would save others. At least they would have a chance then. If they rioted here on Triumvirate, a stronger possibility the longer they remained, they would simply be massacred.

He found Hadling's building and entered the foyer, which was deserted, hot, and stifling. A sign said the elevators were operable only to the sixth floor that day, and he rode one that far, wondering about the people who lived at the top, on the sixteenth floor. From the sixth floor Benedict climbed three flights of darkened stairs, the air more stifling than in the foyer.

The ninth-floor hall was stuffy and stale, but he had smelled worse, and it was cleaner than he expected.

Bare metal showed through worn spots in the carpet, and some of the ceiling lights were out. His footsteps were loud, and echoed off the walls whenever his heels struck metal instead of fabric. He came to Hadling's door, and knocked.

A dark young girl of eight or nine years opened the door and stuck her head out. She looked up at him, and her eyes widened. The sound of other voices, indistinct, floated out from the interior. The girl stared for a few moments, then slammed the door shut. He listened to her footsteps, short and rapid, retreat. Before he decided whether or not to knock a second time, the door opened again.

An older girl looked out at him, perhaps fifteen or sixteen years of age. She was darker than the first, with deep brown, tightly curled hair, a flattened nose, and soft brown eyes, as much a young woman as a girl.

"Help you?" she asked.

"I'm looking for Gird Hadling."

"Name?"

He hesitated, then said, "Benedict. Benedict Saltow."

"Wait." She closed the door softly, and he heard the lock click.

The silence in the hall was cold and hollow, as if all the apartments on both sides were empty, deserted. He wanted to drop all his screens, let the feelings of the people around him inside to reassure him that he was not alone. It was an odd feeling, since being alone was what he usually wished for. Benedict kept the screens intact.

The older girl opened the door, nodded, and stepped aside to let him in. As he expected, the apartment was small and cramped. The front door opened directly into the living room, which was three meters square at most. Half a dozen worn chairs and as many cushions were scattered about, and a small video set was stationed in the corner. There were no windows.

"This way," the girl said. They went past three small rooms and through another door into the kitchen. Hadling was seated at a table set against one wall, feeding a small child strapped into a tall high-backed chair with padded support cushions. He did not turn or look up when Benedict walked in.

"Seat, Benedict, with you a minute."

Benedict sat in the chair furthest from Hadling, leaned against the wall. The girl went to the sink and started cleaning plates and utensils. There was a large window on the opposite wall, but the building behind it was so close and tall that the light coming in was dim and gray. Still, it was enough so the atmosphere in the kitchen was less oppressive than the rest of the apartment. The table and chairs were made of hard plastic and metal, legs dented, the finish chipped and dull. The walls were covered with children's drawings, and the stove and fridge were old but clean.

Benedict heard the front door open and close, then two boys ran into the kitchen. They stopped when they saw him, but did not appear to be frightened. Both were about twelve years old and thin, one a pale blond and the other a redhead.

"Johann," the blond said.

"Hiro." The redhead.

"I'm Benedict."

They came forward and put out their right hands. Benedict shook each hand firmly.

Hadling put down the spoon and unstrapped the child. Benedict saw now that it was a girl, maybe four or five. She did not seem to have much control of her head or limbs, and her eyes blinked spasmodically. Hadling lifted her out of the chair and swung her back and forth a few times, one hand firmly supporting her neck. She smiled and made a noise in her throat. He walked over to the two boys and they reached up and around with their arms, locked hands. Hadling lowered the girl so they carried her while supporting her head and body at the same time.

"Back to Leila," he said. He went with them to let them out the front door. When he returned he spoke to the girl at the sink.

"Nita, watch. Back in hour, maybe."

The girl nodded, continued washing without looking up. "Somewhere else to talk," Hadling said to Benedict.

As they walked toward the front door, the young girl who had first opened the door poked her head out from one of the bedrooms. She remained silent, staring, but Hadling went to her, tousled her hair. She grinned and pulled back inside the room.

They walked down the eight flights of stairs and passed through the empty foyer. Outside, a warm drizzle had begun, but the streets were just as crowded; people put on hats, or moved under cover, or just got wet, but for the most part no one moved inside.

Hadling brought Benedict to a small restaurant about a five-minute walk from the apartment. Inside was noisy and crowded. Music played from somewhere in the back, though Benedict could make out little more than a thumping bass line that vibrated the air. They slid into a small booth by a window and ordered coffee from the waitress. She brought two cups almost immediately. The coffee was weak, acidic, and did not set well in Benedict's stomach, but it was hot. Hadling smiled, took out a small flask of brandy from inside his coat, added a twist to each cup. It helped the taste, and helped Benedict's stomach a little.

59

Richard Paul Russo

"Surprised see you," Hadling said. "Surprised initiative, find me, trip here."

"Your family?" Benedict asked.

"A sense." His smile faded. "I'm only family they have. Not the one feeding, Brie. She's Leila's. A friend. Having rough time, financial, emotional. Partner dead or gone, unclear. She won't talk it. I help with Brie." He shrugged. "The others, my family, yes. They have no one else."

"Why, Gird?"

Hadling breathed deeply. As he spoke, the clipped dialect gradually lessened, making it easier to follow.

"Here on Triumvirate, almost ten years. Can leave anytime I wish, plenty of credit, good jobs if I want. Education good. Experience. People here," and he waved his hand around, gesturing toward everyone in the restaurant, "can't leave. Stuck, trapped. No money, no credit, no jobs. So no food, or very little. I'm trying to help." He sighed, looked out the window. The rain was heavier, and slanted now with a strong wind. "Why? Could give my personal history, but not sure it's relevant. I *know* why, but would take too long to explain. Important to me, though. That's enough." He turned back to Benedict. "I know I can't help all, can't do much, but what I can, I do. So, the kids. Parents killed or gone, no family, on the streets, stealing, begging, starving, sick in the rain. No one cares. No, not true. Here they care, but can't do anything. Those with money, means, don't care. I take them in, do what I can. Keep them from dying, maybe."

"But why stay here? Take them somewhere else, better area, bigger apartment. Maybe get them some schooling."

Hadling shook his head, drank some of his coffee. "What happens I die, or the money goes? They'd shift

60

back to a place like this, but not knowing how to survive anymore. I do what I can, *here*. If I can help them learn to get out on their own, terrific. They do it themselves, though. Understand?"

Benedict nodded. Much of what he had learned about survival came from growing up alone on Triskele, his parents dead; learning how to make it day to day in an urban jungle that did not allow for mistakes. In many ways, he did not wish any of it had been different.

A disturbance in the street caught their attention, and they both looked out the window. At first all they saw were people moving out of the roadway and onto the walks, most confused, some apparently frightened. A flicker of orange appeared, and several cries could be heard. The noise level inside the restaurant dropped, and people moved to the windows and doorways to watch.

Two crashes sounded, and a sheet of flame spread along the edge of the roadway. A group of men and women came right behind it, marching along the middle of the road. They each carried a basket of small brown canisters, and they yelled at people on both sides of the street. Periodically one of them would throw a canister to the ground, the canister would burst, and a stream of orange flame would emerge.

Hadling pushed out of the booth and stood. "Got to stop before goes full scale!" He started squeezing through the people in the restaurant blocking the doorway.

Suddenly, just as the group passed the restaurant, a larger group appeared from behind, chasing the first group. A struggle broke out as the newcomers tried to wrest away the baskets, tried to stop the people from throwing any more canisters. As the fighting continued, more people from the walkways converged on the two groups. Two canisters burst into flames amidst them, and a figure staggered out of the crowd, his clothing afire. Two people tackled him and rolled onto his body, smothering the flames.

Benedict saw Hadling break free from the restaurant doorway and head out toward the road. But he hesitated as the fighting appeared to wind down, and the flames subsided. Several people had confiscated all the canisters, and carried them away. Those who had been throwing the canisters were bunched together, hands bound behind their backs, and they were led along the road and out of sight. Hadling headed back for the restaurant as other groups of people worked at putting out the small fires that remained. By the time Hadling sat down again, the street had returned to normal.

"You could have helped, Benedict." He asked for more coffee, and poured two twists of brandy into each cup, shaking his head.

Benedict didn't say anything. What could he tell Hadling? That he didn't see any point? A riot now, or two weeks from now, what difference? It only delayed what was inevitable.

"Two and a half years ago, there was a riot here," Hadling said. "Similar situation, a community of Scandinavian refugees from some colonization attempt that had self-destructed. The one on Windover, if you know it."

Benedict nodded. He'd heard of the colonizing disaster, and he'd heard of the riot.

"They'd been here for over three years," Hadling went on. "A lot of them had died, situation was getting worse all the time. One day a few went berserk, like those out there just now. Only instead of stopping them, everyone else joined in. Turned into one massive riot that spread from building to building, constantly growing. The Triumvirate Security forces coptered in, attacked from the air. Didn't try to control it, just cleared it out. Dropped incendiaries, frag-bulbs, sonics." Hadling closed his eyes, shook his head, then drank all his coffee and brandy. "Over eight hundred people killed. Johann's parents. Hiro's entire family, including six brothers and sisters."

They sat in silence for a long time. The waitress brought more coffee, but they did not drink any of it. Benedict felt ill again.

"Now," Hadling said. "Why are you here? Why track me?"

Benedict did not say anything at first. He had just wanted to say good-bye, spend some time with Hadling once more. Somehow, something else had come of it. He did not understand what yet, but he felt different.

"I'm leaving Triumvirate tomorrow," he said at last. "I wanted to tell you, say good-bye."

"Leaving for where?"

Benedict smiled. "I haven't been told."

"Won't tell me why, will you?"

Benedict shook his head. He stopped smiling. "Gird, I don't know if I'll be back here on Triumvirate again."

Hadling looked steadily at him for a long time, then nodded once. "Hope something good, Benedict."

"So do I." He turned and watched the rain cleansing away the last signs of a riot that had not happened. "So do I."

8

HIS NAME, FOR THE MOMENT, WAS STENNET REESE AGAIN. That's what was on all the documentation Ryker had given him. It would be easy to remember.

In the morning, Benedict left his single bag in a wall cube in the spoke terminus lobby, then went into the Blue Danuub one last time. After nearly two days without rain in Winterside proper, the clouds above were dark and heavy, but there was no rain yet, and he wondered if it would hold off until he was gone.

He ordered a chilled fruit salad and a bowl of cream sherbroth, but he could only eat half the fruit, and the broth was so greasy he gave up after two spoonfuls. His stomach was in rebellion again.

Earlier, he had called Tereze, but she had nothing new for him on Ryker. He told her to contact Jean-Philippe, tell him he would help, if possible. She accepted his decision without comment, then again told him to do what he could, and not worry about what he couldn't. And warned him to watch his back with Ryker.

Benedict had the fruit and soup removed, then ordered a bottle of clearwater. The sky grew darker, like dusk, and the lights moving along the spoke shaft were as bright as they were at night. He would soon be in a pod himself, hurtling up toward the hub.

He did not want to go.

His resolve had faded. He wished Hadling would come by, sit at the table for a while, have a drink. They could talk, or just sit and watch the people leave and arrive, knowing that neither of them would be going anywhere.

The clearwater was cold, and soothed his stomach. He even wished Tereze would appear, perhaps try to talk him out of going. But she was right, he needed something. He did not want to go, but he had to. And maybe . . . maybe something good *would* come of it.

He had time, though, if only an hour or two. He sat with his hand on the bottle, and watched the lights of the spoke, emerald stars rising into the clouds above.

PART TWO
Riotmark

1

HIS BODY HAD TO ADAPT TO FREQUENT CHANGE. BUT BENE-
dict had been through it all many times, and though
there was discomfort he was only vaguely aware of it.

First was the initial thrust of the pod as it accelerated toward the hub. Then there was the drop-off
sensation of floating internal organs as the pod quickly decelerated and gravity dramatically decreased
near the hub.

Next came the zero gee of the inner docking wheel
and the jumpliner cabin, followed two hours later by
hard, twisting thrust as the ship tumbled away from
Triumvirate and accelerated toward the first step-off.
Most passengers chose to be completely sedated for
the duration of the trip, but Benedict rode through
without medication, the gee forces muted by a gel-
foam cradle.

Finally came the most disorienting changes of all as
the ship reached the step-off and jumped quietly out

of the universe. For two shipboard days, everyone conscious moved about in a semidaze, as though the nonuniverse outside the ship was leaking through to the interior, affecting passengers and crew alike.

After two days came the nearly solid mental jolt as the ship dropped back into the universe, between ten and a hundred light years from the step-off. Then the process began again.

Three jumps were needed to reach Wilder's Station, the jump terminal above the plane of the Nightshade system. Wilder's Station was only a fraction of Triumvirate's size, with little traffic other than the Flex cargo ships. It served only Nightshade and the three sparsely inhabited, and barely habitable, worlds of another nearby system—Homer, Ovid, and Virgil. There were no open skies in Wilder's Station, no hotels or restaurants or parks, no streets or buildings or athletic stadiums. It was a solid spoked wheel tunneled through with a webwork of enclosed corridors, small rooms, and cargo holds. Only the crews who ran the station and worked the docks resided at the station, usually in nine- or twelve-month shifts. No one lived there permanently, and no one traveled to Wilder's Station for a luxury vacation.

Benedict and Ryker saw nothing of the station but the two inner docking wheels. They disembarked from the liner, checked the transfer of their bags, then shuttled in a long, serpentlike train of open carts to the opposite side of the hub, where they waited for a conventional propulsion ship to complete its cargo loading. There was no cafe to wait in, no restaurant or bar. They waited with several hundred other people in a large, wide corridor filled with cushioned seats and food and drink dispensers in the walls, many of which were out of order.

Though Benedict wanted to be alone, Ryker sat

beside him, smoking. Benedict closed his eyes and eased Ryker's presence into the background, transforming all the nearby conversation into a dull, meaningless buzz punctuated by the knocks and clatter of food and drink ejected by the dispensers.

He tested the strength of the inner screens and filters, but was not reassured by their apparent solidity. A seizure was due soon, he was certain of that. How long would he be able to keep them from Ryker? And what would Ryker do if he learned of them? If they were far enough along, Benedict hoped, Ryker would not be able to do anything.

At last a voice crackled over the com system to announce the boarding of the Nightshade ship. Within an hour Benedict was alone again, strapped into the bunk of his small cabin, ready for the three-day flight.

The seizure struck two days out. If it had to come, Benedict thought as the first waves of emotion swept through him, this was the best time for it. He was alone, and though overwhelmed by the unfiltered emotions of passengers and crew, most were fairly subdued, by either sedation or sleep.

He crawled into his bunk and strapped himself down, then trembled and sweated through the unusually long seizure, nearly an hour. Compared to the last one, it was mild, but it seemed to continue endlessly, and he felt sick inside, helpless with a dread he suspected was his own.

The seizure ended gradually, his control over the filters and screens returning over several minutes rather than all at once. When they were all back in place, secure and seemingly impregnable, Benedict felt hollow and drained, but without relief. Exhausted, he drifted into a fitful sleep.

The ship docked at an orbiting station above Nightshade. This time they had only an hour wait as Ryker managed to get space on the next shuttle out of the station. Caught in space between night and day, they dropped into the atmosphere and descended toward the city of Riotmark.

2

THE SHUTTLE GLIDED IN TOWARD THE CITY AT DAWN. Through the small window at his left, Benedict watched the glass in Riotmark's buildings appear to burst into flames with the rising sun, a painful glare of bright orange and white.

They approached over the rocky plains southeast of Riotmark, an expanse of fused silicate littered with small stones. Even from a great distance Benedict could see the Morgan'de River weaving through the city. A few kilometers to the south, the Morgan'de became a chute of unnavigable rapids ending in an enormous waterfall before the river became calm again. To the north, the wide river emerged from the vast tract of jungle, still blanketed by fog, then flowed into the city. Occasionally Benedict caught glimpses of the much smaller western tributary, the Qua Tri, which joined the Morgan'de in the heart of Riotmark.

As they descended, Benedict could make out details of the spaceport. Shuttles, planes, copters, and space freighters were scattered with apparent randomness among the beaded strings of ground vehicles and the various structures—loading facilities, hangars, gantries, maintenance sheds, and the tentacles of the terminal protruding from the city proper along the edges of the port.

Their descent steepened, and the shuttle approached the head of one of the barium yellow, crisscrossing runways. His view of the river and the jungle vanished behind the metal and glass of the buildings, and the shuttle began to vibrate with a long loud shudder. The ground came up quickly, the shuttle nose lifted, and a few moments later they touched ground. Braking systems punched in with a loud, extended hiss, pressed Benedict against the restraints.

The shuttle slowed, then turned and taxied in toward the port. The sun was rising, and the sky was clear. Benedict tried to imagine what it would be like to breathe open air for the first time in more than a year.

Four hours later, Benedict and Ryker emerged from the subterranean customs and examination chambers into the cool, sterile air of the main terminal. Ryker seemed more at ease, and carried his field pack at his side. They rode moving walkways along the terminal arm toward the main entrance. The terminal was busy, crowded with people walking and running in all directions or waiting in long lines. Eventually they reached the long, gliding entrance doors and stepped out into the city.

The air, though heavier with the humidity and slightly higher pressure, felt freer than that on Triumvirate. It was late morning, and already quite warm and muggy, but Benedict felt a fresh, gentle surge of energy that seemed to lightly crack the shell of his paralysis.

They walked to the transport loop, and Ryker waved in a cab, a small gray car with a quiet engine. The driver was a stocky, short-haired woman who did not even glance at them. The trunk lid swung open, and Ryker put their bags inside. They climbed into the back seat and Ryker gave the woman two names, presumably streets. Without a word, the driver pulled out of the loop and onto the road.

Here near the terminal, high-rises overwhelmed the skies, office buildings and exclusive residentials with metal and glass and polished stone shining in the morning sun. Riotmark had its share of wealthy, Benedict knew. Nightshade was the exclusive source of Flex, and Riotmark was the largest exporting city on the planet, the Morgan'de River a lifeline to the breeding grounds and distilleries deep in the jungle.

The walks were crowded with expensively dressed men and women, and vehicle traffic was heavy. There was a distinct absence of greenery, as though this part of the city was trying to deny the existence of the jungle at its borders. Benedict rolled down the window, and heard the chop of helicopters overhead. He looked up and saw two copters, one moving toward the spaceport, the other hovering above a building, tail swinging back and forth. Covered passageways connected the building with two others nearby, and Benedict thought he could see movement behind the tinted glass.

"Most of the city isn't like this," Ryker said. "This is where the money is, ninety percent of the city's wealth in about ten percent of the area."

Benedict rolled up the window to cut off the city's sounds. "You've been here before?"

"Once or twice," Ryker said.

"And how long are we staying?" Benedict asked. Would Ryker tell him they weren't leaving?

"Long enough." Ryker did not say more.

As they traveled westward through the city, the height of the buildings began to decrease, and occasionally Benedict could see the superstructures of the port facilities on the left.

The cab slowed, and they approached what looked like a border checkpoint. Elaborate gates crossed the road, manned by security personnel. Open lots on the far side of the gates were filled with vehicles in various stages of disassembly, still more security people searching among the pieces.

"We won't be going through that," Ryker said.

The driver brought the cab to the curb; Ryker paid the woman, then they got out and retrieved their bags from the trunk. The cab made a quick full turn and headed back toward the terminal.

Going through the checkpoint, they and their bags were only perfunctorily searched. Benedict could see that, were they crossing in the other direction, it would have taken an hour to get through. People were led into cubicles, presumably for full-body searches and scanning, while bags and clothing were sent through a series of machines.

"What are they looking for?" he asked Ryker. They were walking down a narrow street just past the checkpoint. The buildings and streets deteriorated rapidly on this side of the crossing, and traffic was much lighter, though there were more people on foot.

"That narrow strip of the city, the one we just left, is very exclusive. The Triola District. They demand safety and security. They try to keep Flex and arms out, so anyone or anything coming in is thoroughly searched. The search when leaving is just a formality."

They turned a corner and Ryker approached a rusting, aged pickup truck parked in the shade of several large ferns. He put his pack in the bed, then unlocked the front door. Benedict put his own bag beside Ryker's pack, and got into the truck when Ryker unlocked the passenger door.

The engine started immediately, ran smooth and clean, and Benedict knew the truck had been far better maintained than the exterior indicated. Ryker started driving toward the west and then, as they neared the river, turned north onto a road that followed the course of the Morgan'de.

Ryker drove slowly along the rough, narrow road. Houses and buildings along the bank of the river stretched in a line periodically broken by vacant lots. It looked like a war zone, though the destruction did not appear to be recent. Fire and explosives had done the work, and the ground was often cratered or burned clear of vegetation. A significant number of buildings remained intact, however, or had been rebuilt. These were usually surrounded by stone and metalwork barriers, and evidenced the presence of field generators and other security systems. There were numerous well-protected docks where the buildings met the river.

"We'll be crossing the river soon," Ryker said.

Benedict looked up and saw a bridge ahead of them and to their left, narrow and built of wood, spanning the river over a series of stone or concrete pilings. A steady line of slowly moving traffic crawled across the bridge, high above the water. The river was about two kilometers wide at that point, and the bridge looked frail and delicate, a spider's web across empty sky.

As they approached, Benedict saw that the bridge, too, was damaged. Shattered timbers hung uselessly from the side, the railing was broken periodically by jagged openings, and even the pilings looked as if chunks of rock had been knocked loose by explosives.

"Not the safest bridge I've seen," Benedict said.

Ryker laughed. "It's come down before. Actually, it's been intact since the river wars ended a few years ago. And it's a hell of a lot safer than a ferry."

At the entrance to the ramp leading up to the bridge was an access control checkpoint. Only one lane of traffic moved in each direction across the bridge. Ryker maneuvered into the forked line waiting to move through the gates. Half a dozen men and women worked the checkpoint, dressed in tan jumpsuits and armed with cutters. One collected toll fees while another, watching a bank of flashing colored lights, gestured to each vehicle—hand down to wait, fist up to drive onto the bridge. The others walked about, inspecting vehicles, staring at drivers and passengers.

It took fifteen minutes to reach the gates. Ryker paid the toll with several coins while two men looked into the truck bed, then moved up to the mass scale. The colors on the board flashed, shifted from reds to blues, the controller's fist went up, and Ryker urged the truck forward.

They drove up the ramp and onto the bridge, and Benedict had his first full view of the Morgan'de River. The water was mud-brown, and flowed swiftly though the river was so wide. Whitecaps chopped across the surface in the wind. Boats and ships of all sizes traveled in both directions, some of the bigger ships clearly armed, and Benedict suspected the smaller boats were armed as well. Maneuvering in and out of the river traffic were a number of light, open-air craft manned by uniformed men and women, with mounted guns.

A few of the larger ships had two or three boats as

escorts, and Benedict could sense the blanket of tension that lay over the entire river. Even the smaller boats, many of which were certainly capable of great speed and maneuverability, traveled slowly, cautiously along the river. Men and women walked stiffly on the decks, alert and tensed. Occasionally one of the small boats would veer gradually out of the main stream of traffic and head for one of the private docks on the banks, and all attention on the river seemed to shift in its direction, as though everyone was waiting for something to happen. Benedict knew most of the river traffic was concerned with Flex in one way or another; that meant the river was afloat with potential fortunes and, consequently, potential death.

Far to the south, the spaceport met the river; the massive docking facilities and warehouses were visible even from this distance. River traffic was heaviest there, the docks and piers and ship decks flurries of motion.

When they reached the other side of the river, Ryker turned north once again. There was much more greenery on this side, pockets where jungle vegetation flourished between buildings and houses, some uncontrolled, some cultivated. There was far less damage to waterfront buildings; most were intact and appeared to be occupied. Small hotels and restaurants were located only a few meters back from the river, and seemed to be fairly busy.

No skyscrapers rose here; no massive, gleaming structures of glass and steel. Although some of the commercial buildings were built of stone, concrete, and metals, most of the houses along the side of the road were constructed of fired wood, clay, or brick. The majority of windows had no glass, were open to the heat and humidity and covered with mesh screens.

Several kilometers up from the bridge, Ryker turned off the road and drove up to a squat, four-story riverfront hotel built of stone and wood. The wood was weathered, but not rotting, and though a few chunks of stone were missing, the building looked stable and intact. Dense vegetation flanked both sides, blocking the view of the river. Ryker parked the truck under a metal overhang, and they carried their bags into the lobby.

"No more luxury hotels," Ryker said. "We keep low visibility from now on."

"Why? We're not staying here long. Thought we were just meeting our two colleagues, then shipping offworld again."

Ryker hesitated a moment, just inside the lobby, then said, in a low voice, "We are. But we're coming closer. We can't attract notice."

Ryker took care of everything with the desk clerk, and Benedict wandered about the small lobby. The tiled floor was warped, and the wall paint had bubbles. A tiny shop in one corner sold packaged food and drinks, cheap paperbooks and cassettes, cubes and a few crystals, pocket newspads, and rows of junk. A curtained doorway led to the hotel dining room, which looked nearly empty. Perhaps it was the time of day, he thought. Between meals. More likely, the food was bad.

The elevator took them sluggishly to the top floor, where they had three adjacent rooms, one for a woman named Renata, who was, according to Ryker, to arrive in two or three days. The fourth member, their guide, would be coming later. Ryker took the middle room, gave Benedict the key to the one on the right.

"Meet at the dining room in two hours, for dinner."

Benedict shrugged. "If I'm hungry."

Ryker banged a fist on the corridor wall. "It's time to start doing what I tell you to do, understand?"

Intense anger radiated from Ryker, broke through Benedict's filters and screens, a rage cut through with an almost desperate panic. For a moment, Benedict thought Ryker was going to lose control, and he had no idea what the big man would do. But Ryker's anger quickly subsided, and though it continued to smolder, it remained subdued.

"All right," Benedict said. "Two hours." He turned away, unlocked his door, then quickly closed it behind him, cutting Ryker off as he began to say something more.

The room was smaller than he had expected, and that was fine with him. The narrow bed occupied a third of the floor. A single chair was set in a corner beneath a wall lamp. Facing the river were two wide, heavy, floor-to-ceiling screen doors, letting in the light and heat and humidity from outside, and revealing a short, railed balcony. Benedict put his bag on the bed, opened the screen doors, and stepped outside.

The Morgan'de River flowed past below him, a grayer brown in the declining afternoon light. River traffic was heavy, the patrol boats already blazing with light. A long, flat barge remained motionless just upstream of the bridge, a string of yellow lights glowing around its perimeter. Something was happening on deck, and a crowd shifted back and forth, but he was too far away to see any details. Clean, damp odors wafted up to him—burning coals and moist leaves and the faint aroma of cooking fish.

His stomach grumbled, protesting again. He had not eaten all day, but the thought of the hotel dining room made him queasy. The food would be badly cooked, too rich and heavy, and inevitably over-priced. Screw Ryker, he thought. He would find dinner elsewhere. The food would be better, and so would the company.

On the other hand, defying Ryker right now might be stupid, Benedict thought, and he wondered why he was being so damn stubborn. Was he deliberately trying to provoke the big man? He didn't think so. There was just something inside Ryker that Benedict found almost repulsive, and that he could hardly stand being exposed to. So he would avoid Ryker as much as possible, and take his chances. Benedict turned away from the river, came back into the room, then left the hotel.

3

THE SUN HAD SET, AND THE DARKNESS OUTSIDE WAS KEPT back by the amber glow of streetlamps. Benedict sat at a window table in a tiny, loud restaurant called the Khun Da. The slatted blinds over the open window had been raised, and he watched the frenetic activity of the street increase as night came on, letting the complex mixture of emotions wash over him.

The Khun Da was crowded, though there were no more than a dozen small tables packed closely together and a short, five-stool bar in the back. A constant babble of voices filled the restaurant, almost drowning out the hiss of cooking food and the clatter of pots, glasses, and wood utensils. The flame of a red wax candle fluttered in front of Benedict, and the smoke rose with a heavy, spiced scent. The restaurant, with walls and floor of black wood, was dark, lit only by the candles at each table and three overhead oil lamps shaded by thick orange coverings.

Benedict sipped at the hot, bitter tea and watched the people on the street. The food had been delicious, hot and filling and, unfortunately, heavily spiced. His throat burned slightly, and already a brief, sharp pain had flared just under his sternum.

The walks on both sides of the street were thick with people, most, like the other customers in the Khun Da, dark-skinned with black or dark brown hair. They were dressed in light clothing for the heat, and spoke rapidly in Thainamese, the Southeast Asian polyglot that dominated much of the western side of the river, though English was the official language of all Nightshade. Across the road was a string of shops selling music equipment, clothing, cameras, body bands, and much else. On the left corner was a stunner arcade with a waiting line backed out onto the walk; vague forms jerked violently in the window booths.

Children wandered among the adults, often running along the curbs, darting in and out of shops and bars. A few of the children wheeled porta-carts filled with smoked fish and called out items and prices as they pushed them along.

The waiter brought a fresh pot of tea to the table and offered Benedict a cigarette from a variety canister. Benedict shook his head.

Several sharp, loud shouts broke the air, words he did not understand, and the sound and emotional levels out on the street abruptly changed. They rose briefly, then dipped, and most movement ceased. Before he saw anyone, Benedict heard rapid, light footsteps from down one of the nearest side streets, and a sliver of twisting panic cut through him, growing sharper and closer. He abruptly flipped up his screens and filters, cutting off the approaching fear, and a young, pale-skinned, blond girl sprinted around the corner and down the crowded street. Heavier footsteps could be heard behind her.

A hand reached out from the crowd, jerked the girl to a stop, then pulled her off the street and into the throng so she disappeared from view. Movement started again, people began milling about as though nothing unusual had occurred.

A trio of Riotmark police, "skitters," Ryker had said they were called, came around the corner, cutters in hand, and slowed to a walk. They scanned both sides of the street, their helmet visors down and partially darkened. Halfway along the block, they stopped in the middle of the street.

"Heyya!" one of them yelled. "Where the hell is she?"

No one answered, or even looked at the three skitters. One remained in the street, gaze flitting back and forth while the other two each took one side and began to search among the people, peering into the shops, restaurants, and bars.

Benedict drank his tea, and ignored the tall, burly skitter who came in and searched the Khun Da. The officer did not question any of the other customers, but he approached Benedict's table, looked down at him.

"Where is she?"

Benedict glanced up. "Who?" He could barely see the man's eyes through the gray, tinted visor.

"The girl, you must have seen her. Know, running down the street." Benedict did not respond. "Young, about thirteen, skinny blond."

"I didn't see anything."

"Shit, I don't expect anything out of the flids, but you're not one of them, dammit. So where's the girl?" Still Benedict did not answer. "I can flip your ass in for a few hours, you like that?"

"I said, I didn't see her." Benedict turned away from him and brought the cup of tea to his mouth.

"Fuckin' tar." The skitter shook his head and stalked out.

The sound of a copter shuddered through the night air, and Benedict looked up to see the dark form hovering above the street, ringed with green blinkers and shining a bright, wide cone of light up and down the street, over the rooftops, between buildings. The three officers gathered together in the road, one talking on a comlink, the other two talking to each other.

After another ten, fifteen minutes of searching, the copter rose, banked away, and flew toward the south and out of sight. The three skitters turned and headed back in the direction they'd come from. The one who had searched the Khun Da turned back to Benedict and made a gesture, digging fist into shoulder, that Benedict assumed was obscene.

Several minutes later, when the skitters were out of sight, people moved away from one of the fish carts. Two women opened the lower storage compartment and helped the blond girl out. She had been curled tightly to fit inside, and she had to work at her legs and arms for a minute before she could stand unaided. By then, a large gap had appeared around the girl, the people visibly avoiding her.

The girl stood, looked around, tried to say something, but everyone ignored her. She staggered in one direction, then another, apparently confused. Why did they avoid her? Was it racial? Yet, they'd helped her. Then, as the girl wandered along the street and came nearer, Benedict saw it.

The signs were clear: the heavy tremor in her left arm; the sallow cheeks and dark lined skin beneath her eyes; and the way her mouth and tongue worked constantly, as though chewing something. She was a Flex addict.

She was so young, and so far advanced, that Benedict felt ill. Probably she had already passed the crux, and didn't have long to live. Christ, what a waste.

The girl saw Benedict and hurried across the street to his window, limping slightly. Despair and a desperate need radiated from her, penetrating his filters.

"You," she said. Her voice was a cracked gasp. "You speak English, right? You can tell me . . ."

She was cut off by Benedict's waiter, who had rushed outside and now grabbed her by the arm. He pulled her away from the window, not roughly, but firmly. "No, please, my customer," he said. "Go."

He released her arm, pushed her gently, and the girl stumbled, then righted herself. She nodded twice and walked slowly away, but she turned her head and kept her gaze on Benedict, continuing to radiate intense need and despair until she was far down the street. Then she sprinted down an alley and was gone.

4

WHEN BENEDICT RETURNED TO THE HOTEL, RYKER WAS furious. He was in the lobby, pacing, struggling to control his anger. His eyes were hard and bright, his hands and arms trembling slightly from the tension. Benedict looked at him, headed for the elevator. The big man strode across the lobby and blocked his way.

"Where have you been?" His voice was a clenched whisper.

"Out. Getting something to eat."

"I told you to meet me, we would eat here at the hotel. I told you, it's time you started following orders. Now."

Benedict glanced over at the desk clerk, who quickly dropped his gaze to a stack of newspads.

"I think we'd better talk somewhere else," Benedict said.

"Yes, we're going to talk. Outside." He walked out of the lobby and into the night. Benedict followed.

They walked in tensed silence through the lush

greenery on the side of the hotel, Ryker leading the way along a narrow path headed toward the river.

They emerged from the trees on a flat shelf of earth and moss five or six meters above the river. The drop was nearly vertical, the bank face supported by a network of metal cables. The river was almost empty of boats. As Benedict watched, though, two vehicles started across from the eastern side, creeping forward, green lights atop each.

Ryker seemed to have calmed during the walk, but there was still an undercurrent of anger. He stood at the edge of the bank and lit a cigarette, gazing out over the river.

"Quiet tonight, without the fog. With no cover on the water, no one will try anything," Ryker said. "Usually don't, this part of the river, fog or no." He turned and faced Benedict. "We can't keep with this crap anymore."

"I agree."

A faint, distant rumbling sounded from the south. A few moments later, a wide tail of flame rose into the night, pushing an invisible freighter up toward one of the stations.

"We have to reach a . . . compromise." Ryker's voice was strained and controlled. "You're not indispensable," he continued. "Important, yes. But there is a point beyond which you're not worth the trouble. I'm not saying you've reached it, but if something doesn't change, you're going to get there damn quickly. I don't want to leave you behind when we leave Nightshade. I don't want to have you killed further on."

"I know we're not leaving Nightshade," Benedict said.

Ryker stared at him a moment, then nodded. He drew in deeply on his cigarette. "I have, perhaps, been expecting too much. You were right on Triumvirate, neither of us is going to change. We have to deal with that." He paused, as if waiting for some response.

Maybe it *was* time to chip out something that would work, time to cut it a little straighter. Benedict could feel Ryker's inner struggle, knew how difficult it was for him to give up anything. "I'm listening," Benedict said.

"We cannot have two people in charge, and the one in charge is me. That's one aspect of this that has no flexibility. Especially once we get out there." He gestured toward the north. "I need to know that my decisions are final word and will be accepted, that my orders will be obeyed. Beyond that, I'm open to your suggestions."

Benedict looked across the river at the lights of the eastern part of the city. He knew Ryker was sincere in his offer of compromise, that he was trying to be reasonable. It gave Benedict some hope for the expedition, but he knew Ryker could not be trusted. The big man still flew along the edge, ready to crack; the tension remained, set to explode, and that would not change.

"All right," Benedict said. "You're in charge. You make all the decisions. But until we leave here, my time is my own. If there are trips to make, people to meet, you let me know when and where, and I'll be there. Briefings, planning sessions, stock runs, whatever you need, I'll help with. But the rest of the time is for me."

Ryker flipped his cigarette into the river, then lit another. "I can go with that," he said. "But realize something, Benedict Saltow. I think it's necessary, I *will* have you killed, or kill you myself."

Benedict nodded. "I know." He turned away and

started back into the trees, leaving Ryker alone on the edge of the dark river.

Benedict lay motionless in the heat, the sheet and blanket thrown back. He wore only a pair of shorts, and he listened to the night sounds that entered through the screen doors. Water dripped from leaves, the river whispered against the banks, and faint music played nearby.

Sleep would not come. He was tired, but his thoughts remained active, restlessly shifting from one thing to another. Getting out, shipping off Nightshade and back to Triumvirate or some other world, was still a possibility, an option he had not yet closed. He would have to leave in the morning, though, if he was going to do it. Another day here and he would have begun too many things, made too much of a commitment.

But knew he would not leave. Why think about it? Close the option, think about going on, what would be next. He still couldn't relax, couldn't shut down.

Benedict dropped a few screens, let in the filtered, subdued pains and joys of the hotel guests. The murmur of emotion, kept dull and at bay, helped calm his thoughts, slow them until they moved sluggishly through his mind, finally bringing sleep.

5

THE NEXT AFTERNOON, BENEDICT RETURNED TO THE NEIGH-
borhood of the Khun Da, trying to track down a name
Jean-Philippe had given him. He rode a crowded
public jit through the hot streets, the air inside stifling
despite the open windows. The jit dropped him two
blocks from the restaurant, and he strolled leisurely
along, looking for street names and numbers.

The streets were as crowded as they had been the
night before, but in the midafternoon heat the movement was more lethargic, and many people did not
move at all—they sat at outdoor tables, benches, or
on the ground, their backs against building walls.
More children were about, and several approached
him, offering to sell cigarettes, food delicacies, various
drugs, the services of their brothers or sisters or
themselves. None of them begged.

A few blocks past the Khun Da, he turned down a
narrow street called Palace Lane. A minute later he
found the address Jean-Philippe had given him, a bar

with no name. Benedict walked in, slid onto an empty seat at the back counter. The place was dim, lit with orange candles and fuzzy blue lights in the corners. A tapstress came over, and he asked for the house beer. When she put a full mug in front of him, he put a coin on the bar.

"I'm looking for Tuong Pham," he said.

"What's your name?"

"Stennet Reese. I'm a friend of Jean-Philippe Blanchot."

The woman did not reply. She took the coin, gave him change, then went through a doorway into the back of the bar. Benedict drank from the warm beer. He turned so he could look out the window. Four women sat at a window table, drinking a dark blue liquid from tall, thin glasses. All four wore dresses not quite knee-length, which was short for this part of the city. One of the women looked at him, blinked twice without expression, then returned her attention to her companions.

The tapstress returned, motioned for him to follow her. Benedict left the beer on the counter and followed the woman through the back doorway. She led him along a narrow corridor, past the kitchen, then out into an open courtyard.

The courtyard was lined with ten or twelve tables, all occupied. A low circular garden in the center ringed a quietly bubbling fountain. A man sitting at one of the tables with an attractive young woman put up his hand, beckoned, and Benedict approached the table, the tapstress retreating into the bar.

The young woman remained seated, but the man stood, held out his hand. Benedict shook it, and the man gestured at the vacant seat between him and the woman. Benedict sat.

"My name is Stennet Reese," he said.

The man nodded. "I am Tuong Pham. This is my wife, Tuong Nhi." The woman bowed her head slightly. "She speaks English better than I," Pham said. "So. You know Jean-Philippe."

"Yes. I worked with him. On Dante's Eye."

Pham nodded slowly once, sighed heavily, then said, "Can I help you with something, Stennet Reese?"

"I need to acquire several objects without official registration. Quietly, and at reasonable cost. Is it possible you can help me with this?"

Pham's expression hardened, and he spoke rapidly for a minute in Thainamese. Before Benedict could say he did not understand, Nhi began to translate.

"My husband says that it depends on what objects you refer to. There are some things he can help with, but others he will refuse. If you want Flex, he will help you with nothing. Neither of us will have dealings with anyone if Flex is involved. There can be no discussion of that."

Benedict shook his head. "I assure you both, I have no interest in Flex, or in any other drugs. I need a mini-cutter, for one. Also I want to check into the possibility of a transceiver graft. There are other items, but definitely no Flex. No drugs."

Pham seemed relieved, and his face relaxed. He spoke rapidly in Thainamese again.

"Such items we can help you with," Nhi translated. "Pham does not directly handle such matters, but we know of a man who does. This man, Nguyen Du, is like us, will not touch the Flex trade, but can arrange for other items. We do not need to know exactly what you want, you talk to Du about that."

Pham leaned forward. "I call myself, arrange it," he said. "Wait, please." He stood, went inside the bar.

Benedict and Nhi sat in silence. She offered him tea. He accepted, and she poured a cup for him. After three or four minutes, Pham returned.

"You can see him. Now." He looked at his watch. "My shift, in a few minutes. My wife will take you."

"My thanks," Benedict said. "One further question. May I leave you with something for your assistance?"

Pham shook his head. "Du will care for all." He waved his hand. "Go now, he will not wait."

Benedict and Tuong Nhi stood, the two men shook hands again, then Nhi led Benedict out of the courtyard, through a narrow passage. A minute later they were out on the main road, walking in silence.

Fifteen minutes after they left the bar, a man called to Nhi from a small open window. He was visible from the chest up and, as with the girl the night before, the signs of Flex addiction were obvious. He was more advanced than the girl, his entire body caught in tremors, the bruised skin stretched over his skull and bones.

Nhi slowed, then approached the man. He spoke with difficulty, and Benedict was not sure he would have been able to understand him even if he spoke English. Nhi, however, seemed to have no problem, and the two spoke back and forth for a few minutes. Nhi sighed heavily, searched through a pocket strapped inside her shirt, and withdrew a thin sheaf of paper currency. She folded it twice, handed it to the man. He bowed his head, spoke a few words more, then withdrew into the darkness of the room.

"Pham's brother," Nhi said when they resumed walking. "My first husband. That is why we will not touch Flex."

95

"How long?"

"Three months. Perhaps a few weeks more. Better he was to die tomorrow."

She said nothing more, and they walked the rest of the way in silence.

Tuong Nhi led Benedict through a maze of narrow alleys, tunnels beneath brick and clay, staircases and enclosed corridors. Shadow and heat played against each other with each turn. Finally she stopped in front of an unmarked wood door on the ground floor of a three-story building. She knocked three times, paused, then four times more. A panel slid back in the door, then closed, and the door swung open. Nhi tipped her head forward.

"Go in. They will bring you out, show you the way."

"Thank you for bringing me."

She nodded, face expressionless, and turned away.

The corridor inside was dark and windowless, and though he could not see anyone, Benedict stepped through the doorway. The door closed behind him, a dim light came on in the ceiling, and he saw a man at his side, a short, stocky redhead with a heavily muscled body and a puffy face.

"This way." The redhead spoke in a deep, harsh voice. Benedict after sensing the man's essentially peaceable intentions, followed him along the corridor, through a door on the right, then up a flight of stairs and into a room, which was empty except for a single chair by the small window.

"Clothes off," the man ordered.

Benedict stripped, and the heavy man went carefully through his clothes, laying out each item on the chair. "No identification?" he asked.

"Not a chance," Benedict answered.

The man nodded, crossed the room, and popped open a wall cube. He retrieved two cylindrical objects, each capped on one end with colored glass. He flicked a switch on each, and blurry violet light emerged along with a faint hum. The man ran the lights over every square centimeter of Benedict's body, holding them so the wide beams were always in partial contact with each other.

"What are you searching for?" Benedict asked.

"M-E grafts and implants."

Micro-electronics, Benedict thought. Transceiver grafts. He had never seen detectors that were so portable.

When the man was done, he put the detectors away. "Dress, and we'll go."

They passed along another corridor, then into a larger room. This room was at the corner of the building, and two large windows filled most of the two adjacent walls. In front of one of the solid walls sat a man behind a simple wood table. The man was young, not much over thirty, and handsome. He kept a thin, dark moustache, short hair, and rested both hands, palms down, on the bare table. What Benedict picked up from the man was repellent, a kind of sick, slimy hunger.

"Nguyen Du?" Benedict said.

The man nodded. "Sit, please."

Benedict sat in the single empty chair, and the redhead left the room. There was silence for a few minutes, the two men watching each other.

"No identification," Nguyen Du said. "In honesty, most of my clients don't have that foresight. They do not carry weapons, but do have identification. No one thinks to take the risk of being stopped by the skitters without it." He paused. "You are not with the skitters." It was a statement, not a question. "My friend Tuong Pham says you need my services."

"I need several things, and these items must be unregistered, purchased without permits, and there must be no record of transaction." Benedict paused, waited for a response.

"That is not a problem," Du said. "Only price could be." He smiled, his skin and lips tight. "What items?"

"I need a seven-charge mini-cutter. Kruger, if possible. The 9-K. Also a Frensi heat knife, 200-millimeter. Finally, ten bands of drop pearls, quarter shots."

"Is that all?"

"Yes."

"Pham mentioned a transceiver graft."

"It was a consideration. I've decided against it."

Du smiled again and nodded. "It is much easier to work with someone who knows exactly what they require. But are you certain there is nothing else you need, or want? For pleasure purposes, perhaps? Entertainment? Flex? Trickle?"

Benedict did not reply immediately. He looked at the young, handsome man who, if he was wise, would retire from this business before he reached forty, a very wealthy man.

"Pham says you don't traffic Flex."

Du shrugged. "Yes, I know how he feels about it. Because of his brother, who . . ."

"I know."

"So I don't tell Pham and Nhi. I don't want to disillusion them. Besides, I keep the brother alive."

"Yes?"

"Yes, truly. He is far past crux. Withdrawal, no matter how sloped, would kill him."

"I'm aware of that."

"So I keep him alive." The smile again.

Benedict nodded. "Understood," he said. And you pull a fine profit doing it, he thought. But he did not say any more about it. There was no purpose with a man like Du. It wouldn't change anything, it never did. "No," Benedict said. "I don't want anything else."

"Then let us talk price."

"Yes," Benedict said. "The price."

Sometime after midnight, Benedict walked along a subterranean passage of rounded metal walls, ceiling, and floor that echoed his footsteps. A trickle of water ran along the concave floor, and the passage was lit by pale blue eye-lights spaced in two rows along the ceiling. This was, he had been told, the only safe exit from his last rendezvous, where he collected the Frensi heat knife now taped to his boot and hidden by his trousers. The Kruger K-9 was secured to a pocket inside his shirt, and the drop-pearl bands were strapped around his legs and arms where they would not impede movement. Several times he heard scraping sounds behind him, or what sounded like echoing footsteps other than his own, but nothing appeared, and the sounds always faded.

He emerged at the river's edge, two or three kilometers south of the hotel. Benedict climbed the steep, rocky bank, then sat on the upper shelf, gazing out over the river at the dense constellations of light in the eastern city.

The shell of his paralysis had cracked even further now, and he felt it was ready to give way completely, disintegrate from around him. The weapons he carried reminded him of Mesa, of Triskele, DreamVeil and Carthage, Dante's Eye and Bell's World. They brought to the surface memories of the energy and vitality he'd had on those worlds, an intensity he had needed for survival, and most important, the sense of purpose he'd had. Those feelings were returning slowly to him, but he wondered if it was really a good thing. He supposed that would depend on what he did with them.

After a long time he stood, worked his way through the trees and ferns to the main road, and started walking back to the hotel.

6

BENEDICT STOOD ON THE BALCONY, THE ROOM DARK BEHIND him, and watched the lights come on in irregular bursts across the river as twilight deepened. The water flowed past beneath him reflecting distorted visions of the electrified city. The sky was overcast, hiding the stars.

Ryker knocked, came into the room. He switched on the wall lamp, then joined Benedict on the balcony.

"We meet Renata tomorrow morning," Ryker said. "She's arriving by boat, coming down the Qua Tri. She's been upriver, in the jungle."

"Why? Part of this project?"

Ryker's voice hardened. "No. She's like you, more independent than I like. I had told her to stay in Riotmark until I returned. I shouldn't have expected her to." He tapped his knuckles on the balcony rail. "We'll have to be up early tomorrow. The boat comes in just after dawn, and it's an hour drive, maybe more."

Benedict looked to the north, but it was too dark to see where the Qua Tri joined the Morgan'de; the gate system across the Qua Tri, which kept ship traffic on the two rivers isolated from one another, was just around a bulging headland so its lights were not visible, just a faint glow in the night.

Ryker held out a thick, glossy sheet of papris. "This is what she looks like."

Benedict took it from him. He stepped inside the room, tilted the photograph so he could see it in the light from the wall lamp. The photo was a black-and-white, shot from the chest up and apparently on the run, though the focus was sharp, the face caught head-on. The first thing he noticed was the scar. A thin line of white, it started above her left eye and lanced straight down and through the brow. It gapped over the eye, then picked up again just below it, shifted toward her nose, then cut back to the middle of her cheek, where it ended with a slight twist.

Renata had thick dark hair, large eyes, and her expression in the photograph was hard. Benedict found her attractive, and was particularly fascinated by the scar. It added to the attraction, and said much about the person wearing it, for it was the kind of scar that was easily and cheaply removed. For whatever reasons, Renata obviously chose to let the scar remain.

"She still have the scar?" he asked.

"Oh yes. It's a part of her."

Benedict expected him to go on, perhaps explain, but he didn't. Ryker came into the room and closed the screen door.

"Why is she with this project?" Benedict asked.

102

"Like you, she's a survivor. And this is her world. She knows the lines, knows the jungle." He paused, quickly lit a cigarette, his fingers trembling slightly. "Actually, I wanted only three people in the expedition. But my employers, the people financing this, decided the optimum number for our group was four." He shrugged, neck and shoulders tight. "Their money, they get what they want." Ryker inhaled deeply from the cigarette, and the corner of his mouth twitched. "You'll get a wake-call in the morning, I've arranged it. Be ready a half hour later."

Benedict nodded, and the big man walked out without another word. Benedict held the photograph to the light again. Renata. He looked forward to meeting her.

Despite the fog and the early hour, Benedict was warm, and pushed his shirt sleeves above his elbow. Ryker looked at his watch, then lit a cigarette as they walked up a metal ramp and onto the docks.

The docks were far smaller than the facilities on the Morgan'de at the spaceport. Six wood piers jutted out into the Qua Tri, the longest about fifty-five meters, a third of the way across the river. A wide boardwalk fronted the piers and extended along the riverbank, a cluster of short huts and shacks at each end. Seventy or eighty people moved about the boardwalk and out on the piers. While many of the pier slips were empty, two thirty-meter barges were docked along with half a dozen small boats. A crew of men wearing black pants, no shirts, and brightly colored reflecting head-bands worked at one of the barges unloading webbed crates and transporting them to a corner of the boardwalk, back from the water.

Ryker pointed to the longest pier. "Her boat should

tie up out toward the end." They crossed the board-walk, took the three steps onto the pier, and headed out along it.

The pier was several meters above the water, and swayed slightly under their feet. The Qua Tri had much more color in its waters than did the Morgan'de. A rich, almost black silt, tinged with red, flowed languidly beneath the piers, eddying around the pilings.

A harsh, deep whistle sounded from upstream, followed by two different warning sirens. At first Benedict could see nothing, then a carrier boat appeared out of the fog, flanked by two smaller security boats with guns trained on the carrier. All three boats moved slowly, floating with the current.

"Son of a bitch," Ryker whispered. "That's her boat."

Benedict sensed the tension around them, and he noticed a number of uniformed skitters mingling with the crews on the boardwalk. There were probably others as well, out of uniform. Workers and bystand-ers began to slowly withdraw from the long pier, and the boardwalk gradually cleared. Even the crew un-loading the barge stopped working, retreated to the barge's main deck, and watched. A small contingent of skitters came onto the pier and headed toward the end.

"Time we left," Benedict said.

Ryker nodded. "Agreed. Casually."

They turned away from the river and walked back toward shore. The six skitters approached, then went past without a word. When Benedict and Ryker stepped down from the pier and onto the boardwalk, Benedict spoke quietly.

"If this has something to do with Renata, do we try

to get her out of it, or forget her, leave, go on with the expedition without her?"

"We can't go without her. I would, but . . . those with the money . . ."

"Then get the truck, pull it as close to the board-walk as you can, stay at the wheel. If this doesn't have anything to do with Renata, we can just meet her and go. But I suspect it does, so we'll have to do something."

Ryker shook his head. "Well, this is why I hired you. Truck'll be ready." He strolled off the boardwalk and into the street.

Benedict walked over to the webbed crates that had been offloaded from the barge. Although a few of the crew stared at him from the barge deck, no one said anything. He searched for the skitter van, spotted it backed up against the boardwalk directly across from the long pier, then turned his attention back to the carrier and its escorts.

The boats were nearly dead still in the river, drifting in toward the pier. Most of the passengers and crew appeared to be on the carrier's main deck, lined along the rail and looking down at the escort boats or up at the skitters on the pier. Probably no one knew what the trouble was.

The skitters waiting on the pier had donned their contour helmets, visors down. What did they expect? A riot? The boat drifted in, and ropes were thrown onto the pier, taken up by three of the skitters. They pulled the boat in, let it bump slightly against the pilings, then tied it off.

A single ramp was dropped to the carrier's main deck, and the skitters descended quickly to the boat, blocking the passengers who tried to disembark. Angry shouts broke the air, and the skitters pushed back several passengers, waved weapons, and snapped orders until everyone calmed down.

One of the security boats tied up and the officers climbed a ladder onto the pier, then joined the others on the carrier. The second boat motored slowly back and forth along the perimeter of the carrier. Two skitters stayed at the ramp, weapons drawn, while others began a search of the big boat.

The fog had almost completely cleared, and the sun cut through to the river in slices between the taller buildings in the east. Crowds lined the north bank to watch the events on the carrier.

Benedict shifted position, breathed deeply to calm himself. It could be a long wait, and it was possible he would be unable to do anything even when the wait was over. He glanced back, saw the rusted green truck slowly backing in toward the boardwalk far from the skitter van. The quiet rumble of the truck engine continued a minute, then ceased.

The barge crew resumed unloading their cargo after several minutes, but they ignored Benedict, and waited silently for him to move whenever he was in their way. He paced a short stretch of the boardwalk, remaining close to the stacks of webbed crates, the only cover available.

The heat increased as the search continued, and sweat began to drip from under his arms, down his face. The tension and anxiety were building on the docks, and in the crew and passengers of the carrier, and Benedict temporarily strengthened his screens and filters to block them out. Inside his mind, behind the screens and out of the heat of the day, was a cool, empty stillness which he let spread throughout his body. When he felt ready, he lowered the screens again to stay in touch with the flow of emotion around him.

The atmosphere shifted abruptly. A rolling murmur swelled on the carrier, and a knot of skitter officers pressed through the passengers to the ramp. A single person walked in the middle of the knot, a helmetless head of dark hair visible.

Two officers remained on the boat guarding the ramp while the angry passengers pressed against them. Two more officers split from the group as it stepped onto the pier, and returned to the ramp entrance to help with the passengers. The five remaining officers formed a tight circle around their prisoner and marched along the pier. When they had nearly reached the boardwalk, Benedict could see that their prisoner was Renata.

She wore a black single-suit lined with lockpockets, contour boots, and her arms were behind her back, secured at the wrists. Her head was up, and her gaze shifted from one side to another. Benedict recognized the process: the constant search for options, analyzing and evaluating. She would not recognize him, but he tried to think of a way to catch her attention without drawing that of the skitters. Renata's gaze did fix on him for a moment, and he gave the slightest nod, but was not sure she caught it.

Two of the skitters hurried forward to the van and opened the doors, leaving three with Renata. It had to be now.

Benedict drew the cutter from inside his shirt, dropped to his knees against one of the webbed crates, and hit full charge, briefly noting the barge crew hurrying back to the barge for cover. His cutter beam arced half a meter above the ground just to the left of the group, and he brought it right. The beam hit the legs of the first two skitters, Benedict jacked down the charge as it crossed Renata, then jacked it back up as the beam struck the third skitter's legs.

The three skitters crumpled, one of them firing a wild shot with a gun, and Renata jumped over the nearest. Her hands still bound, she ran directly toward Benedict and the cover of the crates. When she reached him, he grabbed her arm and swung her around behind the crates. "Arms out," he said. Renata, crouched beside him, held her hands out from her back. Benedict grasped her wrists and cut through the straps with the heat knife, freeing her hands.

"The green truck's ours," he said. He leaned to the side to see where the skitters were.

The two at the van had dropped over the side of the boardwalk, only their visors now in view. The three he had cut down scrambled frantically on hands and knees toward the pier, while the four who had stayed with the carrier were already up the ramp and running toward the boardwalk.

"We've got no cover," Renata said. The scar on her brow and cheek seemed to glisten with the sweat.

"And no time," Benedict replied.

"So we run like fire."

"That's about it. Hold a sec." He shifted to his left, fired toward the van. Two shots were returned, neither close, then the two helmets dropped from sight. Benedict burned the cutter beam into the boardwalk, and smoke rose. "Now!"

They shot to their feet and ran toward the truck. Benedict heard the engine running again, and the clunk of gears shifting. He and Renata ran zigzag paths to the truck. Shots from guns sounded, and he felt the heat of cutters lancing past them. As they neared the edge of the boardwalk, the truck began to move forward.

Something struck Benedict's calf, a sharp, hot pain,

and he stumbled, then hit the ground, rolling with his momentum. Renata reached the end of the boardwalk and jumped across the narrow gap and into the truck bed, dropping to her belly. Benedict pushed up to his feet, ignoring the burning in his leg, and rushed forward. The truck had stopped, far from the board-walk now, and Renata was on her knees, waiting for him. Benedict jumped. He hit the edge of the truck, crashing a shin against the tailgate, and Renata grabbed his arm and pulled him in as the truck shot forward.

They lay flat on the truck bed as Ryker pulled away from the docks. The shots continued, and the rear window shattered. Benedict covered his head and closed his eyes against the shower of glass, then felt himself rolling into Renata as the truck turned a corner. He could feel the glass on his face and in his hair, and kept his eyes shut.

After several more turns, and two or three stretches at high speed, the truck slowed, then jolted to a halt. Benedict shook his head and arms, then brushed at his face and rose to his knees. Carefully he opened his eyes, brushed the remaining glass from his clothing and skin.

Ryker had pulled the truck into a grove of broadleaf trees, out of sight from the air and a few meters back from the road. Ryker emerged from the cab, and Benedict and Renata climbed out of the bed.

"I lost the van right at the start," Ryker said. "Had to get under before the copters showed."

Benedict leaned against the truck and raised his pant leg. A bullet had struck him, not a cutter beam, and while it did not enter his flesh, it had cut out a groove a centimeter deep and four or five long. Blood oozed from the wound and dripped down his leg.

Renata took a sheet of cloth from one of her lockpockets, handed it to him. "We probably shouldn't stay with the truck," she said.

"I agree," Ryker answered. "But we need it. Or we need to know if it's found. They can trace it back to the hotel."

Benedict tied the cloth over the wound to stop the blood flow, then pointed across the street toward the corner. "There, a cafe. We can get something to eat and drink, and watch the truck." He let the pant leg drop back down, then straightened and put out his hand. "Benedict Saltow," he said.

She took his hand, smiled. "My hero." She laughed, shook her head. "Renata Birk." She nodded toward Ryker. "Who's the guy with the beard? Your chauffeur?"

The blast of anger from Ryker cut through Benedict's filters for a few moments until he was able to shut it off. But the big man did not say a word.

"Let's go," Benedict said.

They headed toward the cafe in a heavy silence.

7

A FULL MEAL EATEN, TWO BOTTLES OF WINE FINISHED, THEY sat at an outdoor table, still watching the truck and the road. Copters had appeared overhead in the past hour, but all were long gone. No one had approached the truck, and not a single skitter had come down the street. Benedict had washed out the wound in the back rest rooms, and though his leg ached, the bleeding had stopped. Ryker was smoking, and the waiter brought a small pot of coffee for Benedict and Renata. Renata took one sip of the coffee, grimaced, and pushed her cup away.

"Canal water," she declared. "*I* make good coffee. Think we can leave soon? Truck looks all right."

"Yes," Ryker said. "We can leave."

"We need to chip by a place, pick up my bags."

Ryker shook his head. "Not worth the risk. They're looking for you. You can replace anything you need."

"How do you know what I can replace?" Her voice

had a hard edge to it. "It's safe enough. And I'm going, with or without you. Faster with the truck, though."

Ryker stared at her, silent for a few minutes. He lit a fresh cigarette, though one still burned in the table bowl.

"Why were the skitters waiting for you?" he asked.

Renata shrugged. "Apparently, I made a mistake upriver. Maybe two. Mistakes I wasn't aware of, or I wouldn't have been on that damn pig boat waiting to be taken up."

"What mistakes? And what were you doing upriver? I had told you to remain in Riotmark."

"My business, what I was doing. And what mistakes. It's going to stay mine."

Ryker's face tensed, then he forced a stiff smile. He turned to Benedict. "I'm going to have to work out an understanding with her, like with you."

Renata turned to Benedict. "What's he talking about?"

"What he said. An understanding. Of who's in control, who makes the decisions."

"Don't tell me the chauffeur makes the decisions."

Ryker's smile trembled a moment, then cracked as he spoke. His voice was soft but controlled. "Same thing I told Benedict. You had best listen, Renata. You, too, can easily reach a point where you're not worth the aggravation. I'll kill either one of you if I need to. Or both."

A long, tense silence hovered about them. Renata stared at Ryker a long time. The white line of her scar seemed to harden its edge, become more prominent against her dark skin.

"Well understood, Mr. Ryker. Now, shall we go pick up my bags?"

Ryker crushed out his cigarette, left money on the

table, and finally nodded. They rose from the table, left the cafe, and returned to the truck.

As they drove into the southwestern part of the city, the roads became rougher, the paving cracked and pitted and poorly maintained. Abandoned warehouses and factories lined the streets. Renata directed Ryker into an alley between two derelict buildings of crumbling stone. Halfway down the alley, she told him to stop in front of a bent metal door.

While Ryker and Benedict waited in the truck, Renata worked at the door locks with a set of metal instruments she had retrieved from one of the single-suit's lockpockets. The door opened, and Renata slipped inside.

As they waited, Ryker continued his tense silence. The big man sat nearly motionless, hands gripped tightly on the wheel, eyes hardly blinking. His breathing was slow and regular; Benedict sensed that behind it was not calm, but rigid control.

Renata emerged from the building with two brown leather shoulder bags and a small valise. She tossed her bags into the back, then climbed into the cab. "That's it," she said. "I'm yours, Mr. Ryker."

Ryker started the truck, put it into gear, and, still without a word, shot forward.

A half hour later, as they drove through a busier, commercial area, Ryker pulled over to the side of the road.

"I have a call to place," he said. "Wait here. I should be back in a few minutes." He stepped down from the truck and went into a bar across the street.

Renata leaned against the door and looked at Benedict.

"How's the leg?" she asked.

"Good enough." The wound was beginning to itch

more than hurt, and he rubbed at it. "What do you know about Ryker?"

"Probably no more than you. He doesn't volunteer much about himself. Nothing at all, in fact."

"All right. But you're perceptive, you know which pikes to hit. Twice with the chauffeur comments, and you're not firing blind—you've been too damned accurate. The point being, you must know the edge he's flying, and you push too much. He goes over, I don't want to be around. I've lived this long because I've learned to avoid situations like that, not escape from them."

Renata nodded. "You're right about him. And I do dig it too deep. I . . . misjudged." She slowly shook her head. "I must be losing a drift. What happened on the boat today, never should have. Another mistake." She smiled. "Getting old. Time to retire."

"Old?" He smiled back. "What, thirty-four, thirty-five?"

"Thirty-nine. For life it's not old. But for this shit it is." She breathed deeply. "Question. You know what Ryker's like, why the hell you working with a zerko like him?"

"Why are you?"

She smiled again, nodded. "All right, Benedict. Someday. Maybe we'll tell each other histories, yes?"

"Perhaps." He looked over at the bar. No sign of Ryker.

A young blond girl walked past the truck, and for a moment Benedict thought she was the girl from the other night, the Flex addict at the Khun Da. But when she turned, and he saw her face full-on, he saw she was someone else.

Ryker returned to the truck. His movements were more animated, his entire demeanor more relaxed.

INNER ECLIPSE

"Ryker," Renata said as he got into the truck. "I was off line earlier, I accept that. I'll keep a cap on it."

Ryker started the truck, moved out into traffic. He smiled. "That's all right, I understand. It was a tough mix out on the docks this morning. Fresh start, for all of us. We have to make two or three stops, collect a few supplies, then we go somewhere private to talk." His smile broadened. "In three days it begins."

What begins? Benedict wondered. He looked at Renata, who shrugged and gave him a hint of smile. He didn't know what to think of her yet. That was the biggest problem of this entire expedition, he decided. He knew too damn little about any of it.

They moved through the afternoon heat of Riotmark, and he tried to push all the concerns out of his thoughts. But with Ryker on one side, and Renata on the other, peace was impossible.

8

THOUGH IT WAS MIDAFTERNOON, THE ASHY HAZE IN THE AIR gave the impression of dusk. Ryker, Benedict, and Renata stood on a solitary, ruined wall of stone. Several other ruins were scattered about, but most of the buildings in all directions had been razed. Stone, cement, and tangled metal rubble littered the earth, dotted with charred wood. Smoke still rose from mounds in the distance. The truck was the only vehicle in sight, and there were no signs of other people.

"They started the fires four days ago," Ryker said. "A day or two, they'll move in to clean up, build from scratch. Cheapest way to do it."

Renata dropped to the ground, picked up a piece of charred bone, turned it over in her hand. "Looks human."

"Possibly," Ryker said. "They don't always manage to clear everyone out."

Renata tossed the bone aside and it clattered across a broken slab of concrete. "I see why you chose this place to talk. It's *very* private."

They were in a southern district of Riotmark, two kilometers west of the Morgan'de. The smoky haze kept visibility low, like dry river fog.

Ryker sat on the highest part of the wall, and Benedict found a depression a few meters away to sit in, facing the big man. Renata stayed on the ground, standing just below Benedict, her shoulder against the wall.

The ash in the haze dusted Ryker's black hair with gray; sitting atop the stone wall with ruins all around him, a slight breeze trembling his long hair, he looked a natural part of the environment, a man who had found his place in the world. In some ways, Benedict thought, it was too bad Ryker could not remain there forever, a human sculpture in a neverending dusk.

"In two days," Ryker began, "our guide arrives in Riotmark. His name is Gerad, but he's known on the rivers as Blade. He is one of the best freelancers the Flex market has ever had, and there is probably no one on Nightshade who knows the jungles and mountains better than he does. More important, he's had actual contact with these creatures. He knows where they've been seen, and what they look like. Two contacts himself." Ryker lit a cigarette, drew on it a few times before going on.

"Our trip will take a long time, weeks at minimum, and we might be out there for months. We'll be traveling as free-lancers with Gerad, fully certified with Timons, Ltd. They're one of Nightshade's largest Flex combines. That association will give us some protection, though all free-lancers are at risk in the jungles. It gives us river access, though, and that's the most important aspect. We'll be able to make connections at their distilleries or way stations, berth for the night, take on a resupply. We'll travel by boat up the Morgan'de." He stopped, tipped his head. "At some point, we'll go by foot. You'll learn exactly where as we go along." He looked at Benedict. "You understand why we won't go by air?"

Benedict nodded. "I know something of this world. I assume it's not worth the risk."

"It's not," Renata said. "I've known two people who tried to fly into the jungle. They're both dead." Her voice carried no feeling, and Benedict looked down. Her face showed no more emotion than her voice.

"When do we leave?" Benedict asked.

"Day after Gerad arrives. He should have a boat locked in for us, fully supplied, all necessary equipment. We'll leave early in the morning." He stood, took a few steps along the wall. "Weather will be a slight problem. Rainy season is coming, but we should be able to get in pretty deep before it hits." He dropped his cigarette, crushed it with his boot. "You both need to be reminded of something. From now on, I am in charge. You do what I tell you to do, go where I tell you to go. My word is now law." When there was no response, Ryker lit another cigarette and smoked it in silence, looking out over the ruins.

Benedict climbed down from the wall, then he and Renata returned to the truck.

"We didn't come out here for a briefing," Renata said. "You realize that?"

"He sure didn't tell us anything. Why, then?"

"He brought us out here to give us that last message. Fit his purposes well, I think, when I found the bone." She shrugged. "Got it?"

Benedict nodded. They stood beside the truck and waited in the failing light for Ryker to descend.

THE NEXT DAY, RENATA TOOK BENEDICT TO AN AQUARIUM in the Monsoe District, west of the Morgan'de, and north of the Qua Tri. The terrain was dominated by jungle rather than buildings, and roads were narrow dirt passages cut through the dense foliage, vegetation often encroaching on the cleared earth. On foot, Renata led the way along deserted winding roads, the trees often so thick overhead that all direct sunlight was blocked. Occasionally, small clusters of huts and shacks appeared on the side.

The aquarium stood in a large clearing, a U-shaped building of rotting wood, discolored stone, and grime-encrusted windows. A derelict fountain emerged from a stagnant pool covered with thick green scum.

"Nice place," Benedict commented. "Showing me the prime attractions of Riotmark?"

Renata silently led the way into the left wing. A listless young man seated at a table took several coins from Renata, pocketed them, then waved toward the interior.

The left wing was lined on both walls with two levels of illuminated Plexiglas tanks filled with water and dully colored fish. There were no other people in the wing, and as they walked slowly past the tanks, watching the lifeless fish, Renata talked.

"These are all river fish," she said. "Why they're so drab, colorless. Everything in the aquarium is local, what they trap in the rivers, the canal, in the jungle. There are reptile and amphibian enclosures in the central wing, more fish on the right. Just as drab as these. There *are* colorful fish on this world, mostly in the oceans. There's an incredible aquarium in the Triola District. Several stories, huge tanks with rigidly controlled environments, and thousands of beautiful, colorful fish and exotic plants."

She breathed deeply, then stopped in front of a dark tank, the sides coated with algae. A long fish with pale green stripes and a suckerlike mouth crawled along the glass, eating the algae and leaving a cleared trail behind it.

"You don't like Ryker, do you?" she asked.

They moved on, past more brightly lit tanks of small gray, disc-shaped fish that darted rapidly from side to side, all changing direction in unison.

"No," Benedict answered.

"Nor do I. Maybe with that in common, we'll get along."

"Yes, maybe."

"He told me you're a First."

"Yes."

"Some people thought I had potential when I was a child. Arranged for examination sessions."

"And?"

She smiled. "I tested out null. Not a trace. Sometimes I wonder what it's like, what it would have been like for me." Her smile faded. "Most of the time I'm glad I'm not."

They reached the end of the hall, and the central wing stretched to the right.

"What's this all about?" Benedict asked.

"I feel the need to know you better. This is my way."

"Here?"

She pointed down the central wing. "This way. What I really wanted to show you is in here." She led the way past glass terrariums, some dry, most with pools of water or dripping with heavy mist. She stopped before a small, unlabeled terrarium. Inside, weaving among dark green plants crowned with red flowers, was a two-headed snake.

Mounted next to the terrarium was an illuminated X-ray plate revealing the snake's single spinal column and the two short, branching segments leading to the two skulls. Inside the terrarium, tongues flicked out of both mouths, one more rapidly than the other. The left head appeared to be dominant.

"Is this why you brought me here?"

"Yes."

"Like Ryker? Is this supposed to be a message of some sort?"

Renata shrugged. "I don't know, Benedict. It seemed to be important. I thought you would understand."

When she said no more, Benedict nodded. "I suppose I do," he said. He returned his attention to the snake. Yes, he was certain from the way it moved that the left head was dominant. As he watched, it led itself counterclockwise around the interior of the terrarium, either unaware of or purposefully ignoring the right head, which it periodically smashed against the glass walls as the snake traveled the boundaries of its world.

10

BENEDICT SAT IN A CHAIR ON RENATA'S BALCONY, WAITING for the sun to rise. A second chair was set against the opposite rail. A warm morning breeze drifted past, shimmering with a crackle of damp electricity.

"Maybe we'll get a little early rain," Renata said. She stepped out onto the balcony, handed Benedict a mug, then sat in the other chair. "Linsok coffee. No one brews it better, or faster, than I. We'll never lack it on the river, in the jungle, wherever. I'll cover it."

Benedict sipped at the coffee. It *was* good, hot and very strong without a bitter sting. "Hired," he said.

Renata smiled, shifting the twisted tip of her scar.

Across the river, the sun's curved edge broke above a high, wide office building, a glaring corona above the dark structure. It continued to rise for a few minutes, the glare softening as it broadened, but before a fourth of the sun was visible, clouds moved across it and shut off its glow. Dawn seemed to transform instantly to early evening.

"Actually, might not rain," Renata said. "The clouds are probably dumping water on the jungle, might be able to cross the city and the plains without dumping more."

"Have you lived here long?"

"Most of my life. Been offworld a few times, maybe half a dozen other worlds for short periods. But I was conceived and born on this planet. Grew up partly in Riotmark, ten years in Blass. Blass is safer, but Riotmark is a better place to feel alive."

"Family?"

"Yes." She did not say more. Then, "Are you reading me?"

"What do you mean?"

"You're a First. Do you read me when we talk, to see if I'm lying? Do you read me to know what I'm feeling?"

Benedict smiled and shook his head. "It's not that simple. I could, if I wanted, open enough to sense whether you were lying or not, but . . . It's difficult, making that determination. Almost like mind reading, which is impossible."

"I know," she said, looking directly at him. "I wanted to see what you would say."

"To see if I would lie to you."

"Exactly."

"I have no reason to lie to you. As for reading you, to pick up what you're feeling . . ." He shook his head. "I don't do that with people. They deserve that privacy."

"Except . . ." she started for him.

Benedict paused, then nodded. "That's right, except when it's crucial to my continued existence, or that of something or someone important to me. Then I won't hesitate."

"Fair enough."

The clouds continued to move slowly overhead, rolling like slow-motion ocean waves. They now covered the entire city, but no rain fell.

"Why do you keep the scar?" Benedict asked.

Renata didn't answer immediately. Her expression remained fixed, her gaze on the river below. "A fine question, Benedict. People don't ask me that. They ask *how* I caught it. You, though, know the important question." She turned to face him, still no change in her expression. "You might ask me again in a few weeks. I may know you well enough by then."

"Fair enough," Benedict said. They both smiled.

Someone knocked sharply at the door, two loud clusters of sound, then the door opened and Ryker walked in. He crossed the room and came out onto the balcony, breathing heavily.

"Glad you're both here. I won't have to run this twice." He frowned, made a crushed sound in his throat. "I've received a bubble about Gerad. He's been clinicked, and he's going to be in for a while. Someone almost killed him. A few days minimum, maybe as long as a week before he'll be out. We've been put on hold."

"Dead on for the start of the rains," Renata said.

"No goddamn choice," Ryker answered. "We don't go without him."

A dull throbbing began in Benedict's chest. It was as if, just at the mention of delay, the paralysis began to take hold of him again, his momentum lost.

"We're going to have to wait longer than a few days, aren't we?" Renata asked. "He may be out of clinic by then, but he won't be in condition to take us into the jungles."

"He'll have to be," Ryker answered. "We cannot wait any longer. He's a gutter, he'll make it. But it still means we have a few days to wait out, keep ourselves

126

low." He faced Renata. "Particularly you. The skitters are still looking for you, count on that. Make damn certain they don't find you." He tapped on the balcony railing with his fingers, then slammed it twice with his palm. "Damn every . . . Run it easy and careful for a while, we'll be fine."

Renata nodded. Ryker turned to Benedict.

"Any questions, problems? You're damn quiet."

"Nothing to say. Tomorrow, or next week, I'll be ready."

"Hope so. We won't be leaving anyone behind now. Not alive." Ryker pushed away from the railing. "I'll keep you both on line about this." He went through the open screen door, across the room, and out.

"You all right?" Renata asked. "You look . . ." She shrugged. "This delay a problem for you?"

Benedict shook his head. He sipped at the coffee, which was now lukewarm. "No, it doesn't matter." He held out his mug. "I could do with some fresh coffee, though."

Renata stared at him a few moments without moving. "You look like you need something," she said. She stood, took his mug. "See if coffee helps." She went inside.

Benedict watched the clouds, which had thickened, become nearly black. The heavy, stale feel of the air was broken by a few drops of rain. Another minute, and the warm rain began to fall steadily. Benedict remained in his chair, his head tilted back so the rain washed down his face, and he thought about Tereze Abouti. She, too, had said he needed something. He closed his eyes, listened to the rain on the balcony, on nearby windows. They were both right, but that didn't help. Nothing did. Benedict sat in the warm rain, and waited.

11

BENEDICT WALKED THE STREETS OF RIOTMARK THROUGH
the rain and the night. He had no specific destination
in mind—just away from the hotel, away from Renata
and Ryker. That was all that mattered for now. He
needed to keep moving, maintain an energy level high
enough to hold back the paralysis he felt returning,
clawing at him. If he stayed at the hotel for the next
few days, he would succumb to it.

After an hour of walking, he found himself at the
Khun Da. He went in, ordered food, but ate little. His
stomach was sensitive to the spicy food, and he had
little appetite. He remained at the table another half
hour, drinking tea, then finally called up the energy to
leave, continue wandering.

Benedict wore a poncho with the hood pulled back,
and the rain was warm and light on his face. It felt
soothing to his cheeks and forehead, running in
rivulets along his skin, dripping from his hair. He
took to watching the people on the streets, following

the subtle flow of movement. Male and female body hawkers avoided him, as though they all sensed his need for isolation.

Not far from the Khun Da, Benedict saw the blond girl from his first night on Riotmark. This time it *was* the same girl, the Flex addict. She bounced along the street ahead of him, her hands slapping nervously against her thighs, her gait awkward. Her head jerked from side to side, her attention shifting constantly.

Remembering the utter despair he had felt in her the other night, Benedict followed as she turned a corner onto a crowded street lined with restaurants, bars, cinedomes, and music clubs. She came up behind a young couple, matched their pace. Benedict knew what was coming.

The girl inched closer to the couple with each step, and stayed with them, her hands at her sides, until the couple was jostled by people walking in the other direction. At that moment, the girl slid one hand under the flap of the woman's bag, and the other in the man's rear lockpocket, which hadn't been completely secured. A moment later, hands buried in her own pockets, the girl calmly retreated from the couple, drifting back and to the side. She stopped and leaned against a building wall.

Benedict stopped a short distance behind her, watching. The girl waited a minute, then crossed the street and entered a public com booth. Through the opaque divider, he could see her using the phone.

Benedict did not understand his fascination with the girl, his intense curiosity, but he did not fight it. When the girl completed her call and left the booth, Benedict continued to follow her.

She backtracked several blocks, then entered a cinedome showing a set of four-minute video fugues. Benedict remained on the street in the rain, a strange energy rushing through him. He wanted to help the girl, he understood that part of the drive; it was, he thought, something Hadling would do. But he also knew he could *not* help her, just as he could not help Tuong Pham's brother, or the woman Ryker had cut on Triumvirate, or the woman who had opened the door to him that same night and sat slumped on the ground in the rain beside him. Yet he stayed outside the cinedome, waiting.

When the girl emerged a half hour later, she seemed a different person. She was not so frenetic, her movements were now graceful and fluid, and she walked with assurance through the streets, her face glowing with a life that had earlier been missing.

The girl headed north, and Benedict kept pace. Before long they left the night-life area, and the streets were darker, less crowded, and eventually almost deserted. Benedict dropped back, but kept her in sight. A public jit drove past, and the girl flagged it. Benedict hurried to catch up, and climbed on just behind her.

The girl walked to the rear and Benedict sat in one of the middle seats facing to the side so he could keep her in sight. The jit rattled ahead, growling in the rain. They had not gone far when the girl made her way forward and sat beside him.

"I know you," she said. "You were there. Night the skitters were on me."

"Yes, I was there."

"You following me?" Then, before he could answer, "Why?" And, "I don't care, just wondered."

"Maybe," Benedict answered. "I don't know."

"What's your name?"

"Reese. Stennet Reese. Yours?"

She tilted her head, looked at him, and smiled. "No it's not, but that's good enough. Call me Silky. It's my

130

tag if not my name." She jumped up and yelled at the driver. *"Next block, Tinker!"* She turned to Benedict. "You getting off with me?"

The jit drifted to the right and jerked to a stop. Silky went to the door, still looking at him. Benedict nodded, and joined her.

Outside, it was still raining, but the air was quiet. Amber lamps lined the streets, illuminating decrepit buildings of rotting wood and crumbling stone. He heard the sound of rain on water, and looked to his right. When he saw the reflection of the amber lamps on a wide channel of water, he realized they were at the Qua Tri Canal.

"Change of mind?" Silky asked. "Don't want to be in the Canal Zone?"

Benedict smiled. "No, no change of mind. This is a good place for now. A fine place."

Silky gave a snort. "Oh, yeah, a fine place. It's where I live. I guess it's home."

She turned and headed west along the edge of the canal, and Benedict walked beside her, the lamps and the canal lighting the way through the night and the rain.

PART THREE

In The Canal Zone

1

THE NIGHT AIR WAS QUIET EXCEPT FOR THE RAIN HITTING THE ground and the water. A gentle creaking of wood sounded from the canal, and the dark shape of a small boat drifted past, poled along by a solitary figure. A covered oil lamp swung freely from a support arm and sputtered when the rain blew in and caught it.

"Almost midnight," Silky whispered. "Why it's so quiet. This part of the Zone drops after dark. Other parts . . ." She smiled and bobbed to a silent rhythm. "When it starts to kick me, we'll go to the Spectre, okay?"

"All right," he answered. Whatever the Spectre was.

The buildings along the canal varied greatly in size, from one-story shacks to stone buildings of five or six floors. Most, even in the dark, looked dilapidated. He would have thought they were all abandoned except for the faint lights that flickered in some of the windows, the vague sounds of footsteps inside the buildings, the occasional cries, shouts, or laughter from within, and the shadows of movement in open doorways.

"Siiiiilllllllky . . ."

The cry, high and plaintive, floated down from a window above them.

"Siiiilllllkyyy . . ."

Silky stopped her bobbing, but continued on.

"What's . . . ?" Benedict started, but she cut him off.

"You don't hear that, understand? I don't hear it, and you don't hear it." She did not pick up the pace, but her gait became stiff and tense. "I don't hear it, I don't . . ."

Her voice trailed off into a low, unintelligible mutter. The cry came once more, much quieter, then near silence returned. Silky did not mention it again.

A few minutes later, Silky turned from the canal and into a dead-end alley between two buildings. The alley was so dark Benedict could not see the ground or walls; metal and glass crunched underfoot. Silky's blond hair was barely visible, a dim reflection of light in front of him.

She stopped, and Benedict heard the quiet clink of metal on metal, a twisting scrape followed by a heavy click. The door in front of Silky opened slightly.

"Wait," Silky said. "Let me . . ." She reached in through the opening, moved her arm up, and scrabbled about inside with her fingers. "Okay." She withdrew her arm and pushed open the door. "Stay close behind me." She closed the door after him, and a loud snap sounded. "And keep quiet."

A stairway began immediately to their left, dimly lit by a pale glow from somewhere above them. Silky started up, and Benedict followed, listening to the hollow echo of silence in the stale, warm air. The stairs made two quarter turns, then ended on a

136

narrow landing. Silky unlocked the single door, opened it, and they stepped into a hall lit by blue overhead lights. She locked the door, motioned for silence.

They passed three doors on their way down the long hall, then stopped in front of the fourth. Silky unlocked the door, pushed it open, and they went inside.

The room was dark, weak illumination coming from the window facing the canal, and Benedict took only a few steps inside. A glow flared, and Silky turned up the flame of an oil lamp. She set it on the square wooden table in the middle of the room, and Benedict closed the door to the hall.

The room was larger than he'd expected, about six or seven meters square, with a high ceiling. There was a second window on the wall facing the canal, but it was boarded over. Walls and floor were bare wood streaked with dark mold. There was a bed in one corner under the open window, a neatly folded stack of sheets and blankets at its foot, several wooden chairs around the table, and a bare mattress on the floor beside the door. In the opposite wall was a doorway into a kitchen, and in the far corner was a door to what he assumed was the bathroom.

"Home?" Benedict asked. He took off his poncho and hung it over one of the chairs.

"Yeah, home." Silky went into the kitchen, lit one of the two stove burners, then put a kettle on the flame after shaking it to see if there was water. "We had to be quiet coming in because of Lady Deebo," Silky said. "She lives down the hall. Weird lady. If she's awake, she doesn't hear a popping thing, but if she's asleep, the tiniest noise wakes her up. And when she wakes up, she howls." She returned to the front room, laughing. "You should only hear it, nothing sounds like Lady Deebo, nothing. She's harmless, though, and she keeps the gas and power going in this building." Silky waved at the stack of blankets and sheets. "And Lady Deebo keeps that stuff clean for me. Like I was her girl."

Silky went to the bed, reached under, and pulled out a pile of clothing. She sorted through it, tossing a pair of pants, a shirt, and some shoes on the bed. She straightened, then stripped off her wet clothes and turned around to face Benedict, naked. She held out her arms.

"You like it?"

Her skin was pale, almost translucent, and spotted with bruises, some fresh, others old and fading. She was thin, the outlines of her ribs clear so Benedict could have counted them had he wanted, and her breasts were small, nipples light and puckered. She had little hair between her legs, and her hips were narrow, like a boy's. Benedict smiled, shook his head.

"Get dressed, Silky."

She looked down at herself, up at Benedict, then at herself again. She shrugged, grabbed the dry pants, and pulled them on.

Water boiled on the stove. Benedict went into the kitchen and turned off the burner. There was little to the kitchen—a stove, a discolored sink, and two sets of cupboards, one on the wall, the other on the floor and topped with a tiled counter. "What's this for?" he called. "Coffee, tea? Something else?"

"Dinner," Silky called back. "Hold on."

Music began to play, at low volume but fast-paced. Silky came into the kitchen carrying a portable cube player. She set it on the counter, adjusted the volume up a little.

"Have to watch the volume," she said.

"I know. Lady Deebo."

Silky grinned. "Got it." She opened a wall cupboard, removed a bowl, then rummaged through the shelves. "I know there's some in here. Lady Deebo's always leaving a carton." She gave up, tried the lower cupboard. "There." She withdrew a dark red packet, ripped off the top, and poured dry, powdery flakes into the bowl. Benedict poured hot water into the bowl, and Silky mixed with her fingers. "That's enough. Lady Deebo keeps me stocked with this stuff, says it's nutritious. One packet a day will at least keep me alive, she says. Want some?"

"No thanks. I've eaten."

Silky walked into the front room, still stirring with her fingers, and sat at the table. Benedict sat across from her and watched her eat the thick, gray mixture.

When she finished, Silky tipped her head forward and belched, long and loud. She started to giggle.

"You'll wake Lady Deebo, belching like that."

Silky belched again, giggled harder, and put her hand over her mouth. She picked up her bowl and staggered into the kitchen, still laughing.

"If there's hot water," she said, "I'm taking a bath. Take one with me?"

Benedict shook his head. Silky shrugged, and went to the small door in the back. She opened it, entered the bathroom, and lit another oil lamp before she moved out of sight. Water began to run. It continued for a few minutes, then Silky stepped out, nude again.

"It's hot. I'm going to take it while I can." She scampered into the kitchen, picked up the cube player, and took it back with her. "Check on me once in a while, make sure I don't drown. I'll probably be a while."

"Sure."

Silky smiled, looked down as if suddenly shy, and withdrew.

Benedict crossed the room to the open window and

stood with his arms on the sill, gazing out into the night. The water continued to run in the bathroom for several more minutes, then ceased. When it did, he could again hear the sound of the rain outside, spattering against the building and the window frame.

Why *was* he here? The question had been nagging at him all the last hour, and he was beginning to reach some answers. Hadling was part of it, he thought; he supposed he was trying to learn how Hadling helped others, and why Hadling was able to succeed when he had so often failed. But there was more to it than that, he *knew* there was, though he wasn't even sure he wanted to admit just what it was.

He turned from the window, looked at the open bathroom door, listened to the quiet sounds of water moved by fingers, hands, feet. He *identified* with Silky. That's what it was more than anything. They were different, yes, but that first night he had seen her, and been hit by that heartbreaking despair . . . It was a despair, with life, that seemed so much like his own, and he felt it somehow formed a strange, powerful, and painful link between them. And he thought that perhaps by helping her, he would be able to help himself. But whatever it was, he knew that, at least for a while, he would not leave her.

2

AN HOUR LATER, SILKY WAS OUT OF THE TUB, DRESSED, AND bouncing around the room like a loser in a stunner arcade. Her energy level was up and nearly out of control. The lamplight glittered from her eyes, and her mouth had begun to work, swallowing and swallowing.

"Starting to kick," she said. She slapped at her thighs, grinned. "To kick, to kick, you ready to go, Stennet Reese? Ready to hit the Spectre? It's starting to kick, yeah, I've got to go, you said you would, you want to?"

"Sure. The Spectre, Phantom, wherever you want to go."

Silky giggled. "It's just a rip club." She switched off the cube player and blew out the oil lamps. "Quiet again," she said as she took his arm, led him to the door.

They padded silently along the blue-lit hall, out onto the landing, then down the stairs to the alley door. Before going out into the alley, Silky showed him the alarm system hooked up to the door.

"Sets automatically when the door closes. You open the door enough to get your arm in, then disconnect it like this." There was just enough light for Benedict to see what she did above the door. They stepped out into the alley and Silky locked the door. The rain had stopped, but the night air was still warm and damp. Silky held out a metal block with keys.

"Take these," she said. "They're my extra set. You know how to get back in now." Her energy had stepped up another notch, and she bounced as she spoke. "When the backlash hits, I want you to bring me home, all right? I don't want to wake up in a pit somewhere, in bed with some fucking deckhole. I've done it enough, and I can do without. Okay?"

Benedict took the keys, pocketed them. "I'll bring you back."

"Thanks." She started off down the alley, and Benedict followed.

From a block away, they could hear the music coming from the Spectre, fast-paced rip that echoed from the buildings on both sides of the street. Inside would probably be an overwhelming light extravaganza, colored lasers keyed in to the beat. Already Silky was dancing with the heavy bass line that vibrated the air as they approached.

Dark green neon blanketed the wall above the single entrance. THE SPECTRE was in black relief against the neon just above the doorway. They stepped into a small foyer where Benedict paid for their admits, then through another door and into the main club.

They entered an explosion of colored lights and sound and the swirling of heavy odors. An elevated platform, covered with small tables, ringed an open dance floor which was fairly crowded. Most of the tables were occupied. Above and behind the platform, on a deep stage, was the rip band. All five musicians were masked in dark blue and wore glowing blue single-suits lined with fluorescent silver. One played percussion, one a stand-up base, one a guitar console, and the other two worked on a massive synth-bank. Multicolored light erupted from the stage, pulsing with the beat, and reflected off faceted mirrors set in the club ceiling and walls.

Silky immediately leaped onto the dance floor and began twisting to the music, arms in the air and swinging down with each percussive beat. Her long blond hair flipped wildly from side to side.

Benedict made his way through the tables and chairs and sat at one on the edge of the platform, next to the metal railing. He had a clear view of the entire club and could see Silky out near the center, dancing madly. Although there were a few couples on the dance floor, most people danced either solo, like Silky, or in groups of three or four.

When the song ended, Silky bounded over to his table, grasped the metal railing. Even now she couldn't stop moving; her legs shook and her head bobbed to a regular rhythm.

"You aren't going to come out and dance with me, are you?"

Benedict shook his head and smiled.

"Figured. Watch me, though, okay?"

"Sure."

The next piece began, a fast bass line joined by a sharp, staccato drum, and Silky darted away.

A waitress stopped at his table, leaned over to ask what he wanted. Benedict ordered a mag scotch, over, and settled back in the chair.

Smoke filled the air around him, and he smelled the pungent odor of pseudo-Flex. At most of the nearby tables people were smoking—cigarettes, inhalers, electric water pipes. His head throbbed from the music, the lights, and the thick, heady smoke. Out on the dance floor, Silky bobbed and twisted and swung her arms and legs in time with the rapidly accelerating beat.

The waitress brought the large tumbler of scotch and Benedict asked for another. When she left, he drank deeply from the cold amber liquid, relishing the smooth burn as it flowed down his throat and into his unsettled stomach. By the time the waitress had returned, Benedict had finished.

He slowed with the second scotch, almost regretful that he could always control his drinking. Sometimes he thought it might be peaceful to drink himself into oblivion. For now, though, the scotch eased his depression, soothed the throbbing in his head, and allowed him to relax.

Silky was a cyclone of energy. She would pay for it later when her body's resources became depleted, but now she shook her head frantically, and her hair whipped about, masking her face, twisting around her neck. Her legs pumped up and down, and her arms kept an alternating pace with them.

With each song she seemed to accelerate, her motions became more abrupt and violent. She pounded at her legs with clenched fists in time to the music, and Benedict wondered how many of her bruises were self-inflicted.

In between songs she did not stop dancing. Instead, she whirled in place, waiting for the next song to begin. Several other dancers did the same, bouncing around the dance floor between songs as though afraid to stop moving.

Just as Benedict was finishing his third drink, Silky leaped high into the air, twice straight up with her arms stretched toward the ceiling, staggered for a moment, then collapsed to the floor. She did not get up, and the dancers spun around her, giving her space.

A young man dressed all in green and black approached her, squeezed through the dancers, and picked her up under her arms. He lifted her only partway off the floor, and dragged her to the back of the club. Benedict got up from the table, skirted the dance floor, and walked quickly toward them.

"What are you doing with her?" he asked. He had to shout above the music.

The man in black and green stopped, glared at Benedict. "What do you think?" he shouted back. "Shipping her out. Can't have her lying around in here."

"I'll take care of her." Benedict's voice was hard and tight. "She's with me."

"Yeah?" The man looked down at Silky, then back at Benedict. He released Silky's arms and she crumpled once again to the floor. "Fucking perv." He pointed down a green-lit corridor. "Take her out the back."

Benedict leaned forward, keeping his gaze on the man, and carefully picked Silky up from the floor. She was even lighter than he had expected, and he gently laid her over his shoulder. The man jabbed a finger toward the back. "Now," he said.

Benedict strode along the narrow corridor, around one curve, and pushed open the door at the end. Outside, the door swung automatically closed and cut off most of the music. The quiet was solid and heavy, marked by the solid thump of bass from inside. It was raining again.

Benedict followed the alley out to the main street.

He considered waiting for a cab, but didn't see any around, and didn't know if they even ran in the Canal Zone. He decided to walk.

The streets near the Spectre were busy, but though a few people watched him closely as he walked by them with Silky on his shoulder, no one approached him, no one asked what he was doing. No one said a word.

About two blocks from Silky's building, he passed an all-night liquor and smoke shop. He hesitated, then went back and walked in. Even here in the store, with Silky still draped over his shoulder, the clerk said nothing except to give him the price of the bottle of scotch and the package of plastic cups. Benedict walked the remaining two blocks through the rain, tired and depressed.

He had no trouble with the alarm, or any of the locks, even with Silky in one arm, a bag in the other. Inside Silky's apartment, he put the shop bag on the table, fumbled for the lamp and matches with his free hand. He lit the lamp, then carried Silky to the bed. He set her on the floor, and put sheets and blanket on the mattress. Silky mumbled occasionally, but did not awaken. Benedict removed her wet clothing, then eased her between the clean, cool sheets. Almost immediately she curled into a ball so her knees nearly met her face; short, quiet noises emerged from her open mouth.

Through the window, Benedict saw that the canal was nearly deserted. A single boat, lit by two lamps, moved slowly downstream. Three people stood on deck, talking and smoking, and quiet laughter rose from them.

He took Silky's wet clothing into the bathroom and hung it on the tub. He sat at the table and fiddled with the oil lamp; it sent up sporadic puffs of smoke. He stared at the twisting flame, the curling smoke. After a few minutes of staring, he opened the bag, took out the bottle and cups. Benedict twisted off the cap, poured the scotch, drank it down quickly, and poured another.

He turned the chair so he could watch Silky. She did not move in her sleep, and had become silent. Though she would sleep for a few hours, he knew she still had one more cycle to go through, another energy kick and the subsequent backlash collapse. The second cycle would not be quite as intense as the first, but after the second collapse she would probably sleep for twelve, fourteen hours or more, then wake up to a full day of feeling relatively normal and healthy before she would need her next pop.

Benedict stayed awake another half hour, slowly sipping at the scotch. Eventually he recapped the bottle, put out the oil lamp, and undressed in the darkness. He took one of the extra blankets, lay on the mattress beside the door, and dropped quickly into sleep.

Benedict woke to Silky's nude body climbing over him under the blanket. Before he could move she started kissing him hungrily, and had one hand down his shorts, reaching for his genitals. Benedict grabbed her hand, pulled it away, then gently pushed her face from his.

"Come on, Stennet, I need it now, isn't this why you're here?" She reached behind his head, tried to pull his face to hers. For a moment, still slightly disoriented, Benedict's filters relaxed. Silky's desperate need broke through, became his own, and he almost responded by pulling her down atop him. But the filters snapped back up, the need stopped, and he pushed Silky away, more firmly this time. He rolled to the side, slid his legs over the mattress, and sat up.

Silky lunged for him, wrapped her arms around his waist, and kissed his belly, trying to pull herself onto him. "I have to, Stennet, I have to . . ." The next cycle was kicking in, and her energy level pumped higher and higher. "This is why you followed me, isn't it? I know it is, I know . . ."

Benedict grabbed her by the shoulders, broke her grip around his waist, and held her away from him.

"No." He spoke firmly, with restrained anger and despair. "No, that's not why I'm here. Now don't."

Silky squirmed, twisted away, and retreated a few steps. She panted heavily, and her eyes glittered in the gray morning light.

"Then why?"

Benedict didn't answer. He did not know what to say.

"I'm going to screw somebody, don't you understand? Better you than some deckhole stranger. I *have* to. See? And soon, like now. Stennet . . ."

"No, Silky." He left no doubt in his voice.

"Don't make me go find it on the streets," she pleaded. "Don't make me!"

Benedict remained silent. He slowly shook his head.

"Then damn you to shitting hell!" she screamed. She stumbled backward, staggered to the bed, and hurriedly worked on pants, a shirt, and a pair of shoes.

"Silky . . ."

She scrambled to the table, picked up the cube player, and threw it at him. Benedict just got his arm up to deflect it from his face, and a sharp pain shot up from his elbow. A blur of motion streaked by him and out the door. Silky slammed the door behind her, and Benedict could hear the pounding of footsteps running down the hall. She continued to scream obscenities at him until the second door slammed shut and cut off her voice.

Benedict stood, went to the window. Silky emerged from the alley, turned to the right, then continued along the canal at a rapid walk. She did not look back.

From down the hall, a long, low howling began.

3

THE HOWLING WENT ON FOR HALF AN HOUR, OSCILLATING IN arrhythmic waves. Each time Benedict thought it was about to subside, it surged again with renewed strength. Finally, afraid the howling would break down his screens and allow the woman's pain through to him, he left the apartment.

In a nearby shop, Benedict bought vacpacs of meat, cheese, vegetables and fruits, and a variety of dehy food packets. At another store he bought a second bottle of scotch, two newspads, a paperback novel, and several packages of sweet, hard candy, knowing Silky would crave sugar when she got back or when she woke after sleeping half a day. Finally, he tracked down a music store and picked up three new cubes and an extra set of cells for the player.

Outside, the clouds had swept past overhead, leaving clear skies and a growing, humid heat in the midmorning sun. As Benedict walked along the canal, a light mist rose from the water, delicate tendrils of disintegrating smoke. A few small open boats moved slowly across the calm surface.

When he returned to Silky's room, an aging, heavy-set woman was seated at the table, drinking Benedict's scotch from a plastic cup. Her long, coarse hair was completely gray, and she wore a heavy brown kaftan. The skin of her face was puffy, pale but colored with splotches of broken veins like tiny patches of purple lichen. Her swollen feet were bare.

"Where's Silky?" she asked. She poured herself another cup of scotch.

"I don't know. Out, somewhere." He took the bags into the kitchen, put them on the counter, then returned to the front room and sat across from the woman.

"You must be Lady Deebo," he said.

"Are you fucking her?" the woman asked.

"No."

The woman looked at him without moving, then slowly brought the cup to her mouth. Her fingers were thick and bloated. She drank, put down the cup. "Yeah, I'm Lady Deebo. Why *aren't* you fucking her?"

"She's a kid." Benedict poured himself a drink.

"Yeah, she's a kid. Fourteen. Doesn't stop some people. And she's gone die soon, hear me you, she's gone die."

"I know."

Lady Deebo snorted. "I am too, to speak. It's just taking me a hell of a lot more years."

"Is that good or bad?"

The puffy-faced woman laughed, the sound coming harsh and deep from her throat. She reached into a pocket of the kaftan, removed a slightly crumpled cigarette, and put it in her mouth. Benedict lit it for her with one of the lamp matches.

"Thanks." The laugh subsided. "Why you here, then? If you aren't putting it to her?"

"I don't really know." He wanted to say more, to somehow justify himself, but there was nothing else to say.

"I like that girl," Lady Deebo said. "Understand that now. And I do what I can to take care of her, keep her alive, yeah? You aren't going to be good to her, I'd just rather you left now, got it?"

Benedict nodded. "I'll do all right by her."

Lady Deebo looked steadily at him, then tipped her head forward. "Fair enough. Wasn't really worried, any. Silky's got a crazy sense 'bout people, hooks the good ones, stays away from the bad." She drank the rest of the scotch. "You want to fuck *me*? Won't cost you much, and though I'm not too trif to look at, I'll do you just fine in bed."

Benedict smiled, then shook his head. "I think I'll just stay here until Silky gets back."

"We can do it here, you want. Silky comes back, hell, she knows what it's about."

He shook his head again, no longer smiling. Lady Deebo nodded, concentrated on smoking her cigarette and watching the smoke rise toward the ceiling. Benedict wanted to talk more with her, but did not know what to say.

She pointed at his cup. "You haven't had a drop."

"Not in the frame, I guess."

Lady Deebo sighed, reached across the table and picked up his cup, drained it. "Shika, this is dying." She pushed herself up from the chair, grabbed the bottle. "Mind I take this?"

"Go ahead. My treat. Enjoy."

"I will, I will." She shuffled to the door, turned around. "Take care of her," she said. "Take care."

"Yes."

Lady Deebo nodded, breathed heavily several times, then moved down the corridor. A minute later Benedict heard a door open, close, then silence returned to the building.

Footsteps dragged along the hallway, nearing the open door. Benedict sat at the table, reading a newspad, and he turned at the sound. Silky appeared in the doorway, slumped, her eyes only partially open. She held on to the door frame for support, and smiled.

"Hi, Uncle Stennet." She pushed herself forward, staggered to the table, and dropped into the chair beside him. She saw the hard candy and ripped open a packet, jammed the stick in her mouth, and sucked furiously.

"You all right?" Benedict asked.

Silky nodded. "Tired," she said, the candy in her mouth. "Very . . . tired." Still sucking at the candy, she noticed the new cubes. "For me?" Benedict nodded. Silky fumbled with the player and pushed in one of the new cubes by a rip band called the Shadow Prophets. A slow, somber bass line emerged from the tiny speaker, and Silky bobbed her head lethargically with the rhythm, sucking at the candy with each beat. Her eyes gradually closed; she started to tip forward onto the table, then jerked upright. The candy stick fell from her mouth, hit the edge of the table, and dropped to the floor, sticking in place. "Sleep. I need sleep."

She carried the cube player with her as Benedict helped her to the bed. Silky lay on top of the blankets while Benedict took off her shoes, shirt, and pants. She held the player to her ear, eyes closed, and rolled her head from side to side. Benedict slid her between the sheets, laid a blanket loosely over her.

"Good-night kiss, Uncle Stennet," she murmured.

"I'm not your uncle, Silky."

"Yeah, you are. Why not? Sleep kiss, please." Her eyes were still closed, and her grip on the player relaxed.

Benedict leaned forward, kissed her softly on the forehead.

Silky smiled. "Sleep, sleep," she whispered.

Benedict returned to the table, glanced at the newspad. He could do with some sleep himself. Silky would be out twelve hours or more. He closed the hall door, locked it, then lay atop the mattress, fully clothed. For an hour, perhaps longer, Benedict lay in the growing heat, unable to sleep, and listened to the faint, tinny music from the player and the sounds of the street and the canal drifting in through the open window.

4

WHEN BENEDICT WOKE, IT WAS NEARLY MIDNIGHT. HE HAD slept fitfully, disturbed by a series of shifting, connected dreams. Awake, he could not remember most of it, but through some of the dreams he had watched a short motion picture in a cinedome, the two primary roles portrayed by Tereze Abouti and Gird Hadling. After the film had ended, he had tried to contact Hadling to congratulate him on his fine performance, and ask him how he had done it. But despite major efforts, he had been unable to find Hadling, and was still searching for him when he woke. The feelings of frustration and disorientation stayed with him as he rose and washed up in the tiny bathroom.

Benedict went to the window, glanced out into the darkness, and wondered what Ryker and Renata were doing, wondered if they had any idea where he had gone. He turned and looked at Silky. She continued to sleep soundly; the cube player still lay by her head, the music fast and quiet, the cube replaying for perhaps the fifth or sixth time. Benedict reached down and touched it off. Silky did not move, and her breathing remained deep and slow.

He lit the oil lamp, and two squat candles he found in a cupboard, then sat at the table with the paperback novel he'd bought the day before, and started reading.

It was more than an hour later when Silky woke, struggled to sit up on the edge of the bed. She blinked several times, scratched her side and stomach, then both arms. Her face was haggard, and dark crescents shadowed her eyes, a contrast to the pale skin. She trembled slightly, though it was not cold in the room, and managed a partial smile.

"You're still here."

Benedict nodded. "Can I do something for you? Fix something?"

"You can fix me a new head." She slid off the bed and onto her knees, dug through the pile of clothes. She put on a pair of brown shorts and a T-shirt, then leaned against the bed. "I'm okay. I'm used to this." She stood, using the bed for support, then staggered into the bathroom.

Benedict picked up the book again, opened it to the page he'd been reading. The novel, written by an author whose previous work he had admired, was practically unreadable. Benedict could still admire the technical virtuosity displayed, but the writing seemed so intellectual and calculated that it had become lifeless. Benedict simply could not bring himself to care for anyone or anything in the book.

Silky came out of the bathroom and went into the kitchen, put the kettle on the stove. She opened a cupboard, whistled, opened another cupboard, then stuck her head around the doorway.

"Stennet, all this food! You buy it?"

"Sure. Everything is simple to cook, and most you can eat cold, you want. It's all packed so it will last."

"But it'll take me weeks, *months*, to eat all this!" She shook her head, laughing.

"It's not really that much."

Silky leaned against the wall and frowned at him. "Why *are* you here, Stennet? Why are you doing all this?"

"Would you believe me if I said I really don't know?"

"I guess. But what are you going to do? You moving in, or what?"

"That depends, Silky. If you want me to, I'd like to stay here for a while, just a few days."

She started to smile, then the frown returned. "Wait. You going to try to be my parent? Tell me where I can go, when to come home, what to do, all that? Because you can jitter that, you want to do that you can take off right now. I like you, Stennet, and I *would* like you to stay, but I do what I want, what I have to do, and I don't need anyone getting in the way. Not now."

Benedict nodded. "My promise, Silky. I won't try to be your parent."

She smiled finally, scratched her forehead. "Can I call you Uncle Stennet then?"

"Isn't an uncle like a parent?"

She shrugged. "No. Besides, it's different with you. I just want to call you that, if it's okay."

"You want, Silky, it's all right with me."

"Thanks . . . Uncle Stennet." She went back to the stove, took the boiling water off the burner. "One more thing. My body is starved for food."

"The cupboards are full, Silky."

"Take me out somewhere, please? Not a dress-up, just somewhere with good food, and a lot of it."

"All right. Pick the restaurant, and we'll go."

Silky walked over to him, gave Benedict an awkward hug, then stepped back. "Thanks."

It was three in the morning when they returned to the apartment. Silky put water on for tea, and Benedict opened the second bottle of scotch. He sat at the table, poured some of the scotch into a cup, and sipped at it. It did not taste as warm and good as it had the night before. Silky made her tea, then sat on the bed, her back against the wall, drinking it. Though sounds came in through the open window from outside, the building was quiet.

"I met Lady Deebo," Benedict said. "While you were gone."

Silky grinned. "Yeah? What did you . . . ?"

She was cut off by a buzzer sounding twice. There was a long pause, then the buzzer, a small mutebox above the door, sounded three more times in quick succession. Silky jumped up from the bed, hurried to the table, and set down her mug.

"That's Tanker, with a packet for me." Silky's face had picked up a flush of energy. "Wait here, be right back."

Benedict went to the window, and when he put his head out, he could see the entrance to the alley. Two or three minutes passed, then a man and woman emerged from the alley and walked past below the window. In the light from the nearby streetlamp, Benedict could see their faces, which had so many similarities that he wondered if they were brother and sister.

Silky came back into the room carrying a small

packet with two Flex cartridges, and held it up for Benedict to see.

"Two pops. It's a freeb from Tanker. Sometimes he comes around, gives me one or two." She skipped into the kitchen, and Benedict heard her rummaging through the cupboards. When she came back into the room, her hands were empty. "I'm in good shape now," she said. "With that, and the three others I have left, it'll be almost two weeks before I have to . . ." She stopped, looked at Benedict.

Benedict almost finished the sentence for her, but said nothing. There was no reason for it. Silky shrugged, picked up her tea and returned to the bed, sat close to Benedict. He leaned on the windowsill and drank from his scotch.

"Why does he give you freebs, Silky?"

"To help," she said. "To make it easier for me. They do that for some of the other Flexies too."

"Who does?"

"Tanker and his friends. I don't know, Tanker's the one who brings mine."

"Do you know where they get it?"

"No, and I don't care." She grabbed his arm, scowled at him. "Hey, what spins? I thought you weren't going to be a parent? Or are you some kind of skitter squeeze?"

Benedict shook his head. He'd never heard the term before, but he had a good idea of what it meant. "I'm sorry. I did promise. That's me. I ask a lot of questions."

"It's okay," she said. She stuck out her mug, grinned. "I could use some more tea. Make it up to me."

"Sure." He made another cup of tea for Silky, and refilled his own cup with scotch. Silky took the mug and lay prone on the bed, letting the steam rise into her face. Her eyes slowly closed.

"I'm tired," she said. "Going to have to sleep again soon. Only a couple of hours, though. But then I'll need a pop. You might not want to stick around, I get a little . . . I don't know. Blitzy."

He looked down at her thin, frail body, at the visible bruises, the pallor of her skin.

"What happened, Silky? How did you get on the Flex?"

She cocked her head, glared at him, and her face twisted with pain. She sat up, then abruptly threw the full mug across the room, tea spraying as the mug tumbled through the air. The mug hit the floor, bounced into the wall, and shattered.

"What's *wrong* with you, Stennet? You can't *help* me. Why you want to know how I got started, or how? The reasons don't matter anymore, don't you understand? Even if they were gone it wouldn't change anything. I'm past the crux, you *know* that. I'm going to die, dammit, and that's all there is. I'm going to . . ." Her anger seemed to leave her, and she stared at him a long time before finishing, her eyes dull and lifeless. ". . . die," she whispered. The word hung in the air, then her face twisted and she turned away and began to cry. Despair welled from her, breaking through his screens and rolling through him with an awful ache.

What *was* wrong with him? Benedict wondered. Why couldn't he let it be? He approached the bed, reached out and touched her shoulder. Silky shrugged him off, pulled away from him.

"Leave me alone, Uncle Stennet. Just because you feel so shitty, no reason to lay it on me. Just leave for a while, please." Keeping her face turned away, she felt around the bed for the cube player. Still crying, she turned it on, pushed up the volume, and held it against her ear. "Go away, please," she repeated.

Benedict stepped away from the bed. He crossed to the table, set down the plastic cup, then walked out of the room, closing the door behind him.

5

HE WALKED THE CANAL IN DARKNESS FOR AN HOUR, PERHAPS
longer, until he was certain he was near the junction
where the canal rejoined the Qua Tri. Ahead was one
of the few footbridges that crossed the water to the
I-Zone: "I" for Inner, for Island, for Isolated. Border-
ing one side of the Canal Zone, it *was* a kind of island,
he thought, ringed by the canal and the river. Benedict
climbed the ramp onto the bridge, and started out
over the water. Though the sun would be rising soon,
the darkness now was a comfort, a warm and heavy
presence enfolding him.

Halfway across the bridge he stopped and leaned
over the rail, facing upstream. The roadways along
both banks were deserted, amber lamps casting frozen
shadows. A light rain would have been welcome, but
the sky was clear above him, and the bright silver of
stars shimmered in the night.

Three or four kilometers away Silky would be
sleeping, the cube player beside her, replaying contin-

uously. Maybe he should just leave, find some other place to stay. He had left the hotel to be alone, and perhaps that was what he should do—travel on to the outskirts of Riotmark, into the sparsely populated fringes of the western jungle where he could be alone when the next seizure struck, within range of only a few scattered people.

And, if he did that, maybe he should just stay out there, never return to the hotel, never see Ryker or Renata again; forget about searching for other intelligent beings; forget about it all. He could live the rest of his life in the jungle, alone, rarely seeing people. The seizures would probably be mild, perhaps barely noticeable. Without people around him, the seizures might cease altogether.

Benedict slowly shook his head. The life of a jungle hermit was not for him. It would be existence, but not necessarily life. It was not a much better alternative than suicide. It was not the kind of escape he needed.

Three boats, side by side, came into view and drifted toward him, oil lamps swaying with the gentle swell of the water and the slight breeze. Three people crouched around an open fire on the middle boat's deck, frying something in a large pan. As the boats approached the bridge, the three people looked up at him, their gazes locked onto his eyes until the boats passed beneath the bridge and out of sight. The heavy odor of pseudo-Flex smoke rose and hovered about him, then gradually dissipated. He pushed back from the railing, decided he'd be better off staying out of the I-Zone, and retreated along the footbridge. With a glance back at the three boats downstream, he started back west along the silent canal.

Dawn had begun to illuminate the sky, an orange and gray break in the darkness behind him, when

Benedict heard the first shots. A pained cry followed, both sounds from deep within the I-Zone, across the canal and ahead of him. More shots broke the air, interspersed with screams and angry yelling, still somewhat distant. In some way attracted to the noise, Benedict continued westward, headed toward the disturbance, and listened to the growing swell of sound. A sensation of highly charged particles whispered past, a sign that the disturbance was increasing in intensity. He could feel impending riot, he had been involved in or around enough similar situations, and then the swelling panic and anger leaking through his filters and screens confirmed it. Benedict slammed all the barriers solidly into place, secure and impenetrable, and stopped walking, trying to decide on the best course.

Suddenly the sky filled with copters, some passing by directly overhead, others flying in from the southeast, fifteen or twenty whirring shadows outlined in pulsing green. The beat of their blades was loud and steady and vibrated the air. Most of the copters converged a few blocks into the I-Zone from the canal, and ten blocks further up. They hovered and dipped, search beams blazing, crisscrossing the fading darkness with bright shafts of light. Other copters, one or two at a time, continued to arrive from other parts of the city.

Shouts and cries and rumbling sounds grew, cut through with gunfire and shattering glass. A shower of sparks descended from one of the copters, followed by an explosion and a burst of orange erupting from a building half a block from the canal. Several copters, almost in concert, swerved toward the canal; they sprayed lines of tracers in all directions, and one fired a second missile that burst across the roof of a building at the canal's edge. Chunks of stone and splintered wood rained onto the canal roadway, and some splashed into the water.

Though the riot was in the I-Zone, its edges clearly threatened to spill over across the canal, and Benedict hurried for the nearest building. In the shadow of an alcove, he pressed against stone walls, head out just enough to follow what was happening.

Groups of fleeing people began to appear across the canal, running chaotically up and down the streets and along the canal bank, shouting and swinging fists, some firing weapons. A squad of uniformed skitters, in full riot gear with visors lowered and armed with guns and cutters, came out from one of the streets and gave chase to the nearest group.

Several copters swooped toward the canal, streaming tracers and bullets at the people running below them. Suddenly one of the copters twisted away, started spinning out of control, apparently hit from below. As it dipped toward the ground, still spinning crazily, it fired off two missiles. One hit the water, but the second headed out across the canal, almost directly at Benedict.

He had time to drop to the ground, cover his head, then the missile struck the building with an explosion that shook the ground beneath him. Stone fell all around him, bounced off his back and arms and legs, then something struck his head, shooting silver through his eyes, and Benedict was out.

When he came to, Benedict found himself half buried in rubble from the building. The air was much quieter, though there was still plenty of noise. His arm burned fiercely. He could see a long red streak on his skin, and a burned-out flare on the ground a few feet away.

He dug himself out of the shattered stone and

stood, legs and arms aching, his head throbbing. The canal roadway looked relatively peaceful, people walking in both directions, so Benedict started back toward Silky's apartment.

He slowed as he passed a destroyed bridge. Only a few meters of the metal structure remained on this side of the canal, jutting out into empty air just above the water. Squads of armed skitters milled about on both sides of the canal. The shooting and explosions seemed to have subsided, but several buildings across the way in the I-Zone were still burning, and it did not look as if anyone was attempting to put out the fires.

Several bodies had been pulled from the canal on the south bank, and were laid out uncovered on an open stretch of grass near the water's edge. Three skitters stood guard while others talked to pedestrians walking by, or stood together in small groups, smoking and talking.

Benedict approached the line of bodies and tried to appear merely curious. Though some were partially burned, he recognized two of the wet bodies. One was Tanker, the other the woman who had been with Tanker in the alley. None of the others were familiar.

A skitter came up to him, cleared her visor.

"You know any of them?" she asked. "We're trying to make identifications, and we would appreciate any help."

I'm sure you would, Benedict thought. He shook his head and continued to look over the bodies. "No, I don't think so."

"Are you sure?"

He waited a moment, then nodded. "Yes, I'm sure."

The skitter kept her gaze on Benedict a long time.

"What happened to you?" she asked. She pointed at the burn on his arm, at a bleeding cut, gestured vaguely at his dirty, torn clothing.

"I was beaten," he said. "Tuckered by three kippers in a building back there. Maybe you could come, track them down, get my money back."

The skitter did not reply for some time, then put a gloved hand to Benedict's chest and shoved. "Just get the fuck out of here, gawker."

When he arrived at Silky's place, the room was empty, the building unnaturally quiet after the shattering noise of the I-Zone. Benedict stripped off his clothing, found he was bleeding from several cuts and scrapes. The burn from the flare had blistered. A bruise was starting to swell on his forehead. He washed up in the bathroom, discovered there was no medication, no bandages.

He got a clean cup and poured himself a full glass of scotch. Too much drinking in the last couple of days, he told himself, but it didn't stop him from draining the cup and pouring another. When he finished the second, he dropped onto the mattress by the door and lay on his back, staring up at the stained ceiling. His body was exhausted, but his mind remained active, unable to relax or shut down. Benedict lay without moving, listening to the quiet sounds outside, absorbing the warmth of the scotch and the growing heat of the day.

6

HE WAS AWAKENED SOMETIME IN LATE AFTERNOON BY THE quiet click of the door. Silky stepped into the room, leaned over and kissed him on the forehead. She bounded into the kitchen and came out with a piece of hard candy in her mouth, rolling it from one cheek to the other. Nervous energy kept her moving; she was in the first kick phase of her new pop, though not nearly as frenetic as the first time he'd met her.

As he dressed, Silky danced around the room, first to the bed to get the cube player, then back to the table to pick out another of the new cubes. She punched out the old cube, pushed in the new one, and turned up the volume.

"Want some tea or something?" she asked.

"Maybe some of the cheese." What he really wanted was some of Renata's Linsok coffee. He still felt tired, his head foggy with a dull ache at the base of his skull and a sharp throb from the lump on his forehead. The blisters over the burn had not broken, but he should get to a clinic, put his arm in a unit for an hour or two. He could also do with a long, hot bath. Benedict stood, tried to remember if he'd bought any coffee the day before. Yes, some instant.

In the kitchen, Silky rummaged through the cupboards. Two packages of cheese were on the counter, and she moved cans and boxes around, searching for something.

"I'm looking for clean plates," she said. "But I guess Lady Deebo hasn't been by to do the dishes for a while. Everything's under the sink, dirty." She closed the cupboard, looked at him closely. "What happened to you?" She gently brushed her fingers over the bump on his head and the blisters on his arm.

"A misunderstanding," he answered. In a way, it was true. He smiled. "I'm all right."

She handed the cheese to him. "Take this in, I'll wash a couple plates."

"A mug for me too. I'm going to fix some coffee."

Fifteen minutes later, they sat at the table, a plate of sliced cheese between them, a steaming mug of coffee in front of Benedict, a mug of tea in Silky's hands. The Flex backlash was hitting her, and her energy level was dropping. Benedict took a slice of cheese, bit into it. The flavor was strong, with a pleasant bite. The coffee was just tolerable.

"Crazy stuff happening in the I-Zone today," Silky said. "Skitters all over the canal, copters in the sky, shooting and explosions, smoke like something burning, buildings or what. Probably another damn skitter push. They never leave us alone."

The image of the dead bodies along the canal rose in Benedict's mind. He watched Silky nibble at a thick slice of cheese, her eyes half closed.

169

"Tanker's dead, Silky."

She stopped chewing, her eyes widened. "Stennet, don't do things like that, joke with me, not about . . ."

"I'm not joking, Silky. I saw his body. It happened during the I-Zone riot. They pulled him out of the canal. He was dead, Silky."

Her face twisted, not with grief, but with fear. She pushed back from the table, stood, and started pacing. "Oh, shika, what am I . . . ?" She stopped and spun around to face him. "Are you sure it was Tanker? Wait, how could you know, you've never seen him. How do you know it was Tanker?" Her voice rose to a shrill, desperate plea.

"I *have* seen him, Silky. When he brought you your freebs, I saw him through the window as he left. I didn't know his name until you told me, but that's who I saw by the canal this morning." He paused, watching Silky's face tighten. "He's dead."

She shook her head violently, rubbed at her thigh. "No, no, he can't . . . what am I going to do now?"

"Silky . . ."

"No, Stennet, you don't understand, how much easier he made it, it's getting harder all the time for me, and now . . ." She resumed her pacing, and Benedict remained silent. She stopped in front of him. "Can you give me a couple bones? I need to go talk to some people, Tanker's friends, I have to find out what's going to happen, if I'll be . . ." She hesitated, then shrugged and said nothing more.

Benedict took bills from his pocket, handed them to her. "Careful, Silky. I don't know why he was killed. Watch for skitters."

She nodded, pocketed the money. "Thanks, Uncle

Stennet. I'll be back." She started for the door, came back and kissed him on the cheek, then left.

Benedict remained at the table and sipped at the lukewarm coffee and fingered the cheese, his appetite gone.

7

BENEDICT SPENT PART OF THE NEXT MORNING AT A CLINIC ON the edge of the Canal Zone, healing the burn and cuts on his arms. When he left, the burn area was still pink and raw, but the blisters were gone, and the pain was barely noticeable.

He roamed the Canal Zone for several hours, walking up and down narrow streets and wide roadways, through small parks and vacant lots, familiarizing himself with the deceptively well organized layout of the Zone. He noted the locations of shops, bars and restaurants, service outlets, hotels, dayclubs and nightclubs. He saw only two cinedomes all afternoon, and one of them was boarded over. There was not a single stunner arcade in the Canal Zone as far as he could tell.

Toward late afternoon, the air hot and muggy and stifling without a hint of breeze, Benedict bought several newspads and sat at an outdoor cafe to read them. They only depressed him further, however, and as dusk fell he left the cafe, recycled the pads, and headed back toward the canal.

It was nearly dark when he reached the apartment. The oil lamp was burning, and Silky lay on top of the bed, fully clothed and asleep. Benedict noticed two fresh bruises on her left arm, and dried blood on her pant leg. Her mouth was partially open, and her hair was damp, matted against her forehead and cheek.

The scotch bottle was still on the table, and he opened it, then recapped it without pouring any. He put out the lamp, felt his way to the mattress, and sat on the edge. The night air was quiet, but filled with faint, unidentifiable sounds that drifted in through the open window. At the sound of a boat poling past along the canal, he thought of how peaceful and relaxed it would be to drift up and down the canal, netting a few fish to sell to restaurants, going to sleep with the gentle rocking of the water, without worries and at peace with the world.

But it wasn't real, and he knew it. Perhaps somewhere else, though even that was unlikely, but definitely not here in the Canal Zone, not in Riotmark. Not anywhere on Nightshade, unless it was deep in the jungle, away from all human beings. Was it possible that *there* he would find peace?

Dreams scattered, twisted away from him with the prodding of a small hand. Gray and white gave way to darkness, and the dry voices of the dreams became a warm, damp whisper.

"Uncle Stennet," the whisper called to him. The small hand shook his shoulder. "Uncle Stennet, please."

Benedict opened his eyes, momentarily disoriented.

He faced a dark rough wall; it was still night, the air warm and humid. The hand continued to shake him.

"Uncle Stennet, wake up, please wake up."

He rolled away from the wall and faced her. She knelt on the floor beside the mattress, barely visible in the dim light. The dull reflections of tears glimmered on her cheeks.

"Are you awake, Uncle Stennet?"

"What is it, Silky? You all right?"

She sighed heavily, her hand still gripped on his shoulder, though she stopped shaking it. "I'm scared." Benedict waited, but she didn't say anymore.

He sat up on the mattress, his feet on the floor and his knees sharply bent. Silky fell against him and wrapped her arms around his chest, pressed her face to his side. Her nails dug into his skin, she trembled, and Benedict strengthened his inner filters and screens, afraid of letting her feelings through.

"What are you frightened of, Silky?" He put his arm around her shoulder and held her tight.

"Just hold me, please."

"I am, Silky."

She became quiet, her tears dripping down his side. The night was nearly silent now, hardly a sound drifting in through the window. The minutes slipped by, heavy and slow.

"I'm afraid of dying," Silky finally said. Then she shook her head. "No, not exactly, not so much dying, but how I'll die. I have two ways to go, and I'm afraid of both of them." She released her hold, eased back and wiped her wet face with her T-shirt, then looked up at him. "I talked to some of Tanker's friends, and they don't think they can help me, not for a while. The skitters are making it too hard, too many people killed in the I-Zone riot. That's going to make it that

174

much harder for me, I *counted* on the freebs, they helped me get through without going all the way off. Now, I don't know, and I'm afraid of what happens if I miss a pop, and then can't get another, and . . . I've seen someone dying that way, and . . ." She couldn't finish. A tremor shuddered through her, and she twisted her fingers in her hair. "The other way . . . You ever see someone dying from the Flex itself? Shika, weeks or months of barely functioning, riding the cycles, no more sliding periods, not eating, so mindshot they can't hardly talk. That's my other choice, Uncle Stennet, and I'm afraid of that too."

Benedict thought of Tuong Pham's brother in the dark window. "I understand," he said. He did not need to lower his screens to know what she felt; he fought a similar fear himself—the fear of losing all control of the screens and filters and shields, being constantly in a state of seizure, dying slowly as a raving madman.

"Uncle Stennet?"

"Yes."

"Why are *you* scared?"

"How do you know I'm scared?"

"I don't know, I can just feel it. Why are you?"

"I don't really want to talk about it."

She nodded, then said, "Uncle Stennet, I want you to do something for me."

"What?"

"If I live that long, if I get like that with the Flex killing me, so you can tell I'm never happy, that I'm not a person anymore, I want you to kill me. I mean it, Uncle Stennet, I want you to end it for me, because I'll be too mindshot to know I should kill myself, and I don't want to go on like that, I don't, I really don't . . ."

175

She started crying again, and held on to him once more. He held her in return until the shaking subsided and she was quiet and still against him.

"I can't do that for you, Silky," he began. "I'm going to be leaving Riotmark in a few days. I won't be around."

"Then come back when you're done," she pleaded. "See how I am, come back once in a while to see how I'm doing, so you'll know when it's time, so you can take care of it for me."

Benedict shook his head. "I'm sorry, but I don't know if I'll ever be back. You can't count on me, Silky. I'm sorry, I really am, but you just can't."

He thought she was going to start crying again, but she remained silent. She leaned back from him and sighed deeply. They watched each other in the pale light, and Silky nodded, tried to smile.

"It's okay," she said. "I'll be fine."

Yes and no, Benedict thought, but there was nothing he could do about it.

"Can I stay here the rest of the night, Uncle Stennet? The mattress is big enough, and I just don't want to sleep alone right now, I just want you to hold me." She hugged herself and shrugged. "I'm still scared."

Benedict hesitated at first, then realized there were no good reasons to turn her down, and plenty to let her stay. "All right, Silky."

He slid over and moved against the wall, lying on his side facing her. Silky left her pants and shirt on, crawled in next to him, then turned so her back was to him and curled into the curve of his body, a small ball huddled against him. Benedict put his arm over her, and she took his hand in both of hers, squeezed. She kissed his fingers, then held his hand against her

176

throat. Within a few minutes her breathing was slow and regular. Soon after, Benedict drifted toward sleep himself, warmed by the small, soft body beside him.

8

AT DAWN, SILKY WAS CHARGED AGAIN AND UNABLE TO remain still for more than a few seconds. She bounced around the apartment, whistling and snapping her fingers. Benedict wanted to sleep, but she tugged and poked at him, and pestered him to take her out to breakfast until he finally agreed.

They emerged from the building into the shadowed alley, and Silky had just locked the door when a figure stepped out from behind a stack of broken crates. It was Renata.

She wore a single-suit, this one dark brown, and a leather bag was slung from her shoulder.

"Hello . . . Stennet," she said.

"Renata."

She turned to Silky. "You must be the infamous Silky," she said. She put out her hand. "I'm Renata."

Silky shook Renata's hand, but remained guarded. "I don't know you. How do you know my name?"

Renata smiled. "I was looking for Stennet. I was

told I'd find him with Silky. So then I had to find Silky. I learned that Silky lives here, I wait the night through in the alley, and you two come out, so you must be Silky."

Silky turned to Benedict. "Is she why you wouldn't go to bed with me?"

"No." He glanced at Renata, who grinned broadly. "She's a professional colleague. Would you mind an extra person at breakfast?"

She stared at Renata for a minute. "Why do you keep the scar?"

Renata nodded, and continued to grin. "I like you, Silky. Same as Stennet, you know the right question." She put her hand on Silky's shoulder and scowled. "I keep it because it makes me look mean." Then she smiled again, softly.

Benedict looked at Renata, wondered how much truth there was to her answer. Some, probably.

"You want to have breakfast with us?" Silky asked.

"Love to."

Silky smiled, turned to Benedict. "Sure, let's take her. She's all right."

As they walked along the canal, Silky and Renata talked, already at ease with each other. Benedict listened to them and watched Renata, pleased, for some reason, that she had tracked and found him.

They ate on the second-floor balcony of a restaurant a block from the canal, at a wooden table by the railing where they had a clear view of the street in both directions, and could see the heads of pilots guiding their boats along the canal. They ordered plates of eggs and cheese and baked bread, a pot of coffee for Benedict and Renata, and tea for Silky. Silky managed to eat more than either Benedict or Renata.

The plates were empty, and they had just ordered

fresh pots of coffee and tea when someone on the street called up to Silky. She looked over the railing. A woman on the street waved at her to come down, and Silky yelled for her to wait a minute.

"That's Mishka," Silky said. "A friend of Tanker. I've got to see what she wants. Maybe I'll be back, probably I won't. If not, I'll see you later, somewhere." She shook hands with Renata, leaned over and kissed Benedict on the cheek. "Good-bye, Renata. Bye, Uncle Stennet."

Silky hurried off, and a few moments later appeared on the street. She talked with the woman for several minutes, then looked up, waved, and headed down the street with her.

"*Uncle* Stennet?"

"It's what she wanted to call me."

Renata nodded. "She's a good kid. Damn shame she's past the crux. Damn shame she ever got on the Flex in the first." She dumped the cold coffee from their cups into Silky's empty mug, then poured fresh coffee for both of them.

"Was it hard to find me?" Benedict asked.

She gave a half shrug. "It took a couple days. Riotmark's a big city. But no, not really. You weren't trying to hide, and that was all the difference."

"Ryker send you?"

Her expression hardened. "I would not have tried if he'd asked. I thought you would have understood that."

Benedict breathed in, nodded. "I'm sorry. It *was* an unnecessary question. Call it overactive caution. It's a habit I have, one I'm not interested in breaking." He smiled. "I *do* try to bypass it for certain people, when I know them well enough."

She nodded back. "All right, Benedict. Accepted

and understood. I tracked you for several reasons. Something to do while we wait for Gerad. A way to needle Ryker without pushing too far. He wasn't pleased when you took off, and when he finds out I've gone too . . ." She smiled.

"You're not going back?"

"Not for a while. Be at least another couple of days before Gerad's released from clinic." She tapped her leather bag. "I packed enough to hold me."

"Where are you staying?"

"Nowhere, yet. Been on the streets. No worry, though. I won't drape anywhere near you, you don't want me to. And I won't shadow. But there is another reason I tracked you. I'd like to spend some time with you, alone, without Ryker. I think I'd like you if I knew you better." She paused. "I might even let you know *me* a little more. Think on it."

"I will."

They sat without speaking, and Benedict watched the boats slip past at the end of the street, canal traffic apparently back to normal after the riot. Half the balcony tables were now empty, and it was much quieter than it had been earlier. The balcony was still in shade, but the air was growing warmer.

"About you," Renata said. "Staying with Silky?"

"For now, yes. She has an extra bed."

"You really think that's a good idea?"

"What do you mean?"

"Don't know that it's fair to her." She paused, but when Benedict did not respond, she continued. "So I've only just met her, but I've picked up a lot, and I've known other people like her. Now she calls you 'Uncle.' All right, not a problem, but it's a sign. She's come to depend on you for emotional support. She's pretty damn independent, because she's had to be,

181

but at the same time she's vulnerable. The longer you stay with her, the more dependent she'll become. If you were going to be here permanently, that would be different. But unless you've made a complete change of plans, you're going to be leaving this city in the next few days. That's what isn't fair to her. She's done all right on her own up to now, and she'll be fine on her own in the future . . . if you let her." Renata breathed deeply once, then leaned back in her chair.

Benedict thought of the night before, of Silky coming to him. It was not that she had asked to stay the night, but that she had asked him to end her life for her if it became necessary. No, not *if*, but *when*. That was a lot to ask of someone, too much for most people. It showed tremendous faith and trust, and she had asked *him*. And he had let her down, in a way.

"I'm not suggesting you stop seeing her altogether," Renata went on. "Just that you shouldn't . . . Look, there's a place nearby, a private roomer. I know it well, it's the sort of place that discourages inquiries, if Ryker were to start looking for us. We can get a couple of rooms there, stay until Gerad is out and we're ready to go, but we'll still be close enough to Silky."

Benedict breathed very deeply and slowly once, and nodded. "Your point is well made. And you're probably right." He gazed down at the street, searching for a glimpse of Silky though he knew she was nowhere close. "Let's go to this place you know. I can go back later, tell Silky why I'm leaving and where we'll be." He pushed his coffee cup away and stood up from the table. "And I would appreciate it if you would make some of your Linsok coffee. I'm tired of sludge."

Renata smiled, and nodded. "A deal," she said. She stood, dropped a bread crust in her coffee, and they left.

The roomer was called the Waterfront, a two-story building of unfinished wood fronting the canal just half a kilometer from where the canal split off from the Qua Tri. Standing in front of the building, looking upstream, Benedict could see the gate system that diverted the water into the canal. He and Renata walked up to the screened porch, crossed through it, and entered the front hall.

Inside were dark wood walls and floor and a fabric-covered ceiling that dangled thick strings of varying lengths. Across from them was a stairway, and next to it a wooden desk, now unoccupied. On the left wall was a screen window, and on the right a doorway that opened onto a large room furnished with several padded chairs and a sofa, and a few small tables. In one corner of the room was a fireplace.

Renata stepped up to the empty desk, reached behind it, and pulled at something. Two minutes later a short, white-bearded man emerged from a previously hidden door in the room, and approached them. Though he was old, muscle still rippled beneath his light T-shirt. He grinned, reached out and squeezed Renata's hand.

"How ya, R. Got your rooms ready. I can take you up now. This the friend you talked?"

"Yeah, Kreole, this is Stennet. Stennet, this is old friend Kreole, runs this place." The two men shook hands. "Take us up," Renata said.

The short man gestured with a closed fist and led them up the narrow, twisted staircase, then along the echoing hall. Near the end of the hall, he pushed open a door.

"Rooms adjoining, double door between," Kreole said. "Single balcony."

The room was large, simply furnished with a bed, two chairs, a small table, and a single standing lamp.

An oil lamp rested atop a tall dresser. Through the large screen door could be seen the wide balcony with a table and three chairs.

"I'll take this room," Renata said.

Kreole opened both doors on the left wall, and they all walked through to the next room, which was furnished much like the first. Kreole handed Benedict a key, gave another to Renata. He pointed to a lever next to the hall door.

"You need anything, Stennet, pull that. Toilets, showers at the end of the hall. R can tell you anything else you need to know, so I'll leave." He nodded, then went out into the hall. His heavy footsteps echoed, fading gradually into silence.

"They leave you alone here," Renata said. "The way I like it." She returned to her room, leaving the adjoining doors open, and tossed her bag onto the bed. Benedict opened the screen door and stepped out onto the large balcony which was connected to Renata's, though each half had its own table and chairs. Renata joined him.

"You want coffee now? I'll make you a cup."

Benedict shook his head. "Maybe later."

"Fine. I'd rather take a shower."

"I could use one myself."

"All right, how's this? Showers, then I'll take you up to the Qua Tri, we'll have some coffee on the river."

"All right. A shower, then a walk."

Renata went inside. Benedict stayed on the balcony, gazing out over the canal. Boat traffic was heavier here than in front of Silky's apartment, and the pilots deftly guided their craft in complicated patterns around one another. The high sun above him blazed brightly, giving everything a bleached look. Tired, and faintly depressed, Benedict turned and went back inside.

184

9

BENEDICT FELT WEAK, SUFFUSED WITH AN INDIFFERENT lethargy, and he found it difficult to put one foot in front of the other as he and Renata walked upstream along the canal. Though he had just showered for the first time in several days, he was already sticky with sweat. The late morning sun burned through the thick, damp haze, and Benedict felt the sun and haze as a pressure on his skull, not painful but enervating. He refused to pick up his pace to match Renata's, and she finally slowed to walk at his side.

"Hope you're not like this in the jungle," she said. "You'll be worthless."

"I'll be fine." He smiled. "Blame it on inertia. Once we leave this city and start moving, I'll do just fine."

As they neared the river, and the gate system controlling water and transportation flow, the canal became more congested; the boats moved more slowly, often stopping completely as they waited for signals from the controllers. Boats destined for the river were directed off to a narrow side channel that cut across the tip of the I-Zone and entered the Qua Tri downstream from where the canal branched off the river. Boats transferring from the river to the canal had a similar channel on the opposite side, cutting from the river upstream of the main canal. Chaotic docks and piers jutted out into the canal and the river all around the junction, and activity was constant, especially the transfer of cargo to and from boats too large to change waterways.

Renata and Benedict skirted the docks and headed upriver along the incoming side channel. The paved roadway, free of all vehicles except hand-drawn carts and cycles, curved at the junction to follow the river, which was still lined with piers and docks upstream. The bank was crowded with tiny stalls. Fish was cooked in the stalls for consumption, or smoked for storage and shipping. White smoke spiraled up from fires and coals. As they walked past, Renata pointed out the way each monger cooked the fish. A few boiled the fish in kettles with vegetables and algae, others steamed the fish, and some charred it on open racks hung close to hot, red and white coals.

"Let's go down by the water," Renata said. She led the way down a narrow path and onto a shelf of rocks and driftwood at the water's edge.

Renata knelt in the shelter of the bank, took several items from her bag, and set up a tiny portable stove.

"Told you I can make coffee anywhere," she said.

Benedict watched her work, her movements smooth, rapid, and efficient as she prepared a special flask, measuring water and fine grounds, adjusting four or five settings on the flask. Within two minutes the flask was half full with hot, rich coffee, which Renata poured into two cups. She handed one to him, then broke down the stove and flask and repacked them. They sat beside each other with their backs against the dirt bank, quite warm from the sun.

"It's been quiet in the Canal Zone recently," Renata said. "You came at a good time. Except for a riot in the I-Zone, it's been unusually calm. You hear about it?"

"The riot? I heard about it. Got caught on the edges of it."

"What happened?"

"Don't really know. I was walking along the canal when it broke loose. Didn't move quickly enough, next I knew I was buried under the rubble of a building."

"That where you picked up the head bruise?"

He nodded. "A few other wounds, nothing major."

"You got out, though. A lot of people didn't."

Benedict gazed across the river, at the dense jungle infrequently broken by a dwelling or a glimpse of a narrow unpaved road. He could almost hear the boom of throbbing music from the underground chamber filled with caves and rope bridges.

"I still don't know what started it," he said. "Newspads were not illuminating."

"They rarely are. Information access in this damned city is pretty strictly controlled by money or power. Still, almost certain the reason was Flex. Flex is the major cause of most everything in this twisted city. Some like to think it's even the cause of life itself." She laughed and shook her head, but her expression gradually hardened, her gaze became unfocused.

"What *is* the way with Flex?" he asked. "I've picked up the impression that it's legal to acquire, process, and sell if you're trading offworld, but that it's illegal for personal use."

"That's it," Renata answered. "Way it lays, possession of Flex is illegal unless the intent is to ship offworld. And you have to be certified, attached to one of the authorized exporting firms. How the combines keep all the control, the money. That's why even the free-lancers, like Gerad, are tied with a combine. And why we'll be certified with Timons. If we weren't, we wouldn't get far upriver. We might not anyway." She tossed what little coffee remained in her cup into the river, stepped down to the water, and rinsed out the cup. She remained kneeling, staring into the water. "Sometimes, this place is just a fucking hole."

"Why do you stay here?" Benedict asked. "You've been offworld. Why did you come back? Or why not leave again, the way you seem to feel about this world?"

Renata turned to face him, gave a half smile while shaking her head. "You know someplace better?"

Benedict shrugged. "Depends on what you mean by better, I suppose. There are places with different problems. That would at least be a change."

"I don't know. There *are* better places, I imagine. But it's not that simple. I have reasons to stay here." She returned to sit at his side again. "I'm sure *you* have reasons. Besides, Nightshade and Riotmark do have certain . . . attractions." She tapped the empty cup against her knee. "I have ambivalent feelings, about what I want. Times I wish it was always calm and peaceful, that I could spend my life relaxed, way I am now, sitting by the river in the heat. Glide along day to day, no worries, no problems, die at an old, old age." She smiled and shrugged. "The other side, though. In this city, on this world, if you move in certain spheres, survival is predicated on maintaining the sharpest edge, an intensity that at times is ecstatic. I like that too. So I go back and forth. If the other reasons didn't exist, I might stay here anyway."

188

Benedict finished his coffee, rinsed the cup in the river, and gave it to Renata. She put the two cups away, and they sat side by side, watching a patrol craft jetting upstream. The sun was almost directly overhead.

"I have to go," Benedict said. "To Silky's. Talk to her, explain why I'm leaving."

Renata nodded, shouldered her bag. They climbed the bank and onto the main roadway.

"Will you come with me?" Benedict asked. "Afterward, maybe we can go somewhere, talk."

Renata nodded. "Sure."

Benedict nodded in return, and they started downriver toward the canal.

10

THEY WALKED TOWARD SILKY'S APARTMENT IN THE growing afternoon heat. The high, light overcast now only occasionally blocked the sun, which otherwise reflected brightly from the canal water. Benedict's clothes, though loose-fitting, clung to him with his sweat, but he noticed that Renata's dark single-suit, though tighter, did not cling at all, and she seemed to sweat far less.

"What's the suit made of?" he asked. "Hylotex?"

She nodded. "All my single-suits are custom-made, most comfortable clothes I've ever worn. I've got a couple for the cold, too, and a shadow-suit, same material the Black Phantoms wear, absorbs light so you're practically invisible in the dark. Useful, at times."

"I imagine."

"Before we leave the city, you want I can bring you to someone, have a couple of suits made for you. Very expensive, but worth it. They'll be better than what you're wearing now, guarantee."

"I'll let you know."

"You don't sound enthusiastic. Like being uncomfortable?"

Benedict smiled and shrugged. "Maybe. Sometimes it's a good reminder."

"Of what?"

He did not answer, and they continued on in silence.

They reached the old three-story building, and turned down the side alley. High, sharp sounds came from inside the building, muted by the walls.

"You hear that?" Benedict stopped in front of the door, listening.

"Sure. Sounds like . . . someone calling out?"

"Yeah." Benedict unlocked the door, reached in to disconnect the alarm, and they moved inside. The sounds were louder, now clearly a voice crying out for help. Then there was silence.

Benedict and Renata started up the stairs, taking them two at a time. Halfway up, Benedict halted, a hand gripped on the railing. Mindless fear cut into him from above, followed by only slightly milder panic from another source. He pushed up the inner screens, strengthened them; the fear and panic snapped off momentarily, then returned, slightly weaker. The two tremors of emotion oscillated inside him, as though the screens wavered, shifting up and down, and he could not completely shut out the emotion coming at him from above. Christ, he thought, can't have a seizure now. Not now. It was too damn soon!

"What is it? What's wrong?" Renata prodded him with her hand. "Come on, Benedict. Move!"

He forced himself forward, the fear and panic

vibrating through him. At the top of the stairs he
hesitated again, but with Renata's hands digging into
his back he went through the door and into the
corridor. The first door, to Lady Deebo's room, was
open; harsh gasping sounds emerged with choked
whimpers. Benedict stepped inside the dim, stifling
room, Renata just behind him.

Silky knelt on the floor beside a twitching figure. It
was Lady Deebo, lying on her back, her eyes wide, one
hand gripped around a table leg, her mouth opening
and closing, a fish gasping out of water. A bottle of
scotch, probably the one he'd left for her, lay on its
side nearby.

"Uncle Stennet!" Silky cried. She jumped up
from the floor, grabbed him. "Do something! She's
dying!"

Benedict did not move. He still fought to keep out
the desperate, uncontrolled fear swelling from Lady
Deebo, and Silky's hysterical, lost panic. He watched
Renata hurry past him, drop to one knee beside the
gasping woman. She touched Lady Deebo's throat
with her fingers.

"Stroke, maybe," Renata said. "Respiratory failure,
I don't know. She needs help fast." She spun around.
"Is there a phone in here, or another room? We've got
to call the van-meds, *now*. Stennet? Silky?"

Silky still hung on to Benedict's hand, wild and
almost uncontrolled, jerking at his arm. Benedict was
unable to move. He stared at Renata and Lady Deebo,
only vaguely seeing them.

"I don't know!" Silky managed to cry out. "I don't
have a phone, I don't know if there's . . ." She
couldn't finish. She looked up at Benedict and jerked
once more on his arm. "Uncle Stennet, you've got to
help. What's the matter?" She stared at him, tugged

once more. "Oh, shika, Renata, he's not going to be able to help at all."

"Benedict! Benedict, what in hell is wrong with you? We've got to get meds here fast, and I need your help. Pop out of it, will you? Benedict!"

Silky released his hand, still staring at him. "Benedict? Is that your name, Benedict? Don't . . . don't . . . be so . . ."

All the filters and screens disintegrated, and Benedict knew he had lost the fight. For the first few moments he was able to identify and distinguish all that rushed inside him: the paralyzed fear from Lady Deebo; hysterical and confused panic from Silky; more confusion, linked with anger and concern from Renata; from another room nearby came a dark, painful grief and loneliness; from upstairs, one source emanating physical pain, despair, and self-attempt, and a second source matching the self-contempt and adding confusion and building tension as orgasm approached. And with the final explosion at climax, all the emotions in the building mixed together completely inside Benedict, fueled from outside, from anyone and everyone in the nearby buildings, on the streets, or gliding across the canal.

Benedict cried out once, doubled over, and collapsed to the floor at Silky's feet. He heard her scream, saw her grab her own shoulders with clenching fingers, then back away from him. Renata, too, moved across his vision, though he could not concentrate enough to fully comprehend what she was doing. He felt her hand on him, felt her shake him, heard her call his name three or four times, but he could not respond. Then she seemed to be shaking Silky, who quieted, and saying something, blurred words drifting through the air. Silky ran out, her footsteps vibrating in his head, then Renata knelt again at his side, checking his pulse perhaps, his breathing. Her face twisted with confusion. Then she was gone, back to Lady Deebo.

He burned inside. The seizures had never been this bad, he thought. Or . . . But then he could barely hang on to that idea before it was swept away in the pain now rushing through him, acid in his veins.

Benedict's vision blurred, his hearing collapsed in a disintegrating wave function, punctured by a shrill ringing. Sand filled his mouth and throat, the stench of rotting meat plugged his nose. With the burning came flashes of orange and red and violet across his eyes. One moment he knew he was on Lady Deebo's floor, and the next he could not remember who Lady Deebo was, or what city surrounded him, or upon which world he circled what mysterious sun.

A very small part of his mind detached itself from, and looked down upon, the swirling chaos of emotion that was tearing him apart. He wondered if he was dying. Perhaps this time *everything* had collapsed, every possible perceptual barrier, and the sensory overload would at last be complete, would at last kill him. And then he wondered if it mattered.

Maybe it was time to die. Maybe he'd had enough of this life, of being a part of humanity. Maybe death was the escape he now needed.

No.

NO.

His own answer to himself was firm. He did not want to die, and though he knew he *would* die someday, he hoped he would never want it. Death was an answer to nothing. Life was at least a web of possibilities.

But, he realized, he might not have a choice now. The fire inside him grew, his vision flared out in a brilliant red-orange flash of an exploding sun . . . and then came a solid black, blocking out all light, and then there was nothing at all.

11

BENEDICT CAME TO INSIDE A HEAVY SILENCE. HE OPENED his eyes, recognized the stained ceiling of Silky's apartment, but only after he had gazed at the ceiling for a long time did sounds begin to leak into his awareness. Voices from outside the building, distant and faint, filtered through to him, then the sound of someone shifting position within the room. Benedict turned his head and saw Renata seated at the wooden table, holding a mug, watching him. Benedict sat up, leaned back against the wall. He felt drained, but all the screens and filters were up and solid, locked securely in place.

"How you feel?" Renata asked. "Want some coffee? I made some a few minutes ago, should be hot."

"I'm all right. A little shaky. Coffee sounds good."

She got up from the table, went into the kitchen, then returned and brought him a steaming cup. Benedict sipped at the strong coffee, only peripherally aware of the taste. Stark, flame-colored images and fleeting sensations from what had happened in Lady Deebo's room flickered through his mind. He had never lost consciousness during a seizure before, and did not know what it meant, if anything.

"Where's Lady Deebo? Is she . . . ?"

"She's not dead yet," Renata said. "I talked to someone at the clinic, physician in charge. She's alive, but no one knows for how long. Her vitals are shot, apparently."

"Not surprising."

"Did you know her real name?"

"No."

"Ilitia Deebolovski. Lady Deebo's a hell of a lot easier to say, but it sure doesn't ring the same."

"And Silky?" Benedict asked.

"She's gone. Don't know when she'll be back. All this flaked her. She shot up. Tried to stay around until you woke, but she couldn't handle it."

Benedict nodded. He stood, spilling some of the coffee, and walked over to the table, sat across from her. A slight weakness still pervaded his limbs, and his chest and stomach felt hollow, but he felt more relief than anything else.

"How are *you* doing?" he asked.

Renata smiled. "Consider I had three people to take care of, I'm doing just fine."

Benedict turned toward the open window. He guessed it was almost dusk. Sleep and food were what he needed, but he could not decide which should come first. He looked at Renata.

"Aren't you going to ask me what happened?"

"No."

"Why not?"

"It's yours. You want to talk about, I'll listen. I won't pretend I'm not curious, or that I wouldn't prefer to know, but it was obviously more than

197

physical. Something private. If you never talk about it, fine."

"But what about our expedition? Going upriver, into the jungle. You'll go with me, where we could depend on each other for our lives, knowing it could happen again?"

Renata shrugged, then breathed deeply. "I trust you, Benedict." She pushed back from the table, stood, and smiled. "Come on, you look hungry. I'll buy you dinner, then we can go to a fine music club I know near the Waterfront. A trio there like you've never heard. What say?"

Benedict looked at her, uncertain. Trust? What had he done to earn it? He finally nodded, and stood up to leave with her.

Fagan's Place, a music club several blocks from the Waterfront, was nearly full though the sun had only recently set and the music didn't start for an hour. Renata knew the manager, and she set them up at a private table near the empty stage where they were isolated—by wood pillars and hanging plants—from the rest of the club. Renata ordered a bottle of the house ale, and Benedict, after some hesitation, ordered a scotch. Slow and easy, two or three drinks might help smooth him out. He usually didn't trust alcohol after a seizure, but this time he just didn't care.

They spent most of the next hour in silence, though they did talk occasionally about Silky, about Riotmark and Nightshade. He felt comfortable with Renata, more comfortable than he had felt with anyone in the last seven years, with the single exception of Hadling.

By the time the band came onto the stage, every table in Fagan's Place was full, and people stood along the walls. When the first musician stepped onto the stage, the sound level dropped to near silence, and continued until all three were on stage. The main lights came down, and muted orange bathed the trio.

On the right, a very dark woman with short, coarse hair sat on a stool, holding a saxophone. Center stage, to the rear, another woman sat enclosed in a maze of percussion—drum kit, bells, wooden blocks of various sizes and shapes, strips and sheets of metal, strings of alloyed bars. On the left, a thin, graying man sat at a piano.

The dark woman brought the saxophone to her lips and blew two long, painful notes, the second abruptly cut off by a screech of metal from the percussionist. Silence for a minute, then the pianist started, a slow, simple, minor-key progression. The percussionist joined on the drums, the saxist cut in once more, and the evening set began.

Renata was right—the music was unlike anything he had heard before. It was not so much the individual pieces, most of which came out of recognizable traditions, but the overall impact and effect of the set that was so compelling and unique. Much seemed to be improvisational, and many of the pieces were in minor keys. Some were jazz or neuro-jazz oriented, some were from the ethereal schools, a few more were classical, and one or two were even influenced by current rip music. Most of the transitions were brief, atonal segments that Benedict found strangely effective and moving.

Throughout the set, individual pieces or passages called up images, sensations, and memories of his life. He felt once again the disorientation of a stellar jump, the nonuniverse leaking through his body, shifting his sense of reality. The multicolored explosions of an electrical storm on Dante's Eye flashed around him.

Cool, dark water enclosed his face from a time he had nearly drowned in one of Triskele's underground reservoirs. Once he saw simply the star-filled universe laid out before him, an image from a week he had spent in an orbiting observatory several years before, watching the painfully sharp and clear, never-ending skies of night.

Pleasant memories surfaced, but so did moments of pain, and one of the atonal transitions brought back his feelings from the first time he had killed someone. Fourteen years old, trying to survive in Triskele after his parents had died, he was attacked one night in the stairwell of a deserted building. Benedict had shoved a knife deep into the man's sternum even as the man's own knife bit deeply into Benedict's shoulder. In his first total empathic episode, he had felt the man die, and had been sick for days afterward. Those sensations always returned in later years when he was forced to kill again; the nausea became muted and more controlled as he grew older, but it was always there, and, though he had not killed anyone in years, he experienced it once again, adrift in Fagan's Place, trapped by music.

The set ended around midnight. Benedict and Renata sat at the table without talking for a long time. The musicians left, Fagan's Place slowly emptied, and finally the manager stopped by and gently asked them to leave.

12

Renata made coffee and they sat out on the balcony in front of her room; they had not spoken since leaving Fagan's Place. The warm night air was clear, and the stars flickered distinctly above them. Benedict realized for the first time that he missed seeing a moon. Nightshade had none.

"I envy them," Benedict said.

"The musicians?" He nodded. "Why?"

"Hard to explain. I felt both hopeful and inadequate listening to them. I've been trying all my life to . . ." He shrugged to himself. "Sometimes I don't know what I've been trying to do. Whatever it is, I haven't been successful, and I've given up trying."

"But the envy you feel?"

"To be able to move people that way, the way they moved me, even someone as cynical as I am. For several hours tonight I did not have any awareness of where I was in a spatial sense. No awareness that I was on Nightshade, in this damned city, in the Canal Zone." He paused. "I envy that."

"I understand," Renata said. "They even made an amateur musician of me. About three, four years ago, I had just returned to Riotmark after being offworld a while. One night I ended up in Fagan's Place, and they were playing. I'd never heard them before, never heard anything like it. By the time their set had ended, I was ready to try it myself. Few weeks later, I was in the jungle, came across a band of free-lancers, and one of them was playing a soontari. A kind of flute. I thought of Fagan's Place, asked the free-lancer to let me try it. He taught me the basics, even made one for me, and I've been playing it ever since."

"You want to play it now? I'd like to hear you."

Renata shook her head and smiled. "Not tonight. Sometime. I never play in the city. It really belongs in the jungle."

Neither spoke after that for a long time. The silence was comfortable and easy, but Benedict felt a growing tightness in his chest. It was time to talk to Renata about the seizures, to at least explain what they were. She had a right to know, after the last two days. But he did not know how to approach it, and he wished he could just let it go.

He turned and gazed out over the canal. Streetlamps reflected off the surface of the water, moving in distorted patterns as the boats moved past cleaving the water and adding reflections from their own swaying oil lamps.

"I do not want to be an empath," he finally said. "I want it to end." He paused, then went on. "The first time I had a seizure, like the one today, was seven years ago." He continued to look at the water, and when Renata did not respond, he resumed. "I had been on Mesa for two years. The reasons I was there

were gone, and I had shipped offworld, to Triumvirate. I had a home then, but I wasn't going back. On a
world called Rose. I made arrangements to sell it. I've
never had a home since, and I'm not sure I'll ever
want another." Renata still did not say anything, and
he went on.

"What the seizures are . . . You know something
about empaths, you said. Most people think we read
emotions the way they might read a newspad, or listen
to what another person is saying. It's not like that at
all. We do more than sense emotion, we *feel* it. The
emotions and feelings of others actually become our
own."

"I understand, Benedict. I've known another First,
and she talked a lot about it."

"Then you know there are controls, filters and
screens, so I can regulate what comes in. Some
empaths call them barriers or shields. Maybe that's
more apt. Well, I can keep all the screens and filters up
so nothing at all comes through, or I can adjust them
to focus on a single individual, or several people, or
everyone around me, at different levels of intensity."
He sighed heavily and turned to look at her. "When
these seizures strike, I lose all that control. The shields
come down, the filters and screens collapse, or disintegrate, something, I don't really know what happens,
they just disappear, and I become completely exposed
to the full force of the emotions of everyone within a
kilometer or more. It's an additive effect, and so
quickly overwhelming I become paralyzed. Like this
morning. Sometimes it's over soon, sometimes it goes
on a long time, but eventually something clicks inside
me, the filters and screens snap back into place, and it
ends. Everything back to . . . normal.

"I had that first seizure, and then not another for a
year and a half. Then it was a year, then nine months,

seven months, five . . . They've been coming closer together, especially in this past year. The last one was about two weeks ago. I have no idea when the next one will be. Soon."

Renata did not say anything for a while. She looked down at the cup in her hand, turned it one way, then another, then set it on the table.

"Why are you telling me all this?" she asked. "I imagine you haven't told many others."

"I've told no one."

"Then why me?"

"In the jungle, up the river, we'll all depend on each other. You deserve to know."

"But you won't be telling Ryker."

"No." He breathed heavily again. "When it happened this morning, I had no choice but to know you much more deeply than I had before. This afternoon, you said you trusted me. I trust *you*, Renata."

Again she didn't respond at first. Then, "Come to bed with me, Benedict."

The tension in his chest returned. It was something he wanted to hear from her, but had been afraid of hearing. He was not prepared for it at all.

"It's been a long time," he said.

"Seven years?"

He smiled. "Yes. Longer, actually."

"Then it's been long enough, Benedict."

"It's not that easy."

"I know."

Silence returned. Benedict wanted to tell her no, that it wasn't a good time, maybe later would be better. He wanted to take the easy way, go back to his room, alone, spend the night in restless sleep.

Renata stood. "I'm going inside, Benedict." She looked at him a few moments, then turned and went into the room. Benedict got up from the chair and followed.

A single oil lamp lit the room, and Renata turned it low; exaggerated, vague shadows played on the walls. She slipped her boots from her feet, set them under a chair. Benedict approached her, touched her cheek with his fingers. Renata put her hands around him and on his back, pulled him slowly but firmly to her. Their faces came together, tilted, and mouths touched, then pressed tightly to each other. Renata took his hand, placed it on a small tab on her left shoulder.

"Just a single zip-trac for the whole suit," she said.

Benedict manipulated the tab, then eased it down, opening a seam in the single-suit all the way from her shoulder, down her side, then across and down the inside of her thigh, knee, calf, and finally to her ankle. She stepped out of the suit, and Benedict laid it across a chair. Renata wore nothing beneath it.

A scar the length of his middle finger shone just above her left breast, thin and white in the darkness.

"This to make you look mean too?" he asked. He brushed it gently with his finger.

She smiled, reached down, and pulled his shirt up over his head. He removed his boots and socks while she supported him, and loosened his trousers, which he then slipped off and dropped into the chair.

They stood beside the bed, holding each other, their shadows wavering across the bed and wall. He kissed her eyebrow, her cheek; she kissed his throat and shoulder. They sank to the bed, then shifted to lie side by side, still holding one another.

Benedict's heart beat rapidly, and he heard the sound of rushing blood in his ears. The tightness remained in his chest, but her warmth, the soft touch

205

of her fingers on his skin, eased the tension, uncoiled the tightness so that it flowed out along his limbs and dissipated into the night.

He watched the shadows flicker across her skin, kissed them as they fluttered, searched the light and dark places of her warm body. Renata's hands and lips were soft, pleasant needles marking his skin, comforting him, coaxing him into her.

When he entered her, there was the warm, moist sensation he had never quite forgotten, yet had never totally remembered either. A shudder arced briefly through him, as though he was momentarily chilled, then all the tension in him was gone, and they moved easily together, hands and feet and mouths exploring.

The thin layers of their sweat mingled, formed a single coating between them, slick and hot as they pressed against one another. Her breath blew warm and soft across him, faster and faster while his own breath came harder, and sharp from within his chest.

But then, just before he climaxed, Benedict shifted his attention and strengthened his inner screens and filters, afraid he would lose control of them. And later when she, too, climaxed, Benedict again distracted to strengthen the screens, afraid he would relax his control at the sudden intense surge of feeling from her, afraid of letting that emotion inside him, afraid of what he would discover about her, or about himself.

Afraid.

Listening intently, Benedict could just hear the lapping of water at the canal's banks, or perhaps against the hulls of boats moving past. The Waterfront was nearly silent, as if there were no other residents. Perhaps there weren't; he'd seen no one except Kreole since they'd been here.

Renata moved beside him, her skin warm against his.

"What happened on Mesa?" she asked.

"An old story. And one I don't want to talk about. Not now."

The oil lamp sputtered, threatened to extinguish. The tight, clenched knot had returned to his chest, and he could not dispel it.

"I'm tired," he said. "I need to sleep." He swung his legs over the side of the bed, sat up, his bare feet on the warm hardwood floor.

"Stay," Renata said. "The bed's big enough for two."

He shook his head, turned and smiled at her. "Not yet." He leaned over, kissed her softly on the mouth, then harder when she returned it. He eased back and stood. "Good night, Renata."

"Good night, Benedict."

He put out the sputtering lamp, then went through the double door to his room, leaving the doors open. An oppressive despair weighed on him. The knot still clenched in his chest, he crossed the room and climbed in between the sheets of his empty bed.

13

WHEN BENEDICT WOKE, IT WAS NEARLY MIDDAY. HE FELT sluggish from sleeping in the heat, his head stuffed with cotton, his limbs heavy and awkward. He looked into Renata's room, and it was empty, but there was a sheet of papris on his pants, marked with black letters.

Gone for a while. Errands. Back sometime. R.

Benedict showered and dressed, then went out into the damp heat of the day. He wandered upstream along the canal, thinking of Renata, recalling the smell of her damp skin, the shifting patterns of shadows across her face from the lamplight. Already it seemed to have happened a long time ago, and yet at the same time felt so immediate that the tensed knot returned to his chest, clenched in pain.

The heat and humidity suffused him, drained his energy so that he wanted to sit on the bank of the canal and cease all motion. What he needed was a few days of taxing physical labor, he decided. Purge the toxins, cleanse the fatigue from his limbs, clear his head. Benedict headed for the canal/river junction and the maze of docks and piers where he knew he could easily latch onto daily temp jobs, the kind of jobs he needed.

Within a half hour he was in the dark hold of a river freighter, loading massive crates onto swing platforms that were then hauled out of the ship and unloaded onto waiting trucks. He did not know what was in the crates, and he did not care. Muscles straining, working side by side with three other men in the hot, stifling hold, sweat streamed from him, leaching his strength, but leaching his enervation as well. The flow of water from his body seemed to be a cleansing that drained and somehow purified him.

Three hours later the job had ended and he'd begun the next, cleaning fish in the hot sun with six other men and women, working on a boatload of pardos from upriver, preparing them for a packing firm. With a long, sharp knife, Benedict sliced into and gutted one fish after another as the swirling water of the cleaning tables washed the entrails into the covered grinders. As he worked, an ache spreading through his arms and shoulders and tightening his neck, he listened to the other workers talk or sing or tell jokes, and matched their curses with his own at the heat, the low pay, and the occasional cuts received from his own knife.

They finished the job just before dark. The foreman paid them in cash, then issued work chits which would give them access to one of the dock shelters where they would be provided a cot for the night. Before going to the shelter, however, Benedict joined his six co-workers at a nearby tavern for dinner and several rounds of cold ale, most of which he paid for himself. Half drunk and physically exhausted, Benedict made his way with one of the women and two of the men to the closest dock shelter.

Renata was seated in front of the old building, watching him approach. Benedict stopped next to her while his companions went into the shelter.

"Don't have trouble finding me, do you?" Benedict asked.

Renata stood, shook her head. "You really want to sleep here tonight?"

"I don't know." He took the work chit from his shirt pocket. "Don't want to waste this."

"Waste it," she said.

Benedict glanced in through the open door, at the dark forms of bodies and cots scattered about the huge room, then pocketed the chit. "It's not so bad," he said.

"I know. I've slept in plenty. Let's go."

They walked slowly along the canal, in and out of the cones of light from the streetlamps. The sky was hazy above them, the stars barely visible as muted, dull flickers.

"I'll be glad to leave this city for a while," Renata said. "The river and the jungle . . . some ways they're a lot simpler. Not necessarily less dangerous, but simpler."

"Is something bothering you?" Benedict asked.

"Not that I want to talk about." She turned to him and smiled. "You and I are alike in that way, so many things that are too damn hard to talk about. We'll have to be a long time together before we know very much about each other. If not for the fact that we have at least some trust in one another . . . Well, time and patience."

A series of explosions shook the air, then smoke and flame began to rise from inside the I-Zone. The distant crack of weapons fire drifted across the canal, echoing from waterfront buildings, and the blinking green lights of skitter copters began to weave into sight, a kilometer or two away.

"There again," Renata said. "A follow-up operation to the riot. Smaller, probably, but we'll have a fire show tonight." She paused, then turned to face him. "You avoiding me?"

Benedict shook his head. "No. I just needed some time alone, some hard labor. That why you tracked me again?"

"No. And you should know that. Had to find you because we've got to get back. Gerad's being released from clinic tomorrow, and we leave the next morning."

They stopped in front of the Waterfront, which once again was dark and silent.

"How do you know?"

"Talked to Ryker today."

Benedict looked up at the darkened windows of the second-floor rooms. "He knows where we are?"

"No. I called him. Felt we owed it to keep in touch. Good thing, he'd have gone over the edge he's flying if Gerad had been released and we hadn't shown for several days."

Benedict nodded. "Glad you were thinking, since I wasn't."

"He wants us back tomorrow, but he'll settle for first light the next morning, when we leave. Says he's got everything ready."

"He seems to be taking it all pretty smooth."

"Not really. With us, yes, but not the expedition. Seems to be some kind of new time pressure. Gerad's not really ready, impression I got, but Ryker pushed his release. Don't know what it is, but Ryker's pushing up the whole time schedule as much as he can."

Benedict nodded. He gestured toward the building. "Let's go in."

Upstairs, they sat on the balcony in front of Benedict's room, watching the red and orange glow of flames deep in the I-Zone, listening to the dull, infrequent explosions and the faint staccato of gunfire.

"I have to find Silky tomorrow, before we leave," Benedict said.

Renata slowly shook her head. "Kid's had a rough few days. Her friend, Tanker, is killed. Lady Deebo's going to die. And now we're leaving."

"She'll be all right. She's damn tough for a fourteen-year-old kid. The only reason she's lived to be fourteen."

Renata put her hand on Benedict's arm, squeezed. "Yeah, I like her too," she said. "And you're right, she'll deal with it, come riding out the top."

"Sure, for whatever little time she's got left." He sat without moving, watching Renata. The pressure of her hand on his arm was reassuring, and somehow helped to ease the ball of tension that had knotted inside his chest again when he'd seen her in front of the shelter.

"Will you sleep with me tonight?" he asked.

"Sleep? Or sex?"

"Both."

She moved her hand down his arm to lock her fingers with his. "I'd like that very much."

They stood up from the table, went into the room, and slowly undressed in the light of a single oil lamp. Benedict put out the lamp, and they climbed into bed with only the dim glow of the streetlamps providing any light. For a long time they lay quietly in the darkness, hardly moving. Renata's breath was warm in the hollow of his neck, and as his eyes adjusted to the darkness, he watched the faint, nearly indistinguishable shadows shifting across her skin.

It seemed to Benedict that Renata started to speak several times, but she never said anything.

"What is it?" he finally asked.

"I don't know if I should say anything. Last night, you closed yourself off, you closed *me* off. I could sense it."

"It's hard, Renata."

"I know." She brushed the bridge of his nose with her fingertip. "I know, Benedict. I just want to tell you, ask you not to be afraid."

He nodded, and they were silent, and they held each other tightly in the warm darkness.

14

THE DOOR TO SILKY'S ROOM WAS OPEN. BENEDICT LOOKED in, Renata looking over his shoulder. Silky lay on her bed, awake but motionless, the cube player by her head, the volume high. Benedict knocked on the open door, and he and Renata stepped inside, but Silky did not move. Benedict crossed the room, reached forward, and touched Silky's arm.

"Hi, Silky. I came to talk to you."

She reached up to turn down the volume, but continued to stare at the ceiling.

"They wouldn't let me in to see her," she said. "They said it was my age, but I know. It's because I'm a Flexie. I told them, I told them she was my . . . my mother, but they didn't believe me. Or didn't care. They just don't know." She closed her eyes and turned toward the wall. "I'm sick of it all, I'm sick of everyone, even you, Uncle Stennet. Or Benedict, whoever in shika's hell you are."

Benedict sat on the bed, glancing at Renata, who shrugged and sat at the table.

"Yes, Silky, my name *is* Benedict. Shouldn't be a surprise. You remember the first time we met, you told me you knew Stennet wasn't my real name. It was all right then, and nothing's changed." He knew that what he'd just said wasn't true, and was not surprised when she didn't respond. Almost everything had changed for her in the past week.

Silky remained facing the wall, and spoke quietly, her voice muffled. "Lady Deebo's going to die, isn't she?"

"Probably. If she doesn't improve in the next few days, they'll disconnect the life support systems. Her physician doesn't think she'll make it on her own."

Silky twisted her fingers, slowly made a tight fist, then started hitting at the wall, softly at first, then harder and faster. Benedict resisted stopping her, and he let her pound at the rough brick, over and over, each punch accompanied by a tight expulsion of air. Eventually she slowed, and after a time, stopped. Finally she turned to face him and sat up.

"So they don't think she'll make it on her own. Fucking butchers. What about *me*? You think I can make it on my own?"

Benedict nodded. "You'll have to, Silky. Renata and I are leaving before dawn tomorrow. We'll be leaving the city, and I don't know when we'll be back, if ever."

Silky did not say anything, just slowly and mechanically nodded her head, staring at him. She slid off the bed and walked stiffly into the kitchen, then came out carrying a large meat knife. Rust spotted the blade, and Silky wiped it twice on her pants, then tucked it into her back pocket and covered it with her shirt.

"Let's go," she said. Her voice was cold and hard. "I've got one more thing to take care of. I want you to come with me, case I have trouble getting back."

"Silky, what are you . . .?"

"Shut it, damn you! You tell me I have to make it on my own, so let me do what I have to do. Just come along, and don't ask anything, don't say a word." She started for the door, looked at Renata. "You too." Then she was out the door and marching with determination along the corridor. Benedict looked at Renata, and they quickly followed Silky out of the building.

Outside, Silky led the way eastward along the canal. She walked quickly, her gaze straight ahead, silent but emoting a swelling rage and frustration that Benedict had to strain to keep blocked. He and Renata kept pace, just a few steps back.

Fifteen minutes of steady, silent marching passed, then Silky slowed and stopped in front of a tall building facing the canal. She stared up at the second or third story of the dark wooden structure, as if waiting for something. A few minutes later, a familiar cry drifted down from the third-floor window.

"Siiiiilllllllkyy . . ."

Benedict remembered the cry from the night he'd met Silky on the bus, and he remembered how Silky had trembled at the sound, trying to ignore it, pushing on through the night as the cry followed her. Now, though, she did not ignore it, and she did not walk away to leave it behind.

"Siiiiilllllllkyy . . ." came the cry again.

"All right, bitch!" Silky yelled. "You want me, I'm coming up! This time I'm coming!" Silky started forward, the knife now in her hand, and headed for the door on the ground floor.

"Silky, wait . . ." Benedict began.

216

She whirled, pointing the knife at him. "*No!* Stay back." She turned away and continued toward the door.

Benedict stepped forward, felt Renata's hand on his shoulder, holding him back.

"You've already made a decision with her," she said. "You're leaving tomorrow. Whatever this is, she has to deal with it on her own. You *know* that."

Benedict turned and looked at Renata, sighed once, and nodded. Yes, he knew, but that didn't make it easy. Renata put a hand on his shoulder and squeezed.

They stood near the canal bank and watched the building, listening and waiting. Silky had left the door open, but nothing could be seen inside except darkness. The air all around them seemed heavy and unnaturally quiet. If there were any boats moving on the canal behind them, Benedict could not hear them.

The voice called Silky again, fainter this time as if it was directed into the building. A brief silence followed, then someone cried out, screamed and screamed, the sound oscillating for several moments. Then the screams abruptly ceased.

Silence returned to the building, and Benedict and Renata waited, motionless.

Silky appeared at the door, the knife in her hand. She stumbled toward them, tears streaming down her cheeks, dripping to the dirt and onto the knife. As she came closer, Benedict studied the knife, felt a painful relief when he saw there was no blood on the blade. Silky kept coming, crying louder now, then passed them and stepped to the edge of the canal. She hesitated a few moments, then threw the knife into the water.

"Why couldn't I do it?" she whispered. "Why couldn't I just kill her and end it all, why couldn't

I . . . ? Why is it she . . . loves me?" She turned, staggered forward, and collapsed against Benedict, hugged him tightly. "Oh, Uncle Stennet, Uncle Stennet, hold me, please hold me . . ."

Benedict held her tightly as she shook against him, her hands clawing his shirt. Silky hugged and pressed against him for a long time, crying steadily. Renata stood a few steps back, watching them, her face expressionless but tight. Eventually Silky's trembling subsided, and her crying eased. She released her tight grip, but did not let go of him completely.

"Take me home, Uncle Stennet. Please." She wiped her face on his shirt, then backed away. "I want to go back home now."

Benedict started to nod when the plaintive cry came down from the window again.

"Siiiiillllkyy . . . Siiiiilllllkyyy . . ."

Silky began to cry again. "Now, Uncle Stennet, *please*," she managed between sobs.

Benedict put his arm around her, while she held on to him with both of hers, and they started upriver along the canal, Renata beside them.

"Who is she?" Benedict asked.

"My mother," she whispered.

She squeezed him tighter again, Renata put a hand on her shoulder, and the three of them walked on until the cry from the window could no longer be heard.

PART FOUR

Up The River

1

IT WAS OBVIOUS GERAD SHOULD NOT HAVE BEEN RELEASED from the clinic.

He was just over six feet tall, but thin, his knotted muscles delineated like an anatomical drawing. Black shadowed his eyes; dark blue and violet of fading bruises stained the dark, yellow-toned skin; thin pink lines of still-healing scars etched his lower arms and left cheek. Both wrists and thumbs were taped. His short black hair was choppy and unkempt. Still, in the man's stance and bearing, and in the well-defined muscle, Benedict could sense Gerad's physical and mental strength, and began to understand why he was called Blade.

Gerad stood near the truck, smoking a cigarette, gazing through the foliage toward the river. The rear window had been replaced, and the truck bed was filled with packs and crates and tightly wrapped bundles, equipment and supplies Ryker had acquired while Gerad was in the clinic and Benedict and Renata were in the Canal Zone. Duf bag in hand, shoulder bag at his side, Benedict skirted the truck and approached the free-lancer.

"Gerad? I'm Benedict." He put out his hand. Gerad turned, took it, and squeezed firmly.

"Ryker says your name's Stennet. Stennet Reese."

"It's what my idents say, and the name I'll give to anyone who asks. But to you, and Renata and Ryker, I'm Benedict."

"That your real name, or another pseudo?"

"Does it matter?"

Gerad smiled and shook his head. "Shit, last that matters in this fucking place."

Benedict put his bags in the back of the truck. Renata emerged from the hotel and joined them; as she packed her own bags among the others, Benedict made the introductions.

"Don't mean to be rude," Renata said, looking at Gerad. "But you look like you could do with another day or two in the clinic."

Renata the diplomat, Benedict thought to himself. Just like with Ryker. But Gerad did not appear to take offense; he laughed and flicked his cigarette butt to the ground.

"I feel like I could use a week," he said. "But the man says we go now. I'll make it. First few days on the river won't be dead shit to worry about. I'll rest then." He lit another cigarette, leaned against the side of the truck. "Where *is* Ryker? He's the one in such a damn hurry."

"Paying the hotel bill," Renata said.

Gerad snorted. "That's one thing he's good for, paying the bills."

Renata turned to Benedict, raised an eyebrow, and smiled. Benedict shrugged.

222

The midday air was heavy with the humidity, and the thick cloud cover threatened rain. They stood silently near the truck, waiting for Ryker. Gerad smoked, and Renata gazed at the clouds. Benedict leaned against the truck and rubbed at the growing whiskers on his face, which had begun to itch.

"What put you in the clinic?" Renata asked. "Ryker said someone almost killed you."

Benedict looked at Gerad, saw the thin man breathe in deeply on his cigarette, then shrug. At first he thought there would be no answer, but Gerad took another hit and said, "Carelessness." Hard and sharp, and then nothing else.

Ryker appeared, shoving his way through a group of people heavily laden with baggage. One woman dropped both of her bags as Ryker brushed her aside. She turned and opened her mouth; but on seeing Ryker, closed her mouth and remained silent.

"Everything's set," Ryker said as he approached the truck. His face was blank, but tightly set, his skin and muscles like stone. "Let's *go*."

Gerad climbed into the back of the truck atop all the supplies. "I'll ride back here. Can lay out and sleep, and I sure as hell need some." The cigarette hung from the corner of his mouth as he shifted the bundles and worked a place for himself among them.

Ryker got in behind the wheel, Benedict sat beside him, and Renata, after some hesitation, finally joined them. In the rearview mirror, Benedict saw cigarette smoke curling up from the bundles. Ryker backed out from under the overhang, swung the truck around, then pulled out onto the main road, headed for the bridge.

Two hours later they had crossed the bridge and were headed back north. Rain had begun falling, and

223

Gerad had wrapped himself in a poncho, still content to ride in the bed. Ryker was silent, but radiating a tense desperation. Renata, on the other hand, was asleep, her head resting against the window.

To his left, Benedict saw where the Qua Tri entered the Morgan'de. The long, grilled barrier across the Qua Tri, which prevented boats from transferring rivers in either direction while allowing water, silt, plank, and fish through, was marked by strings of blue lights flickering dully in the dim afternoon light.

A half hour north of the Qua Tri, the first docks of a large wharf area appeared. A long string of piers jutted into the river, the piers lined with mismatched light poles, railings, and ramps. Masts and fishing rigs and cabins marked the presence of a large variety of boats, and despite the rain the docks were crowded with people, many huddled near the small wooden shacks that dotted the piers.

Ryker steered the truck down a twisting, rock-paved narrow road leading toward the docks, then onto a slightly wider road running parallel to the river, fronting the main boardwalk area. Renata opened her eyes and sat up, and Benedict saw in the mirror that even Gerad was up and alert, watching over the top of the truck. Somehow the free-lancer managed to keep his cigarette lit even in the heavy rain.

Ryker pointed upriver. "Our boat's there. Can't see her yet, but it's there. Or someone's going to have real problems."

Supply and tackle shops, repair sheds, and a few restaurants lined the road to their right. Ryker worked his way through the slower traffic and parked vehicles, then at the second pier from the end of the wharf he drove up a wooden incline and onto the boardwalk. He spun the truck around and backed out halfway

224

along the pier. A man waved at them from the head of a ramp leading down to the water and a large, weathered boat.

The boat ran ten or eleven meters in length, painted white and dull blue, the paint peeling away from the pale wood. A small enclosed pilothouse rose above the deck in front of the main, lower cabin. The man who waved at them scuttled over to the truck as Ryker cut the engine and opened the door.

"Mr. Ryker? Remember me, I'm Bill Farlow, we met a few months back." Water ran from the short, stocky man's hat and down the length of his steel-blue coat.

Ryker nodded. "Everything okay with the boat?"

"Sure, Mr. Ryker. Just like Blade asked. You want to load her now?"

Ryker grabbed his poncho from behind the seat, shaking his head. "Christ, of course I want to load now. Why do you think I've got the truck out here?" He looked at Benedict and Renata. "All right, let's get this done so we can go get something to eat."

With the rainfall growing still heavier, and the sky darkening as the already hidden sun dropped, they unloaded the truck. Gerad remained aboard the boat, showing them where to store each crate or bundle, lashing them down or checking to see that each piece was properly packed. Bill Farlow was little help and spent most of the time avoiding Ryker. When they finished, Ryker told Farlow to stay with the boat until they got back from dinner.

Farlow sighed and shrugged, then shook his head. "I can't. I'm late already. You were supposed to be here earlier today, that's what they told me. I have an appointment, a meeting, I can't . . ."

"Look," Ryker cut him off. He jabbed a large finger at Farlow's face. "We have to eat, and watching the

225

boat is what you were paid for, and we can't leave the boat with all our supplies. You'll stay."

Farlow continued to shake his head, slouching as though trying to retreat from Ryker. "I can't, I told you."

"I'll stay with the boat," Gerad said.

Ryker spun, chopped his hand through the air. "No! This asshole was hired to watch the boat, he'll watch the goddamn boat!"

Farlow shook his head again. "No I won't. And what can you do to force me? Kill me?"

"No. But I'll tie you to the deck rail with a gun pointed at your head . . ."

"Ryker," Gerad cut in. "I said I'll stay with the fucking boat. Let him go."

Ryker hesitated, then grabbed Farlow with both hands and lifted him from the deck. He heaved Farlow onto the ramp, and Farlow sprawled onto his hands and knees, grabbed a railing to keep from pitching into the water. His hat fell, floated below him. "Move your ass out of here, Farlow. I see you again I'll probably kill you."

Farlow scurried up the ramp and onto the pier, a lopsided grin on his face. The rain slicked down his hair and spattered his face, but he didn't seem to care. He hurried away.

"Let's eat," Ryker said.

As they walked up the ramp through the rain, Benedict turned back to look at Gerad. The freelancer remained on deck, gazing out on the gray river, his face half shadowed by the poncho hood, smoke rising from the glowing end of his cigarette.

After they ate, Ryker left to drop the truck with someone, reminding them that they were leaving at first light, and that Gerad still wanted to talk with them. Benedict and Renata remained in the restaurant, drinking liquers and looking out at the rain and the docks and the boats. The wind had picked up and the rain fell in slanting silver sheets that spread into golden, sparkling cones beneath the dock lights.

"He pulled Gerad out of the clinic too soon," Benedict said. "It's a hell of a risk. If Gerad doesn't make it, we'll have serious problems."

"Ryker must have some reason, he's not over the edge yet. But he's panicking. Or close to it. Time pressure, something like that. I wonder what it is."

Benedict shrugged. "It's something. Maybe something that happened while we were in the Canal Zone. Worries me, because I don't see how we can find out what it is. Ryker won't tell us."

"Then we can't do much except go on, can we?" Renata smiled. "No point worrying."

Benedict studied her face, her smile. He couldn't stop worrying; there were too many things hidden by too many people. Including Renata.

"Why are you with this expedition?" he asked.

Renata's smile slowly disappeared. "Want to spring that question back at yourself? Are *you* willing to tell *me*? If we'd had a few more days in the Canal Zone, maybe we could have talked it. But we didn't. This isn't the place, it sure as shika is not the time." Her fingers tightened around the liqueur glass, and Benedict thought she might crack it. But the glass held, and her grip relaxed. "Maybe somewhere up the river, or in the jungle. But don't count on it." She pushed the liqueur glass away from her. "Let's go back to the boat."

"I'd wanted to stay a while longer."

"Then stay." She stood, pushed her chair in, then hesitated. "See you at the boat."

He watched her retrieve her poncho and leave.

227

Outside, she came into view, walked across the road, and climbed onto the boardwalk. Instead of returning to the boat, she walked out along the nearest pier. Out near the end was a small shack with a flashing sign angled so he couldn't read it. Renata opened the door, letting out a strip of yellow light, then entered and closed the door behind her. She did not emerge, and after fifteen minutes passed, Benedict left the restaurant, and returned to the boat alone.

2

"THE MOST IMPORTANT THING ON THE RIVER IS, YOU DO what the fucking skimmers tell you to do."

They'd waited over an hour for Renata, but when she finally returned to the boat, no one asked her where she'd been. Now all four of them sat around a single table in the boat's galley, windows open and screens closed. The rain had let up, but still pattered lightly on the roof above them and on the decks; louder was the dripping of overflow from the roof and the deck rails. Ryker and Gerad both puffed on cigarettes, and smoke filled the tiny room. Gerad had laid out a map, but hadn't yet referred to it.

"But don't ever call them skimmers to their face," Gerad went on. "They are Officers of the Morgan'de River Security Patrols no matter what river they're on, and you call them 'Officer' or by rank if they've made a point of it. Easiest thing is to let me deal with them. I've been shucking the skimmers for years, know a lot of them personally, and I know how they

think. Thing they want most is obedience, even for
some shit-ass order. So do it. Long as they don't get
any shit, though, they'll let us do what we want." He
turned to Renata. "For you, don't worry. We've
bought your name and all your records *out* of their
computers. You'll be fine.

"Now, tomorrow morning before we leave they're
going to board us, make an extensive search of the
boat and all our supplies. They'll repack it all just the
way they find it, and with nothing missing. Unless . . .
You got anything illegal stuffed away, don't worry.
They expect to find unregistered weapons, illegal
drugs, and they won't conf any of it. They just want to
know what's on the river. Flex, though, is out, so if
you have any, dump it in the river tonight. They'll cut
this trip before it starts, they find any. Only other
things they won't have are anything resembling atom-
ics or those new vibrationals, but I don't think any of
you are stupid enough to carry that kind of shit
around with you." He grinned. "Or am I wrong?"
When he received no answers he laughed, lit a fresh
cigarette, and went on.

"Ryker says I can't talk about destinations, ulti-
mate or otherwise, so I won't give you any details. We
will be stopping at Timons' facilities—lysium farms,
breeding pens, distilleries, trapping centers, or way
stations. Sometimes. Two reasons for these stops.
One, we'll be able to resupply if we need to. The other
reason is appearance. It's what most free-lancers do.
It's what I do once in a while, when I'm teamed or
alone, so we'll do it too.

"But do yourselves, and all of us, a blessing when
we stop at these places, or any others. I tell you to stay
on the boat, you stay on the boat. I tell you to stay on
company grounds, or on certain trails, or off certain
trails, do it. I don't give advice for a pump. Not into

power licks. I tell you to do something, it's because it's safer, it'll keep you out of shit. Believe me, there's plenty of shit on the rivers. But Ryker tells me you two are 'survivors.' His word. I guess I know what he means. If he's right, then you know enough to believe what I'm telling you. Any problems?"

"No," Benedict said. Renata remained silent.

"Good." Gerad tapped the finely creased, unused map. "This map isn't good for much. Brought it out to show you, give you an idea what the rivers are like, where the Morgan'de comes from, what feeds it. It's all right for the Morgan'de itself, but maps of the tribs become obsolete from year to year. With the regular flooding and draining, the fucking things are always changing course, tearing out new trails, widening or narrowing or disappearing altogether. Even the farms, pens, and breeding grounds shift around during the year. Only the distilleries are permanent, and that's because they're built to float. For what it's worth, the map will be here." He stuck it into the cupboard above and behind him.

"That's really most of what I have to say. Couple of little things. I'd stay out of the water. You want a good rinsing off, use the shower on the boat, or stand in the rain, but don't swim. Not that the water's bad, or some river creature will take a bite out of you, though that might happen. What you have to worry about are the skimmers. They're suspicious bastards, think everyone's trying to pull something on them. They take target practice on anything in the water that looks even vaguely human.

"Okay. Last line is, I'm here to show you anything you need to know. You've got questions, ask. Things get pretty fucked up on the river sometimes, and in the jungle, shit, it's like madness let out of its cage. We just use our damn heads, though, don't do anything

231

stupid, we'll be all right. Most people who get killed out here, they were stupid, trying hot-ass licks and tricks."

Gerad leaned back, sucking in on his cigarette. His face was haggard, and he looked close to collapse.

"One more thing. Nothing concrete, but the feel of the river is off. Different from when I was last on it. I don't know what it's about, maybe after a few days on the water I'll have an idea. Stay alert. First three or four days will be almost empty, it can lull you into false security. Bad news out here, remember that. Don't let it put you to sleep, or you might not wake up." He coughed several times, clamped his eyes shut. When the coughing stopped, he looked at them again and shrugged. "That's all I've got to say. We should get some sleep. The skimmers'll be here at first light. We get up at five, be ready for them."

Ryker leaned forward, his maned head almost looming over them. He looked tired, and tense, and Benedict noticed new shadows under the big man's eyes.

"Just a few words," Ryker said. "Time is a bigger concern that it was before. Don't even ask me why, I won't talk about it. But it is. We'll be pushing it as much as possible without getting the skimmers on us. No delays, no extra stopovers, no sight-seeing. Just keep that in mind." Ryker slid off the bench seat, nodded once. "This meeting is over." He turned and retreated into one of the two small cabins in the rear.

"You two can share the other cabin," Gerad said. "I prefer to sleep on deck when it isn't raining, or in the spare bunk out here." He tapped the wall panel above the table. "So tonight it's in here." He smiled. "Forget Ryker, don't let him bother you. We just do the job, go on." He lit a cigarette and shook his head. "Good night."

Their cabin was lit by a small overhead light, and was low and narrow. The two bunks were built into one wall, and in the other wall were two screened portholes. Benedict opened them, stood in front of one, breathing deeply of the fresh air, listening to the rain which had become a light drizzle. He could see the pier beside them, deserted now, illuminated by the golden, misted cones of light. In the distance, barely visible, was the dull glow of the sign over the shack Renata had entered. He still couldn't read it, and wondered if he would have time in the morning. He wondered if it really mattered.

"Which bunk you want?" Renata asked. "Upper or lower?"

He shrugged. "It doesn't matter."

"Then I'll take the top. My preferred position."

He turned to her and smiled. "Yes?"

She smiled back, then stripped off the single-suit and pulled herself into the upper bunk. Benedict undressed, piling his clothes on the floor, then reached up to turn out the light. He got in between the cool, thin sheets and lay on his back, the dark surface of the upper bunk just above him, within reach.

"Benedict?"

"Hm."

She paused a few moments, then said, "Sleep well."

"Good night, Renata."

He lay in the warm darkness, two dim circles of light in the wall across the cabin like giant, screened eyes, the hiss of rain behind them. There was much unsaid between him and Renata, but he did not know where to start, and so remained silent. It was a long time before he slept.

3

THE RAINS HAD CEASED DURING THE NIGHT, BUT A DENSE mist hung over the river, rising only slowly from the surface of the water. Morning was dark gray, marked with the amber shafts of light along the piers. Benedict stood on the bow deck of the *River Nova*, watching the skimmers lounging near the gangplank, talking and laughing while their colleagues continued to search through the cabins. Benedict had learned the name of the boat when he overheard one of the skimmers talking about it, and now he leaned over the deck rail to see the faded gray letters on the hull. Ryker was below deck, and Gerad sat on the roof of the pilothouse, smoking and talking to one of the skimmers. Renata had been pacing the decks, above and below, shadowing the skimmers, and now joined Benedict at the bow.

"Gerad was right," she said. "They found contraband, all my stuff, probably yours. They left it, didn't say a word."

"Odd place, this world."

"So is every world. You know that."

He looked out across the river, but the mist was so thick he could not see the opposite bank. The light was increasing, however, and the fog slowly thinned in the growing heat, a giant ground-level cloud sluggishly evaporating beneath the rising sun. Renata touched his shoulder.

"Might want to take a casual look two piers down," she said. "See a familiar face."

Benedict turned and gazed downriver along the docks. Out toward the end of the second pier over, a girl or young woman stood against a light post, behind and just out of the cone of light. A dark, hooded poncho draped the thin figure, obscuring most of the face, but Benedict recognized her. Silky.

"Don't worry," Renata said, facing the opposite bank. "She knows enough not to wave or call."

"Why is she here?"

"Benedict, you know why. She's here to see us off."

"To let us know she's all right, and she'll stay all right."

"Sure. She's a good kid."

Silky turned and walked along the pier, then stood at a railing, looking away from them.

"She knows we've seen her."

"Yes."

They were silent for a while, then Gerad waved them over. As they joined him near the foot of the gangplank, Ryker came up from below.

"Documents check," Gerad said.

While the skimmers checked the idents and free-lancer certification, Gerad joked and talked with them. They knew him well, apparently; they called him Blade, and they traded sex and Flex jokes. Body searches were next, thorough but relatively courteous.

Satisfied, the skimmers gave Gerad a thick plastic card, then disembarked.

Ryker then called Benedict and Renata down into his cabin for one more personal search. He brought out a set of portable M-E detectors like those that had been used on Benedict two weeks before. Ryker scanned them both in silence, slowly and thoroughly, and Benedict thought of what would have happened had he arranged for a transceiver graft. Ryker might have wanted to rip it out of Benedict's body with his own hands before killing him and dumping him in the river.

When the scanning was finished, Ryker nodded his approval and waved them out of his cabin, then locked himself in. Benedict and Renata went back up on deck. Gerad was in the pilothouse, starting up the engines. Benedict and Renata cast off the lines, then joined Gerad. There was just enough room for three, cramped and close.

"There *is* something odd on the river," Gerad said. "Skimmers sense it too, but they don't like talking about it. Been a lot of years now, but nobody wants the river wars to start again. There's enough shit at night without worrying about the day." He put out his cigarette and lit another. "Probably nothing will happen on the big river. But once we start up the Qua Met . . . shit, who knows?"

The *River Nova* had drifted from the pier, and now Gerad engaged the engines and reversed the boat in a tight half circle so they faced the open river. He shifted, throttled forward after a pause, and they moved slowly away from the docks. When they were clear, Gerad turned the boat upstream and increased the throttle, and they were on their way.

As they pulled away from the docks, Benedict looked back. Silky stood at the end of the pier, gazing after them, her hood pulled back so her hair was free, fluttering in the light breeze. Benedict's chest tightened; with guilt, he realized. Seeing her grow further away from him, he knew that Hadling would not be leaving her behind like this. But he *wasn't* Hadling, he could not stay, though in some ways he wanted to, and so he continued to watch the motionless figure until the mist thickened between them, then enveloped her completely and she was gone from view.

By midmorning the mist had lifted so both banks were clearly visible, but the sun remained obscured by thick clouds that held a constant threat of rain above them. As the boat continued upriver, Riotmark's aspect gradually transformed.

Ryker was still below, and Renata sat on a bench in the stern, gazing at the changes they left behind. Gerad maintained a steady, leisurely pace—as fast, he said, as the skimmers would allow.

Benedict stood at the bow, watching the city change. The western bank was residential, the people who lived there poor, and the dilapidated buildings fought a losing battle with the dense jungle growth. Staircases, ladders, and ramps led down to floating docks, but there were no boats in sight. Men, women, and children stood or sat on the docks, fishing or hauling nets and traps out of the water.

The eastern bank, however, had been completely cleared of jungle, as had all the adjacent land as far as Benedict could see. Back from the vacant bank were the upper-class residential districts, large houses landscaped by plants either from other parts of Nightshade, or from other worlds.

As they continued northward, the eastern residential districts gave way to silos and garners and glass greenhouses interspersed with elongated, open fields of cultivated plants—low, squat, broadleaf bundles; staked vines; bulbous dwarf trees; and tall swaying stalks of green and yellow. Eventually the fields and storehouses, too, gave way, this time to a bleaker industrial zone. Smokestacked factories rose between brick and metal buildings. Docks reappeared, constructed at the ends of rail lines leading from the plants and factories. Cargo boats, twenty and twenty-five meters long, were berthed at the docks.

Boats and ships of all sizes passed them headed downstream. The *River Nova* occasionally overtook slower boats as they continued upriver. During the overtaking, passengers and crew members of both boats would watch each other, but no words would be spoken, no gestures made, no silent messages passed other than "Keep away."

Just past noon, Gerad had Ryker take over the wheel. Benedict watched as Gerad staggered down into the darkness of the galley, face pale and drawn, shadowed eyes barely open. He looked bad.

On the western bank, all signs of habitation disappeared. The lush foliage of the jungle grew right to the water's edge, branches or vines sometimes dipping into the river. Once in a while a face would appear, or the flash of hands and arms, occasionally a fishing rod.

The industrial districts on the eastern bank gradually blended into the sawmills and lumberyards of the northernmost section of Riotmark. Wide canals had been dug out of the bank, and most were filled with flotillas of unhewn trees waiting to be pulled up conveyors and into the mills. Sawdust and a constant whine, loud and pervasive, hung in the air.

As they neared the end of the canals, they skirted a float of logs being maneuvered into a slip by two small

238

but powerful tugs. The massive logjam shifted slowly but accurately toward the canal mouth.

Once past the sawmills, the city dwindled quickly. A few scattered buildings still appeared, small and far apart, dotting the encroaching jungle. By midafternoon the last vestiges of Riotmark had vanished, and the jungle reigned supreme on both banks. Ryker picked up speed, and they left the city behind.

A brief, intense squall struck in the late afternoon, forcing Benedict and Renata inside. When the squall passed, they emerged from the galley and looked out onto a jungle transformed.

On both banks, the jungle was now heavily dappled with bright blue, as if the squall had dumped dye upon the trees and bushes. They had reached the first of the lysium fields.

The word "field," implying a clearing of the land, was a misnomer. The jungle had not been completely cleared before planting, since direct sunlight withered and killed the lysium plants. Instead, irregular rows were cleared beneath and between the larger, thick-canopied trees that shaded the jungle floor, and the lysium planted in every available space. The bright blue of their upper leaves stood out even against the rich greens and yellows and reds of the rest of the jungle.

"How much do you know about Flex?" Renata asked. "And lysium?"

"The basics, I guess. The cured leaves from the lysium plants is pseudo-Flex. Mild hallucinogen. Flex itself is distilled from the saliva of animals that feed on the lysium." He shrugged. "Not much else."

"Did you know the strength of Flex in saliva varies among different animal species?"

"No."

239

"Significantly. Biologists, zoologists, have worked together a rough evolutionary model for the jungle mammals, ranking them according to presumed intelligence. Nothing concrete, but a working model. Going from it, the hypothesis is, the higher up the evolutionary ladder, the greater the strength of Flex in the saliva."

From her intense expression, it seemed to Benedict that Renata was trying to imply much more than just the facts she had given him. Something was forming in his thoughts, but his mind felt sluggish, tired, and nothing coalesced.

"Don't you realize what Ryker and Timons are really after, searching for these intelligent beings?"

"Commercial exploitation. He's admitted that."

"Oh yes, commercial exploitation, but not in the way he's implied."

Then the shifting came, and the connections snappped into place. "They're hoping these creatures feed on lysium," he said. "They're hoping if the pattern holds, that they'll have a prime source of Flex."

Renata slowly nodded. "Exactly. Don't know how they plan to work it, but I'm sure they've got it lined. Maybe try to hide the discovery. Or claim the creatures aren't intelligent. I don't know."

Benedict nodded. "Even if they turn out not to be a source for Flex, whoever finds them will make out, one way or another."

"Trif, isn't it? Nice to know the contribution we'll be making to the cultural and ethical advancement of humanity."

"You knew this, Renata, you feel this way, why the hell *are* you a part of it?"

"That same damn question. I'm in it for the money."

"I don't believe you."

"Are you reading me?"

"I don't need to."

She breathed deeply and shook her head. "Still not the time or place." She turned and headed toward the bow.

Benedict remained where he was, and in the waning light of the day watched the lysium fields sweep past.

A half hour later, Gerad emerged from below, nodded to Benedict, then scanned both riverbanks for two or three minutes. He looked a little better, Benedict thought. Rested and relaxed. Gerad nodded again.

"About forty, forty-five minutes before we dock for the night. Sun's just about set, so the skimmers'll be antsy, but we're close enough."

"Where are we stopping?"

"A kind of trading center. Nonsponsored. A place for people to stop, eat, put in for the night, whatever." He lit a cigarette, continued to watch the jungle and the river, then headed for the pilothouse to take over from Ryker.

Darkness came quickly to the river, as though it flowed out of the jungle itself like a dense fog. Ahead, on the right bank, Benedict saw lights and the vague outlines of a few piers, and perhaps buildings set back among the trees. He moved forward to join Renata and Ryker outside the open door of the pilothouse.

As they approached, the docks and boats became more distinct. Half a dozen piers reached out into the river, only a few slips still available. Most of the boats were small, only one or two larger than the *River Nova*. Several skimmers paced among the docks, and one waved, directed them to an empty slip between two smaller, open boats. Gerad maneuvered the boat in, quickly and smoothly, bumping slightly against the pier. The skimmer who'd waved them in approached, helped them tie up. Gerad handed him their boat card.

"A little late, aren't you?" the skimmer asked.

"We got delayed," Gerad answered. "You're new here, aren't you? Don't recognize you."

The skimmer swung a portable terminal up from where it hung at his thigh, and popped in the plastic card. He punched several keys, watched the terminal, then tapped at several more keys, ejecting the card. He handed it to Gerad.

"Food shacks close at nine, the bar at midnight. Yes, I'm new. You've been here before, then you know where everything is. Leaving in the morning?"

Gerad nodded.

"Then I won't see you again, unless there's trouble tonight." He clamped the terminal to his thigh. "Good evening." The skimmer turned and strode away.

"I *haven't* been here before," Ryker said. "You want to tell me where the bar is?"

"What about something to eat first?" Gerad said.

Ryker faced him, silent for a minute, half his face lit by the orange pier lights. "I didn't ask you about the food shack. I asked about the bar."

Gerad shrugged, then pointed inland. "Paths are all lit. Main one branches there, by that ugly green statue. Left to the food shacks, right to the bar."

Without a word, Ryker stepped off the boat and onto the pier, and stalked toward the lighted path.

"You go on," Gerad said. "I'll stay with the boat, fix something for myself in the galley." He smiled. "I'm assuming you want to eat rather than drink."

"How about we stay here, join you for dinner?" Renata said.

"Sure. I'm a damn good cook. You want to try me out."

"Better than the food shacks?"

"Much better." They started down into the galley. "One thing, though," Gerad said. "Don't try to pump me with him gone. I don't like him much either, but he's in charge. My employer, and yours, is paying him to be in charge, to make the decisions. I abide by them, better you were to do the same. Trouble, that one." He grinned. "We all have things the others will never know, and even Ryker doesn't know everything I've got up here about this trip." He pointed at his head with the cigarette. "How I keep myself useful. So don't bother." With that, they went below to eat.

4

BENEDICT WAS AWAKENED BY A SLIGHT ROLL OF THE BOAT, A clomping sound, and a dulled thud followed by a low, drawn-out groan. For a moment he thought it was Gerad, somehow falling out of the hammock he'd strung on deck. But the groan had been too close, and now he heard it again, just outside the cabin door. He sat up, his head brushing Renata's bunk.

"You awake?" she whispered.

"Yes. Did you hear that?"

"Something."

He stood, opened the door, and looked into the galley. A light had been left on, and it illuminated Ryker, facedown on the floor between a cabinet and one of the table benches.

"It's Ryker," Benedict said. "Hurt or drunk. Or both." He knelt beside the big man, struggled to turn him onto his side. The smell of alcohol was strong on Ryker's breath, and he moved his arms and hands at

Benedict, weakly swatting the air. There were no signs of violence, no blood spots or cuts, not even a bruise. Ryker muttered and snorted once. He seemed to be breathing easily.

"Do we help him to bed?" Renata asked. She stood in the doorway.

"No . . . need," Ryker mumbled. He opened his eyes, rolled back onto his stomach, then slowly pushed himself up to his knees. "I'm all right."

Benedict helped him to his feet, and Ryker staggered forward to his cabin door. Benedict motioned to Renata, who nodded, retreated, and closed their door. Benedict helped Ryker across his cabin to the lower bunk. Ryker dropped onto it, sitting hunched with his head touching the empty bunk above. Benedict closed the door, cutting off the galley light, then leaned against the wall, watching the big man in the dim light that came through the portholes.

"I don't trust either of them," Ryker said. "You I trust a little . . . don't know why."

I don't know why either, Benedict thought. You shouldn't. He remained silent, content to wait for Ryker to speak.

Ryker reached under the bunk, withdrew a small full bottle. He uncapped it, drank some.

"Last night of this," he said. He drank some more. The pier lights cast pale shadows across his face. Ryker slowly shook his head, then looked up. "Secondary option," he said. "Support. What shit is that? Underestimate me, no understanding, worst of all, the underestimating. Bad for them. Bad for Klidowska." He twisted his head away from the bunk, upended the bottle above his mouth, and drank the rest of it. He recapped the bottle, slid it under the bunk. "I won't do it. I *will* find those bastards." He paused. "And when this is over, I'll be able to buy my own . . ." Ryker breathed deeply, then looked at Benedict. "You ever pilot a solo scouter?" he asked.

Benedict shook his head.

"I did once," Ryker said. "Nothing so . . ." He smiled and nodded. "Nothing like it, nothing so beautiful, nothing so absolutely alone." He paused again, gazing out the porthole. "Stars and stars and stars and a never-ending night. Sometimes no stars at all, just . . . a bubble in space, with hollow, delicate sounds. And orbiting worlds no man or woman has ever seen." He nodded again. "That's peace, Benedict Saltow." The smile was gone, but Ryker seemed completely relaxed, more so than Benedict had ever seen him.

"Go, Saltow." Ryker's voice was calm and quiet and content. "Go," he repeated. "Last time I'll have peace this trip. Let me enjoy it."

Benedict nodded, and left the cabin without a word. He switched off the galley light, then returned to his cabin and slid into bed. The night air outside was almost silent, but he lay awake, unable to sleep, listening to Renata's quiet breath and the gentle sounds of the river flowing past beneath them.

As the *River Nova* continued upstream over the next three days, the rain season broke upon them with full force. Rain fell two or three times each day, and on the third day poured for nine hours without a break, a gray veil of water draped permanently over the boat.

They passed lysium fields, distilleries, way stations, and skimmer centers, and one vast breeding colony of poraks, the main Flex animal source. From the river, they could see the huge network of open-air cages and pens built onto a partially cleared hill sloping gently upward from the west bank. The squat, dark-furred quadrupeds paced lethargically within their small confines, large eyes open to the sky. Complexes of saliva-milking machinery sparkled among the pens, a brilliant array of shiny metal geometrics in a brief appearance of direct sunlight.

During the second night, while docked at a small Timons-owned way station, gunfire and scattered explosions split the darkness. Next day, word along the river was that two unattached boats loaded with base Flex had tried to drift downriver under cover of the darkness and the heavy fog. They'd been spotted, and in the firefight two skimmers were injured, one skimmer craft slightly damaged. Both renegade boats had been sunk, all crew members killed or drowned.

On the afternoon of their fifth day out from Riotmark, they reached the last major river port, Gateway. The Morgan'de, which several kilometers upriver split into a number of narrow branches, re-formed just above Gateway, all the branches joining within a hundred meters of each other to widen the river to nearly two kilometers. The large freight ships, unable to navigate the twisted, narrow, and often shallow channels, traveled no further upriver than Gateway. There they docked and waited for the smaller boats to bring cargo to them from the upper Morgan'de and all its northern tributaries.

Gerad, at the wheel again, skirted the port and the heavier lanes of traffic around it. Once past the dock facilities, he steered the *River Nova* into the far-right channel and punched up the throttle against the swifter current.

The right bank was a solid thicket of jungle, but the left was a long island of constantly changing topography. A dry, barren beach of white sand gave way to rocky mounds scattered with brush and spindly trees, which in turn gave way to jungle as thick as that on the right, then later returned to bare sand; and the changes continued as they went on. Occasionally, as they passed clear areas, they could see signs of the next channel over—either a glimpse of the water itself or the cabins and masts of other boats.

An hour and a half later, the channel met two others, and soon after joined the remaining branches, and they were on a wide, slower Morgan'de River again.

River traffic was much lighter than it had been below Gateway, and often there were only one or two boats in sight, occasionally none at all. For nearly an hour they moved upriver under clear skies; but as dusk approached, so did clouds.

Darkness came quickly with the heavy clouds, and before long a steady rain began. Benedict stood in the pilothouse next to Gerad; Renata was at the tip of the bow, huddled in her poncho. Ryker, as had become the routine when he wasn't piloting the boat, was below.

As they came around a long, wide bend in the river, Gerad pointed upstream with his cigarette. On the right bank were the lights and short piers of a way station, but then Benedict realized Gerad was pointing further upstream. He scanned the bank upriver until, in the rapidly failing light, he just barely made out a break in the trees that indicated a junction with one of the Morgan'de's tributaries.

"The Qua Met," Gerad said. He pulled back his hand, put the cigarette in his mouth, and talked as he smoked, both hands on the wheel. "Tomorrow morning we'll start up that river. It'll be different, believe me, from this river. Hell of a lot more interesting."

"And more dangerous?"

Gerad laughed. "Of course. The station up ahead is owned by Timons, so we'll resupply a bit, eat a free meal, dock the night." He throttled up and headed directly for the lighted docks.

Gerad pulled the boat into one of the empty berths. A skimmer wearing a Timons badge strolled out along the pier, then waved.

"Hey, Blade!" he called.

Gerad looked at the man, expressionless, then cut the engines. Ryker emerged from below, and they all clambered onto the pier.

"Jesus, Blade," said the skimmer. "You look like skitter meat. What the hell happened to you?"

Gerad stared, hard and cold, and Benedict wondered what was between them. "I asked too many fucking questions," Gerad said. He stuck out the boat card. "Process this."

There was silence for a minute, everyone motionless, the rain pouring down on them. The skimmer nodded, ran the card through his terminal, then returned it to Gerad without a word. Ryker broke the silence.

"We're hungry. The mess still open?"

"Another hour. You know where it is?"

Ryker nodded. He strode toward the gravel path, followed closely by Gerad, then Renata and Benedict.

"Hey Blade, what the fuck's the tale?" the man called after them.

Gerad didn't reply. He flipped his cigarette high up and back, and Benedict watched it spin through the air and hit the dock with a sizzle just in front of the man. Gerad lit a fresh cigarette without pausing. "Fucking squeeze," he whispered.

The station consisted of several geodesics set among the trees, each lit by a distinct pattern of colored lights. Through the thick foliage only pieces of the patterned outlines were visible. The gravel path, illuminated by covered flame torches, split into three branches. Ryker led the way down the left, a narrow trail cut through thin trees and wide-leaved ferns, then into a large, maroon-lit dome.

Inside were ten or twelve large tables, about half of them occupied, and a contoured counter, behind which stood two heavy men in cream-colored smocks.

Open troughs of steaming food lined the counter. The two smocked men filled four plates, not giving them a choice. Benedict took a tray, looked at the food scooped onto his plate; it looked like the slush Silky had fixed for herself that first night. His hunger, which had grown all afternoon, swiftly vanished.

They sat at an empty table, and the babble of voices around them quieted.

"That Blade over there," someone said. "Want to stay away from him, don't touch him, he's sharp. He'll cut you, you're not careful. Oohhh, look at that blade shine."

There was laughter from several people, but most remained silent. Gerad, without turning around, answered.

"Yeah, and I'd cut your balls off if you had any, chica."

The laughter was louder this time, but underlaid with tension. The smoldering anger twisting the face of a tall, dark-skinned blond two tables over marked the speaker. The man was large, strong, and glared at their table. Benedict watched, prepared for a confrontation, but as the laughter trickled away, and the big man remained seated, Benedict realized nothing was going to happen. At least not here, not now. Benedict wondered why.

Gerad kept his attention on the food, and ate methodically. "Tastes like shit," he said. Still, he continued to eat.

"Then why eat it?" Benedict asked.

"A formality here," Gerad answered. He grinned. "*Etiquette.*"

Ryker had taken a few bites, then quit, and now sat wordlessly, his gaze circling the interior of the dome. Renata, like Benedict, had eaten nothing.

Just before Gerad had cleared his plate, a tall

woman in a pale green uniform walked in, and the dome went silent. She approached their table.

"Gerad. Ryker. Tuoco will talk to you. Now."

Ryker breathed deeply, closed his eyes. "And what if we don't want to talk to Tuoco?" he said.

Gerad put his hand on Ryker's shoulder. "Heya, nothing to push, Ryker. The man wants to talk, we talk."

Ryker hesitated a minute, then opened his eyes and nodded once. He and Gerad followed the woman out of the dome.

"Trif," Renata muttered. "We get this mob on our own."

They sat at the table, moving food about their plates without eating. The tension persisted within the dome, but no one said a word to them, no one approached the table.

"Do we wait here for them?" Benedict asked. "Or just go?"

"Let's go back to the boat. Get something edible."

They stood up from the table, started for the door when someone called out to them. Benedict recognized the big blond's voice.

"Wait a drift, pooners," the man said.

"Is that a compliment or an insult?" Benedict whispered. Renata smiled but said nothing.

"You tell the Blade something," the man went on. "You tell him he's going to hear from the Black Swede again. He might just be target meat for the skimmers."

Benedict stopped, turned to face the big man. "We're not messengers," he said. "Seems Blade was right, you don't have the balls to tell him that yourself. Waited till he's gone, saved your ass." He turned back and started for the door, Renata at his side.

252

"Shika, you complain about *my* diplomacy." But she was still smiling.

Nothing more was said to them as they left, nor did anyone follow. Outside, it was still raining, and they hurried along the path through the trees. The rain was warm on Benedict's face, and he kept the poncho hood down so the rain slicked his hair and ran freely over his skin.

Near the boat, an odd tinkling sound rustled the air, like off-key wind chimes, and there was the high-pitched sound of rain on free-swinging metal. Benedict and Renata emerged from the trees, stared at the *River Nova*. Shifting glints of light flashed at them through the rain.

Wire was strung all over the boat, from deck railings to pilothouse antenna, from cabin posts to deck rings, from railing to railing, up and down and across in a complex network. From the wires hung misshapen pieces of sheet metal cut in irregular designs, Flex syringes, a porak milking collar, and fifteen or twenty broken knife blades without handles. In the slight breeze, the wires bobbed and shifted, metal clinked against metal, and the rain pattered in gentle tones upon everything.

"We've got to cut it all down before Gerad gets back," Renata said. "Don't know if he's a spooker, but can't take the chance. Shit." She picked up the pace and they hurried to the boat.

"What is it?" Benedict asked.

"Talismans. A hex on the *River Nova*, on Gerad. Lot of river and jungle people acquire a very odd sort of mysticism living out here." They boarded carefully, worked their way between strings of wire and dangling, sharp metal. Renata went below, came back up with two sets of wire cutters. "Don't know if Gerad believes in this shit, but if he does, even a little deep inside, it can throw him off. Blunt the edge."

"Self-fulfilling prophecy."

"Like that, yes." She handed him wire cutters. "Just cut it and deep it."

Much of the metal was sharp, jagged-edged, and the wire was so strong and fine it could slice flesh; Benedict learned that on a finger he nearly lost. He climbed onto the pilothouse, cut through the highest wire tied to the radio antenna. The string dropped to the deck with a loud clatter. Renata cut the other end, then fed it overboard and into the river as Benedict moved across the roof, cutting every wire that was either tied to the roof or looped around some part of it.

They worked quickly, but there was an incredible maze of wire, and Benedict wondered how whoever had rigged it had managed to do so much in so little time. Probably it had been prepared days ago, ready for their arrival.

When the boat was clear, the cutting tools put away, and Benedict and Renata were below checking the galley and cabins for other "talismans," footsteps sounded from the pier. They came up on deck, saw Gerad and Ryker approaching the boat.

Ryker stepped aboard, and Gerad was about to follow when he stopped, his gaze fixed between the boat and the pier. He knelt, reached toward the water, then drew his hand up. In it was a triangular piece of jagged metal that had snagged on the boat, still attached to the wire. As he pulled it up, the string of wire, metal, blades, and syringes followed. Shining streams of water dripped from it, and the metal pieces rattled against each other. Gerad held the wire out away from his body and looked at Benedict and Renata.

"What is it?" Benedict asked.

"How much was on the boat?" Gerad asked in return.

Ryker looked back and forth, confused. Benedict, too, tried to appear puzzled.

"What do you mean?" he asked.

Gerad shook the string. "How much of this stuff was hung on the boat?"

"Somebody answer a goddamn question," Ryker said.

"There wasn't anything on the boat," Renata said. "We must have picked that up from the river somewhere, hooked into it."

Gerad dropped the string of wire and metal into the river and shook his head. "Don't run me that shit. I know what it was, and what you're trying to do. Don't worry, I don't take with all that hoo-doo crap. But I *know* what was on this boat." He glanced back at the geodesics. "Shit. Fucking waterbrains." He brought his cigarette to his mouth, but it had gone out in the rain. He tossed it into the river, then came on board and went below.

"What's he talking about?" Ryker asked.

"I don't know. Ask him," Benedict said. Renata just shrugged.

Ryker sighed. "No, I'm not going to ask him. I withdraw the question. Too damn much other shit to worry about without adding this." He glanced first at Renata, then at Benedict. "Things are happening on the rivers. Deep in the jungle. People doing crazy things. People tensed and wired up. There's power in the air, people don't know how to handle it. Not Flex this time, it's the creatures. Thing is, almost nobody knows it, nobody knows what's charging up the atmosphere. That makes everyone dangerous, because they don't know what it's all about, so they don't know what to do. Take that as a warning. It could get rough from here. Or just strange. Nobody knows."

"Not even this person, Tuoco?" Benedict asked.

Ryker grinned. "Especially not Tuoco. You don't even know who he is, do you?"

"No."

"It doesn't matter." He turned away and went below without another word.

"Much to look forward to," Benedict said.

Renata shrugged and smiled. "I never wanted to be bored." She laughed. "Let's go below, see if we can get Gerad to cook something. I'm still hungry."

Later that night, or very early morning, Benedict woke from a dream that remained vivid for several minutes, though it seemed to constantly shift and change as he thought about it. There had been strings of wire, hung with bells, and they had been strung like a web among trees deep in the jungle, either as a trap or an alarm. Somehow, though he was far from the river, the *River Nova* was nearby, floating on water within sight of the wires. He stood on the deck of the boat, which wasn't very much like the *River Nova* when he looked closely at it. Sometimes, though, he was standing against one of the trees, on soft earth, his fingers touching the nearest bell, tapping lightly. When they began to ring, he woke.

He lay still in the bunk, listening to the rain on the cabin roof. Then he heard footsteps on deck. Benedict dressed quietly, then moved in silence through the empty galley and stopped at the open hatch. Slowly he put his head out and looked from side to side.

Gerad was on deck, naked in the rain. He was bent over, closely studying the deck railing, running his left hand along the wood. In his right hand was something shiny. He stopped, plucked at something with his fingers, then brought the shiny object—wire cutters —forward, and snipped. He brushed at the deck railing, then moved on.

No, Benedict thought to himself, this man doesn't believe in the hoo-doo at all. He wondered if removing every last trace of the wire strings from the boat would be enough to satisfy Gerad, to put him at ease. Probably not.

Tired, and now slightly depressed, Benedict turned away and silently returned to the cabin.

6

BENEDICT WAS AWAKENED AGAIN BY THE VIBRATION OF THE boat's engines. He staggered onto the deck in the dim predawn light, not yet completely awake. Gerad's profile was visible in the pilothouse, cigarette smoke rolling up into the orange overhead light. Benedict joined him.

"In a hurry?"

Gerad shrugged. "Couldn't sleep. Thought I'd just get us on the river. A controller should be here in a minute."

Light steam rose from the surface of the water, and the cloud cover seemed thick and unpenetrable. There was no rain yet, but Benedict was certain there would be before long.

Soon, the sound of footsteps crunching gravel drifted through the pale light, and a security man walked onto the pier. His Timons badge flashed as he moved.

"Blade," he called. "I'll check you out now."

Gerad left the pilothouse and handed the man their security plate. The man put it through his terminal and returned it. He and Gerad shook hands, then gripped each other's shoulders. They spoke quietly, and Benedict could not make out anything they said. After several minutes they clasped hands again, and parted.

The Timons man cast loose their lines, and Gerad returned to the pilothouse. He engaged the engines, then steered the boat slowly away from the pier and out into the river. Though Gerad did not look back, the Timons man stayed on the pier, watching until, obscured by gray light and rising steam, he was gone from sight.

Benedict stayed in the pilothouse with Gerad, but they remained silent as they moved through the dawn. They were alone on the river, not a single boat in sight, and the river was silent except for the quiet splashing sounds of fish, the hiss of water sliding over sand, and the quiet animal sounds from within the jungle—birds awakening, tiny furred creatures moving high in the upper canopy, larger creatures pushing invisibly through the undergrowth.

They reached the mouth of the Qua Met, and Gerad steered the boat into the tributary. Once past the mouth, the Qua Met was much narrower than the Morgan'de. The water appeared to be deep, and flowed swiftly beneath them, but there would have been room for no more than three boats the size of the *River Nova* to travel side by side.

The jungle on both sides of the river was denser than that along the Morgan'de. Most of the time there was no visible bank on either side of the river. Vines and looping tree branches and islands of thick grass and moss trapped by other branches trailed in the water. Occasionally an open area of bare rock would appear, usually topped by some vague creature staring at them through the steam.

The river turned and twisted constantly, with few straight stretches. With the sun, if it had yet risen, completely hidden by clouds, Benedict soon lost all sense of direction. At times it felt as if they were traveling in circles, and in some ways he would not have been surprised to emerge once more onto the Morgan'de. Still alone, they pushed on upstream.

By midmorning, Benedict was sweating freely, the air warmer and more stifling than it had been on the big river. The sweat felt good on his skin, though, as if it drew his fatigue with it as it oozed from his pores.

Renata, who had slept late, had joined them on deck, bringing up coffee and a stack of toasted sandwiches. Soon after they ate, they heard the quiet motor of a boat, and a minute later a skimmer craft appeared, coming around the bend ahead. The boat was low and open, much shorter than the *River Nova*, and fairly narrow. Three skimmers stood on deck, one stationed at a mounted gun, another at the wheel, and the third alone at the stern, signaling to them.

Gerad slowed, but did not stop. The skimmer craft passed them, then swung around and came alongside, matching their pace. The skimmer signaling them was a large woman, who pulled herself up onto the *River Nova* and approached the pilothouse. She was nearly as tall as Ryker, and built much the same, with thick, blond hair.

"I'm Major Yllondia," she said.

"Stennet Reese."

"Renata Birk."

"And I'm the Man of La Mancha," Gerad said.

Major Yllondia smiled. "How are you, Blade?"

260

"I've been better, Wilka." He kept his gaze on the river ahead while talking to her.

"You look like hell, Blade."

"Should have seen me a week ago. Comparison, I look wonderful now."

"Glad to hear it. Listen, Blade, sure you want to go up the Qua Met? Why not try free-lancing somewhere else?"

"What's the problem?"

"Don't know. Something's trembling. No one knows what, or exactly where. Easier to wait a few weeks, let it blow up or blow over. Not interested in pulling your skinny ass out of the river."

Gerad shook his head. "Wilka, be serious. You ever see me back away possible trouble?"

"No. Don't expect it this time. Just my way of warning you." She shrugged, then looked at Benedict and Renata. "Either or both of you want out, we can fix rides back to Riotmark for you."

Neither said anything, and the big woman shrugged again. "It was just an idea. Someday I'll learn to keep my nose out of it all."

"Hope you never do," Gerad said. "I've always appreciated your warnings. One of the reasons I'm still alive, imagine."

"Shit." She shook her head. "Just watch it, all of you. Hope I see you on your way out." She dropped off the boat and onto the skimmer craft. The craft shot forward, cut around to face downstream, then shot past them. Major Yllondia held two fingers up and chopped the air with them, and Gerad returned the salute. A minute later the skimmer craft was around a bend and gone from sight.

Just before noon, the rain began, and did not stop all day. They passed way stations, trading centers carved out of the jungle, skimmer checkpoints for downstream traffic. But everything was smaller than on the Morgan'de, and less frequent so that for long stretches of time there was nothing to be seen except water and jungle and the dark skies pouring rain upon them.

The river itself was so cloudy nothing deeper than a few centimeters was visible. Animals did make their presence known, however, occasionally by surfacing, more often by leaving trailing wakes behind them as they swam along just beneath the surface of the water. Serpents were the most common on the surface, usually less than a meter long and no thicker than Benedict's thumb. They whipped along, usually in groups of ten or twelve, heads slightly raised, moving easily against the current.

Larger, underwater animals put in brief appearances, smooth, curved backs breaking the surface and sucking water down with them as they submerged. Birds crisscrossed the river high above the boat —bright, wide-winged fliers in groups of three or four, and smaller blue and white birds in flocks of forty or fifty that would dip in unison toward the river, wings flapping frantically, then skim along just above the water for half a minute before rising into the air and disappearing into or over the trees.

Benedict and Renata remained on deck most of the afternoon, either huddled in ponchos or inside the pilothouse with Gerad. Ryker, though, stayed below except when he made offers to relieve Gerad. Gerad refused each time, though as the day went on his exhaustion became more and more noticeable. He said it was too dangerous for someone who didn't know the river, and eventually Ryker stopped offering; he remained below the rest of the day.

They docked that night at an unsponsored station

called Oasis. According to Gerad, it was run by a private group completely divorced from the Flex trade, and contained the most diverse facilities on the Qua Met, perhaps on any of the Morgan'de's tributaries.

"Nightshade's *Last Chance Saloon*," he said. "One last pocket of 'civilization' deep in the jungle. Half a dozen eating places, as many bars, a cinedome, couple of music and dance clubs, three gambling houses. Specialty shops supplying luxury items to permanent jungle and river residents. And two establishments where you may have your pick of company, male or female, but very expensive and almost certainly not worth the price. But . . ."

They stood on deck, with the boat tied up, and looked inland. Oasis itself could not be seen from the docks, but in the heavy twilight the glow from all its lights was like an electrified mist above the trees. Lighted paths cut through the jungle from the piers.

"If you want to go in, a final night of entertainment, then go," Gerad said. "I'm staying with the boat. I can do without."

"Not interested," Renata said. "I thought I was getting away from this when we left Riotmark."

"Benedict?"

He shook his head. "I'll stay."

"I'm going," Ryker said. He was staring into the jungle, along the lighted paths. "I'm sick of the boat. I need *something*." Without looking at them, he climbed onto the pier, and headed for the paths leading into Oasis. Within a minute he had disappeared into the trees.

Just before midnight, the rain started in again. Gerad, Benedict, and Renata were on deck, talking, and retreated below to the galley. Gerad was hinting at sleep when the quiet was shattered by a gunshot. Shouts sliced the night air, growing closer, and then there was a sound like animals crashing through undergrowth.

The three of them hurried onto the deck. The first thing they saw was Ryker, limping slightly, barreling toward them along a path from out of the trees. He clutched his left arm with a hand that also gripped a knife. As he reached the docks and started out along the pier, bootsteps crashing on the wood, a group of figures emerged from the jungle in pursuit.

There were several men and women in the group, and as they ran toward the boat, Benedict saw they were all naked from the waist up, skin painted in swirls of dark color.

Ryker leaped onto the boat, stumbled, and rolled across the deck, finishing up on his knees, still holding his left arm. One of the painted men, as he jumped onto the pier, threw a knife that just missed Ryker and buried itself deep into the pilothouse wall. Gerad stepped in front of Ryker and aimed a gun at the painted men and women running toward them. Benedict and Renata joined him, Benedict drawing his cutter, Renata pulling a gun from her single-suit. Ryker's pursuers slowed as they continued out along the pier, then came to a stop directly beside the boat.

"They call themselves Reclaimers," Gerad whispered.

The Reclaimers stood silently for a few minutes, watching. Their bodies were swirled with dark purple and indigo, their faces striped with deep greens, eyes shadowed in black. They were armed only with knives.

"What clicks?" Gerad demanded.

One of the Reclaimers stepped forward. He pointed

his knife at Ryker, who was still on his knees. "We claim that one. Killed one of ours. A woman, back at Oasis."

"Why?"

"Because she wouldn't fuck this stinking porak. All we want, him. No one else."

Gerad shook his head. "Understand, but can't do it. We need him. Gladly give him another time, but now we need him, see." He held up his gun, pointed at Benedict's cutter, at Renata's handgun. "You've got more people, but we've got guns. Too many will die for nothing. We'll be gone in the morning. Best we can do."

The Reclaimer looked at Gerad a long time, then glanced at Benedict, Renata, and finally at Ryker. One of the others started forward, but the man put out his hand to stop her.

"No," he said to the woman. He turned back to Gerad. "All right. But understand. We only claimed him." Again he pointed at Ryker with his knife. "Now, we see *any* of you . . ." He made several quick gestures with the knife, a slash and thrust followed by a snapping twist.

Gerad nodded. "We understand."

The Reclaimers backed away, keeping their gazes on Ryker and the boat. A few onlookers had appeared, and several dock security people, but they all moved aside to give the Reclaimers free passage. When the Reclaimers reached the trees, they finally turned away and vanished into the jungle.

Gerad turned to Ryker. "How's the goddamn arm?"

Ryker remained silent. Blood dripped from his arm and Gerad shook his head. "Let's clean that up. Shit, I'll have to pump you with antibiotics, the crap that'll grow in that wound out here. Jesus Christ."

"She . . ." Ryker started. But he didn't finish. Instead, he turned away from them and went below.

The rain had let up slightly, but still continued as a steady drizzle. Ryker, the wound cleaned and disinfected and bandaged, his arm shot with antibiotics and a strong sedative, slept heavily in his cabin. Renata, Benedict, and Gerad sat in the galley, gazing out through the open hatchway, listening to the hiss of the rain.

"No worry about the Reclaimers," Gerad said. "They try anything tonight, swimming up to the boat, like that, I've got pressure sensors rigged all over the boat. They're set now."

"Who are they?" Benedict asked. "What are they trying to reclaim?"

"Earth's heritage, they say. Whatever that is. No one really knows. They're always just better avoided."

"Was it worth saving Ryker?" Renata asked.

"No choice." Gerad turned to blow smoke out the porthole beside him. "He knows too much I don't. He's got the real connections. I've been kept in shadow. Without Ryker, we just as well turn back."

"You sure you *can* turn back?" Benedict asked. "You're running trouble on this river. Maybe even on the Morgan'de. Enemies you've made this trip. The Timons man. The Black Swede. Now the Reclaimers. Or is that the way it usually winds out here?"

Gerad laughed. "No, it's not usual. Doesn't matter, though. And why I need Ryker alive. We find these creatures, whatever they are, I'll get paid enough to leave this whole fucking planet, go to any other planet I want. Tell you, I'm good at what I do, free-lancing for Flex, but I'm damn sick of this filthy jungle." He breathed deeply, shook his head. "No, not the jungle. The jungle I love. It's the people in it. I've had it with this pit of a world and all the deckholes living here. Get paid, going to find a clean, unexplored world somewhere, where I can be left alone."

"You really think it'll be better somewhere else?"

"No. Not if there are people there. But looking for something else is a hell of a lot better than sitting in the shit. Isn't that the main line, searching for something else?" He grinned. "You two, example. Neither of you is in this just for the money, that's obvious. So you're both looking for something out here. Don't know what it is, and don't care. Hope you find it. But I'm going to be doing my looking in some other solar system. I just have to worry about getting back to Riotmark alive so I can collect and ship out. You're right, Benedict, these new enemies . . . And I've still got an old one. Probably have to stay off the river coming back, go the whole thing on foot through the jungle. Take me two or three months. Safer for you too, that way. Maybe when we're finished we can all go back together."

"Ryker too?" Benedict asked.

"Only in a casket." Gerad ground out his cigarette, lit another.

Silence returned to the galley. Outside, the rain continued to fall.

$$\overline{\underset{\text{—}}{7}}$$

THE RAIN DID NOT STOP ALL NIGHT, AND IN THE MORNING IT kept the sky dark, the visibility poor. Departures were delayed, and the *River Nova* was the third boat to leave, which appeared to bother Gerad. "We've got a long way to go today," he told Benedict. "We change boats tomorrow, and I want to be at the station tonight so we can make the transfer first thing in the morning. We're going to have to push it today."

Gerad kept the boat's speed up all morning, though it was clearly capable of even greater speeds. The river narrowed as they continued upstream, but the convoluted nature of its course, and the high density of jungle on both banks, changed little. The way stations continued to decrease in size and frequency, fewer boats were on the river, and even the number of skimmer craft dwindled. On the other hand they passed an increasing number of minor tributaries, all too narrow and shallow for the *River Nova*, some little more than trickles of silver water flowing from the dense undergrowth.

The rain continued all morning. Gerad was intent and unapproachable in the pilothouse, his attention locked on the narrow, twisting river course, navigating the boat through tight bends, around fallen trees drifting downriver, in and out of the occasional stone mazes near shore, avoiding submerged rocks. Despite the rain, Ryker remained on deck, his bandaged arm encased in plastic to keep it dry. He paced constantly, as though all the inactivity of the past few days, when he had stayed below, now broke out into a need for movement.

Just after midday, Gerad slowed the boat, then maneuvered into a small, shallow inlet cut into the right bank, and dropped anchor. He asked all three of them to remain with the boat while he was gone, and showed them a siren to sound if anything serious occurred. He said he would be gone no more than an hour, but refused to say where he was going, or why.

After Gerad had disembarked and plunged into the jungle, Renata disembarked as well. She fixed a spot for herself on the bank of the inlet under a large fern, wrapped herself in a poncho, and sat without moving, watching the river. Benedict remained on board with Ryker in the shelter of the pilothouse. Ryker smoked a cigarette, staring into the dense jungle.

"I don't trust him," Ryker said.

"He saved your life," Benedict replied.

"Doesn't matter. I still don't trust him." He pointed with his cigarette toward Renata. "Don't trust her, either. We have to watch both of them, especially when we get into the jungle. I'd weigh anchor and take off without them if I thought we could go it alone. But we need Blade."

"Not Renata?"

"No. We don't need her." He didn't say any more.

Ryker's thick beard and long hair usually obscured most of his face, but close to him in the pilothouse light, Benedict could see the toll the pressure was taking on Ryker. The skin under his eyes was almost black, darker now than the shadows under Gerad's eyes. His face was drawn, lines more prominent than before, and his eyes constantly shifted from side to side, restless and driven, perhaps, by paranoia. Ryker was still the one they had to watch.

"How's the arm?" Benedict asked.

"What?" Ryker looked down at his bandaged arm as if he'd forgotten about it. "It's all right, wasn't much." The big man shrugged. "I don't know . . . I'm not sure why I . . . last night, that woman." He lit another cigarette, hands trembling slightly. "It's all the way, out here. This expedition. No limits, too much at stake. Sometimes I guess that makes it hard to . . . maintain . . ." He shrugged again, and returned to silence.

As they waited for Gerad to return, several boats passed them, one traveling upriver, the others down. But though the people on deck stared at the *River Nova*, and at Benedict and Ryker, no one called to ask if there were problems, no one called to offer help, no one said a word.

When Gerad returned, and boarded with Renata, he seemed more energetic, and much of the tension strung through him appeared to have eased. They weighed anchor, Gerad started the engines, and soon they were back on the river, headed upstream. It was when Gerad lit his first cigarette in the pilothouse that Benedict noticed something new.

On Gerad's wrist, which before had been completely bare, was a wide band of wood and leather, both the wood and leather inscribed with intricate, repetitive designs. Several times during the first half hour on the river, Benedict saw Gerad rub the band with his fingers.

A talisman of his own? Benedict wondered. Something, perhaps, to counter the strings of wire and metal that had been rigged on the boat. Benedict hoped it was exactly that.

Darkness fell, and they were still on the river. Gerad turned on all the boat lights so the skimmers would not think they were trying to hide. Before long they were approached by several skimmer craft, two of which pulled directly alongside while the others remained at a distance, their guns trained on the *River Nova*.

Upon being boarded, Gerad explained that they'd had engine trouble, and that they hadn't stopped earlier because he had an important meet with someone at Waullen Station just ahead, and he had miscalculated, thinking they could reach it before dark.

The ranking officer did not really seem to care about Gerad's explanation, in fact seemed completely unconcerned about the entire matter. He told them the boat would be escorted to Waullen Station, and then they and the boat would be thoroughly searched. "Purely standard procedure," the officer said. His voice was totally void of malice or anger.

Waullen Station consisted of two small, poorly lit piers, and there was only one other boat docked for the night. A single security officer was visible, and when he saw all the skimmers escorting the *River Nova*, he returned to a small hut on the riverbank.

As promised, the boat was thoroughly searched, and then body searches were made, idents inspected. Finally the ranking officer processed their security

271

plate, thanked them for their patience, and released them. The five skimmer craft, all brightly lit, motored away from the station, and within minutes were gone, returning the station to silence.

"I suggest sleep," Gerad said. "Orly and Bullet will be here long before dawn to take us to the new boats. We'll need the rest. Tomorrow . . ." He shrugged. "Tomorrow, things change. Anyone want to back out now?"

He was answered with silence.

PART FIVE
Into The Jungle

1

STILL DARK AND STILL RAINING WHEN THE TWO MEN ARRIVED. Orly was the taller, and older, his hair completely gray. Bullet was short and thin, hair only half gray. They had a large wooden cart with them.

Orly and Bullet held a tarp over the cart as everyone else worked at transferring all the supplies from the boat. It did not take long to unload the boat, then cover the cart tightly with the tarp.

Standing on the pier, ready to leave, Gerad waited for several minutes, gazing at the boat. The boat was dark but for the single orange pilothouse light.

"Probably the last time I'll ever see it," he said quietly. "A lot of years, a lot of rivers." He sighed and lit a cigarette. "Let's go."

Orly and Bullet insisted on pulling the cart themselves without help. Orly gave Gerad and Ryker two covered oil lamps, then he and Bullet led the way down the pier, along a stretch of cleared riverbank, then into the heavy darkness of the trees.

Orly and Bullet talked constantly on the half-hour march through wet, stifling jungle, as if they had not spoken to anyone but each other for months. Benedict realized they probably hadn't. The trail was narrow, with vines and leaves brushing at their faces, branches catching at arms and legs. Water fell steadily upon them, but there was no way to know whether it was rain or just heavy dripping moisture from the trees above. The fuzzy yellow lamplight bobbed and shimmered in front of Benedict, the light fragmented by the dense foliage.

Bullet talked about their house, which he and Orly had built by hand eighteen years before, and to which they had recently added an extra room. Orly talked about the new paintings he'd been working on, and the homemade beer and wine that were almost ready in their cellar. Back and forth they talked, practically without stopping, and Benedict smiled to himself at the two men. Ryker, just in front of him, cursed and muttered something about "the damn little fags."

When they reached the river, it was still dark, but the rain had stopped, though the jungle behind them continued to steadily drip water. Sheltered in a camouflaged slip were two long, slim boats like canoes. They were called pirogues, Gerad said. The stern was flat and mounted with a small prop motor with a long handle for steering. Two paddles were clamped to the inner walls of each pirogue, and in the bottom was a slightly raised, slatted floor.

Benedict had piloted similar craft on other worlds, and said he'd take one with Renata. While Bullet and Orly watched, supplies and bags were divided between the two boats. By the time they had lashed everything down, covered them securely with waterproof tarps, dawn was beginning to leak onto the river.

It took five minutes to get through good-byes with Orly and Bullet, but finally they were aboard the pirogues, and the two older men pushed them out into the river. Benedict started the motor—a quiet purring—then waited for Gerad to start upriver before engaging the prop. Gerad gave Bullet and Orly one final wave, then throttled up and headed the pirogue upriver. Benedict engaged the prop, and followed.

After the loud engines of the *River Nova*, the pirogues seemed strangely silent, and with no sounds from other boats on the river, the quiet had a solid, disturbing feel to it. In the pirogues they were much closer to the steam rising from the river, and it coiled up and around them as they glided across the water.

Benedict had to keep the motor at full throttle to stay with Gerad and Ryker. The pirogues rode high in the water, and at times seemed to be skipping over the river, riding a cushion of air. The rising steam and dim light kept visibility low, but Benedict just followed Gerad.

Once, Gerad put out his hand, waved it downward, and slowed drastically. Benedict followed suit, cutting his speed in half. Almost immediately, Benedict heard the sound of boat engines, and a few moments later a boat the size of the *River Nova* came around a bend upriver. The boat roared past, its wake bobbing the pirogues, but when the wake had flattened and the boat was both out of sight and out of hearing, Gerad accelerated again, and they were at full throttle once more.

The gray light brightened gradually, though the thick clouds overhead still hid the sun. They had been on the river an hour and a half when Gerad slowed and signaled for Benedict and Renata to come alongside.

"Break out the paddles," Gerad said. "Couple of minutes, we're going to cut the motors if the river's clear, let the boats drift downriver. We've just passed the trib we want, but I want to go into it in silence. It's almost completely hidden, I want it to stay that way. Just follow us when we make our move, and dig in hard. Remember, there'll be a sudden change from floating downriver to paddling upriver. The trib isn't that big, but the current is still fairly strong. All right?"

Benedict and Renata both nodded. They continued upstream for a minute, Gerad listening intently, then he cut the motor, and Benedict did the same.

They brought the pirogues around, then Benedict and Renata backpaddled to let Gerad and Ryker drift on ahead. The current was swifter than Benedict had expected, and the pirogues rode so easily with it that the jungle slid quickly past them, becoming a blur of color-streaked green.

They drifted around one wide bend, then one much tighter, and Gerad signaled. They dug in with the paddles, Gerad and Ryker leading the way toward the right bank.

At first Benedict could see no opening at all, and it looked as if they were headed for a solid thicket of jungle and rock. Then he saw the swirling of current emerging from dense foliage that hung in the river growing across the mouth of the tributary, thick and tangled.

Ryker and Gerad hit the thicket of branches and crashed through it. Benedict steered for the same spot and they, too, crashed through overhanging vines and branches, breaking off leaves and twigs. The branches and the current brought them momentarily to a standstill, but he and Renata dug in harder with the paddles and moved slowly forward. They broke

278

through and jumped forward, now easily overcoming the force of the current. Just ahead, Gerad and Ryker were paddling upstream near the right bank where the current was weakest.

It was like entering another world within the world of the jungle. The river was quite narrow, perhaps five meters across at its widest, though it appeared to be fairly deep. The jungle on both sides was dense and unbroken, but now more colorful. The deep greens were broken by spectacular flushes of bright red, shimmering yellows and oranges of huge petaled flowers, and the less frequent blooms of brilliant blue from lysium plants. As they continued upstream, headed deeper into the jungle and further from the Qua Met, animal sounds grew louder and more varied. Chitters and squawks, high-pitched hooting, and long, mournful cries punctuated the air. For the first time, Benedict felt they had finally left civilization behind.

The river, dark and serpentine, seemed almost alive as it twisted and turned through the jungle beneath rolling clouds. They continued to paddle silently, watching and listening to the world close in around them.

"What happened on Mesa?"

They were using the motors again, but Benedict had let the pirogue drop back from Gerad and Ryker so he and Renata could talk without being heard. She had turned around to face him, and a light rain had begun; her face was shadowed by the hood of her poncho.

"A revolution," Benedict said.

"Masakita?"

He hesitated, surprised, before answering. "Yes, that's who we helped. You've heard of him."

"I've heard his government isn't much better than the one it replaced."

Benedict sighed and nodded. "You heard right. I believed in him. In Masakita. So many people did. Karl, Likra, and I. We gave everything we had to that revolution." He paused for a long time, then went on.

"Karl had known Masakita for years, believed in him, almost more than anyone else did. And I'd known Karl for years. He contacted me, brought me to Mesa to meet Masakita. I listened to Masakita, and I joined his cause. The revolution was a success. And Masakita's regime was nearly as bad as the previous." Benedict shrugged. "Makes for major disillusionment."

There was quiet for a while, then Renata said, "But you're a First Order empath. You must have been able to read Masakita, to know what he felt. To know if he was sincere. Wouldn't you have known you were supporting a fraud?"

Benedict smiled slightly and shook his head. "That's the worst of it, really. He wasn't a fraud. His intentions, believe me, were the best, and were sincere. He truly wanted a better life for the people on Mesa."

He stopped talking, looked at the jungle on the right bank. The tall, thick-trunked trees back from the riverbank and rising above the rest of the jungle reminded him of the stately palms surrounding the government quarters on Mesa. The long, low buildings flanked a river that, once past the lines of tall palms, flowed into, and was swallowed by, the desert.

"What happened then?" Renata asked.

"I'd like to be able to say that, once Masakita came to power, he lost control over the other members of his new government, and that they alone were responsible for what happened. But it wouldn't be true." He shook his head slowly. "Masakita himself, before he came into power, would not have believed himself capable of what he later did."

He thought back to the small, thin man, eyes dark and heavy the night before the first major push against the old government, and compared that memory to one of the same man many weeks later, those same eyes now bright and hard, charged with lightning, it seemed, as he ordered the public disembowelment of all previous government officials.

"I suppose I didn't fully understand him. Or I underestimated his potential for change. Retribution, vengeance, those had never been goals with him. They weren't what drove him at all. But when the opportunity arose, all his pent-up rage and indignation exploded, took over. His first act was to order the public disembowelment of everyone who had been an official of the previous government, even minor supervisors and clerks. No trials. No discussion. A complete purge, divorced from guilt."

Benedict watched the river slide past beneath them, clearer than the Qua Met so that at times he could see flashes of plants or fish beneath the water. He felt he understood the fascination philosophers had with rivers, the fascination these flowing streams of water and life held for poets and writers and painters, for artists of all kinds.

"It wasn't just rage," Benedict continued. "Fear was a large part of it. Fear of being deposed. Fear of corruption in his government. Fear of losing everything he had worked for. Fear that fed on itself, I guess, and on him."

He breathed deeply several times. "Masakita even tried to have the three of us killed. We survived both attempts, though Karl nearly *was* killed the second time. And somehow we managed to get off Mesa alive." Benedict paused, his gaze drifting among the trees, the lush plants, the explosions of color.

"I haven't seen Karl at all since then, but apparently he's never been able to forgive either Masakita or himself. Bitterness and guilt. From what I understand, he's made a cripple of himself. He's been almost completely bedridden the last seven years, willing his body to remain broken."

They continued upriver for several minutes in silence. The rain became heavier for a short time, drenching them, then lightened until it was just a drizzle misting down upon them.

"And is that what you've done?" Renata asked.

"What?" A block of tension leaped into his chest.

"Made yourself a cripple."

The block tightened, twisted inside him bringing pain. "What do you mean?"

"With your seizures, Benedict. Purely coincidence they began just after Mesa? Unlikely at best."

Benedict did not respond. The tension spread from his chest to his arms and legs, made it almost impossible to move. But he managed to twist his hand and increase the throttle to its maximum. The pirogue lurched forward, and within a few minutes, all passed in strained silence, they had caught up with Gerad and Ryker. Benedict kept their boat close, just a few meters away, where they could no longer talk in private.

2

EARLY AFTERNOON THEY APPROACHED A SECTION OF THE
river that narrowed and tumbled through a jagged
maze of rocks and boulders, then fell about two
meters into a small round pool before it narrowed
again. They motored into the pool and a mist almost
as heavy as the drizzle from the clouds, and beached
the pirogues on the left bank. Once they had emptied
the pirogues of water, Gerad opened a small box in
the bow of each boat. Inside were shoulder pads and
handles that locked into depressions in the pirogues
so they could carry the boats on land. A path had been
cut into the trees his last trip, Gerad said, and should
still be relatively clear. The pirogues on their shoulders, they headed into the jungle.

The trail was barely visible, but they could move
slowly along it, and only had to stop twice to clear
through the densest sections. The path wound
through the trees without apparent pattern, but a half

hour later the trail opened out onto the river just above the short run of rapids, and they resumed their journey upriver.

Not long afterward, the rain stopped. The cloud cover dissipated, and the sun shone freely upon them. The temperature, already warm, rose steeply. They kept the boats in shaded parts of the river whenever possible.

They saw no other boats on the river the entire day, and no signs anywhere of other people. Large winged insects materialized in the bright sunlight, hovering above the river or darting across it, colored wings flashing the sun like crystals. Strange, shiny creatures with bare yellow skin and large unblinking eyes seemed to drip from branch to branch in the trees at the water's edge, then drip into the river itself, disappearing from view and never, that Benedict could see, resurfacing.

Just before sunset, Gerad steered into a narrow inlet carved out of the right bank. He cut the motor, raised the prop out of the water, then he and Ryker used the paddles to continue on. Benedict and Renata followed closely behind them, a new and heavy quiet descending on them without the purr and vibrations of the motors.

The inlet was shallow and barely wider than the pirogues. The water was stagnant, blanketed with a thick layer of leaves and flowers and clusters of tiny black insects. Vines and looping branches hung over the water, frequently brushing at their faces.

The further in they went, the darker and more stifling the air around them became. Only glimmers of the sky could be seen above them at first, and then none of it at all. Even the sounds of animals, birds, and insects were muted. Finally, with the river long out of sight, Gerad stopped.

They climbed from the pirogues and drew them partway out of the water. A trail led away from the inlet, narrow and overgrown. They brought food and sleep-sacks, and followed Gerad through the trees to a small hut tucked between two large trees. Gerad knocked, which struck Benedict as an odd gesture. When there was no answer, they went inside.

The hut was a single room with glass windows in each wall, two chairs, and a wood-burning stove in one corner. There were no other furnishings, no foodstuffs or utensils, no decorations or bits of writing or any other signs of habitation.

Gerad cooked dinner with his own stove, and they ate in silence, the hut lit by a single oil lamp that cast large, vague shadows on the walls and ceiling. The darkness outside felt like a warm and heavy presence weighing down on the hut.

After they ate, Benedict decided to go out, and took one of the handlights.

"Don't go far," Gerad warned. "Too damn easy to get lost."

"I won't. Just want some fresh air."

"Want some company too?" Renata asked.

Benedict shook his head and left the hut.

He made his way along the trail and back to the inlet. Water dripped from the trees all around and above him. A bird cried out in the distance, and another answered. Insects clicked and whirred about his face, and some battered themselves against the handlight. When he reached the pirogues, he climbed into one and switched off the light.

The night felt heavy, pressing in on him from all sides. His stomach burned from the food, and his head throbbed with a gentle rhythm, as if it was expanding in the warm darkness with each of his heartbeats.

The jungle's sounds—insect noises, fish splashing and bubbling, bird cries, the steady dripping of water—grew louder, closing in with the heat, the humidity, and the black night, enveloping him. His vision slowly adapted to the dark, but he still could see no more than vague forms and wavering outlines. A flying animal swooped down, startling him, and fluttered its wings about his head. It piped shrilly in his ears, and Benedict swung at it with the handlight, never connecting, but the creature rose and flapped away.

Benedict remained motionless for a long time, feeling the pulse at his throat, willing it to slow just as he willed his breath to slow. Gradually he relaxed, finding comfort in the darkness, in the animal sounds,and in the heavy, damp air like steam in his lungs.

Above him, high in the thick canopy, was a small opening in the leaves, and he could see two bright stars in the clear sky. He thought of Karl, somewhere out there, circling a star that probably was not visible from any part of this world. Karl Ruhman. Why didn't Karl just kill himself? Why didn't he end all the pain, the guilt, the bitterness? Did he feel a need for punishment, for suffering as penance?

Thinking of Karl reminded him of Renata sitting in the bow of the pirogue, looking at him through the rain when he would not respond to her accusations, her expression hidden in shadow. Benedict breathed in deeply, held it for a few moments, then slowly, slowly released it, fighting back a new block of tension that threatened to rise within his chest.

She could not be right, he thought. No.

He remained in the pirogue, staring up through the

tiny opening, staring at the two flickering points of clean, white light. Benedict opened himself to the jungle, gradually lowered the internal screens, let in the emotion in the air around him. From the hut came the feelings of Ryker, Gerad, and Renata, and one by one he blocked them out, until all three were gone, and then he opened himself to whatever else was out there in the jungle.

There was nothing at first, then a glimmer of emotional presence touched him, plucked at his heart. He focused in on it, but it came from too far away, and he could not tell from how many people it came, nor what emotions it carried.

And then, a sudden burst of strange, dark and confused emotion struck him like a heavy blow to his chest. For a moment he lost his grip on the pirogue, and the craft rocked as he lost his balance. He slipped off the seat, dropped to his knees on the floor of the boat, then gripped the sides for support. Inside himself, he quickly erected the screens and filters, all together, until he'd completely blocked out the strange, foreign burst of emotion, and he was alone again.

What was it?

Benedict did not move for several minutes, then worked back up to a sitting position. He controlled his breathing which, like his pulse, had become rapid and ragged. When he felt calm again, and more prepared, he opened himself once more to the jungle.

Nothing.

He lowered the screens one at a time, keeping his three companions blocked, and after a minute or two picked up the faint, distant glimmer he'd first detected, but nothing else. He remained seated, open and "listening" intently to the jungle, but the strange, explosive burst of emotion was gone, and there were no hints of it anywhere in the night.

Benedict stayed in the pirogue a long time, waiting, but nothing came again. Above, the clouds had returned, and the two bright stars had disappeared from view.

3

THEY WERE ON THE RIVER EARLY NEXT MORNING, DRIZZLE and clouds once again obscuring the sun, though the air was still warm. The river continued to narrow as they motored upstream, and sets of rapids became more frequent. Though a few were navigable in the pirogues, by noon they had portaged past four much rougher passages.

Just past midday, Gerad signaled for silence. They cut the motors to a quiet purr, and moved slowly upriver for fifteen, twenty minutes. When a tiny strip of dirt and rock appeared on the right, they beached the pirogues, and disembarked. Gerad faced the dense vegetation and whistled a loud, complex pattern, then repeated it. Ten minutes later, he whistled the pattern twice more.

Silently, and without warning, three women emerged from the trees. They remained motionless for a moment, then approached Gerad and embraced him, laughing and smiling.

All three women looked to be in their thirties. Two were black-haired, one a blond, and the hair on all three hung to their calves. One of the black-haired women was pregnant, probably no more than a month from giving birth. They were all dark-skinned, and dressed in knee-length robes of a light, opaque fabric, and were barefoot.

Gerad introduced the three women to Ryker, Benedict, and Renata, explaining that the women had no names; they had renounced all such labels when they moved into the jungle nine years before. Gerad untied a thick bundle from one of the pirogues and held it up for the women to see. They smiled and nodded at him, and Gerad slung it over his shoulder.

The women led them along a wide path through the trees. The trail, hidden from the river, was well maintained, and they hiked along it in silence. Eventually the trail opened onto a large clearing that was not natural. Several stumps from trees that had been cut down were still visible. On the far right was a large garden, but the bulk of the clearing was occupied by their home.

The house, an odd building of irregularly shaped walls and strange projections jutting from the roof, had been built around the shell of a helicopter that had either crashed or been shot out of the sky. The main cabin, its spiderwebbed glass still in place, served as an entrance to the building, which was constructed of rough-hewn logs, sheets of metal and plastic, alloy drums, thick branches, and wide-leaved fronds. Lights around the oval opening on the pilot's side of the copter blinked steadily, alternating red and blue. Metal spikes and coils of wire decorated the copter roof, and streaks of silver paint crisscrossed what remained of the body and tail.

The women entered first, and waved them in.

Benedict followed Renata through a narrow passage just behind the pilot seats, which were still intact and bolted solidly to the frame. Two human-shaped bundles of branches and leaves were belted into the seats, each topped with a large piece of dried and shriveled fruit for a head.

They were led through a series of chambers, each connected by low, narrow halls. The halls were brightly lit by strings of minnow lights woven into intricate patterns on the walls and ceilings. The first chamber was empty and unlit, dark with no windows. The second chamber's walls were covered with oval canvases, each painting with a dark green background of molds, the foregrounds abstracts in varying shades of red. The third chamber was a hanging garden of flowering vines suspended from a latticed roof open to the sun and rain. Water pooled on the floor, and Benedict moved cautiously through the wet vines which hung to his waist, careful not to knock off petals or buds.

Finally they were led into a large hexagonal room, the roof a clear dome upon which the rain fell. The walls were a solid surface of clay, bare and unbroken by windows. Cushions were scattered about the room, and the women invited them all, except Gerad, to sit on one side of the room, while they and Gerad sat on the opposite side around a square wooden table.

"They want to talk to me alone," Gerad explained, sitting down with the women. "In private. But they don't want to be rude, so you're welcome to stay, as long as you remain on that side of the room." The pregnant woman nodded in confirmation. Gerad shrugged. "I need to talk to them." He shrugged again, and turned to the women.

Benedict sat on a cushion with his back against a wall, and watched Gerad with the women. First

Gerad brought out a pack of cigarettes, offered them.
Each woman took two and put both in her mouth.
Gerad lit the six cigarettes, then one for himself.
Soon, clouds of smoke were rising from the table.

Next, Gerad put his bundle on the table, untied it,
and began removing the contents, showing each item
to the three women. Packets of cigarettes, small tins of
food, cells and music cubes emerged from the bundle
to smiles and approving nods. When the bundle was
empty, the items handed out and inspected and
stored under the table, the three women and Gerad
began to talk. Their voices were so low Benedict could
not make out a single word.

"We've seen more damn freaks on these rivers,"
Ryker said.

"I'm sure these women would agree," Renata replied. She had taken three cushions, propped them
against the wall, and now leaned back against them
and closed her eyes.

Ryker stared to say something, but cut himself off
with a short hard sound, and smiled. He looked at
Benedict, who shrugged, then lit a cigarette. He
turned his gaze to the clear dome above and the
spattering of rain across its surface.

Gerad and the women talked and smoked for over
an hour, voices never rising enough to become intelli-
gible, the discussion punctuated regularly with laughter. Renata appeared to sleep through it all, and Ryker
smoked one cigarette after another, his gaze constantly fixed above them. Benedict remained motionless,
observing them all.

Finally the discussion ended, and the women stood
up from the table. Gerad signaled for Benedict,
Ryker, and Renata to follow, then the three women
led them further into the building, through two more
narrow halls and two more chambers—one chamber

filled with wood carvings, the other a brilliant display of red and violet phosphor lighting.

"Where do they get all the power?" Renata asked.

Gerad laughed. "They've got a generator driven by a perma-sealed nuclear power pack. Converted from a starship drive. Don't ask me how they got it, or how they converted it. All I know, it's here. They'll have power another twenty or thirty years."

They entered a long, wide room with a kitchen at one end, more cushions and several short tables at the other. One of the two longer walls was entirely of glass, revealing a large courtyard and garden. Tall, thin black stones rose from the ground amid a profusion of flowering bushes, and a tiny stream swirled in and out of the stones.

Warm beer was served all around, and they all dispersed among the tables, sitting on the thick cushions. When everyone was seated, the blond woman gestured to Gerad, and they left the room together.

The two dark-haired women sat at one table, sharing a single tall glass of beer. They watched their three guests intently, but remained silent. Benedict, Ryker, and Renata each sat alone at separate tables, sipping at the beer. The warm beer flowed easily down Benedict's throat, and it eased the tension in his belly.

When it was clear that Gerad and the blond woman were not coming back soon, Ryker waved toward the doorway with his beer glass.

"Where did they go? What are they doing?"

The woman who was pregnant leaned back, rubbed once over her rounded belly. The other woman said, "Hopefully, they will conceive a child for us."

Ryker stared at the two women. "You mean they're off screwing?"

The two women did not reply, though their expressions tightened. Ryker put down his glass, leaned forward, and stared at the woman who was not pregnant.

"Why don't *we* go off somewhere and try to conceive a child, all right?" Ryker grinned.

The woman stared back at him, cocked her head. "You *are* a big man, strong. Good health except for the cigarettes, but so with Blade. And I think, if Blade is with you, you with Blade, you are reasonably intelligent." She nodded. "Perhaps it would make a good mesh. Your manners are not a matter of genetics." She slowly rose to her feet.

Ryker's grin vanished, and he shook his head. "No, wait, I wasn't serious. It was a joke."

The woman stepped from behind the table and approached him. "That is not an offer to joke about," she said. "And it was, I think, a good offer." She stopped in front of Ryker, held out her hand to him.

"Sit down," he said. "Back at your table. I'm not going anywhere with you."

"But . . ."

"I told you, I wasn't serious. Damn you, woman, just go sit back down."

"I think we should try." She bent forward, reached for Ryker's hand. He pulled it back.

"Don't touch me, you goddamn freak."

But the woman persisted, reached forward again and took his hand in hers. Ryker jerked his hand back, then swung it forward, forming a fist and striking the woman on the side of her face as he came to his feet. The woman staggered, dropped to her knees, and Benedict and Renata both quickly stood and stepped forward.

"Christ!" Ryker held up both hands, palms out. "Hey, I'm . . . I didn't . . . I told you not to touch me. I am sorry, I lost . . ."

Ryker apologizing? Something new, Benedict thought.

Ryker reached down to help the woman to her feet, but she pulled away from him, backed away along the floor, watching him closely. When she was far out of reach, she slowly rose to her feet on her own. She returned to her table and sat beside the pregnant woman. Ryker nodded once, and sat down again as well.

The next twenty minutes stretched on in heavy silence, the air charged, and yet somehow sluggish in feel. No one moved from their seats, and the two women did not once take their gaze from Ryker.

When Gerad returned, alone, he looked at everyone in the room, puzzled. "What the hell happened in here?"

"A misunderstanding," Ryker said. He set his empty glass on the table. "Are we ready to go? This isn't supposed to be a pleasure trip." He stood.

Gerad turned to the two women. "Are you all right? What happened?"

"Nothing," said the woman Ryker had hit. Her cheek had started to swell. "But this man Ryker is no longer welcome in our house. Your other two friends are welcome in the future."

Gerad turned back to Ryker. "What the fuck did you do?"

"The woman said. Nothing."

"It is past, Blade," the woman said. "And the tale is irrelevant. It is, however, time for you to leave." The two women stood, embraced Gerad, then walked out of the room.

Benedict and Renata rose to their feet. "Let's go," Benedict said. "Leave them in peace."

Gerad started to ask again about what had hap-

pened, but Renata shook her head at him, and he let it
go. Ryker stood near the doorway, waiting. Frowning,
Gerad led them back through the chambers and
corridors, out through the copter, then along the trail
and back to the river, where they boarded the pirogues without a word, and started upstream in the
late afternoon rain.

They stopped early that day, when there was at least
another hour of light remaining, and went ashore at a
long, wide beach of sand on the right bank. Gerad
said they would be leaving the river, start the next
morning through the jungle on foot. After emptying
the pirogues of all their supplies, they pulled the boats
out of the water, carried them into the jungle, and hid
them under a thick cover of branches, leaves, patches
of moss, and layers of vines.

They set up the tent for the first time that night. It
was just large enough, with their supplies, for the four
sleep-sacks side by side. Gerad took advantage of a
temporary break in the weather to build a fire in a pit
dug out of the sand, and cooked dinner over it. Ryker
seemed distracted, but Benedict felt as if some of the
tension that had been building within the big man had
dissipated. After they ate, Renata made coffee for
everyone, and Gerad gave them another briefing.

"We stopped to see the women today for information. Why I brought the bundle of special supplies for
them. That was part of the price. The other part . . ."
He shrugged, looked at Ryker as if expecting the big
man to say something. Ryker looked back at him with
a calm expression, and said nothing. Gerad went on.

"Those three women probably know more about
what's happening deep in this part of the jungle than
anyone else. They make it a point to keep aware, so
they can avoid contact, avoid confrontation. Why I

talked to them, to learn what's been happening around here recently. Don't like surprises of any kind, especially don't like them out here. Enough damn surprises from the jungle, worry about people.

"What they said wasn't really unexpected. A lot of activity out here lately. By a lot I don't mean hundreds of people tripping around. Three groups have been through here in the last two months. One party of four, and two larger groups of around ten each. All three apparently working alone.

"Thing is, that's too many too close together. For free-lancers. This isn't Flex. At least one of those groups, if not all three, is deep in here for the same reasons we are. And it means they have a head start. Some concern there, but fact is, nobody knows where the hell these creatures are. Probably they know where one or more of the contacts have been made, and will be searching in the same general areas. But tell you, it's a big fucking jungle, and we've got as good a shot as any of them. Also, we know there are other searchers out there, and they shouldn't know about us. And I know this part of the jungle, where we're headed, better than anyone, and that'll give us an edge. And Benedict, you're probably the only empath out here, though I'm not too damn sure how much good that'll do."

Benedict smiled. "Neither am I, if that helps." He thought back to the strange, powerful burst of emotion he'd sensed the night before, but didn't say anything about it.

"Take us a few days, week or so just to reach where I had *my* contact with them. We have to be quiet, and careful. *I* want to be the one doing any surprising. We didn't come all this way to get our asses shot off. Though *you* seem to be trying damn hard for it." He glared at Ryker.

Ryker said nothing. He slowly and deliberately took a cigarette from his pocket, lit it with the blackstone lighter, then stared into the fire. Benedict could see tiny images of flame reflecting in the big man's eyes.

Benedict thought Gerad had more to say, but if he did, he apparently decided to let it go until another time. Instead, they all sat around the fire in silence, drinking coffee or smoking in the warm night, and watching the fire slowly die.

4

BENEDICT SLEPT POORLY IN THE CLOSENESS OF THE TENT, THE air stifling despite ventilation windows of mesh in the tent walls. He dozed frequently, often drifting into a half-asleep, half-awake state in which dream and reality became confused, strangely mingling with one another so he could not distinguish between them.

Rain came during the night, left for a time, then returned to continue through morning until, just after dawn, it ceased once more. Gerad was the first to leave the tent, just after the rain stopped. Through the open flap, and through delicate curtains of dripping water, Benedict watched Gerad carefully shave at the river's edge using a hand mirror and straight razor. Benedict rubbed at his own whiskers, which had now grown into a full beard. He did not miss shaving.

After they ate, they prepared for their march into the jungle. On a fresh, dry sheet of tarp, Gerad laid out all the supplies and equipment, opened all the bundles and crates. There were disassembled automatic rifles and handguns wrapped in sheets of sealtight. There were power cells and heat torches, and a box containing the components of a small but powerful transceiver. Another box was filled with sections of lightweight tubing and four, folded, patterned pieces of waterproof fabric covered with inner and outer pockets. Gerad showed them how to put the sections of tubing together and through the fabric to form the four field packs.

When the field packs had been assembled, they began to methodically pack them. Gerad made all decisions about what to bring, what to leave behind, and distributed the weight according to his own mental calculations of body weight, size, and strength. They switched to the special jungle terrain boots, packed their old boots as spares, and were ready.

The clouds were sparse that morning. The sun broke through them and boiled up a steamy heat from the jungle. They broke camp, loaded everything they would leave behind in the hidden pirogues, and erased all signs of their presence. With sharp, lightweight machetes clipped onto their packs in easy reach, and Gerad leading the way, they set off into the jungle.

There were no paths or trails to follow, but they did not need to clear their way. The thick, tall trees that rose high above them, leaves and upper branches forming a thick canopy that blocked out most of the direct sunlight, grew far apart from each other; below, shorter trees, bright ferns and squat bushes, flowering plants and vast networks of dark vines filled the gaps between the trees, but usually there were openings through the undergrowth, narrow passages through which they pushed or squeezed. Gerad led them in a twisting, irregular path, in and out of the large, towering trees that formed vaulted, hollow chambers in the air high above, around massive moss-covered stones, over fallen trunks disintegrating in the damp heat, the fallen logs alive with weaving lines of dark insects and clumps of bulbous fungi.

The ground was uneven, blanketed by an ever-changing carpet of moldering leaves, softened branches, thick layers of bright green and gray mosses, all of which hid flat earth, or hollow depressions, or rocky ground. With each step there was no way to know what lay beneath that carpet, but Benedict had marched through similar terrain before—on DreamVeil, on Bell's World—and he quickly adapted. He adjusted to the extra weight of the pack, and relearned how to walk through constantly changing ground, his muscles not anticipating, but making instantaneous decisions as his boot touched spongy moss, flat, hard-packed earth, shallow depressions, or jagged rock.

The heat grew, and water dripped steadily from above, though it was not raining. Deep within the lush vegetation, the damp heat was oppressive. Benedict was soon sweating freely, his clothing soaked through with sticky moisture.

They made frequent stops to rest. Each time they stopped, Gerad checked a pad of notations he kept in his shirt pocket, used two different instruments to take readings Benedict could not fathom.

Gerad showed them vines that could be tapped for fresh water. The vines were as thick as a forearm, fell from high among the trees, draping down and then curling into the dense undergrowth. Spaced along the vines were large bulges. Gerad used the machete to cut first above, then below the bulge, letting the lower half of the vine fall to the ground. Then he held the round section of vine above him, tilted his head back, and let the clear water from within trickle into his mouth.

"Running through the vines, the water gets purified, distilled, then stored in these pockets. Perfectly safe."

He also pointed out, as they marched, which fruits were edible, which were poisonous, and which of those edible had an unpleasant taste.

Late in the morning, a heavy rainfall burst from the clouds. They heard it first, descending on the canopy high above them, and it was only after several minutes that the rain worked its way through the upper layers and down along the branches and trunks and vines and leaves to begin falling directly upon them. When the storm ended an hour later, the jungle itself continued to rain on them long afterward, and even when it let up, the steady dripping of water all around them never seemed to cease.

The sounds of the jungle changed as they hiked through it. In some areas there was a heavy, hollow silence as if no other living creatures existed, and all they would hear for long periods of time was the gentle dripping of water, their labored breathing, and the sounds of their own passage. At other times it seemed they were in a densely populated animal preserve, the animal noises like a shell of sound enclosing them. Large, dark-furred creatures watched them from the upper branches, apparently unafraid, yet unwilling to descend for a closer look. Birds clustered among the branches, or swooped through chambers of open air high in the canopy, or darted in and out of complex webs of shimmering vines. Serpents hung from lower branches or slithered along tree trunks, avoiding them in silence. Invisible insects clicked and buzzed in the undergrowth, or whirred past them in a blur of dazzling flight.

Ground animals were less prevalent, and were

heard more than seen, usually crashing through the brush in the distance. Once, however, they surprised a grazing porak chewing on the bright blue leaves of a lysium plant. The porak jerked its large head at their approach, froze for a moment, then waddled quickly away, disappearing into the dense undergrowth.

Before they moved on, Ryker picked several of the largest, brightest leaves, rolled all but one into his shirt pocket, and put the one in his mouth and began to chew on it.

"You might want to do the same," Gerad said to Benedict and Renata. "Would myself, except I can't chew and smoke at the same time, and I'd rather smoke. Just stick a leaf in your mouth and chew. Swallow the saliva, but don't swallow the leaf itself. Wouldn't kill you, but would make you sick."

"What's the purpose?" Benedict asked.

"Reality shifting," Renata answered.

"Not exactly," Gerad said. "Will alter your perceptions slightly. Mostly intensifies them, adds a sharpness. Best thing is, picks up the speed of your reflexes. Also, a slight time distortion, slide you along. Time seems to slow up a bit, but at the same time there's less awareness of time passage, so the day will go sliding by. I say not exactly reality shifting because you won't have anything like hallucinations. Overall, I'd say it just adds an edge."

"But you won't chew it yourself."

"I've got all the edge I need." Gerad smiled.

"I advise against it," Renata said. "But it probably won't hurt you."

Benedict picked a single leaf, folded it twice, then placed it in his mouth and started chewing. They resumed their journey into the jungle.

The leaf had a bitter taste, and he did not feel any changes at first. But after twenty or twenty-five minutes, when the leaf had begun to disintegrate so he had to spit it out, he did begin to notice a slight shift in his perceptions. Sounds seemed sharper, as if they'd been cut from the air, and his vision twisted into a tighter, clearer focus so that everything he looked at glistened, like outlines etched in glass. The odors of the jungle stung his nostrils, nearly bringing tears to his eyes until his nose adjusted to the intensity of the smells. Even his sense of touch heightened, and he thought he could feel each of his pores opening in the heat to secrete a fine film of sweat over his skin.

A gradual increase in intensity continued over the next half hour, though he'd stopped chewing the leaf. Benedict found the extra sensitivity disconcerting; he felt unsure of his perceptions, concerned that at least part of what he sensed was not, in fact, real.

Then, as Gerad led them through a long tunnel of vegetation, the air dark as twilight, the foliage thick above them, Benedict detected a more disturbing change. Strange bubbles of incoherent emotion leaked through his filters, then floated randomly about inside him, never quite attaching and becoming his own. He did not, after a brief initial concern, find it frightening, because he quickly realized that this was not another seizure. He had not lost control, and the screens and filters were firmly fixed in place, but they had somehow become porous, and the peculiar bubbles of emotion now slowly percolated through them.

It was only after mentally observing this for some time that Benedict realized the emotion leaking through was not human. A slice of his own fear shivered through him, but he quelled it, forced himself to remain calm and pay closer attention to what was entering his mind and body.

It definitely did not come from any of his companions; it definitely was not human. It was completely unidentifiable as any specific feeling or combination of feelings, but Benedict recognized, on a deep level, that it *was* emotion of some kind. It was, however, incomprehensible, emotion he had never sensed before, though vaguely familiar.

Then he realized what the familiarity was—what leaked through the screens and filters now was the same as the odd burst of emotion that had struck him two nights before while he sat alone in the pirogue, staring up at the two visible stars in the night sky.

Benedict tried focusing on the emotion, but it remained slippery and incomplete, slick bubbles floating in and out of him, coalescing and then disintegrating. There was no way to determine from which direction they emanated, nor from how far. In fact, there was nothing at all he could learn about the disparate bubbles of feeling that continued to slip in and out through his inner filters. The only thing he *did* know was that they were alien.

In the choking humidity of the jungle, with a strangely heightened perception, and with incoherent bubbles of alien emotion floating inside him, Benedict felt as if he was hiking through an underwater forest. He had difficulty concentrating on his surroundings, difficulty keeping pace with the others, and he stumbled several times, never knowing what it was he stumbled over.

Eventually, though, the effects of the lysium decreased. As he continued to push himself along behind his three companions, who did not seem to notice anything different, his perceptions gradually returned to normal, and his inner screens and filters became less permeable until one final bubble of emotion slipped out and he was alone again with his own thoughts and feelings.

Drained and breathless, Benedict abruptly collapsed to his knees, all strength leaving him. He stared after Renata, who disappeared around a tree, and then he was completely alone. He tried calling out, but had no energy. Instead, he shrugged off his pack, leaned against the soft, moss-covered log beside him, and faded quickly into sleep.

He woke, probably only a few minutes later, to rain on his face. He opened his eyes, saw he was still alone, but a moment later Renata emerged from the trees several meters away and strode quickly to his side. By the time she reached him, Ryker and Gerad appeared as well.

"Benedict, what happened?" She knelt beside him, whispered. "Was it another . . . seizure?"

"No." He breathed deeply, watched the other two arrive.

Gerad looked down at him and frowned. "Never seen that kind of reaction before. You think it was the lysium? Or are you sick?"

Benedict shook his head. "I'm all right now. I think it *was* the lysium." He turned, looked at Renata. She was kneeling in the shelter of a tree, brewing a pot of coffee, shielding the brewer from the rain with her body and poncho. "It was wearing off. I don't know, my energy level dropped out from under me." He pushed himself up, sat on the log. "I *am* all right now."

Gerad slipped off his pack, sat beside him. "Let's rest for a bit, though. Have some coffee, make sure you're okay." Gerad looked like he needed a rest more than Benedict. His face had become haggard again, and his skin was pale except for the dark shadows beneath his eyes.

Benedict nodded. He looked at Ryker, who stood in front of him, chewing on a lysium leaf. The big man shrugged and leaned against a black boulder, but did not remove his pack.

They drank the coffee in the rain, then shouldered their packs, and continued on.

Toward late afternoon they came upon a garden of the water vines, several of which had been cut. Gerad inspected them closely, nodded.

"They've been cut recently," he said. "Not today, they're already healing over. But within the last two or three days. We're close to somebody."

Ryker held up one of the vines, stared at it, then moved to another without a word and cut out a fresh bulb. He held it above his head and drank deeply, letting the water run down his beard. Still silent, he threw the bulb into the brush and stood motionless until Gerad started them off again.

Other than the garden of vines, the afternoon passed without incident. Although none of them talked much, Ryker now never spoke at all. He moved efficiently and wordlessly along behind Gerad, his gaze traveling in all directions, taking in the world around him. He did not smoke a single cigarette during the day, but he chewed one lysium leaf after another until darkness began to fall.

It was still raining when they found a small, flat clearing and set up camp for the night. They stretched a large tarp from several trees to cover most of the clearing, then Gerad built a fire with damp wood dried out with a heat torch. After they ate, they sat around the fire, and Renata brought out her soontari.

The soontari was eighteen hollow wooden tubes wrapped together in a three-by-six block, the tubes of varying lengths and thicknesses. Renata played it by bringing it to her mouth and blowing into the upper openings, moving the instrument from side to side

307

and back and forth. Sometimes she blew through a single tube, but often she blew through two or more, and the notes sounded like a wooden flute, though harsher and more hollow.

Renata played for an hour, perhaps longer. Most of the melodies were slow and mournful, and the music seemed to play off the shadows thrown into the jungle by the fire. A few tunes were more upbeat, but even those carried an eerie quality because of the mournful tone of the soontari's sound and the heavy, stifling darkness of the jungle.

Gerad brought out a container of vodka, offered it around, but they all refused, even Ryker. No one spoke. No one talked of sleep. So Renata played on, while Ryker sat and stared and chewed the lysium, while Gerad drank from his bottle and smoked one cigarette after another, and while Benedict stared into the fire, listening to the notes float away from the crackling flames and out into the night of the jungle.

5

THE SECOND DAY OF THEIR MARCH THROUGH THE JUNGLE was little different from the first. Rest breaks were more frequent, however, and Benedict felt constantly tired, his energy a step lower than the day before. Renata appeared to feel the same, though she kept her pace steady, her movement crisp and efficient; the exhaustion showed in her face.

The exertion was clearly taking its greatest toll on Gerad, though he never complained. Coughing fits struck him regularly, and he popped medication tabs every hour or so, but he pushed on.

Ryker, on the other hand, seemed to thrive in the steamy heat of the jungle. When they stopped to rest, he usually remained on his feet, sometimes pacing, sometimes exploring the terrain nearby. He chewed the lysium leaves constantly, and his mood remained elevated throughout the day.

The jungle itself changed little, if at all. Though their path rose and fell over jagged knolls and into deep, narrow gullies, and occasionally flattened for long stretches, Benedict felt certain their overall progress was a gradual uphill climb.

Trickles of water crossed their path, running downhill between trees and plants, but so insubstantial they could not be called streams. Pools of fresh water collected on the floors of gullies or small valleys, usually covered by bright green leaves and often surrounded by birds and ground animals. The jungle was as wet as it was hot, and there was no way to stay dry; the rain and dripping water did nothing to cool them, the moisture only making the heat stickier, the air more difficult to breathe.

Once, when they pushed through a cluster of lysium plants, and Ryker replenished his stock, Benedict plucked three leaves and folded them into his pocket, thinking about the strange bubbles of alien emotion. He had no specific intention of using them again, but it seemed important to have the option available.

Near midday, a gunshot cracked the air. All four of them stopped, remained motionless, and listened intently. It was impossible to know how far away the shot had been, or from which direction it had come, but they waited for another, or some similar sound. The rain continued to fall, a breeze rustled leaves above them, and bird and insect noises continued, but they did not hear anything else.

Twice more that afternoon they heard sounds that did not seem natural, but nothing as distinct as a gunshot. Both times they stopped to listen, but heard nothing more.

That night when they camped, there was no fire. They ate cold food from vacpacs, and fruit from nearby trees. Renata did not play the soontari, and they spoke only in whispers. They decided to keep a rotating watch through the night, two hours each.

Benedict took the first watch, and sat a few feet from the tent, wrapped within his poncho, his back against the soft trunk of a huge tree. Renata had made a cup of coffee for him before she went in to sleep, and Benedict cupped the mug in his hands, sipped at the hot coffee as he listened to the warm night around them.

The jungle was louder at night, and the world was nearly invisible to him, but he caught flashes and glimmers of light in among the trees, though he did not know what it was he saw. Benedict put his hand to his shirt pocket, felt the lysium leaves wadded beneath the fabric. A part of him wanted to try chewing the lysium again, to reexperience the bubbles of alien emotion percolating through him, whatever they were and wherever they came from. But he moved his hand away without taking one, not yet ready to submit to that loss of control.

Instead, he approached it more directly, and cautiously lowered his inner filters and screens, opening himself little by little to the jungle and the night.

From within the tent came a mixture of sleep-muted feelings distorted by dreams, and he methodically blocked off each of them. At first, there was nothing else. He lowered more screens and strained, reaching out through the jungle. After a time he thought he could sense the traces of emotional presence, far away and nearly out of his reach. He focused on it, caught and pulled himself along the delicate threads until he was certain of its existence. This *was* human, but it was so slight and fragile because of the distance that he could not determine much about it. It did come generally from the northeast, he thought, and from several people, but that was all he could discern.

But that was not what he was searching for, and he

blocked out that presence as well. He lowered nearly all his screens and filters, and waited in the darkness, "listening" intently for the slightest hint of that alien emotion he had now sensed at two different times.

Time passed, and then more time passed until he had no idea how long he had been sitting in the dark, but though he remained wide open all that time, there was only a hollow, empty stillness, and he was alone in the night with only his own thoughts, and his own dark and swirling emotions.

6

THE ATMOSPHERE THE NEXT DAY WAS ALMOST OPPRESSIVE. Cautious and alert, they progressed more slowly through the jungle, creating a layer of tension around themselves with their own apprehension. The vegetation itself seemed more alive than before, exuding a hostile, malevolent air. Animal sounds startled them, the screech of birds elicited jumpy movements and curses. Only Ryker appeared to be unaffected, though he, too, remained constantly alert.

The terrain became steeper, and they continued their slow, upward climb, skirting jumbles of massive boulders, wading a knee-deep swamp, fording trickling streams, and crossing a clearing of tall grasses where they caught a glimpse of the sun burning through a high cloud cover.

Late in the morning, they heard a distinct cracking sound that was almost certainly caused by humans. Following it was a short, loud scraping, tapping, scraping, in a pattern that repeated twice. Then nothing else. The sounds came from the northeast, the direction in which they were still headed, and probably closer than the day before. Ryker held up a hand, signaled them to gather around him. He pointed at Benedict.

"Christ, why we didn't think of this before . . . You're a First, you should be able to find out if other people are nearby, and where. Do it now, Saltow, tell us where they are, and how close."

"It may not be that easy," Renata put in.

"You don't know," Ryker hissed. "He's one of the best there is. He's here because he's a First. It's time he started doing something."

"He's right," Gerad said. "Don't usually agree with Ryker, but this time . . ."

"I've already found them," Benedict interrupted. The others stopped talking, looked at him. "Last night while I was on watch."

"Well?"

"They're out there. Somebody is. They were too far away, though. I have limits."

"That was last night," Ryker said. "Try again now. You should try every couple of hours, so we can track them. We don't want them surprising us, we don't want to stumble onto them before we realize what's happening."

Benedict nodded and breathed deeply. He closed his eyes, not because it was necessary, but to signal the others that he had begun. One at a time he lowered the filters and screens, replacing those needed to block out his three companions.

He was tense at first, sensing the other three watching him as he worked, but he slowly relaxed and opened himself. His perceptual range increased, slowly but steadily, extended out through the trees, reaching, reaching . . . there.

The people were far away, but closer than they'd been the night before, though still too distant to distinguish one from another.

"I've got them," he whispered. "Several people . . . at least five, six, probably more. One of the larger parties?" He paused, trying to pinpoint them. "Several kilometers away, though . . . and somewhere in that direction." He waved his hand in a ninety-degree arc between north and east. Benedict kept his eyes closed, concentrated, but was unable to learn anything more about them.

But just before he started to replace the screens, he caught a different sensation, a low tingling of emotion, the alien emotion that now seemed to come from a great distance, vague and unfocused and weak. It was so weak he could not really lock onto it, and it threatened to dissipate.

Suddenly, though, it blossomed and struck him with great force, exploding in his head and sending fire through his body. He felt himself reeling, losing his orientation. Benedict slammed the barriers back into place, all of them, instantly cutting off the burst, then opened his eyes before he lost his balance. He swayed for a moment, caught himself. Renata put out a hand and steadied him.

"You all right?"

Benedict nodded. "It's the distance," he said. "The extra strain."

"Nothing else?" Ryker asked.

"What do you mean?"

"You couldn't pinpoint them any closer?"

"No. They're just too damn far away."

Ryker nodded absently, gazing toward the northeast. "Then we head in that direction," he said. "We need to find them, learn who they are."

"Why not just avoid them?" Renata asked.

"I hope we can," Ryker answered. "Easier to avoid if we know who they are, and where they are. We're headed in that direction anyway, aren't we?" Gerad nodded. "Safest course," Ryker said. "Any objections?"

There weren't any, and they started off, now at a faster pace.

The oppression lifted, was replaced by anticipation and tension. They moved more quickly through the jungle, knowing they were far behind the other party, but more quietly as well.

Twice that afternoon they stopped while Benedict opened himself and reached out for contact. Though the other group was also moving, the four of them steadily gained ground, and as they did so, Benedict was able to pinpoint them more accurately; Gerad adjusted their course accordingly.

Finally, as darkness approached, Benedict opened himself one more time. The group ahead was now only a kilometer away, perhaps less, and he could distinguish among individuals. The group consisted of eleven men and women, and they were settling down for the night.

The four of them set up camp, ate cold food, then sat together in front of the tent, talking in low voices. The rain had stopped, but water dripped onto the overhead tarp, and the warm air remained humid and still.

"So they're what, a kilometer away?" Ryker asked.

"Maybe less."

"Then we should catch up with them before midday tomorrow."

"And then what?" Renata asked. "I still don't see why, since we know where they are, we don't just circle around them, stay as far away as possible."

"I want to know who they are," Ryker said. "I want to see them, see what they're carrying, what they look like."

There was something off in Ryker, Benedict thought. It felt as if Ryker already knew who they were, and what they were doing out here. Maybe he did.

"I still don't think it's worth the risk," Renata said.

"It doesn't matter what you think," Ryker said. "We're going to continue following them tomorrow, we're going to catch up with them, and once we have we'll just have to see what the situation is. If you don't like that course, and don't want to continue, fine. We'll leave you behind . . . two meters underground."

Renata stared at him a few moments, then smiled. "You would take after that, wouldn't you? All right, boss man, we do it your way."

"I don't need your approval." Ryker's voice was quiet and controlled, but laced with a stinging bite.

"Jesus Christ," Gerad broke in. "We've got enough to worry about without fucking with each other. Ryker's in charge, so we go with his final decision." He turned to Ryker, pointed at him with his cigarette. "But you should listen to all of us before you *make* that decision. I'm with Renata. I think we should bypass them, avoid them completely. Hell of a lot safer. Benedict?"

"I say avoid them."

Ryker remained silent for a long time, smoking a cigarette and looking at each of them. Finally he crushed out his cigarette, and nodded.

"All right," he said. "It's not worth all this. We'll give them wide berth, loop around and pass them." He stood, gazed into the fire for a minute, then turned and went into the tent without another word.

"I'll take the first watch again," Benedict said. He

felt uncomfortable, felt that Ryker had given in too easily.

Gerad nodded. "Same rotation as last night, then." He shook his head and sighed, then withdrew into the tent.

Renata remained outside with Benedict, and they sat against a flat stone several meters from the tent. No rain fell, and very little water dripped on them from the trees. Several openings in the foliage above revealed a clear sky, and a dozen bright stars, their light painfully sharp in the black night.

"Want me to make you some coffee?" Renata asked.

"No."

"He'd like to kill all three of us," Renata said.

Benedict nodded. "I think he plans to. He won't."

"Damn right, he won't. I'll kill that bastard first."

"It may come to that. Gerad's already waiting, ready to do it. We should be too. Tonight, though, we need sleep. You should catch it while you can."

"Yes." She rose to her feet. "See you in a couple of hours." She walked back to the tent, leaving him alone with the night.

Benedict woke in the middle of the night, a hard and driving heat coursing through him. He sat up in the tent, felt the heat solidify into an emotional presence, a wave of alien feeling that shook through him, still incoherent and incomprehensible. He found he could easily block it out, but he let the screens down and allowed it inside him.

It seemed to have color as well as warmth, and it vibrated through him as a deep orange glow. What was it, though? Fear? Love? Happiness? Anger or regret, terror or contentment? Hate or worry or guilt or joy or fondness or disgust? It was emotion, he recognized that quality in it, but nothing else about it was familiar, and like the bubbles that had floated through him two days before, the orange warm glow did not hook into him, did not become a part of him.

Then, as quickly as it had come and awakened him, it left, dissipating into the night. Benedict remained awake a long time, his screens and filters lowered, waiting, but it did not return.

BENEDICT WOKE TO THE QUIET CLICKING OF METAL ON metal. Outside, it was still dark, and nearly silent. Renata lay on one side, Gerad on the other. Ryker's shift, the last.

The clicking continued, punctuated by slides and loud snaps. Benedict recognized the sounds. Ryker was assembling a weapon, probably one of the automatic rifles.

"Benedict?" A quiet whisper from Renata. "You awake?"

"Yes."

"What is that?"

"Ryker. Assembling one of the automatic rifles."

She sat up. "Why?"

"I don't know." All he did know was that Ryker was not going to kill them, not like that, not yet. There was no sound from Gerad, but Benedict was certain the free-lancer, too, was awake.

"We should do something," Renata whispered.

"What?"

"I don't know. Something."

They remained silent in the stifling darkness. The sounds of clicking metal stopped, then a moment later Benedict heard Ryker stand, take a few steps, then stop in front of the tent. More silence, then Ryker moved on, hiking into the jungle and away from them.

"Where is he going?" Renata again.

The sounds of Ryker's passage faded quickly, then were gone.

"Where?"

Benedict did not answer. He did not really want to think about it, about where Ryker might be going, or what he might do.

"We should do something," Renata said one more time. But she did not move, and eventually lay back beside him. "Benedict?" she whispered.

"Yes."

She said nothing more. Benedict lay in the quiet, close darkness, and tried, without success, to sleep.

At the first signs of light, Gerad got up, built a fire, and started cooking breakfast. Benedict and Renata joined him by the fire. No one mentioned Ryker's absence, no one speculated on where he was, or what he was doing.

Rain began to fall, and they ate slowly and methodically in silence, watching the jungle. When they finished eating, they built up the fire again and sat around it.

"How long do we wait?" Renata asked.

Gerad shrugged, said nothing.

They did not wait long.

A loud burst of gunfire broke the morning air, then

a second burst that went on and on, interrupted briefly by shorter, similar bursts and occasional single shots.

Renata stood up, stared in the direction of the sounds, but otherwise didn't move. Benedict and Gerad remained seated, looking at Renata, at each other. There was nothing to do.

"Benedict." Renata turned to him. "Open yourself, find out what's . . ."

"No." He shook his head sharply. "No. You don't know what it's like to . . . die. No."

The gunfire, though more sporadic now, continued for several minutes, then was halted by a loud explosion. Half a minute later a second explosion sounded, followed by another burst of gunfire. Then silence.

There was nothing for ten or fifteen minutes, then half a dozen single shots sounded. Another lull lasted a few minutes, then there was one long burst of automatic weapons fire. Then silence again.

This time the silence remained unbroken, and Renata sat back down. They stayed by the fire, Gerad smoking one cigarette after another, and none of them spoke. They all watched the jungle, waiting for some sign of Ryker. A half hour passed, then an hour, and still Ryker did not appear.

"I hope the bastard's dead," Renata finally said.

Gerad stood, threw his cigarette into the fire. "Let's go find out," he said.

They broke camp, divided the contents of Ryker's field pack between them. Gerad lashed the skeleton of Ryker's pack to his own, and they started off through the jungle.

No one spoke, and they hiked slowly through the trees, headed northeast, spread out whenever possible, searching for signs of the confrontation.

322

Forty-five minutes after they broke camp, at the entrance to a small valley, they came across a body sprawled across a moss-covered stone. The man had been garroted, but there was no sign of struggle, as if he had been taken completely by surprise.

They left the dead man and started into the valley, Gerad leading the way. The valley was narrow, but relatively clear of trees, and there was a natural path along the valley floor, the walls sloping steeply on either side.

Gerad skirted a thicket of lysium plants, then came to an abrupt halt, staring straight ahead. Benedict and Renata came up beside him.

Smoke drifted lazily from the remains of a cooking fire. Strung out along the valley floor on both sides of the fire, some facedown, some faceup, were the bodies of the dead.

They found Ryker halfway up the right-hand slope, wrapped around a tree, his head against a rock. One hand still gripped the automatic rifle. He was barely conscious, and mumbled incoherently as they pulled him to his feet. Further up the slope, Benedict saw a shelf of rock that had been partially destroyed by some kind of explosion.

Ryker had taken a large shell fragment and several chunks of wood and stone in his shoulder. A dark bruise swelled near his temple, and the rest of his body was covered with cuts and scrapes and small bruises, but nothing else very serious. Not a single bullet had found its mark on him. Ryker staggered down the slope, supported by Benedict and Renata, cursing and grunting, gradually becoming more alert.

Gerad built up the smoldering fire, then spent a long time cleansing and bandaging Ryker's wounds.

While he did, Benedict and Renata collected the bodies and equipment and weapons scattered across the valley floor.

Inside one of the packs, Benedict found a portable transceiver and powerpack. While no one was watching, he dragged it behind a tree and, out of sight of the others, wrapped the transceiver and powerpack carefully in a sheet of seal-tight. He dug a hole in the soft earth, laid the bundle in it, then covered it with dirt. He scattered leaves and rocks over the dirt, then returned to the task of collecting bodies.

Benedict worked in a daze, saying nothing to Renata, hardly thinking of what he was doing, and what had taken place just a short time before. There was nothing else to do but go on.

When the bodies were gathered together, Benedict and Renata went through the clothing and checked all the idents. Every member of the group was certified with Timons, Ltd. One of the men was named Maxil Klidowska, and Benedict recognized the name at once.

"You knew they worked for Timons," Gerad said when Renata and Benedict told him.

"Of course," Ryker said. "I recognized some of them."

"Then why kill them?" Gerad asked. "They worked for the same people we do."

"That's exactly why I had to kill them."

"I don't understand."

Ryker shook his head from side to side, as though disappointed in Gerad. "You know how much we'll get paid if we find these creatures. If this other group had found them instead of us, we'd have received nothing but that small support fee from Timons. We're not here for that, we're here for the big money, and nothing else will do. *We* have to be the ones to find them. That means eliminating competition. It's all or nothing, Blade." He shook his head again. "What do you think they would have done to us? Even if they knew we worked for Timons?" He sat up as Gerad finished bandaging his shoulder. "I'm surprised, Blade. You've killed before. You know what survival is out here."

Gerad stepped back from Ryker, lit a cigarette, and stared at the big man. "That's true, Ryker. I've killed. But it's always been in self-defense. I've never slaughtered anyone without reason."

"I just gave the reasons, Blade. It *was* self-defense. They would have killed *us* if they'd had the chance."

By this time, Benedict had put together the pieces —the name Klidowska, and what Ryker had said to him that night he came back to the boat drunk, about secondary options, and support.

"That's not true," Benedict said. "They would not have killed us."

Ryker looked at him, smiling now, and then Gerad and Renata turned to him as well.

"I think I've just worked it out," Benedict went on. "The things you've said that I didn't understand before. What finally did it was this name." He held up the ident. "Maxil Klidowska. One of the dead. We were a . . . what was it you said that night, a secondary option? Support, you said. We were supposed to provide support for this group, weren't we? They actually expected to meet us at some point, didn't they?"

Ryker's smile was gone, but he didn't seem concerned or upset. "Yes," he said.

Silence.

There was nothing more to say. Ryker remained by the fire while Gerad helped Benedict and Renata lay out the bodies in a long, shallow depression in the valley floor. They covered the bodies and supplies with ferns and thick branches and webs of water vines, wide leaves, and clumps of grass.

When they were done, they returned to the fire, put it out, then hiked out of the valley. Gerad took the lead and kept a steady, rapid pace, putting as much ground as possible behind them before darkness fell.

8

WHEN THEY STARTED OFF THE NEXT MORNING, RYKER IN-
sisted on carrying his full pack despite the wounds in
his shoulder. No one objected.

The atmosphere surrounding them, though no longer filled with the stretched tension of the day before,
was again transformed, this time into a dark, oppressive fog that weighed on all of them but Ryker. In fact,
though he had lost much blood, was pumped with
painkillers and antibiotics, Ryker displayed a growing
exhilaration while the mood of the other three remained dark and heavy.

As they marched through the jungle, through down-
pours broken by stretches of light, steady drizzle,
Ryker continued to thrive. His energy pushed up the
pace, indirectly forced Gerad to press on longer and
harder than he would have without the constant
prodding.

The sun did not once make an appearance, but
Benedict didn't mind. He preferred the gloom and the

wet heat; it allowed him to submerge his thoughts, dampen them so that most of the time he could move along in a daze, unable and unwilling to think.

But he could not submerge his thoughts completely, and questions and doubts resurfaced throughout the day, forcing their way into awareness. Was there any real hope of finding the escape he wanted? Even if they found these creatures, who were, very probably, intelligent, then what? That would not change humanity, and there seemed to be no escape from humanity, not even out here in the deep jungle. He began to wonder if, continuing on this expedition, he was losing more than he could ever hope to gain.

When they stopped to eat at midday, Benedict sat apart from the others and, while automatically eating, lowered the screens and opened himself, reaching out for the strange, alien emotional presence he knew was somewhere in the jungle around him.

Minutes passed with only a hollow emptiness vibrating through him, then the first glimmers of emotion touched, then filtered into him. But there was a hesitancy about what he felt, a reluctance, as if the source or sources of the alien emotion somehow had control of what he would be allowed to perceive. The emotion shimmered inside him for a minute or two, never quite congealing, and Benedict, afraid he would lose it, lowered more screens. But the alien presence did not become more substantial, and it slowly began to withdraw from him, either oblivious to or ignoring his efforts to hold on to it. It faded gradually, and steadily, until there was nothing left behind.

Benedict looked at his empty plate, not remembering a single bit of the food, then looked at his silent companions. Whoever the aliens were, *what*ever they were, Benedict really had no doubts of their intelligence, not after what he had sensed from them the past few days. He did not begin to understand anything of what they were like, or what they felt, but he was certain they were more than just animals; they were intelligent beings, and after yesterday's events, that fact only depressed him.

We seem perfectly willing to use and destroy each other, Benedict thought. Those who don't destroy directly allow others to do so. People won't hesitate to do the same to nonhumans.

Then, he thought, maybe there *was* something he could accomplish out here, if not for himself, then for the alien beings, wherever they were. Perhaps Jean-Philippe and his people *were* the only chance these alien creatures had. Which meant the job he had so reluctantly taken on for Jean-Philippe might be, after all, what he needed. It might be all he had left.

Just before dusk, they came to a stream curling down from the southeastern slopes, cutting its way north along a gully of rocks and slanted trees. It was the first flowing water they had seen since leaving the river that could actually be called a stream.

They halted at the water's edge, the stream just over two meters across, and no more than thigh-deep. Gerad took several readings from his two instruments, then nodded.

"This is it," he said. "It leads down, about a day's hike, to a bigger river, a little bit narrower and shallower than the trib we were on, but similar." He looked up into the sky above the trees, visible in patterned openings through sparse branches. "We should probably camp soon, then start following the stream tomorrow."

"What's at the other river?" Benedict asked.

"More traveling," Gerad replied. "We're close, but we've got a ways yet."

A half hour later they found a flat area just big enough for the tent, and set up camp. Gerad started a fire near the stream, using rocks to form an enclosure. Ryker retreated into the tent to sleep, some of his excitement and energy drained by exhaustion that had finally caught up with him. While Gerad tended the fire and made preparations to cook, as usual refusing offers to help, Benedict and Renata walked downstream, well out of hearing of the camp. Renata brought her soontari, and they sat on the bank in the falling darkness.

"You having any trouble?" Renata asked. "Controlling things. Your 'barriers.' With all that Ryker's had you do, I've been expecting you to . . ."

"No," he said.

Animal sounds filled the dusk, a welcome background after the morning sounds of the day before. Benedict watched the water flow past them, bubbling quietly over rounded stones.

"You haven't had a seizure since that day in Lady Deebo's apartment, have you?" Renata asked.

"No, I haven't."

"You're overdue."

He nodded, but said nothing. It had been almost three weeks since that seizure, but he felt more secure than he had in months, perhaps years.

"I don't think you're going to have one out here," Renata said. "You should have had one at Oasis with the Reclaimers. Or yesterday. You were ripe for it both times. But no seizure."

"No seizure."

"Why, Benedict?"

"I don't know." He continued to stare at the water, not looking at her. "I feel it's going to be a long time before I have another." He shrugged. "I've been

330

thinking about it some. I'm certain the time I spent in the Canal Zone, with Silky, with you, has something to do with the change. Like I've acquired a different way of looking at the world, at people. I don't know, really."

"But you had a seizure in the Canal Zone. When you were with me and Silky."

Yes, he thought, and I almost died in that seizure. "Maybe it was my last."

They were silent a long time, then Renata brought the soontari to her mouth and played for a few minutes. The notes were long, sad whispers of sound in the darkness, somehow matching the gurgling of the stream, which flashed dulled scales of light at them. She stopped, held the soontari in her lap.

"Soon after the free-lancer made this for me, and I learned to play it, I went on a long trip through the jungle, deep into the northwestern tracts, past the source of the Qua Tri. I returned with the two scars I've never healed away."

She paused, raised the soontari, but did not play it. Benedict remained silent, waiting. He knew she would tell the story, and did not need any prodding now.

"Reasons I'd gone so deep," she resumed, "are unimportant now. What happened while I was out there, though, *is* important. At least to me." She paused. "I killed two of the creatures we're looking for out here."

She stopped again, tapped on the soontari with her fingertips, an irregular, repeating pattern.

"I was hiking through jungle much like what we've been marching through. Wasn't rainy season, but still hot and damp. Rained every two or three days instead of every two or three hours. Had a weapon in my hands, automatic rifle like Ryker's. I'd had some trouble the day before, expected more. I was tired, on edge.

"I was following a stream. Ahead, in a small open area near the water, I saw one of the creatures. I'd heard what they looked like, caught the rumors they were intelligent, almost impossible to find. So I knew what I was seeing. It was lying on the ground, belly up, and I saw blood leaking from its side. Heard quiet moaning, knew it was still alive, in pain." She paused. "You know what they look like?"

"No. Nobody wants me to know."

"Tall, larger than humans on average when standing. By half a meter. Apparently, what I've heard, they walk both bipedally and on all fours, whichever suits them best. Body and face are completely furred, usually a mottled gray with a pale, bluish tinge. Feet clawed, hands clawed, the hands with three long claws and a roughly opposable fourth digit, also clawed. Head long and large, wide mouth with sharp teeth, long, flat nose, small eyes set deep under a large brow. Large ears covered with tufts of fur." She breathed deeply. "I've seen two very close, you understand." She paused, then went on.

"I approached slowly, cautious. It was big, looked very strong even wounded. When I was a few meters away it turned its head, looked at me. It didn't try to move, but the small eyes glittered and stared at me, and stared. I couldn't read the expression, but it was intense. Maybe it was only pain. I didn't know what to do, so I continued forward. I stood over it, then knelt at its side, looking for the source of the blood." She stopped, breathed deeply again. "I only wanted to help it, if I could.

"I don't know exactly what happened, whether it was trying to hurt me, maybe just reaching out to me, and losing control, or not knowing how strong it was, I don't know. I had reached forward with my free hand and touched its side, parting the fur and trying to find the wound, and it swung its arm up and across its body. Next thing I knew I saw claws coming at my face.

"I didn't move quickly enough. A claw caught me just above the eye, ripped open my skin down to my cheek as I pulled away, then ripped through my single-suit and hooked into the skin below my neck.

"My reaction was instantaneous, instinctual, I guess. I was already rolling back, and I came to my feet a few steps away, brought the rifle up, and started firing, single-shot. I'd put half a dozen shots into it, more than enough, when I heard crashing sounds in the trees next to me. Another of the creatures appeared, headed straight for . . . whom? It's companion, or me? I don't know. Never a chance to find out, because I turned and opened fire on it, shooting until it had crumpled to the ground a few meters away." She blew two long, quiet notes on the soontari, then lowered it to her lap again.

"They were both dead. I felt sick, looking at the two bodies. Sick, the way I felt yesterday walking into the valley. I hadn't wanted to kill either of the creatures. And the more I thought about it, the more I felt the injured one had not intended to hurt me, that it had clawed me by accident. But I'd killed it, I'd killed them both.

"And that's why I've kept the scars, and why I'm out here in the jungle now. May seem insignificant or unimportant to you, but it became imperative to me that I learn whether or not these creatures are intelligent. I need to know so I can come to terms with what happened, with what I did. If they're not intelligent, then I work it out one way. If they are, I work it out another, much more difficult way. It's the not knowing that makes it impossible.

"So I'm here, with this expedition, so I can learn how to come to terms with something I did in the past. And after yesterday, I have something else to come to terms with."

She stopped talking, and after a moment she started playing the soontari again. Benedict wanted to tell her he could answer that question for her, that he knew the creatures *were* intelligent, but he wasn't ready to reveal that to anyone yet. That would have to wait. They all had to wait for something.

9

FOR THREE DAYS THE RAIN DID NOT STOP, DAY OR NIGHT.
They marched gradually downhill now, through what seemed to be an infinite, wet jungle, the rain providing no cooling effects, only making the heat less tolerable, breathing more difficult. The trees became somewhat shorter, the thick canopies no longer quite so high above them, but the vegetation was still so dense that now the jungle seemed to be closing in on them.

The way was clear—follow the stream—and Ryker took over the lead. When the jungle proved too thick to push through without leaving the stream, they waded into the water until they could again pick a path along the banks.

Because it rained continually, the light was always dim, a never-ending steamy dusk broken only by night, which eventually made way for the dusk again next morning. The plant life flourished in the rain and the heat, and at times it seemed they could actually see the plants growing, could watch the mushrooming fungi rise from the ground with bulging heads, could see flowers curl slowly open to receive insects and rain.

Although he and Renata continued much as before, it appeared to Benedict that Gerad and Ryker were following two opposing courses as they hiked on through the jungle. Ryker easily overcame his injuries, the wounds were healing despite the damp, and he continued to thrive in the heat, marching tirelessly from morning until dark, then sleeping heavily through the night. Each day his energy level increased, and he pressed them all harder, urging them on even when they were exhausted.

Gerad, on the other hand, was steadily losing energy and strength. Each day found him more exhausted at its conclusion, and he did not regain much energy with sleep. His mood was low, he almost never spoke, and his eyes were dull and glazed. The edge he had talked about was all but gone. Even his cigarettes drooped listlessly from his mouth, the smoke a languid cloud rising about his head.

And yet . . . and yet Benedict sensed an inner layer of strength within Gerad, a hard edge somewhere inside that would not dull, and Benedict was certain that, in spite of appearances, there was a level on which Gerad had not given up. He was still driven, perhaps no longer by the need for revenge against those who had nearly killed him several weeks earlier, or by the need for enough money to leave this world, but by a need for revenge against the huge bearded man who now led them relentlessly through the jungle. It was not over for him just yet.

At the end of the first day of following the stream, they reached, as Gerad had said they would, a larger river. Though close in size to the Qua Met tributary, it twisted more, was laced with rapids and small falls, dotted with rocks both on its banks and in the river itself, jagged stones jutting up through the swirling water. In this part of the river, any kind of boat would have been useless.

They spent the next two rain-drenched days continuing their downward march, following the river. Twice a day, on Ryker's orders, Benedict let down the screens and searched for evidence of other people, but there was never the slightest hint of human presence anywhere around them.

Still, Benedict knew they were not quite alone, though he never said so. The alien emotional presence was always there when he opened himself to the jungle. Sometimes it was only barely discernible, and seemed to be coming from far away. At other times the sensation, though unfocused and undefined, overwhelmed him with its wild, uncontrolled intensity, and he would wonder if there was an entire tribe of the alien beings directly beside them, hidden in the thickets of dense foliage. But he never learned anything about it, whether it was dim and vague or wild and intense, and he knew that if there was any chance for understanding, he would have to confront them directly.

The morning of their third day along the river, the rain let up, though it did not stop completely. A heavy, warm mist fell upon the river, surrounded them as they moved along the river's left bank. The right bank was high and steep, a rocky cliff draped with thick vines and flowery creepers.

Gerad took over the lead again, tapping into a fresh energy source, and kept the pace steady. He was still grim and wasted, but there was a new determination driving him. His gaze moved rapidly across the jungle, and his eyes were alive again, constantly searching.

Near midday, the terrain became more uneven as the river carved its way through low but steep mountains, and the jungle became even denser. The left bank rose and steepened to match the right, and before long the river was flowing through a narrow gorge, and they marched along upper ledges ten and fifteen meters above the water.

Their progress slowed, and occasionally they had to cut their way through the undergrowth with the machetes. The air became even steamier, so that each breath threatened to become a cough. Benedict lost track of time and distance, was aware only of the dense vegetation surrounding him, and Renata's legs and feet moving ahead and marking the trail he had to follow.

But then, as the high banks began to sink back toward the river, Gerad brought them to a halt. They stood at the edge of the cliff, ten meters above the water, and the river flowing past below them was quiet, its sounds and echoes muffled by the mist still falling heavily from above. Gerad pointed downriver, toward the opposite bank, half a kilometer ahead, to where the riverbanks were no longer cliffs and the river began to move through flatter ground.

"Can you see that flat, huge white rock?" He jabbed at the air with his finger. Benedict could see nothing through the mist, though it occasionally parted to reveal the opposite bank. "That's where I saw it," Gerad continued. "Him or her, I don't know, but it was there, sitting on that rock, gazing into the water. Basking in the sun. No rain that day. It was magnificent, that sight. I'd seen one once before, in a cage. But here, deep in the jungle, in its own environment."

He nodded to himself. "I was further down when I saw it, almost directly across from it. After a while, it stood, and stared up into the sky, motionless for nearly half an hour. Then suddenly, like it was waking up, it turned, looked right at me, though I was completely hidden in the brush. Smelled me, or like that, but it knew I was there. Looked at me for a minute, then turned and disappeared into the trees." He breathed deeply. "Never saw it again, never saw another." Gerad stood gazing at what Benedict still could not see, lit a cigarette, then shrugged and led them on.

A half hour later they had descended to the water's level and walked easily along the river, the white, flat rock now clearly visible ahead. At a wide, shallow stretch of the river, just upstream of the rock, they crossed through hip-deep water, the current tugging at their legs.

On the other side of the river, they hiked the last few meters to the large, flat rock, and walked out onto it. All four of them remained silent, searching the jungle as if expecting one of the creatures to make an appearance. Nothing did.

"The difficult part starts now," Ryker said. "It's too late to do any searching today, but we need to find a place for a semipermanent camp. We stay here for a few days, run an organized, methodical search of the area, and if we don't find anything, move on. We need to be thorough, and we need patience. It could take days, it could take weeks."

"And we might never find them," Renata said.

"We'll find them."

"I know where we can set camp," Gerad said. "I did a lot of exploring when I was here, trying to find another one of them. There's a clearing nearby, not far from the river." Without waiting for a response, he clambered down off the rock and headed into the trees. The others followed.

Ten minutes later they emerged into a clearing almost ten meters across, treeless but carpeted by short bushes and tall grasses. They spent the next two hours clearing ground for a more permanent camp, setting up the tent, building a fireplace of stones, digging out a latrine. By the time they'd erected a large tarp over the tent, and a smaller one over the fireplace, darkness had fallen.

After a hot meal eaten in silence, when the others withdrew to the tent to sleep, Benedict remained by the fire. He built a makeshift chair of damp logs and large, smooth stones, and sat in the darkness, watching the flames and listening to the quiet hiss of the mist that still fell.

He started to open himself, to lower the screens and filters and listen for the alien creatures, but he changed his mind and kept himself closed. He didn't need to listen. He knew they were there, close perhaps. Benedict felt certain he could find them, and that they could find him.

He opened his shirt pocket, took out the lysium leaves he'd put there a few days before. They were falling apart, and he tossed them into the fire. In the morning, or sometime in the next two or three days, he would have to find some fresh leaves.

The lysium would be the key for him, he was certain of that now. He could open himself, and sense them, but could never, unaided, determine distance or direction, or anything else. But the way those bubbles had filtered through him when he chewed on the lysium . . . yes, that *had* to be the key to finally locating the creatures.

He would have to be careful. He did not yet know what he was going to do, but he knew he had to find the aliens without the others knowing he had, and he had to prevent the others from finding the aliens themselves. And then, once he did locate them, he would have to signal Jean-Philippe's people, and hope they came soon. None of it would be easy.

He was tired, his body and mind both worn out. Tomorrow, he thought, tomorrow he could start, maybe tomorrow he would think of a way to do it all.

10

BENEDICT WOKE IN THE EARLY GRAY MORNING, ALONE IN THE tent. He felt groggy, as if he'd slept too long, but he knew he hadn't slept enough. He could hear the crackle of flames, quiet footsteps, the hiss of Renata's brewer, and the whisper of drizzle on the tarps. He lay without moving, almost relaxed, and wished he did not have to begin the day.

When he emerged from the tent, Renata was pouring coffee and Gerad was dishing up breakfast. Ryker sat on a rock nearby, chewing on something wadded in his cheek, and cleaned his disassembled rifle. A small rucksack, partially full, was at his feet. When Gerad held out a plate to him, Ryker shook his head.

"I'll grab something later," he said. "I want to get out early, before we start, do some hunting. The food we brought won't last much longer, and we could be out here a long time. We'll need fresh meat."

Gerad, without replying, turned away and handed

the plate to Benedict. Benedict sat by the fire, and Renata gave him some coffee.

They were almost finished eating when Ryker stood, slipped on the rucksack, and slung the rifle over his shoulder. The Great White Hunter from Earth's past, thought Benedict.

"Anyone want to join me?" Ryker asked. When no one answered, he shrugged, shifted his weight. "I'm off, then. Back soon, we'll talk about a plan for the search." He stood without moving for a few moments, waiting, perhaps, for some response, then turned away. He crossed the clearing, pushing his way through the tall grasses, and disappeared into the jungle.

"I *will* kill him someday," Gerad said quietly. "When this is over, and we no longer need him. Maybe it'll take a year, maybe longer, but I'll do it. I'm going to kill the fucking bastard."

"I thought you were going to leave Nightshade as soon as possible," Benedict said.

Gerad gave him a slight, unhappy smile. "First things first." He put his cup on a rock near the fire and stood. "I think I'll go down to the river for a while, maybe sit on that rock. Need to be alone, do some thinking. Push some things aside until this is finished. Now might be the last chance I have. If I'm not back by the time Ryker returns, come get me." He put on his poncho and walked into the trees.

Benedict and Renata remained in front of the fire, dry under the tarp. The drizzle became heavier until it was a downpour, but as the invisible sun rose higher, the air grew brighter. They sat in silence a long time. Renata dried a few pieces of wood with the heat torch and added them to the fire.

"He'll do it too," Renata finally said.

"What? Kill Ryker?"

"Yes."

"I know. Gives me something to look forward to."

Renata smiled, shook her head. But the smile did not last long, and she looked out across the clearing into the dense jungle.

"Do you think you'll be able to sense these creatures?" she asked.

Benedict hesitated, then said, "I don't know. They're not human, and I'm a human empath, so . . ." He didn't finish.

Renata turned to look at him; stared silently for a time. "I think you're lying," she said. "I think you've already sensed something out there. I've had this feeling the last two or three days, you've been picking something up from them."

"No," he said.

She continued to gaze at him, but did not say anything more.

Benedict got up, retrieved his poncho from the tent, and walked back to the fire. Maybe now would be a good time to go for a walk himself, while Gerad and Ryker were gone. Pick up some lysium leaves, maybe even chew one, start searching. Give him something to do.

"You going somewhere?" Renata asked.

"Thought I'd go for a . . ." A sharp dagger of panic and pain cut deeply into him, ripping through his chest, halting his breath for a moment. He rode it, filtered down, then focused in on it. It was . . . "Gerad," he choked out.

The pain and fear intensified, climbing in huge leaps, and he reached out for support. When he caught empty air, he staggered, dropped to his knees in front of the fire, reached out to the ground to keep from falling further.

"What is it?" Renata asked. "Another seizure?" She was at his side, gripping his arm. "Benedict?"

"No, it's . . . Gerad. He's . . ." The fear, the pain, and the dying itself tore through him, became a sharp, intense pain lodged in his own chest, shooting up through his skull. Deliberately, still very much in control and now filtering the fear, he lowered other screens and filters, reached out. Almost immediately he picked up Ryker's flushed exhilaration, an orgasmic upswell flooding through and out of Ryker to now rush through Benedict.

"Ryker's killing him," Benedict said. He could not move. He threw all the filters and screens back into place, blocking out all feeling. Benedict breathed deeply several times, relief washing through him.

"Where are they?" Renata snapped. "We've got to . . ."

"They're too far," Benedict cut in. "Happening too fast." But he got to his feet, pointed into the trees. Renata started to run into the trees, but Benedict lunged at her, caught her arm and jerked her to a stop. "It's too late," he whispered.

Still holding on to Renata, he dropped the screens and filters once more, and let all the emotion back inside him. Benedict reeled for a moment, steadied himself, then cut down the intensity while staying with the two men.

Already Benedict could feel that Gerad's fear was beginning to fade. The pain quickly reached a peak that blossomed, like a blinding explosion of light, then erupted from Gerad in a single violent burst. The pain rose, and then was blacked out by a billowing cloud that took his pain, his fear, and his life with it. The cloud expanded and rose, black over the bright light of the pain, then all of it rapidly dissipated.

Only a ghost of emotion remained behind in Gerad.

It left him, hovered for a few moments, vague and incoherent, then slowly disintegrated and was gone.

All that was left was Ryker's intense joy, his rush of power. Benedict cut him off, sickened.

"Gerad's dead," he whispered. He felt drained, but still in control. He was still holding on to Renata, and now he released her. He turned away and walked slowly back to the fire, sat beside it. Renata did not move at first, then, after looking once more into the trees, joined him by the fire.

"Why did Ryker kill him?" Her voice was quiet, but tight.

"Because, I suppose, Gerad is now expendable. He brought us to where he'd had contact with these beings, and that was his sole purpose as far as Ryker was concerned."

Renata paced around the fire, nodding slowly. "And what about us?"

"I think he still needs us. To find the creatures. But I'm sure he'll take us out as well, first chance he gets, when he thinks he doesn't need us anymore."

"He'll be back soon."

"Yes."

She stopped pacing, stared at him. "So what do we do?"

He had no answer.

They waited for Ryker to return.

What would Ryker say? What would they say to him? Would all three of them feign ignorance, sit around the fire waiting for Gerad to return, all three knowing he would not? Benedict shook his head to himself. Would they search for him together, then give him up for lost? Or what if they *did* find Gerad's body? Would they begin to search for the alien creatures, pretending nothing had happened? Would Benedict and Renata just wait for Ryker to kill them as well?

The fire was slowly dying, but neither of them moved to add fuel or stoke it. They remained silent, listening to the rain, waiting. Benedict could not reach any decisions, he could not even think clearly.

Ryker appeared, emerged from the trees on the opposite side of the clearing. Erect and confident, Ryker walked with self-assurance across the clearing. Benedict could see the rifle in his hand, which had not been fired, hanging loosely at his side as he pushed through the high grass.

"Didn't get a damn thing," Ryker said when he was just a few meters away. "Didn't even get off a shot. I didn't see . . ."

Before he could finish, Renata's hand had come up, pulling the gun from her single-suit, then the other hand joined it, aimed the gun at Ryker's chest. She fired three times in rapid succession, all three shots striking him in the chest where his heart should be.

The force of the shots stopped his forward progress, and for a brief moment he stood motionless, his eyes wide, his mouth open as though trying to finish what he was saying. Then he fell back, crumpling heavily to the ground with only a harsh, choking sound emerging from his throat. His body quivered for several seconds, then was still.

PART SIX

Inner Eclipse

1

"Twelve people too late," Renata said. "We should have given him to the Reclaimers." She turned and aimed the gun at Benedict.

"Are you going to kill me too?"

"I don't know. Do I need to?"

"Why should you kill me?"

"To protect myself. I really don't know yet why you're here, Benedict. I think it's time you told me." She lowered the gun, put it back in her single-suit. "First, we've got a body to move. This heat, rain, it'll be reeking in an hour."

"No gun on me?"

"I told you once, in Riotmark, that I trust you." She shrugged. "I guess that really hasn't changed."

He stood, and they walked over to Ryker's body. Ryker's hair and beard were slicked down on his face from the rain, his eyes partially open. His chest was a congealing mass of blood, flesh, and bone, and his left arm had a fresh knife wound. So Gerad had managed at least that, Benedict thought.

They each took hold of a wrist, then started dragging him along the ground. But Ryker was so heavy they hardly moved him. His skin was slick from the rain, and their grip slipped easily.

"Christ!" Renata hissed. "Even dead he's a hell of a lot of trouble."

They worked in a regular rhythm, pulling together in short bursts, and succeeded in moving him steadily, if slowly and painfully, across the clearing. By the time they reached the opposite side, and dragged the body into the trees, they both were breathing heavily. Benedict's arms and legs felt weak with the effort.

"We've been dragging around too many dead bodies," he said.

Renata nodded. They stood near the body for a few minutes, resting. "We can bury him later," Renata said. "Better, let him rot. Let the jungle take care of him."

They turned away from the big man's body, and headed for the river to search for Gerad.

They found Gerad propped within the curved root of a tall tree, covered with broken and torn vegetation, not far from the river and the flat white rock upon which he'd seen the alien creature. He had been garroted, and his face was twisted and discolored. His fingers were still tightly clasped around the knife that had found its mark one final time in Ryker's arm.

They left the knife in his hand, but Benedict removed the wood and leather band from Gerad's wrist, and put it on his own. Then they buried him under a thin layer of vegetation and dirt, and, through an oppressive shell of silence, returned to the camp.

* * *

"I came on this expedition hoping to find a race of alien, intelligent beings," Benedict said. "I came hoping to find escape."

"Escape from what?"

They sat in front of the dead fire, waiting for the lysium he chewed to take effect. Benedict had a ball of two leaves in his mouth, and he chewed steadily on it. Another dozen fresh leaves were in his pocket.

"Escape from humanity. I'm a First Order empath, and that will never change. For some reason, that makes being alone impossible, makes isolation unbearable. At the same time, though, being an empath among people, too, has become unbearable. I don't know, I guess I've hoped I could be an empath among an alien race instead, hoped that it would be more bearable than being among people."

"You really think that's a solution? You really think that's what you want?"

"I don't know. I'm not so sure it's even possible anymore. But I also came for another reason which, no matter what else, still holds. Now more than before."

"And what's that?"

"I'm here to help these creatures. I hope we can prevent an intelligent alien race of beings from being exploited, or even destroyed."

"They *are* intelligent?"

"I'm almost certain. There's something about the emotional content I've sensed from them. I don't understand it even vaguely, but there's a specific quality about it that . . . feels like intelligence. An aspect of self-awareness. It's strange, too, because when I think about it, I don't believe there's been anything at all like true empathy with them, at least not yet. I *perceive* their emotion or emotions, but I don't . . . ." He shrugged.

"But you think with the lysium you'll be able to find them."

"If not, it may be impossible."

He was beginning to notice the effects of the lysium. The rain, though little more than a heavy mist, sounded like a storm on the tarps, and a glistening outline had appeared on whatever he looked at. Renata's scar shone at him, a line of bright silver on her face. Benedict spit the leaves out onto the ground, then put two more in his mouth and continued chewing.

"Even if you can find them, Benedict, how do you expect to help them?"

"I won't alone. Won't even be me, so much. If we find these creatures, I'll take Ryker's transceiver and contact a group of people who are waiting somewhere on or above this world. They will be the ones who can really help."

The first bubbles of alien emotion began to touch him, to sluggishly leak through the screens and filters, tiny and hollow. As he mentally observed the elusive, insubstantial bubbles, he told Renata about Jean-Philippe: how Benedict had worked with him on Dante's Eye; the disaster on that world; and Jean-Philippe's proposal on Triumvirate.

By the time he had finished telling her the story, he felt as if his screens and filters were like loosely woven sieves, and the bubbles of emotion were flowing readily into and through him. Benedict stood, gazed into the trees in all directions. They were out there, somewhere, and now it was time to find them.

He lowered all the screens and filters, blocking only Renata's emotions, and opened himself completely to the jungle, and to the alien beings who were somewhere within it.

The bubbles rushed into him as a torrent. They

merged with one another to form larger spheres of emotional presence that drifted through him more slowly, somewhat more defined and substantial, though they remained incomprehensible. But with that added definition and substance came, as he focused on them, a hint of the source, a vague sense of direction and distance.

"We can start now," Benedict said. He stood and looked toward the east. The source appeared to be in that direction, in the lower slopes of the mountains. But how far away? A kilometer? Three or four? Or more? He could not tell.

They each wore a small rucksack. Inside Renata's were torches, food, and other supplies since they did not know how long they would be gone. In Benedict's were the transceiver and power cells. Benedict led the way across the clearing, pushing through the tall grasses, past Ryker's body, and into the trees.

The mist was heavy and warm, and kept the midday sun obscured, though not quite invisible. Benedict chewed steadily on the lysium leaves, and kept all his screens and filters down as they hiked through the jungle. At times he had difficulty concentrating on the terrain, on picking out a clear path, despite the fact that the trees and plants and leaves and ferns and rocks all seemed much clearer and sharper to him. But focusing on the alien emotions, and following them along toward their source, took so much attention that he periodically stumbled over roots or jagged rocks, walked into impenetrable thickets, or tried climbing over impassable boulders that jutted up from the jungle floor.

But Renata stayed close, and caught him when he stumbled, helped find a way through the dense undergrowth or around the imposing stones rising before them. She did not speak unless it was necessary, but his awareness of her presence allowed him to concentrate on the warm, swirling globes and bubbles of emotional energy that flowed into him, coursed through him for a time, then left to be replaced by others.

There were times when he felt he was being internally, mentally explored and observed by the aliens, as if the spheres of emotion were perceptual tools as well as experiential facets of these strange beings. He did not know what inspired the idea, but it somehow seemed reasonable. And as they marched on, he continued to speculate on the nature of the alien emotion and energy inside him, for speculate was all he could do. This was so unlike anything he'd ever sensed or felt from another human being that, no matter how long he observed and experienced it inside him, he came no closer to understanding anything about it.

The terrain became steeper, more uneven, as they traveled eastward. Each time Benedict chewed two leaves to the point of disintegration, he spat them out and replaced them with two others. As his supply dwindled, Renata picked fresh leaves for him.

His perceptions continued to change, until he felt they were no longer just enhanced, but distorted as well, though he could not be sure. He felt certain that it was not the lysium alone that caused the distortion, but was aided toward it by the bubbles and spheres of emotion that continued to move in and out and through his own inner world.

After some time, Benedict realized he had no conception of how far they had traveled, nor for how long. The mist continued to fall about them, a bright gray atmosphere like an enclosed shell surrounding them, moving with them as they advanced. In some ways, too, he had lost touch with his body, and did not know whether or not he was tired. He did feel he had a nearly unlimited source of energy to tap, though where that source was, or where it had come from, was a mystery.

He *was* making progress, though, he was certain of that. The spheres of alien emotion continued to become more substantial and defined, though still far beyond understanding, and he was able to more accurately home in on their source. He and Renata were getting closer, and it would not be long before they found them.

More time (how much? he wondered) passed. He was pushing through a clump of ferns when Renata took hold of his arm, brought him to a stop. He turned to look at her, and she left bright afterimages with each subtle movement of her head, her mouth.

"Do you know where you're going?" she asked. Her voice was a roar, her lips and teeth trailed flashes of light.

"Of course."

"Can you *see* where you're going?"

"Yes. Why? Can't you?"

She shook her head, nearly blinding him. "No. It's night, Benedict. It's completely dark."

He looked around, but the gray light of the mist remained, the same permanent dusk that had accompanied them all day. Was it really night? Had they been traveling that long?

"Night?"

"Yes," she said.

"Can you keep going?"

"Yes."

"Then we go on."

He took a long piece of rope, tied one end to his rucksack, and Renata took the other. Benedict pushed

357

on, now paying closer attention to the path, knowing Renata could no longer help. Occasionally he felt a tug on the rope behind him, and he would slow to let her catch up.

The march through the jungle—up steep slopes and along narrow ravines, in and out of ragged gullies, over rocks and twisted roots and fallen trees, beneath high canopies and vined archways—continued interminably, and yet without a real sense of the passage of time for Benedict. Mostly what he sensed was an ever-increasing intensity in the bubbles and spheres of emotion, and a growing sense of closeness to the aliens themselves.

Benedict reached the top of a densely forested ridge, and stopped. To the right, running along from the far slope of the ridge, was a steep mountainside, nearly vertical, thickly covered with dark green vines and flowering bushes and enormous ferns extending out over open air above a flat stretch of earth at the foot of the mountainside, fifteen or twenty meters below him. Ahead, the jungle was not quite as dense, which allowed him to see bits and pieces of the mountainside, though the upper canopy was still nearly solid above it. Coarse grass, low ferns, and large tracts of moss carpeted the narrow stretch of flat ground.

The rain had stopped, but water dripped steadily from leaves and branches. Benedict stared at the partially visible mountainside, so steep he would have thought of it as a cliff if he could have seen an upper ledge. The now solid, rising swells of emotion, streams and currents of the bubbles and spheres, emanated from the mountainside itself, and after several minutes Benedict realized the aliens were actually inside the mountain.

"What is it?" Renata whispered. "Do you see

something?" She stood at his side, looking down the slope.

"Is it day or night?" Benedict asked.

"Morning."

He nodded. Then, "They're down there."

"Where?"

"In the mountainside. Caves. Tunnels maybe. I've got to go down, get closer."

"Then let's go."

"I need to go alone. I have to see if I can get through to them."

Renata didn't argue. "How long do I wait?"

He smiled. "I have no sense of time, I might stay down there for days. If I'm not back by late afternoon, come down, see if you can find me."

"All right."

Benedict took the last six leaves from his pocket, wadded all six together, then put them in his mouth and began to chew. He put his hand on Renata's shoulder for a moment, nodded once, then started down.

2

HE DESCENDED FROM THE RIDGE.

The slope was steep, and Benedict had to carefully make his way down through the dense undergrowth. Though this part of the jungle had appeared more open from the ridge, and the trees were spaced further apart than usual, within a few minutes the top of the ridge, and Renata, were gone from sight.

The wad of leaves in his mouth was large and solid, and difficult to chew. He wondered if it was possible to overdose on lysium, if he had chewed too many. But he felt it was necessary to push to the limit if he was to have any chance for success, and he chewed harder, swallowing bitter saliva as he continued down the slope.

As he neared the bottom, he began to have difficulty walking, and difficulty finding a clear path. The huge, glowing spheres of emotional energy now seemed to partially manifest themselves on a visual level, obscuring the terrain, or perhaps they just confused his senses. His depth perception vanished, and he would bump into trees that looked to be several meters away; when he stumbled over a stone or root, he would reach out for support to a branch or trunk he thought was nearby, only to grasp empty air and fall heavily to the ground.

His hearing faded in and out, silence followed by a rush of unidentifiable sound. The inside of his nose burned with the intensity of the odors around him, but he could not match any of the smells with specific objects. And his taste became one-dimensional—the stinging bitterness of lysium.

The earth leveled out, and he thought he was near the mountainside. He wandered through tall, thick patches of lysium plants, the bright blue of the leaves burning afterimages into his eyes until it seemed he was wading through a shallow blue lagoon, the water above as well as below.

Finally Benedict stopped, unable to go further. He was not tired, but he could no longer see the way. His vision was filled with shattering crystals of blue, flashes of bright, iridescent green, and a sprinkling of yellow teardrops that glistened as they danced about him. All of this was overlaid, or underlaid, with the shimmering gold spheres of emotion coming from the alien creatures inside the mountain.

Benedict took off his rucksack, let it drop, then sat on the spongy earth, cradled in the dark, musty roots of a massive tree rising high above him. He looked up, trying to follow the tree to its crown, but turned away, overwhelmed by a swirling kaleidoscope of colors and painful shards of light. He closed his eyes and sank back into the roots. There was only one thing left to do.

Fighting back his fear, Benedict gradually lowered the last of the deep, core shields that had always remained as a final protection, and opened himself completely to the alien beings inside the world.

At first, little occurred. He was immersed in a calm, enclosed sea of emotion, a reassuring, if mysterious, presence that surrounded him. Everything vanished except the pale gold emotion-filled spheres now clustered about him. The spheres were accompanied by hundreds of small globules, the globules in turn surrounded by thousands of tiny bubbles of emotional energy that darted and danced in constant, high-speed motion. The spheres and globules remained nearly motionless, silently vibrating outside him, but the tiny bubbles began to freely penetrate, effervescing through him without impact, without effect, and leaving no traces of their passage behind.

As time passed, the larger spheres took on individual identities, or perhaps he was learning to recognize the differences that already existed, learning to distinguish one individual from another. He believed, now, that each sphere belonged to, or represented, a specific alien entity.

The apparent random motion of the bubbles, after time, coalesced into what he thought were distinct patterns, complex and unfamiliar, but patterns nonetheless, which suggested purpose to him. Benedict began to feel certain that the aliens' emotion, at least in the forms of these bubbles and globules and spheres, was able to serve as an active process. They were probing him, exploring and observing, trying to learn.

But Benedict felt hollow through it all, as though the bubbles now passing through him did not quite exist, or that they passed through a void within him, unable to interact because of some inner defect, some inner lack. They passed through him as if they, or he, were almost completely without substance.

The bubbles slowed their movement slightly, stopped penetrating him, and instead began to merge with each other and with the larger spheres outside him as they left him, until there were none left for him to perceive. After several moments of inactivity, the globules, arranged now in clusters, moved toward him.

Each cluster of globules appeared to be associated with a specific sphere, and they only entered him a single cluster at a time. The globules were also more substantial than the bubbles, carried definite resonances of emotion which he could sense, but which he still could not identify.

As each cluster entered him, causing a ripple effect through his own feelings, it broke apart, and the individual globules moved to different parts of his inner self. The globules vibrated, they induced vibrations in his psyche, they swelled with tension and shrank in release, prodded and probed, stimulated random sensations and flashes of fear, pain, desire, contentment, rage, and a dozen other brief, intense feelings that vanished as quickly as they appeared. But the feelings were definitely his, not the aliens', and he felt he was on an emotional surgical table, being explored and dissected by alien surgeons who comprehended nothing of what they saw.

But there was little pain, and no permanent effects. There were no real connections between his own bursts of feeling and the globules, and he wondered if the globules perceived his emotions as only bizarre side effects of their exploration, unable to understand what they were.

As it went on, though, cluster after cluster entering and exploring, he felt they must be learning *something* about him, while he still was unable to learn anything at all about them. He felt helpless, without options.

He could only wait, let them probe and search, and hope that something more would happen, that there would be some kind of breakthrough. He suspected, though, that they had not really learned much about him either, that there were connections not being made, relationships misunderstood, and perhaps incapable of being understood because of the vast differences between him and them.

Eventually the clusters stopped coming, perhaps because they had all been inside him now. They hovered for a time, then merged with the larger, golden spheres, swelling the spheres until they completely filled his surroundings so that nothing else seemed to exist.

The golden spheres shimmered with an emotional intensity that singed him, though there was no direct contact yet. They completely surrounded him, each one melding with another so that, although they were distinct, they were not wholly separate from one another.

One broke from the others, however, and approached. It made contact, touching him with strange electricity, then both entered and enclosed him simultaneously, as if it were operating on two different levels of reality at the same time. And maybe, Benedict thought, it was.

After a moment, the sphere began to shape its essence to match his own, and suddenly a connection was made with a bright explosion of agony that tore through him.

Almost immediately the pain eased, and the sphere recoiled slightly, not, it seemed, in pain, but for some other reason he could not imagine. Perhaps it recognized the overload—that's what it was, Benedict thought, an overload of emotion. Though he still could not identify anything about the alien emotions,

364

it was obvious now that they existed at an intensity so much greater than any human emotion that he could not handle its full force.

The sphere did not fully withdraw, and eventually it began to flow through him once more, again reshaping itself, striving for some congruency. The sphere swelled from within and pressed in on him from without, trapping him between the two aspects. He felt crushed and squeezed, and wondered if the alien was attempting to force some kind of merging. The alien's emotional intensity in both inner and outer aspects climbed a level, then another, causing in him a claustrophobic mental anguish. But despite the increased pressure, which now became painful, the connections remained incomplete, valences were unmatched, wavelengths moved out of phase with each other. Still, the alien increased the pressure, and the pain.

Until now, none of the processes he had undergone, none of the probing and explorations had bothered him, but the persistent, almost violent attempts at merger now underway began to disturb him greatly. The alien did not seem aware of the pain it caused, and Benedict was afraid of what it might do to him out of ignorance. Panic kicked in, surged through with the claustrophobia and the pain.

Benedict tried to fight down his fear without resisting the alien's attempts at a meshing of emotions. He still hoped some kind of connection was possible, some true empathy with the aliens. But the swelling pain and the cold sensation of complete helplessness combined to elicit a tangible, heated panic that struggled desperately for release.

The alien at last seemed to sense that something was wrong, and eased the pressure. A tense stasis took hold. Benedict continued to fight down his fear, while

Richard Paul Russo

trying in every way to acquire some understanding of what the alien was trying to accomplish, some comprehension of what the alien felt, some vague sense of the nature of the alien itself. But there was nothing, nothing at all, as though an invisible but impenetrable barrier lay between them, a barrier that would never come down.

With that realization came a resignation, an acceptance that everything the alien was now trying to accomplish, whatever it was—communication, merging, understanding—would come to nothing, just as his own efforts had come to nothing. Their world was not his world, and that would never change. He was human, and they were not. His fear and despair faded, then dissipated completely, and he waited for it all to end.

Suddenly it was as if the aliens all sensed his resignation, or came to similar conclusions. The glowing sphere of emotion ceased its pressure, and slowly, gradually withdrew, leaving him once again empty.

He thought it was over. He thought they would all withdraw, retreat, but they remained near the outer edges of his being, still surrounding him. Then, one after another, the spheres merged with each other to become one swirling, enormous sphere like a brilliant, hot sun, radiating flames and tendrils of intense, incomprehensible emotional energy.

This massive sphere, which seemed both man-sized and large enough to encompass the entire world at the same time, approached him pulsing with a heat that melted its way through him.

His fear returned with the certainty that he could not survive contact with the combined energies of all those spheres, all those strange, alien beings. He tried to pull back, but could not move.

What were they doing? Panic spread through him.

Stop! he wanted to cry out. But couldn't. Didn't they realize what they were doing? Hadn't they learned anything?

Of course not; he'd already come to accept that. They *didn't* realize what they were doing. They *hadn't* learned anything at all.

He tried again to retreat, to call out to them, to do anything, but he remained helpless. The huge glowing sphere touched him, and his entire being jolted with the pain. Benedict wanted to run, to cry out his agony, but his body did not seem to exist any longer, or he had lost all contact with it. The sphere continued, entering and surrounding him at the same time.

His body returned on some level, engulfed with pain. Within moments, the sphere, burning and swelling and blinding him, was completely inside, and had at the same time completely encased him.

Fire exploded in his heart. It spread rapidly, burning its way along his arteries to every part of his body, then incinerating thousands of tiny capillary networks to cross to the veins and burn its way back to his heart.

Acid washed across his skin, dissolving it in a flash to leave muscle and bone exposed to a thousand needles of pain. More acid ate the marrow of his bones, leaving them cold and hollow and aching.

And finally, lightning erupted within his skull, then crackled along the nerves, setting off an uncontrolled firing of synapses, a raging current shooting out along the nerves and down his spine and out to the tips of his fingers and toes, then back again to his skull, burning out his nervous system without, somehow, relieving any of the pain.

And the pain would not stop. The fire and lightning and boiling acid continued to arc through his body, gutting and destroying him.

Somewhere, deep inside, some tiny piece of him cried out, knowing he was dying.

The sphere exploded and imploded within him, became the raging heart of the sun . . .

. . . then black engulfed it, engulfed him . . .

. . . and he was gone.

3

WHEN HE CAME TO, BENEDICT WAS DRAINED, A HOLLOW shell reverberating with a dull ache. He opened his eyes, blinked them against the gray light. Rain fell nearby, but none on his face. When his eyes adjusted to the light, he saw shimmers of green above him that slowly drifted into focus to become a poncho strung overhead.

He sat up, mildly surprised he was still alive. His perceptions had returned to normal, and most of the pain was gone. He looked at his hands and arms, saw no signs of injury.

What had happened?

A few meters away, he saw smoke rising from a fire, then smelled the strong odor of Linsok coffee, but there was no one in sight. His rucksack lay on the ground near the fire, next to Renata's. She must be somewhere nearby.

Benedict slowly rose to his feet. He was weak, and

did not want to move. A hollow ache continued to vibrate through him with a numbing effect. He started to walk toward the fire when a movement on the left caught his eye. Benedict turned, and stopped.

About fifteen meters away, standing motionless beside a tree, was one of the alien creatures. It looked much as Renata had described—tall and strong and large and beautifully furred in rich shades of gray. It was larger, even, than Benedict had imagined, a full two and half meters tall, with strength that could not be hidden by the thin fur. It watched him from small, deep-set eyes, and stood with an almost regal bearing. The long, powerful forelimbs hung loosely at its side, dark claws emerging from the long, furred digits.

They watched each other in silence, unmoving for several minutes. Then Benedict glanced around, and three or four others were visible, though not as close as the first. Large and gray, all of them gazed steadily at him.

Benedict felt strangely empty, watching them, as if he had lost something he could not replace. The one he'd first seen took a hesitant step forward, then a second step. When, after a minute or two, Benedict did not retreat, the alien resumed its slow approach. The others followed.

Benedict remained motionless as the tall, gray figures moved toward him. Silent, and with steady, calm gazes, they stopped just two meters in front of him.

Nothing happened for a long time. Something *was* wrong, Benedict thought. There was the odd sensation he'd had since regaining consciousness. Something wrong, or something had changed. The air was too quiet. No, that wasn't it, he could hear the rain falling, the sounds of birds and insects, the popping of the fire. But still, it felt too quiet, too empty.

Something was missing.

He began to feel a faint, tickling sensation through-out his body, inside his mind, so muted he wasn't positive it was actually there. But the tickling nagged at him, vaguely familiar, an elusive hint of something he had once known. The stares of the alien creatures grew more intense.

And then it came to him—he was totally blocked off to even the slightest traces of emotion. Even with the filters and screens in place there was always the slightest undercurrent that leaked through—from other people, no matter how distant, and even animals. An undercurrent that provided a constant, quiet background. *That's* what was missing; *that* was why it felt too quiet. Now there was nothing except the faint tickle, and that was something entirely different. The barriers and shields had become completely sealed.

Benedict tried to lower a few screens, and . . . there were no screens to lower. No screens, no filters, no barriers of any kind. They hadn't sealed, they had disappeared, vanished. He was not blocking out emotion; somehow, he had become incapable of receiving it at all.

The idea seemed too absurd, and he could not immediately accept it. He tried opening himself again, tried to grasp and bring down, *tear* down, screens that apparently no longer existed. Nothing happened. Not the slightest trace of emotion entered.

He had lost it all.

Benedict realized, with a numb but calm certainty, that he was no longer an empath.

The alien beings edged closer to him, and a new, softer expression came to their eyes. When they were so close he could feel the warmth of their breathing, their heads towering over him, one reached out and laid a clawed hand gently on his shoulder. A second

Richard Paul Russo

one put a hand on his other shoulder, and another brushed its furred digits across his upper cheek and through his beard.

Benedict felt certain that the tickling sensation came from the creatures now surrounding him, that it was some kind of emotional probe which he was no longer capable of truly perceiving. Maybe it was the bubbles that had once flowed so freely through him. He thought he could sense a sadness in their touch, in the expression of their eyes, and Benedict then realized that they knew what they had done to him.

After a time, the alien creatures pulled back, and slowly began to withdraw from him. They retreated into the trees, watching him for several minutes as they backed away. Then, almost in unison, they turned away and walked into the jungle, and within minutes were gone from sight.

Benedict wandered over to the fire, only vaguely aware of his surroundings. He sat down on a flat, mossy log and gazed into the low, fading flames. When the fire had nearly died, he added a few sticks of dried wood, brought it back to life. It was then that he noticed the flask of coffee on a rock at the fire's edge, still slightly warm, and a covered plate of meat and bread and cheese. Benedict moved the flask closer to the flames, and when the coffee was hot he poured some for himself.

He sat in front of the fire, chewed at the food, and drank from the coffee, and listened to the silence in his mind. He listened, and watched, and drifted through this new silence and emptiness, and tried to imagine what his life would be like from now on.

He thought of Silky, remembered her holding him, crying and scared, asking him to help her, to be there and take care of her when her life became unbearable. It was the kind of thing, he knew, that didn't take

372

being an empath, and he thought once again of Hadling and the people he helped, doing what he could and not expecting more than that.

Maybe that had been his real problem—that he had always just tried to do too much, and had expected too much. He had wanted to help people, make miserable existence more bearable, and maybe being an empath had actually in some ways been more a hindrance than a help. Perhaps he had just been aware of, and overwhelmed by, too much misery from too many people, preventing him from being able to focus on individuals. Maybe *not* being an empath was an advantage. And after all, losing his empathic abilities was what he had wanted for a long time, wasn't it? Well, he had his wish now.

Benedict felt numb still, but beneath the numbness was a sense of incredible relief and release. He suspected there would be times when he would regret this loss, but for now it was, he felt certain, what he needed more than anything else.

Some time later, Renata emerged from the trees and joined him by the fire. She seemed very tired.

"You all right?" he asked.

She gave him a slight smile. "I'm fine. I've been out walking . . . thinking. How about you? When I found you, first thought you were dead."

"So did I." He tried smiling back, managed it for a moment. "In some ways, I suppose I am."

"What happened, Benedict?"

"Have you see them?"

"Yes. There were several standing at your side when I found you, watching over you. When I showed, they left." She gestured with her head. "There's one nearby now, watching us. And a couple of others that seem to be staring at nothing, like they're in a trance." She looked at him. "What happened?"

"I don't really know." He paused, looking at the fire and remembering the flames he had thought were burning him alive. "They tried to communicate with me, I think, on an emotional, or maybe telepathic, level."

"Tried."

"Didn't succeed." He slowly shook his head. "And then, at the end, they did something else. Maybe a different attempt to communicate, I don't know." A shudder rolled through him, a tingle of pain. "What they did to me . . . I don't know why I didn't die." He looked at her. "I've lost it all."

"Lost what?"

"My empathic abilities. I'm no longer a First." He paused. "I'm not an empath at all anymore."

"Benedict, that's impossible. How could . . . ?"

"The last thing that happened, what I thought was killing me. I'm sure they didn't know what they were doing to me." He glanced at the alien watching them from the trees. "They know now, though." He shook his head again, looking back at Renata. "There was just too much of them; too much . . . power, I guess, too much something, far more than I could handle. It was as if they overloaded me, wiped everything out, burned out all . . ." He sighed heavily. "There's nothing left. I am no longer an empath."

She did not say anything for a long time. Benedict watched the tall, gray figures in the dim light, all unmoving and with eyes open. Like Renata had said, in a trance.

"Do you think it'll come back?" she said. "That maybe you'll heal, and . . ." She didn't finish.

"Possible, I suppose." He looked back at her. "But no, I don't think so."

She didn't say anything for a while, just watched him. Then she asked, "How do you feel?"

374

Benedict shrugged. "Empty. I don't know. Relief, too, like an oppressive weight has been lifted from me." He paused. "Will I miss it? Probably. Sometimes. But I don't think I'll need it anymore to understand people." He smiled at her. "I've learned a few things out here."

"We both have."

"Yes?"

She nodded. "I killed two of them several years ago, unintentionally. Yesterday I deliberately killed someone else, after allowing him to kill others. That's going to be much harder to resolve." She turned to look at the silent, motionless figures. "What do we do with them?"

He followed her gaze, watched them standing and staring, seemingly unaware of their surroundings. "Call Jean-Philippe's people in. I think these creatures could have remained hidden from us, but chose not to. They might be capable of staying hidden from other people for years, but eventually they would be found. I don't know if, once found, they would allow themselves to be exploited, but I'm certain a lot of them would die from the Flex people trying. Look." He pointed to one who very slowly and deliberately plucked a large lysium leaf, put it in its mouth, and began to chew. "They seem to live partially in another reality. They might not realize what was happening to them until it was too late. Jean-Philippe and his people are probably their best chance for survival."

Darkness was falling quickly, and the rain had nearly stopped. Renata added more wood to the fire.

"You worked with Jean-Philippe before," she said. "Will you stay here when he comes, work with him and these creatures?"

Benedict shook his head. "I'm going back to Riotmark. I don't belong here. I need to go back to people, and I'll start with Silky, do what I can to help her."

"You know you can't get her off the Flex. That she's going to die soon."

"Yes. But there are things I can do for her."

Renata nodded. "I'd like to go with you," she said.

Benedict smiled. "I'd like that."

They returned to silence. Benedict looked at the three barely visible gray figures, one apparently watching them, the other two off in worlds of their own.

He had lost a part of himself, but most of him still remained, and he would learn to live with that. It would not be so hard now.

Benedict picked up his rucksack, took out the transceiver, and prepared to send messages back to the world.

Ramsey Campbell

☐ 51652-4	DARK COMPANIONS		$3.50
51653-2		Canada	$3.95
☐ 51654-0	THE DOLL WHO ATE HIS		$3.50
51655-9	MOTHER	Canada	$3.95
☐ 51658-3	THE FACE THAT MUST DIE		$3.95
51659-1		Canada	$4.95
☐ 51650-8	INCARNATE		$3.95
51651-6		Canada	$4.50
☐ 58125-3	THE NAMELESS		$3.50
58126-1		Canada	$3.95
☐ 51656-7	OBSESSION		$3.95
51657-5		Canada	$4.95

Buy them at your local bookstore or use this handy coupon:
Clip and mail this page with your order

TOR BOOKS—Reader Service Dept.
49 W. 24 Street, 9th Floor, New York, NY 10010

Please send me the book(s) I have checked above. I am enclosing
$_____ (please add $1.00 to cover postage and handling).
Send check or money order only—no cash or C.O.D.'s.

Mr./Mrs./Miss _____
Address _____
City _____ State/Zip _____
Please allow six weeks for delivery. Prices subject to change
without notice.

BESTSELLING BOOKS FROM TOR